D0446070

"Laugh out loud funny . . . Loved it!"

—CINDY MARTINUSEN,
author of *The Salt Garden*

"Laura Jensen Walker's debut novel, *Dreaming in Black and White*, had me digging out old movies to watch along with Phoebe. A cute and funny read that shows God created each of us according to His purpose and love isn't limited to the few size fours."

—COLLEEN COBLE,
author of *Distant Echoes*

"*Dreaming in Black and White* is a dream of a book, not only delightfully funny but spiritually wise. Laura Jensen Walker has given us a delectable cream puff stuffed with insight, a tasty treat that oozes rich truths. You'll love it!"

—GAYLE ROPER,
author of *Winter Winds* and *Autumn Dreams*

"OK, I admit it. Although I am a guy of the male gender, I read this chick lit book because, deep down, I still find women baffling. I wanted a sneak peek inside the mind of the fairer sex. I was hooked from the very first sentence. But do I finally understand women? As they say in the French Army, 'I feel so much better now that I have given up hope.'"

—DAVE MEURER,
author of *Good Spousekeeping* and
If You Want Breakfast in Bed, Sleep in the Kitchen

"A sweet tale from a grand new author."

—DAVIS BUNN,
author of *The Lazarus Trap*

"*Dreaming In Black and White* takes the best of chicklit, prodigal daughter, and romance stories to create a novel both funny and heart tugging at the same time."

—LAURAINE SNELLING,
author of the Red River of the North series

"I lost track of how many times I laughed out loud. Laura's lead character Phoebe is a hoot and a half!"

—RANDY INGERMANSON,
author of *Double Vision*

dreaming in black & white

[a phoebe grant novel]

laura jensen walker

WestBow
PRESS

A Division of Thomas Nelson Publishers
Since 1798

visit us at www.westbowpress.com

Copyright © 2005 by Laura Jensen Walker

All rights reserved. No portion of this book may be reproduced, stored in a retrieval system, or transmitted in any form or by any means—electronic, mechanical, photocopy, recording, scanning, or other—except for brief quotations in critical reviews or articles, without the prior written permission of the publisher.

Published in Nashville, Tennessee, by WestBow Press, a division of Thomas Nelson, Inc., in association with the literary agency of Alive Communications, Inc., 7680 Goddard Street, Suite 200, Colorado Springs, CO 80920.

Scripture quotations in this book are from HOLY BIBLE, NEW INTERNATIONAL VERSION®, Copyright © 1973, 1978, 1984 by International Bible Society. Used by permission of Zondervan Publishing House. All rights reserved.

WestBow Press Books may be purchased in bulk for educational, business, fund-raising, or sales promotional use. For information, please e-mail SpecialMarkets@ThomasNelson.com.

PUBLISHER'S NOTE: This novel is a work of fiction. Names, characters, places, and incidents are either products of the author's imagination or used fictitiously. All characters are fictional, and any similarity to people living or dead is purely coincidental.

Library of Congress Cataloging-in-Publication Data

Walker, Laura Jensen.
    Dreaming in black & white : a Phoebe Grant novel / Laura Jensen Walker.
    p. cm.
    ISBN 0-8499-4523-2 (trade paper)
    1. Motion pictures—Appreciation—Fiction. 2. Obituaries—Authorship—Fiction. 3. Overweight women—Fiction. 4. Single women—Fiction. I. Title: Dreaming in black and white. II. Title.
    PS3623.A3595D74 2005
    813'.6—dc22

                                           2004022135

Printed in the United States of America

05 06 07 08 09 RRD 5 4 3 2 1

In memory of my beloved father,
David C. Jensen,
who taught me to dream, and who left us way too soon.
This one's for you, Dad.

Here's looking at you, kid.

–HUMPHREY BOGART,

in *Casablanca*

my thighs were at it again.

They whispered behind my back with every pantyhose-clad step I took—a whoosh-whoosh rhythm that sounded remarkably like one of my Mom's old Engelbert Humperdinck records: "Please release me . . ." *Note to self: Renew lapsed membership at gym to lose fifteen extra pounds in effort to keep thighs from getting so chummy. And buy more tan in a bottle so as not to have to* ever *wear nylons again.*

At least not in August.

I juggled my no-carb lunch, laptop bag, morning paper, and designer knockoff handbag as I struggled to hit the unlock button on my key chain. Too late, I realized everything was starting to slide. Holding tight to my laptop, I leaped out of the way of my cascading tall, nonfat double mocha, no foam—but not before the coffee waterfall splattered my chunky heels and nylon-clad legs.

It wasn't just my thighs that were grumbling. My wet ankles also joined in the clamoring chorus of dissent.

No time to run back home and change. I was already ten minutes late—today of all days, when I was due to find out whether I'd gotten the promotion I longed for. So I gathered all my belongings, dumped the rest of my mocha into the street, and tossed the now-empty cardboard cup into the backseat of my last-year's model yellow Bug.

Pulling out of Starbucks, I punched Lindsey's speed-dial number on my cell as I eased into traffic, scrabbling around in the glove box for a little chocolate relief.

"Lindsey Rogers," my best friend chirped in her annoyingly cheerful human resources voice.

"Hey there, Lins, it's me," I mumbled around the dented Snickers bar I'd just inhaled. "You won't believe what just happened." And I proceeded to regale her with my sad tale. "But never mind. Spilt milk, right? Or spilt mocha. So tell me again this guy's vitals and where we're meeting for dinner."

"Pheebs, you're getting forgetful in your old age. You're going to Imperial Gardens, where they have that nice little dance floor at the back. And his name's Colin—as in Firth. As in *Pride and Prejudice* and *Bridget Jones* and *Girl with a Pearl Earring.* He's a tall, attractive, thirty-something salesman from Toledo who comes to town once a month."

Swallowing the last bite of Snickers, I asked, "What's wrong with him?"

"Nothing that I can see. Nice guy, great hair, and *perfect* teeth. Lots of expensive orthodontia there, I'm guessing . . ."

I interrupted Lindsey, who, ever since she'd finally gotten braces on her thirtieth birthday, seemed to be obsessed with everyone else's pearly whites. "You're sure he doesn't have a wife stashed back home in Toledo?"

"Nope, because I overheard him talking to my boss when he was drawing up his life insurance plan, and he got all wistful when Peterson showed him his silver-framed photos of the wife-and-kidlings unit."

"Hmmm. Good looking, single, *and* likes kids? Sounds too good to be true."

It was.

That night, over the moo goo gai pan and prawns in garlic sauce, Colin—who, truth be told, was nothing at all like Colin Firth, though he did have some great Hugh Grant hair—drilled me on the importance of being earnest about life insurance even at my age. The evening started out well enough; he was rather good-looking, pleasant, and polite—didn't blow his nose in the linen napkin, like my last blind date had—which gave me hope. But by the time the fortune cookies arrived, I was afraid I'd do bodily harm to Colin with my chopsticks if I heard one more word about actuarial tables.

In desperation, I asked him to dance, thanking my lucky stars and my mother that I hadn't been raised Baptist. "This is one of my favorite oldies," I said, as Sinatra slid into "Fly Me to the Moon"—wishing all the while I could fly to the moon instead.

"Mine too. I love the standards," Colin said as he spun me energetically around the floor. Very energetically.

"So, Phoebe, tell me," he said as he whirled me around, "Are you a churchgoing girl?"

Removing a chunk of flyaway hair from my mouth, I answered breathlessly, "Yes. In fact, Lindsey and I attend the same church—First Presbyterian."

"You don't say," Colin said, stopping in midwhirl, causing me to lose the little bit of balance I'd tried to maintain while dancing with Mr. Saturday Night Fever, and winding up with my cheek squashed up against his—I knew it!—polyester-blend jacket. "I'm a Presbyterian too. My goodness, we certainly have a lot in common. So tell me, Phoebe . . ."

Oh no. Here it comes. The dreaded blind-date moment every single thirty-something woman hates: "How come a nice girl like you isn't married?"

But Colin surprised me with a slight variation on the theme. "How come a nice, pretty girl like you isn't married yet?"

"Um . . ." Anxious to change the conversational direction, I cast about for some innocuous gambit of singles small talk to divert him. "Gee. You really have great hair, Colin."

Way to go, Pheebs. Now he's going to think you're coming on to him.

Colin beamed. "Thank you. I'll let you in on a little secret, Phoebe . . ." He leaned closer as I tried in vain to discreetly back away from the garlicky waves emanating from the polyester threads. "It's plugs."

"Excuse me?"

"Hair plugs. A few years ago, my hairline really started receding, and one morning as I looked in the mirror I got depressed and began feeling really old. But mother snapped me right out of it at the breakfast table when she suggested I check into a hair transplant." He giggled and winked at me. "After all, she said, if Burt Reynolds can, why not me?"

"Oh . . . you live with your mother?"

How could this evening get any worse?

"Yes, I moved back in with Mom to help her out after Dad died."

"How sweet and thoughtful of you."

Chastising note to self: Stop being so judgmental and quick to assign the dork *label. Any man who's kind and generous enough to look after his mother in her time of need can't be all bad. How's that old saying go? How a man treats his mother is how he'll treat you.*

Looking at him with new nonjudgmental, empathetic eyes, I asked, "When did your dad pass away?"

"Twenty-nine years ago."

"Tw-twenty-nine years? So, did you leave home when you were a child to go to boarding school, or did you just run away to join the circus when you were eight?"

"No, I was in my final few weeks of college when Dad passed."

"Um, Colin, I hope you don't mind my being personal, but how old are you?"

"Fifty-one."

"But Lindsey said you were in your late thirties . . ."

"I know. Everyone thinks that," he said with a smug grin. "Isn't it amazing what a little eye lift and plugs can do? Just call me well-preserved. Plus, I run four miles every morning and spend half an hour each night on the Stairmaster while watching my *Sell That Security* sales tapes.

"But enough about me," he said, with what he probably thought was a flirtatious lift of his eyebrow but actually made him look like Yoda with a rug, "How old are *you*, Phoebe?"

"Thirty-one."

"Hmmm." He frowned. "Well, that's a little older than we'd wanted."

"We?"

"Oh yes. I meant me. Well, Mother and I have been talking lately, and we think—I think—it's time I settled down and got married so as to carry on the family name. Did you know that a recent issue of the journal *Human Reproduction* says that the most fruitful child-bearing years for a woman are before the age of thirty? Do you think a year or so would make that much difference?"

As Sinatra crooned with daughter Nancy about saying "Somethin' Stupid," I made a new note to self: *Kill Lindsey*.

"Gee, I don't know if you can afford to take that chance, Colin. It might be best to go with a twenty-five– or twenty-six-year-old just to be safe. You never know; that first child could be a girl. And look at poor Anne Boleyn—we all know how that turned out. I'd hate to lose my head."

After saying my farewells to Colin in the parking lot and discreetly dodging his eager good-night kiss, I headed home, punching in Lindsey's number as I drove.

"Girl, you are *so* dead. The guy's looking for a broodmare, not a woman. Plus, he's fifty-one."

"Well, how was I supposed to know? He looked thirty-something to me. Besides, look at Michael Douglas and Catherine Zeta-Jones. He's more than twenty years older than her, and they have a great marriage, plus a couple of beautiful kids."

"Colin is no Michael Douglas."

"But he *is* available. Look, Pheebs, you're always whining that there are no decent single men out there. So I find you one—a Presbyterian, no less—who's got a nice steady job, great hair, perfect teeth, and is eager to get married and have kids, and you're still not satisfied."

"Lindsey, the guy's a loser. He's *so* boring. And I'd be afraid that if I ever ran my fingers through his hair I might unplug him or something. But worst of all—he still lives with his mother."

"Picky, picky. Okay, I grant you that he's a little boring . . ."

"A little?"

"Okay, a lot. But at least he's employed—unlike the last guy you dated. And as for the hair, you could work around it somehow. Although I must admit, the mother thing's a little creepy."

"Just a little. Can you say 'Bates Motel'?"

"Okay, okay. So let's cross him off the list and move on. And speaking of moving on, how was work today? Tell all! Did you get the promotion?"

"I *still* don't know. I was supposed to have that meeting with my editor, which is why I wore my best black skirt, red power blazer, and these way-too-tight pantyhose, but something was going on today. Lots of suits coming and going, so Cooper's secretary e-mailed me that it was canceled and we'd have to reschedule for Monday morning."

"So what are you going to wear?"

"Nothing that requires nylons, that's for sure. I was dying today. I'd hoped to run by Nordstrom's after work to pick up one of those cute print skirts they have on sale and pair it with a sweater set, but someone told me I couldn't be late for my very important date."

"All right already. Point taken."

"I'm thinking I'll go the classic route: black pants, white Tommy Hilfiger blouse, and my longer black blazer that covers my hips. Classy, but in control. And not trying too hard."

"Sounds great. Black is always slimming. What about shoes?"

"My new Nine West slingbacks—the pointy ones that make me look thin."

"Sounds good. Oops, gotta run. Teakettle's whistling. See you tomorrow."

"Okay. 'Night."

Turning right onto Lakeshore Boulevard, I enjoyed the view of Cleveland's lights on Lake Erie as I drove through the ritzy part of town. I lived at the other end of Lakeshore Boulevard—the nonritzy end.

But I loved my cute little apartment in the original 1930s brownstone. Normally I wouldn't have been able to afford the one bedroom with high vaulted ceilings, crown molding, and hardwood floors, but the landlord hadn't had time to paint and clean before I moved in, so he gave me a break on the rent in exchange for my doing the work.

I painted the moldings and baseboard a bright marshmallow white and chose a soft butter yellow for the walls—which I then decorated with all my romantic classic-movie posters: *Casablanca, Gone with the Wind, Wuthering Heights,* and *The Parent Trap.* Then I added a couple of black director's chairs, a bookcase, and my pride and joy—a red leather Pottery Barn sofa, on which I was still making payments.

Barely had the door shut behind me when I kicked off my shoes, hiked up my skirt, and finally tore off the offending nylons, which I threw in the trash. After greeting Gabby, my plastic goldfish, I checked my messages—two telemarketers and my mother, wondering how my blind date had gone.

My mother? How did she know . . . ? *Note to self: Do not tell bigmouth brother Jordy about love life anymore, because concerned mother, who worries her only daughter will become dried-up old maid, will immediately order wedding invitations and set up china registry.*

Discarding clothes as I went, I popped Josh Groban into the CD player and headed straight for the tub, where I turned on the taps and dumped in half a bottle of my lavender therapy bath salts. Easing my way into the now brimming-with-lavender-bubbles water, I lay back, closed my eyes, and let Josh take me away to Italy.

I'll bet Josh Groban doesn't have hair plugs. But then again, he's not even twenty-five. Just a tad too young. Too bad. That voice. That hair. Those eyes.

When the Josh-man stopped singing, I picked up the remote from the side of the tub—being careful not to drop it in the water—and started channel surfing on my portable TV. Goldie Hawn in green fatigues filled the screen. *Private Benjamin.* Not the world's greatest movie, but it held nostalgic appeal for me because of my stint in the

United States Air Force—a part of my past my current friends found almost incomprehensible. But who made the rule that said you couldn't serve your country and still like nice shoes? It certainly didn't apply to Goldie. Me, either. So I smiled and settled back in the steaming, fragrant water to watch her comic transformation from socialite to soldier.

Shivering, I awoke in the tepid tub more than an hour later. Goldie was just heading off to her first European army assignment. My skin was shriveled like a spent balloon. Quickly I toweled off and pulled on my *Sleepless in Seattle* nightshirt and my faded pink chenille robe—now grown smooth in spots from years of wear. I grabbed my blow-dryer and aimed it at my hair. As my limp locks splayed every which way under the onslaught, I peered into the mirror. *Hmmm. Maybe it's time for me to think about hair plugs . . .*

Still shivering, I poked the blow-dryer inside my robe for a few warming bursts. Ahh, that was better. My goose bumps finally sat down. Warmed, I schlepped out to the tiny galley kitchen in my oversized slippers and nuked some milk for hot chocolate. When I opened the cupboard for the marshmallows, my eyes alighted upon the red plaid box of Scottish shortbread I'd bought for my upcoming Jane Austen chick flickathon with Lindsey and the girls.

Yum. Wouldn't some rich, buttery shortbread taste delicious right now? Especially dipped into the hot chocolate with ooey-gooey marshmallow clinging to the sides?

In a sugar-fantasy fog I started to reach for the box.

No! Greedy girl. Gluttonous girl. You got that as a treat to share with your friends.

But they'll never know, my sugar-craving inner child whined.

You need to wait. Delayed gratification is good for the soul.

I'm not good at waiting, my inner brat pouted.

I know. But remember your resolution to exercise self-restraint and become more healthy and fit by shedding that extra fifteen pounds?

Yes, petulant inner child agreed. *But after the world's worst blind date, I deserve a treat.*

And closing my ears to my chiding conscience, I grabbed my hot chocolate and box of shortbread—chocolate-dipped, no less—and marched into my bedroom, where I settled myself comfortably beneath my candy cane–striped sheets and matching comforter. There I tore into the pretty plaid box as only a chocolate-starved, hormonal woman can.

One empty box later, I was sated, but not quite ready for sleep.

Who could sleep already after such an evening? Oy. (There are times when white-bread Protestant expressions simply don't cut it.)

I leaned over and rifled through my video and DVD collection on the garage-sale bookcase I'd painted red and black.

In a British frame of mind from the shortbread, I let my searching fingers pause at *Sense and Sensibility*—with the incomparable Emma Thompson and Kate Winslet. *Note to self: Will now exercise self-restraint and save Kate and Emma and the adorably bashful Hugh Grant for movie day with the girls. Will also bypass all other period English movies for said evening to demonstrate strong mental fortitude and solidarity with girlfriends.*

Finally I pulled out the modern-day chick-flick classic, *Steel Magnolias,* which has some of the greatest lines ever committed to film—after *Casablanca,* of course: "The nicest thing I can say about her is that all her tattoos are spelled correctly." "You are evil and you must be destroyed." And "Laughter through tears is my favorite emoti-n."

Two laughter-through-tears-filled hours later, I switched off the TV, still sniffling, and dragged myself out of bed to brush my teeth. *Note to self, upon looking in mirror at dried rivulets of mascara caking my cheeks: Must learn to cry more prettily. Watch* Ghost *to perfect Demi Moore's technique.*

I then scrubbed my face clean of all remnants of mascara and fell back into bed, asleep in seconds.

t he alarm shrilled.

I hit the snooze button, but it kept ringing. Finally it stopped.

Lindsey's voice filled the answering-machine air: "Phoebe, where *are* you? It's eight-fifteen, and we were supposed to meet at the gym at eight. Are you there? If you're there, pick up. Did you stay up late watching your old movies again?"

"Ahwhmpfft," I mumbled groggily into the phone, "be there in seven minutes."

Kicking the covers off, I jumped out of bed, exchanged my nightshirt for an oversized black T-shirt, sweats, and cross-trainers, pulled my hair back with a scrunchy, brushed my teeth, splashed water on my face, and slapped on a little moisturizer and concealer to hide the dark circles under my eyes. Then I bounded down the stairs to my car.

Three minutes later I roared up to the gym and an impatient Lindsey waiting outside. "See, what'd I tell you? Seven minutes flat."

"Which only makes you twenty-two minutes late," she groused. "What time did you go to bed last night?"

"Um—I think it was around two-thirty or so."

"I thought you told me that part of your new fitness resolution was to be in bed by midnight—especially when you have early morning plans."

"It is. And I will. From now on. But you have to admit, Lins, last night was a little unusual. I needed a pick-me-up after that blind date from the netherworld. A blind date, I might add, that my best friend set me—"

"Okay, okay. Give it a rest. Today's a new day, so let's go inside and pump a little iron," my more petite friend said.

"It's what I live for."

Forty-five minutes later found Lindsey and me huffing and puffing our way to the showers.

On the way, Melissa, our blonde, perky new trainer—who was pushing twenty and maybe a size two—high-fived us and said, "Great job, ladies! Doesn't it feel good to get those muscles moving? Before you know it, your stomachs will be washboard flat. Keep up the good work, and I'll see you Tuesday." And with a bright smile and a jaunty wave, she bounced off to her next victim.

As we watched Melissa bound away in her black tights and orange thong leotard, Lindsey looked at me and said, "What's the penalty for murder in this state again?"

"Life without parole. But I think there's a special dispensation for choking by thong of girls who are less than a size four—especially if they're always in an advanced state of perkiness."

Basking in a fit, healthy glow after our showers, we congratulated ourselves on making it through the first day of our workout regime and decided that was cause for celebration.

I snapped my scrunchy in place. "Starbucks. My treat."

After inhaling Frappucinos and blueberry muffins, we headed to our favorite salon for dual pedicures, then over to the mall for a little power shopping. Lindsey, whose thighs aren't on the same close personal basis as mine are, bought a flirty little jean skirt and white T-shirt, while I finally picked up two of the cotton print skirts I'd been coveting, a new pair of sandals, and a silver toe ring.

Hungry again from all that shopping, but wanting to be good and eat healthy, we drove through a fruit and juice bar for a couple of tall smoothies. As we sped down the highway, I slid open the sunroof and popped in a little Shania Twain, then together we lustily sang out, "Man! I feel like a woman!"

There are times when it's great to be a girl.

"Just think, Lins. By this time next week I could be the next Roger Ebert. Wouldn't that be cool? I can hardly wait 'til Monday." I bounced in my seat, inadvertently jerking the car toward the center line.

"Steady, Pheebs. I want to be sure we *make* it to Monday."

Next stop: the grocery store, to stock up on food for our big singles game night at church.

Lindsey and I—who were both members of the leadership team for our No More Lone Rangers singles group—arrived at the church half an hour later, arms bulging with bags of chips, pretzels, M&M's, Mrs. Fields, and Oreos dipped in to-die-for milk chocolate. Just then, Phil and his brother Scott, also members of the leadership team, pulled up in their muddy Jeep. Phil was a nice guy I'd gone out with a couple of times before we both realized we were better buddies than romantic material. He was also the king of practical jokes—and we'd all been on the receiving end at least once. Scott was quite a bit younger and not really a dating candidate, though I knew he had a crush on me.

He leaped out of the Jeep. "Here Pheebs, let me help you with that."

"Hey Scotty, what about me?" Phil slammed his door shut. "You're supposed to help me carry in these cases of soda."

"Ladies first, bro," Scott said, relieving me of the two heaviest bags.

"Here, Phil." Lindsey thrust one of her overstuffed bags at him. "You could take an etiquette lesson from your younger brother."

"So, Phoebe," Scott caught up to me on the steps of the church's multipurpose room. "When are you going to marry me?"

"When God tells me to rob the cradle."

I said it jokingly, but my smile was halfhearted. My date with plug-man had left me a little touchy about romantic possibilities.

Lord, I don't want to be pushy, but could You please maybe send someone who was born in my same decade?

Inside, we found Jake and Christopher, the two other male members of our leadership group, already setting up tables—under the guid-ance of Susan, an eleven-year Lone Rangers veteran. A great WOG ("Woman of God," as the guys in the group had christened her) in her early forties, Susan was the one who'd convinced the senior pastor more than a decade ago that it would be good for the church to have a group where single adults could meet and fellowship together.

For some, Lone Rangers was a G-rated meat market. For others it was about free food or just a respite from lonely Saturday nights. And for some it really did mean a place of sharing and spirituality with other singles.

Jake, a forty-five-year-old, never-married sports-store owner, jock, and resident ladies' man, definitely fit the first two categories. Susan and former missionary Christopher fell solidly in the third. I was a combination of all of the above. Actually, most of us were.

None of us would ever forget the interim singles pastor—married for almost three decades—who'd breezed through the group last year. "Are you here to worship God or to meet a woman?" he'd thundered to the guys. Then he turned to the women and challenged us as well: "Are you here to worship God or to meet a man? You *need* to be here to wor-ship God."

We squirmed in our seats.

But then quiet, gentle Christopher spoke up. "Are the two mutu-ally exclusive? Why can't I worship God *and* meet women? Or am I sup-posed to go to a bar to meet them instead?"

That pastor didn't last long.

Happily, the church ended up hiring Pastor John, thirty-eight and fresh from his honeymoon to the beautiful, thirty-four-year-old Julia— which gave all us over-thirties hope. He didn't come to all the social events, though. A wise man, he delegated and let the leadership com-mittee handle most of those.

As we set up for the party, the talk soon turned to the familiar, million-dollar topic: what we're looking for in the opposite sex. Jake, who'd been watching all those reality dating and fix-up shows, was convinced he had a handle on what women wanted—and in what order.

"Admit it," he said. "You girls want someone who's good-looking, successful, athletic, fun, likes your mother, and will buy you lots and lots of presents."

We presented him with a deluge of marshmallows, Monopoly game pieces, and anything else we could throw that wouldn't cause serious physical injury.

"You couldn't be more wrong, Jake," I said. "Looks and money aren't even on my list. Here's what I'm looking for." I ticked off the attributes on my fingers. "Kindness, intelligence, sense of humor, shares the same beliefs and values, thoughtfulness, understanding . . ."

"And treats us like a queen," we all chorused.

"Not asking for much, are you?" Phil said. "What I want to know is—"

Lindsey cut him off. "And someone who's a good listener."

"Employed," added Samantha, who'd just ended a three-month relationship with a guy who never picked up the tab.

"Must like cats," said Susan, the feline-loving owner of two calicos.

"Kids," said single mom Kim.

"Someone who calls when he says he will," Lindsey added with a pointed glance at Jake.

"Okay, guys, now it's your turn," peacemaker Susan interjected.

"Smart, sweet, fun, cute without makeup, and makes me laugh," said Scott, stealing a sidewise glance at me.

His big brother jumped in. "Attractive, athletic, intelligent, same beliefs. And who gets *The Far Side*."

"Good-looking, in shape, long hair, fun, and spontaneous," said Jake. "And doesn't bring up marriage on the first date."

"Amen, brother," applauded the guys.

All except Christopher.

Lindsey shot him a curious glance. "So, Chris, what would be your ideal woman?"

"Someone kind, with an open heart, and who's secure with herself and her relationship with God."

"Awww," all the women cooed as one.

I looked over at Lindsey. "Hey guys, did you notice that all of you except Christopher mentioned looks?"

"That's right," she agreed. "Men are so shallow."

"No, it's called visual," Jake said. "And we can't help it. That's how God made us."

"Don't go blaming God."

"Yeah," Kim chimed in. "Admit it: You men are all looking for a spiritual Barbie."

"And you want a spiritual Ken." Phil said. "Or Brad Pitt."

"Only if he's smart *and* funny—like Chandler on *Friends*." I batted my eyes at him.

"Hey, speaking of Barbie . . ." Lindsey nudged me. I turned—and so did all the guys—and noticed a Heather Locklear look-alike standing in the doorway, looking around uncertainly.

Jake, Phil, and even sweet young Scott fell all over each other jostling to help the pretty newcomer. Only Christopher remained behind, calmly setting up the pieces on the Monopoly board and separating the houses and hotels into neat little piles.

"So, Chris, how come you're not joining the stampede to Miss Hottie?"

He looked over at the cluster of men and chuckled. "Well, I've never been one to follow a stampede." He shrugged. "And I've learned from experience that what's inside a person is what really counts."

Lindsey sighed. "Christopher, will you marry me?"

At that moment, the rest of the thundering singles throng arrived, and we all put on our leadership hospitality hats to welcome the group and guide them to the game tables.

"Hi there. Are you a Monopoly man, or a Pictionary guy?"

"Ready to take a little Risk?"

"Who's up for some Taboo breaking?"

Since I can't draw, am terrible with anything involving numbers, and don't have a clue about strategizing, I opted for my personal favorite, Trivial Pursuit, and joined the table of two—now three—girls and five guys for our ongoing battle of the sexes.

"Um, this isn't fair, five against three," one of the newer guys said.

"Oh yes it is," Phil said dryly. "You've never played with Phoebe before. But don't worry—I know her weakness. It's called Sports."

I stuck out my tongue at him. "Let's roll to see who goes first. All righty, girls, we're off. Mind if we start with pink? That's my best category."

Three plastic pie pieces later, the guys still hadn't landed on the board. But then we missed a Sports question and they seized control. They lost it two turns later on Arts and Literature.

Now it was our turn.

Phil read the card and groaned. "Who played the title role in the movie *Rebecca*?"

I shot him a triumphant smile. "That would be no one. Rebecca is dead before the story begins. However, Joan Fontaine played the new Mrs. de Winter, wife of Maxim de Winter—played by Laurence Olivier—and widower of the dead Rebecca."

"Who's Laurence Olivier?" asked one of my twenty-something teammates.

Phil winked at me. "He was the Kenneth Branagh of his day."

"Is that the guy who was in the second *Harry Potter*?"

With sincere Christian effort, I refrained from rolling my eyes.

We missed the History question on what year the Titanic sank—told you I'm bad with numbers—but that set off a new discussion among the twenty-somethings, who thought the movie *Titanic* was the most romantic ever made.

I begged to differ. "First of all, Kate Winslet and Leonardo DiCaprio were completely mismatched. They didn't have any chemistry."

Phil nodded. "She's a real woman, and he looks like a fourteen-year-old boy."

"A *gorgeous* fourteen-year-old boy," one of the younger women said.

Her pal sided with her. "For sure. And he doesn't look fourteen to me. He looks perfect. He's a hottie. And he sacrificed himself for her. That was soooo romantic . . ."

"Yes, and I found it especially romantic when he was teaching her to spit off the ship's rail," I said. "I'm sure that most debutantes from the early 1900s found spitting to be a fun and daring new social custom. So let's just take our modern-day sensibilities and insert them into a film that was supposed to take place eighty years ago. No one will ever notice . . ."

"Like the Demi Moore remake of *The Scarlet Letter*," said an unknown voice behind me.

"Exactly! Talk about ruining a great story." I turned around to see who this movie buff who knew his stuff was.

And forgot to breathe.

The nametag on his black polo shirt said Alex, but the delicious fluttery sensation in my stomach said, *This is the father of my children.*

I breathed a prayer of thanks to God for answering my prayers so quickly—but couldn't think of anything to say out loud. I was too overwhelmed by that head of wavy hair, that movie-star smile. And those eyes!

Phil filled the silence as I gaped. "Hi, Alex. I'm Phil. Welcome. Care to join us?"

"Thanks, but I don't want to interrupt your game. I'll just watch, if I may, and get in on the next one." He scooted his chair closer.

The sand on the honeymoon beach is white and sparkling, the ocean a deep, inviting turquoise as I run in slow motion, thighs not touching and white gauzy dress flowing behind me, toward my drop-dead gorgeous husband, Alex, who only has eyes for me . . .

"Okay, Pheebs." Phil interrupted my romantic reverie. "We're in the final stretch now. Get ready to be blown out of the water."

"In your dreams, Phillie."

But for the first time in Trivial Pursuit history, I choked on a pink question and we lost.

Note to self: Pull it together, girl. Do not allow yourself to get distracted by close proximity of gorgeous thirty-something movie buff . . .

Phil crowed and punched the air—"Gotcha, Pheebs!"—and began singing, "We are the champions . . ."

The next game we switched the teams around, opting for a boy-girl, girl-boy effect. Alex wound up on my side, and I fantasized he'd stay there forever, even though we disagreed on a couple of movie questions. He was convinced that *East of Eden* was the last movie James Dean completed before he died, but I knew it was *Giant*. (I tried not to gloat too much.) However, I didn't have a clue which character in *Return of the Jedi* the Ewoks thought was a god. My money was on Han Solo, but Alex gave me a sly wink and said, "All women think that. What is it with that guy anyway?" before giving the correct answer: C-3PO. Between the two of us ping-ponging our answers back and forth, we skunked Phil and company. We high-fived while the rest of our team did a little victory dance.

Wow. We really had a Cary Grant, Rosalind Russell His Girl Friday *kind of synergy going there. I like it. A guy who not only loves movies and literature, but doesn't mind getting down and dirty with sports, either. Can you say "Renaissance man"? Pinch me. I must be dreaming.*

Phil slapped Alex's shoulder, conceding defeat. "Good job, man."

Just then, Lindsey popped over from the Taboo table, flashed me a megawatt smile over Alex's head, and sat down next to him. "Hi, I'm Lindsey. This your first time, isn't it?"

"Yes. I'm new in town."

"Oh? What do you do?"

"I'm in media."

"So is Phoebe," Lindsey said, shoving me forward none too subtly. "She writes for the *Star*. And confidentially"—she leaned toward him and lowered her voice—"we're hoping she'll be the new film critic very soon."

"Lindsey," I protested, but before I could shush her, Alex got a strange look on his face and jumped to his feet, spilling his Doritos in the process. "I'm sorry. Excuse me, but I, uh, I have to go." He rushed off, bumping into a few chairs on the way.

Phil smiled. "Guess he *really* had to go."

The next day at church, Lindsey and I scuttled into the second to the last pew on the right a few minutes late for services. I'd been raised a Lutheran, but after my exposure to the nondenominational chapel in air force basic training, I'd decided I liked a little more oomph in my worship, so I'd found a Presbyterian church that suited me just fine. Lins and I always attended the early morning contemporary service, where some people raised their hands when they sang, but the most my Lutheran background would allow was to raise one hand up—bent at the elbow—while sitting down.

After the service, as we stood up to leave, I caught sight of Alex in one of the back pews on the far left. He looked wonderful in crisp khakis and a navy jacket, although I was a bit disappointed to realize that he was about my height. I usually like them taller, but I was willing to make an exception, so I smiled and nodded, But Alex turned and hurried out, leaving me standing there looking like a bobble-head doll.

"My goodness, Pheebs," Lindsey said. "The effect you have on that man. Maybe it's love at first sight and he just doesn't know how to handle it. "

"Yeah. Or maybe he's just a stuck-up jerk."

Or maybe he just saw that goofy puppy-dog look on my face last night and ran for the hills. *Note to self: In future, practice being more aloof and reserved, especially in company of appealing members of opposite sex who could turn out to be Mr. Right, even if they're not all that tall.*

that kid in *The Sixth Sense* may have seen dead people, but it was my job to write about them. Writing obituaries—or obits, as they're called in the newspaper biz—is the mold in the journalism basement and where every beginning reporter gets her start. Why I was just starting up the newspaper ladder at age thirty-one is another story. Suffice it to say I'd taken a few sounded-great-at-the-moment detours on the way to my finally chosen career. So my particular rung on the ladder involved either the obits or the cops-and-fire log. And I'd done both.

The things you learn: A sixty-two-year-old guy was arrested on suspicion of shoplifting at Saving Soles shoe store—the cops found three pairs of size 13 women's stilettos in his gym bag. Then there was the middle-aged man with serious love handles who ran naked through a symphony concert because the voices in his head told him to. And the Sunday-school teacher who swiped the offering from the first-grade class.

It was enough to ruin a girl's day.

That's why I was more than ready to exchange all this mischief and mayhem for fantasies from the silver screen. Like an actor who really wants to direct, I really wanted to write movie reviews. How great a job is that—to get paid for movie watching? Plus, all the popcorn I can eat.

And today at eleven I hoped to learn that the movie reviewer job—long held by Grady O'Neill, who was retiring in a month—would be mine. My managing editor, Blaine Cooper (whom everyone called Coop), had run a few of my reviews over the past few months. The response had been mostly favorable, except from the handful of thirty-something guys—and one twenty-six-year-old woman—who took umbrage at my writing that the bathroom humor in the comedian-of-the-moment's latest gross-out comedy was perfect for junior-high-school boys.

Coop didn't mind. "If a critic doesn't offend somebody, he or she's not doing her job."

That was the job I wanted. And hoped to get today.

Squeaking into work a few minutes before eight, I hurried to the ladies'—which sported a full-length mirror unlike my home medicine cabinet, which cut me off midchest—to give my interview outfit the once-over: black pants, white blouse, and long black blazer cut to hit just below my fluffy rear-end region for the requisite slimming effect. I must say I looked cool, calm, and confident. Definitely fit the role of the hip movie reviewer. And except for the white blouse, I mused as I exited the restroom, I could've landed a job in New York.

Fast-forward to next spring at the Academy Awards. *As I work the red carpet in my black Vera Wang and hair extensions, I acknowledge the stars whose work I've reviewed over the past year: "Nicole: great job. Loved how you inhabited the character. Fabulous dress, by the way. Meryl: flawless, as always. No one does accents like you. Mel: you made me laugh, you made me cry." And then, across the crowded carpet—Indiana Jones himself. And he's heading my way, smiling that little crooked smile at me . . .*

"Earth to Phoebe. Earth to Phoebe." Sharon, our fiftyish receptionist who had a love affair with the color purple and a knack for outdated catchphrases, thrust some pages at me as I passed her desk. "Here's the obits from this weekend."

"Thanks, Sharon." Indy and his crooked smile dissolved in a fast fade-out.

At my own desk, I skimmed the stack of death notices and I wrote up a few but had a hard time reading one, which meant—every obit writer's nightmare—calling the relatives of the dearly departed to clarify the information.

Tossing up a quick prayer heavenward for sensitivity, I dialed the number on the obit form. "Hello. Please forgive me for disturbing you at this difficult time. This is Phoebe Grant with the *Star*, and I'm writing up the obituary for . . . Harry Finke?"

"The name is Harvey."

"Oh. Excuse me." I cleared my throat. "The fax is difficult to read, and I want to make sure I write this up correctly. Is there someone who can answer a few questions for me?"

"I can help you with that. I'm Harvey's father."

Way to go, Sherlock. Sweat began to bead beneath my bangs. "I'm so sorry for your loss. Is there another family member or friend I could talk to so you don't have to go through this?"

"Nope. Just me. I'm his only surviving relative. My wife passed several years back, and Harvey and I pretty much liked to keep to ourselves. We didn't need anyone else."

Tears pricked my eyes. "What a wonderful relationship you had with your son."

"He wasn't only my son. He was my best friend, the poor li'l feller. I'm sure going to miss him running and jumping around here like he did."

I hate this job. I hate this job. "Just a few more questions, Mr. Finke, then I won't disturb you any longer. Um, how old was Harvey when he passed away?"

"Nine."

The tears mingled with the sweat that slid down my cheeks. "So young."

"Actually, he lived a year longer than expected. Most only live 'til seven or eight. That's the normal life span for his kind."

His kind? It was really starting to get warm in my cubicle. I unbuttoned a button on my blouse. "If you don't mind my asking, um, how did Harvey die?"

"He ch-choked on Wilbur."

"Wilbur?"

"My albino mouse."

Realization slowly began to dawn. (Doesn't it always? The only thing realization can do is "to dawn." But I digress.)

"Mr. Finke, how many legs did Harvey have?"

"Four."

"I see. Did he perhaps have a tail also?"

"Of course. All ferrets have tails."

"A *ferret*? You submitted an obituary for a ferret?" I began flapping my blazer open and shut to try and generate a breeze.

"He wasn't just a ferret." Mr. Finke was sobbing now. "He was my baby."

"Yes, of course. I understand. It's just that, um, well, the newspaper has a policy of only publishing obituaries for human beings."

"Well, that's pretty exclusionary!" He slammed the phone down.

Sweating like a socialite in a sauna, I started fanning myself with Harvey's obit.

Mark, the cynical political reporter in the cubicle across from mine, grunted, "Ferrets?"

"Albino mice, too."

"Welcome to my world, Phoebe."

"Is it hot in here?" I started to take off my blazer, then remembered the pin-sized hole in the armpit of my Tommy blouse. No blazer removal for this girl, no matter how hot it got. Besides, my meeting with Coop was less than ten minutes away, and both professionalism and pride demanded that I keep my fluffier regions fully hidden in the boss's presence.

Just then my e-mail beeped to let me know a new message had arrived. *Oh no. Mr. Finke's discovered my e-mail address and is sending me nasty notes. Next, he'll probably send me a dead albino mouse in a box of Cracker Jacks.*

Relieved to see the address belonged to Ray in Maintenance, I double-clicked to read, "Sorry, folks. The AC's broken, but we're working on it and hope to have it fixed within the next two hours."

"Whew. That's good news," I said, lifting my sticky hair and blotting the back of my neck with a tissue. "Thought maybe I was having an early hot flash."

Millie, the lone female sports columnist and, at fifty-four, the reporter with the most seniority, swiveled her chair to the door of her next-door cubicle, hoisted her ever-present menopausal minifan up high, and said, "Trust me, you'll know."

Checking my watch, I saw that I had less than seven minutes to stanch the unprofessional river of sweat pouring from my body. I raced to the restroom, unbuttoned my blouse, and leaned over the sink. I was in the process of splashing cold water under my arms when the door opened. A leggy blonde who was twenty at best glided in on a cloud of Ralph Lauren Romance.

"Oops. Shower break's over. Love the perks with this job," I said, trying to disentangle my hands from their firmly entrenched position beneath my armpits.

She arched a perfect eyebrow at me and disappeared into the first stall.

Red-faced and dripping, I blotted my bangs with a paper towel, swiped some lipstick across my mouth, rebuttoned my blouse, and flapped both sides of my blazer in a last-ditch attempt to dry off. So much for my calm, cool, professional demeanor.

Breathless, I knocked on the managing editor's door and poked my head in, pretending an insouciance I didn't feel. "Hi, Coop. I'm here for our eleven o'clock."

"Oh, Phoebe, I'm sorry. I forgot," Coop said, looking stricken.

"Not a problem," I lied, all the while inwardly screaming: *How could you forget something I've been sweating bullets over for the past month—not to mention this morning!* "I can come back later if that's better for you."

"No, no. That's okay. Er, Phoebe, I'd like to introduce you to someone."

For the first time, I noticed there was another person in the office. All I could see over the back of the chair facing Coop's desk was a curly brown head. "I'm sorry," I said, cheeks flaming, turning to leave, "I didn't realize anyone else was here."

"Hello, Phoebe," said a familiar voice. The curly head turned, and I saw it belonged to Alex.

Alex of the honeymoon sand. Alex of the flying Doritos. Alex of the fast getaway.

Coop's head swiveled back and forth between us. "Do you two know each other?"

"We've met," I said.

"Yes. Well, I'll leave you two," Alex said, shooting up from his seat and bumping his knee on the desk. "Coop, see you at lunch." He nod-ded awkwardly in my direction. "Phoebe."

And for the third time since I'd met him, Alex the mystery man was gone with the wind.

"I certainly have a way of clearing the room whenever he's around. Maybe it's my deodorant."

"Or maybe it's the lipstick on your teeth," Coop said.

Under cover of my upper lip, I slid my tongue across my not-quite pearly whites. Sure enough, I tasted Fire Engine Red. I smiled sheepishly at Coop, ducked my head, and did a quick front-teeth rub with my index finger.

Coop smiled in return. "So, how do you know him?

"I met him at church this weekend."

"Alexander Spencer goes to church?"

"Yes. But I think he's allergic to the pews because he sure doesn't sit in them long. Or maybe he's just allergic to me. Who is he anyway?"

"Our new publisher."

"What?! What happened to Matthew Rhodes?" (The Rhodes fam-ily had owned the Cleveland *Star* for the past 120 years.)

"He took an early retirement. And the Spencer family bought him out."

"The Spencer family? As in the publishing magnate Spencers?"

"Yes. But, Phoebe, you can't say anything to anyone about this yet.

And I mean *any*one. We won't be making the official announcement until after lunch."

Wait'll I tell Lindsey! Except . . . I can't tell her. Or anyone else for that matter. Coop's probably entrusting me with this confidential information since I'm about to become a member of the columnist elite and, as such, am privy to the inside newsroom track . . .

Suddenly, my smugness screeched to a halt as an awful thought hit me. "They forced Rhodes out, didn't they?"

"They didn't force him out. His doctor said the stress was getting to be too much, so he decided to retire early and enjoy more time with his grandkids. Besides, selling was the only way to keep the paper afloat. As you know, we've been operating in the red for quite a while."

Everyone in the newsroom knew that. There had been no raises the last two years.

"So you're saying we have Alex Spencer and his family to thank for our survival?"

"Basically." Coop looked down and shuffled some papers. "Unfortunately, however, that survival comes at a price. I'm sorry, Phoebe, but this means that I won't be able to give you that reviewer job you wanted—and deserve."

My professional life came crashing down around me and lay in broken shards at my feet. "Bu-but, who's going to replace Grady?"

"No one. The Spencer papers generally use nationally syndicated reviews."

Do not cry! Take a deep breath, count to five . . . and breathe, Phoebe, breathe . . .

I gave Coop a shaky smile. "Well, if I said I wasn't disappointed, we'd both know I was lying. But, it's not the end of the world. Maybe I'll still be able to slip in the occasional review now and then, in between my obits."

Coop couldn't meet my eyes. "I'm afraid your obit slot isn't available any longer either. We have to lay off several people, and there's a brand-new college intern willing to write for free, just to get the experience, so . . ."

My fingers dug into the top of the high-backed leather chair for support. "Let me guess. A tall, leggy blonde?"

"'Fraid so. I'm sorry, Phoebe. You're a wonderful writer, and you know more about movies than anyone I've ever met. You'd make an excellent reviewer. And if it were up to me, you'd always have a job at the *Star*. But unfortunately, you've been here less than a year, and they're laying off by hire dates . . ."

Wanting to put him out of his misery, I fumbled with the doorknob. "I understand, Coop. Not your fault. That's just the way the corporate cookie crumbles. It's okay. Don't worry about it. I'm a big girl. I can handle it. The *Star*'s not the only paper in town, you know."

"That's the spirit, Phoebe. I know this comes as a big shock, but sometimes it's those unexpected shocks that wind up working out for the best. I'll be happy to give you a letter of recommendation, although you may have to wait a few days until the dust settles."

"No problem," I said, lying through my very polite, professional teeth.

"Thanks for being such a good sport about this, Phoebe. You're going to go far. Please remember, though, that this is all still very confidential."

"My lips are sealed." I shook his hand, flashed him a brilliant smile, and made my way back to my cubicle.

Millie was out of hers in a New York minute. "So, did you get the job?"

"I can't say."

"C'mon, you can tell me. I won't tell a soul."

"Really, Millie, I can't. I promised. Now, I really have to go." And grabbing my purse and laptop, I sprinted for the elevator before she could see my glistening eyes.

"Hey Pheebs, what's the hurry?" Mark teased. "Got a hot date with ferret man?"

I forced out a smile and a wave. "I'll never tell."

The elevator doors pinged open, and I was relieved to see no one inside. Once the doors shut behind me, my chin-up facade crumbled. But as the claustrophobic chute approached the lobby, I brushed away the tears and pasted on a fake smile—which abruptly faded when I came face to face with Alex the corporate raider and a posse of glad-handing high-powered suits.

"Phoebe, uh . . ."

I inclined my head. "Mr. Spencer."

One of the suits clapped Alex on the shoulder and said, "C'mon Spencer, time to go make some history." I slipped past the posse and, with head held high, click-clacked my way across the marble lobby to the parking lot outside. I was Katharine Hepburn and Rosalind Russell rolled into one—the strong, independent career woman able to handle professional setbacks with dignity and grace, yet exercise remarkable restraint while all the time wanting to kick that rich, Trivial Pursuit–playing, corporate-raider dirtbag in the shins.

Getting into my car, I cranked up the radio to cover the mewling sounds I was making and headed home.

"I love you, darling."

"And I love you, my darling. You're what I've been waiting for my whole life. I've never loved anyone like this before . . ."

"Right, Carissa." I snorted as I reached for another potato chip. "That's the same thing you said to your seven other husbands. Time to come up with a new line, babe. When *I* say those words, I'm going to mean them. If I ever meet anyone to say them to."

The airbrushed and impossibly beautiful couple moved in for the big clinch, then the soap opera cut to a commercial—a teaser for tonight's local news. "Coming up at five: The Cleveland *Star* was bought out today by the Spencer newspaper chain. CEO Alex Spencer has already taken dramatic cost-cutting steps to turn around the financially struggling paper. Today, thirteen *Star* employees got the news and a pink slip. More at five."

I switched off the TV and burrowed under the covers, scattering potato chips, candy wrappers, and a swath of wadded-up tissues in my wake.

"I'm not a strong, independent career woman," I wailed to my pillow. "I'm a miserable, pathetic failure. This morning my future was bright with the promise of my dream job. And this afternoon, I don't have *any* job. I'm just an unemployed, overweight loser."

The phone and my cell rang simultaneously. I ignored both.

Lindsey's voice punctured the air. "Pheebs, I just heard. I'm so sorry. I tried to reach you at work after reading the news online, and Millie told me what happened. You are *not* a failure, so stop thinking that this instant! You're simply a casualty of corporate downsizing. It has *nothing* to do with you and your abilities, so don't even go down that road. Hang in there—I'm coming over after work. And bringing solace."

Two hours later the front buzzer rang.

Shuffling to the door in my footie pajamas, I opened it to find my best friend holding a brown bag. She enveloped me in a bear hug, then pulled back. "Brrr, it's freezing in here."

"I know. The AC broke at work, and by the time I got home I was sweating like a pig, so I stripped off all my clothes and punched the thermostat down to sixty."

"Thus the footie pajamas. Okay. But can I borrow a robe or something?" Lindsey held the bag aloft. "I can't eat ice cream when I'm freezing."

"Help yourself. Back of the bathroom door."

She returned wearing my chenille robe over her sleeveless summer dress and grabbed two spoons from the kitchen. "Living room or bedroom?"

"Bedroom. It's already a mess, and I don't want to drip anything on the couch I'm still paying for—especially since they might need to come and repossess it now."

We plopped down on the bed—Lindsey cross-legged with my robe bunched around her and me with my back against the wall, knees hugged to my chest.

"Now, tell all," she demanded.

So I recounted every sordid detail of the morning's events.

"I don't believe that creep Alex. What nerve! Although that explains why he sprinted from church so fast."

"*Both* times," I reminded her. "I can't believe I was even remotely attracted to him."

"Well, he *is* pretty gorgeous. Wins two out of three on the tall, dark, and handsome scale."

"Looks can be deceiving. Besides, the short thing combined with the deception adds up to zero as far as I'm concerned."

"I hear ya," Lins said. "Feel the same about Jake."

A few months ago, Jake, the flirt with the smoldering eyes and purposely disheveled hair, had pursued Lindsey with a vengeance—sending flowers, e-mailing cute cards, and leaving fun messages on her answering machine—until she finally agreed to a date. They'd gone out and had a wonderful evening, and at the end of the night, when he took her home, Jake had kissed her on the cheek, squeezed her hand, gazed meaningfully into her eyes, and promised to call.

Which he never did.

The next time we saw him at Lone Rangers, he was flirting with a voluptuous redhead.

Jerk. Creep. Jerk.

"But let's not waste any more time on icky men right now," Lindsey said. "We need to figure out what you're going to do next. We need to make a plan."

"I don't *know* what I'm going to do next," I whined. "Hey, maybe I'm supposed to become a missionary. Maybe God wants me to go dig ditches in Africa and suffer for Him. And maybe while I'm there I'll run into Robert Redford in the jungle and he'll wash my hair and take me for a ride in his biplane while beautiful soaring music swells in the background . . ."

Lindsey rolled her eyes. "You're afraid of bugs. Remember? And snakes. And lizards. And elephants. And I think they have all of those in Africa—times ten. Besides, you'd never make it in the heat. You know how you get all wilty and Blanche DuBois-ish." She mimicked Vivien Leigh's *Streetcar Named Desire* rendition: "I have always depended on the kindness of strangers . . ."

"Okay, so scratch the jungle. Although . . . wait a minute. There is one jungle where I'd be right at home—*The Asphalt Jungle.*"

"Huh?"

"Another term for the City. *The Asphalt Jungle* was this great black-and-white movie from the early fifties set in a major city—Chicago, I think. But I'm talking New York, babe." I jumped off the bed. "One of my journalism pals, Brian, who was at the *Star* when I first arrived, is a sportswriter for the *New York Times.* He always told me to look him up if I came to town. So maybe I should *go* to town, look him up, and see if he can wangle me an interview. This could be my big chance, Lins!"

She pouted. "Pheebs, you're *not* allowed to move to New York and leave me behind."

"No worries—since the chances of my getting a job with the *Times* are next to nothing." I frowned as reality reared its ugly head. "Not sure I can even afford the trip. Gotta try, though. Wonder how much I have left on my plastic? I'm going to e-mail Brian and also check out some of those cheap online travel sites to see what a ticket and hotel would cost. Can't be too outrageous, right?"

It was. After hours of checking every travel site imaginable, I realized the only way I'd make it to New York within the next few weeks was to go by Greyhound and sleep in the bus terminal. Which would leave me with some serious bed-head, not to mention mussing up my power interview suit. Discouraged, I went to sleep. And had the most amazing dream. In it, Lins rode to the rescue with free airline tickets and a hotel reservation that wouldn't cost us a penny.

Only it wasn't a dream.

My best friend cashed in her frequent-flier miles, which netted the two free tickets. And our buddy Phil called in a favor from another buddy of his, which resulted in three nights at a hotel just a few blocks from Times Square. Also for free.

I couldn't take it all in when Lins woke me with the news. "You're kidding!"

"Would I lie to you? The thing is, my boss has been bugging me to use my accumulated vacation days, and since things are slow at the office right now, I decided to finally take him up on it."

"Cool! How fun that we get to go together. And I can't believe the Phil-boy either. I didn't realize he had such connections—did you?"

"It's all that investment wheeling and dealing he does. Plus, I think it's not just his younger brother who has a soft spot in his heart for you, Pheebs."

"Not so, Lins. You, more than anybody, know that Phillie's just a good friend. More like a brother. Just like you—except the brother part. What would I ever do without you?"

"Guess you'll find out soon if you get this job and move away," she said, growing glum.

"Well, you'll just have to move *with* me!" I ran with the pie-in-the-sky possibility. "You can get a great HR job, Lins, and we'll be roomies and take the Big Apple by storm. I can see it now," I said. "We'll both become fabulously successful, respected New York career women, with corner offices and a loft in Tribeca. We'll rub shoulders with Donald Trump and Katie Couric, attend exciting Broadway openings and movie premieres, and meet fun and sophisticated creative types."

Note to self: Will have to exchange colorful wardrobe for basic black . . .

chapter four

Ya wanna hamburger, ya go to Boiger King. Here, ya oider a meat san-wich."

Welcome to New York.

Having taken a taxi from the airport to our Seventh Avenue hotel—"Omigosh, Lins, look: Carnegie Hall is right across the street!"—and too excited and starving to unpack, we dumped our bags in the room and ventured out seeking sustenance. We found it, and more, a couple of doors down at the Carnegie Deli, home of the mile-high stacked meat sandwiches, waiters who *tell* you what you want, and the best—and biggest—cheesecake in the world.

Eyeing the plates of staggering pastrami and corned beef passing by, Lindsey and I decided to split a ham on rye and a megaslice of chocolate-chip cheesecake. "Yum—seventh heaven," I said, licking my lips. "Who needs a man when there's cheesecake—rich, creamy, melt-in-your-mouth New York cheesecake—to be had?"

Lindsey pushed back the plate and groaned. "No more. I'm about to pop."

"Me too. Although I hate to leave that last bite. After all, think about all those poor starving kids in—where is it again? China? Romania?"

"In our house growing up, it was always Ethiopia."

I scarfed down the final cheesecake crumb as Lindsey reached down and pulled an envelope from her purse.

"What's that?"

"Don't know. Phil gave it to me at the airport when you were in the restroom. Gave me strict orders not to open it 'til we were eating our first meal in New York."

"Well, open it already. I'm dyin' here."

She did. And two tickets to *Phantom of the Opera* fell out. We squealed—then tried hard to be cool as several jaded New Yorkers glanced our way and muttered, "Tourists."

"We're going to a Broadway show!"

Lindsey shook her head in amazement. "Not just *any* Broadway show, but *Phantom*. Wow. Who'd have thunk it? The Phil-boy's got some class."

"Why do you think we're friends? That boy has hidden depths."

We began to gather our belongings, and I leaned across the table, cupping my hand to the side of my mouth and whispering, "Hey, do I have any lettuce stuck in my teeth?"

"All clear. How 'bout me?"

"No lettuce, but a smidge of mustard."

"Where?"

"Upper right molar, two o'clock."

Lindsey gingerly licked her pearly whites clean around her braces while under cover of the table I undid the top button of my Guess jeans, grateful I hadn't worn a crop top. Then we rolled out to explore the teeming mass of humanity, bright lights, and honking yellow cabs that is Manhattan. We headed to Times Square, where we discovered theater after theater ablaze with the hottest shows in town and the most beloved old standbys. And tomorrow, *we* were going to see the most famous show of all.

Wow. I can't believe I'm really here! On Broadway. Look, Dad, I made it.

All his life, my father, a glorious tenor who performed regularly in community theater, had longed to go to Broadway and take his family. Our den boasted an extensive collection of soundtracks—everything from *Oklahoma* and *West Side Story* to *Sweeney Todd* and *Les Mis*. I loved listening to my father sing. His rendition of "If I Loved You" from *Carousel* always made me cry. So at the beginning of my senior year, when he talked about taking us all to New York for my graduation, I was thrilled.

Unfortunately, he never made it to Broadway. Dad died of a heart attack three months before I received my diploma.

"Thinking of your dad?" Lindsey asked me softly.

I gave my friend a tremulous smile. "Yeah. Sure wish he could be here with me."

She patted my shoulder gently. "He is."

Much later, as we unpacked, a familiar sensation overtook me. "I'm hungry. Are you?"

"I could go for a little something," Lins said. "We had a really early dinner."

"And that was nearly eight hours ago." We looked across at each other and shrieked, "Room service!"

Digging into the golden calamari, we made our sightseeing plans for the next day—my job interview wasn't scheduled until Friday—and went to bed.

But I couldn't sleep.

Dear Lord, I have to get a job before Pottery Barn repossesses my sofa and I lose my darling apartment and become a homeless bag lady. Although You know I'd willingly give up my cute apartment for even a hole in the wall here. Just for the chance to work and live in the City.

I barely remembered to add, *If that's Your will, of course.* But I did remember. Then, tiptoeing to the bathroom, I shut the door behind me and practiced my introduction in front of the bathroom mirror.

"Hello." I pretended to give a firm, confident handshake. "I'm Phoebe Grant. Grant, as in Cary." As I repeated the familiar words that Dad—who had loved Cary Grant—always said when introducing himself, my eyes misted.

When I finally fell asleep that night I dreamed of Cary Grant and giant calamari with shopping carts overflowing my bed, the nightstand, the entire room—like that old *Star Trek* tribbles episode.

First thing in the morning, neurotic about the job interview, I touched base with my friend Brian, who confirmed again that yes, the features editor had agreed to meet with me the next day. That left the present day for sightseeing—and psyching myself up. As Lindsey and I took the ferry out to the Statue of Liberty, I longed to do a Barbra Streisand and belt out to the world—and one Alex Spencer in particular—not to rain on my parade. But it was raining, so I didn't. Instead, I hunkered inside with Lindsey over a cup of watery hot chocolate and imagined myself a *Working Girl* Melanie Griffith—underutilized and unappreciated, but soon to get my due.

And hopefully, a Harrison Ford in the process.

We left the theater in a blissful fog that night, with Lindsey humming a few bars from the "All I Ask of You" duet between Raoul and Christine. "Boy, wasn't that Raoul gorgeous?"

"Yeah, but I felt bad for the Phantom. He really *loved* Christine and helped her with her music," I said. "It was thanks to him that she even became a big opera star. She could have been a little more grateful. Poor guy. Just because he had a little skin problem . . ."

"And was *crazy*."

"Not really. Just crazy in love. Plus he had that whole tortured artist thing going for him, which I find appealing."

"Too much drama for me. Give me a guy with a steady nine-to-five and a 401(k) any day."

"Lins, you have no romance in your soul."

"Sure I do. But I also like to eat."

The next day, with time to kill before my interview, we took a brief tour of nearby Carnegie Hall, thrilled to think of the talent that had graced its famous stage—Judy Garland, Barbra Streisand, the Beatles, almost everybody who had been anybody. Knowing this was a once-in-a-lifetime opportunity, I lingered as the rest of the tour moved on. Then I took my life in my hands—*this one's for you, Dad*—planted my feet firmly on the stage, and belted off-key to the rafters: "These little town blues . . ."

"Don't give up your day job," someone yelled.

"Already have," I yelled back, secure in the knowledge that in just a few hours I had an interview at—drumroll—the *New York Times.*

The "interview" was a complete and humiliating bust.

I spent six minutes with the assistant features editor—a thin, frazzled forty-something woman dressed all in black with sharp, bird-like features and tortoiseshell glasses. I didn't breathe as she glanced briefly through my paltry stack of clips. She kept looking at her watch. "I'm sorry, but I'm on deadline and can't spare much time. Truth is, you're a good writer—Phoebe, is it?"

I nodded, tugging at my skirt, which was getting way too close for comfort.

"But you simply don't have enough experience to work here. The competition is fierce to get a slot at the *Times.* You need to have a few years writing for a major daily or some top-notch journalism awards under your belt before we'd even consider you. You wouldn't have even gotten this meeting if it weren't for your friendship with Brian."

So much for the loft in Tribeca. Should I slash my wrists now or later?

Seeing my crushed expression, she extended her hand. "Tell you what. Go get that experience. In another couple of years, after you've worked at a major daily and amassed a healthy stack of clips, e-mail me and we'll talk again. Okay?"

"Will do." I shook her hand. "Thanks for taking the time to meet with me." I stopped by Brian's desk to convey my thanks also, but he was out, so I scribbled him a quick note and left.

Loser! What made you think you *could get a job at the* New York Times, *obit girl? Deal with reality much?* Depressed and dazed, I stumbled through the city streets in my Manolo wannabes, not knowing my next step.

Need chocolate. Must have chocolate to cushion rejection, even if it does make skirt strangle thighs.

Fumbling in my purse for change, I found something better.

When I returned to our hotel room, Lindsey was smiling and hanging up the phone. She turned to me, her face pink. "You just missed Phi—Pheebs, what did you do?!"

"Got a haircut," I said, turning to show her all sides of my short, kicky, new do.

"I love it! You look fabulous! Like Audrey Hepburn in that movie you showed me—what was it?—*Roman Holiday.*"

"Exactly what I was going for."

"But how could you afford a haircut *here?*" she asked. "Did you put it on plastic?"

"Nope. It was a total God thing." I told her about my job rejection and how lousy I'd felt, and about how when I was searching for money to drown my sorrows in chocolate, I'd instead found my Express Cuts discount card—which showed I qualified for a free haircut. Seeing my limp locks reflected in the store window, I'd decided a quickie makeover was more important than chocolate.

Lins looked at her watch. "You can have both."

"What?"

She gave me her best hoity-toity smile. "We have reservations for tea at the Plaza."

"The Plaza?"

"Uh-huh. Scones and all. And chocolate. Lots of chocolate."

After my third cup of tea and one of the greatest gastronomical experiences of my life, I set my delicate china cup down on the elegant table and cast a wistful glance around at our luxurious surroundings. "Lins, I was *made* for this city. I simply have to get an exciting publishing job here. I'll wear those cool straight skirts like Doris Day in *Teacher's Pet*—although I'll have to lose ten pounds first. Bye-bye cheesecake. I can do ministry here. I can be what God wants me to be here. Right?" I said. "And I can shop and go to the theater every weekend. And God will give me the man of my dreams, a publishing mogul who'll treat me like a queen and give me a Tiffany's diamond. And I can write while raising our little family of two prep-school children—one boy, one girl . . ."

Lindsey snorted. "You always did have a great fantasy life."

"This is more than a fantasy. I don't care what it takes, Lins. New York is my home. My dream. And I'm going to make it come true. No matter what."

On Saturday, since it was our last morning in New York, we decided there was just one place left to see before going home.

Can you say "out of our league"?

In my current unemployed state, I couldn't afford even one of Tiffany's famous turquoise boxes. But after much deliberation, Lindsey bought a sterling silver key chain—for a mere eighty bucks.

As the trying-to-be gracious saleswoman wrapped the purchase of her clearly out-of-place customers, I leaned over and whispered in Lins's ear. "You be Reese Witherspoon from *Sweet Home Alabama*—you can do a Southern accent better, and besides you've got that cute blonde thing going for you—and I'll be Audrey Hepburn from *Breakfast at Tiffany's*."

"Why, bless your heart," Lindsey said to the saleswoman. "Aren't you just the sweetest thing, wrappin' that for me? Thank you *so* much. Ah'll be sure and tell mah daddy how good y'all took care of li'l ol' me when I was in your fair city." And with a brilliant toss of her Reese-blonde hair, she picked up her key chain and left.

I followed, sucking in my cheeks and stretching my neck—trying to look as Audreyesque as possible. When I caught sight of myself in the storefront window, however, I looked more like a giraffe on Valium. Or with the mumps.

Besides, I'm pretty sure that Audrey's thighs went through their entire lives without ever once being introduced.

chapter five

Over an after-church brunch of Portobello mushroom and goat cheese omelets, Lindsey and I passed out souvenirs: chocolate from Saks for the girls, a Statue of Liberty key chain for Scott, and postcards from the Met for art-lover Christopher. We saved the best for last.

"Phillie, we wanted to get you something really special as a thank-you for everything you did to make our trip so memorable," I said as Lins handed him a bulky package.

He tore into the wrapping paper like a kid at Christmas, revealing a glass snow globe of the Empire State Building with an oversized plastic King Kong climbing to the top. "Wow, you guys, thanks. This is *so* cool!"

"Turn it upside down," Lindsey instructed.

Phil obeyed. And as he turned the globe right side up again, Kong let out a mighty roar that made the rest of the girls at the table jump.

"*Way* cool," our Kong-loving friend grinned, turning his gift over and over again.

Lins shook her head. "Boys and their toys."

"Hey Pheebs," Susan reminded me, looking at her watch, "We'd better get going if we're going to try and watch three movies at your place this afternoon."

Scotty frowned. "Hey, how come we weren't invited?"

"It's a chick flickathon," Lindsey said. "No guys allowed."

"I can understand why you wouldn't want Phil, but Chris and I are more sensitive types in touch with our feminine side," Scott said. "We've even been known to leak a few movie tears on occasion. Right, Chris?"

"Right."

"Sorry, guys. Love ya, but it's girls only today," I said. "We're watching Jane Austen."

"Jane Austen? Forget it, then. I spent a lifetime one afternoon watching one of those with a girl. All anyone ever does is sit around and talk. And talk. And talk . . ."

Phil disagreed. "They do more than just talk, Scotty. They drink tea too." He held up a pretend teacup, pinky extended, and made loud slurping noises.

Christopher got into the act. "Hey, you guys, you're not being fair. There's more action than that. Sometimes they go for long walks in the countryside, or even ride in a carriage to someone's manor house, where they dance, play cards, or listen to someone play the pianoforte. *Then* they talk."

I sniffed. "Better intelligent conversation than all those mindless action movies that need to rely on special effects to make their point."

Phil emitted one of his Tim "The Toolman" Taylor grunts. "Hey guys, don't sweat it. We'll go over to our place and watch some manly, mindless action films instead. How about, uh, *King Kong, X-Men . . .*" He thought a second, then added triumphantly, "and the ultimate guy movie, *Gladiator*. Wanna come, Chris?"

"Only if I can play with the snow globe."

Four hours later, the girls and I had sniffled our way through *Persuasion* and *Sense and Sensibility* and were taking a much-needed food and potty break.

"That Willoughby sure was gorgeous," sighed Samantha, scooping up another handful of M&M's from my coffee table.

"Yeah, but what a selfish jerk," Lindsey said, crunching on a pretzel. "He cast aside the woman he loved in favor of money."

"Do you think he *really* loved her?"

"No," everyone but Susan chorused.

Our resident WOG disagreed. "Yes, he did—in his own way. Just not enough."

I reached for a piece of shortbread—having replaced the box I'd inhaled earlier—to dunk in my tea. "Give me Alan Rickman's Colonel Brandon character any day. *That's* a man with staying power. Someone who will be there through thick and thin, in sickness and in health."

"Yeah. I should have lived back then," said Kim, whose husband had abandoned her and their asthmatic four-year-old a couple of years earlier.

"Nah, you wouldn't have liked it," Susan said. "Women had a raw deal. Just look at the Dashwood sisters. They lost the only home they'd ever known when their father died—simply because they were women."

"That's *so* not fair," Kim said.

Lindsey shifted on the couch as she flipped through my latest issue of *People*. "Who said life's fair?"

With my back to my guests, I sifted through the DVDs and videos. "All right, what next? The Gwyneth Paltrow *Emma*? Or *Pride and Prejudice* with Laurence Olivier and Greer Garson?"

"I thought *Pride and Prejudice* was with Colin something or other," Samantha said.

"Firth," I said. "Wonderful, sensitive Colin Firth. But that's a six-part series, and we don't have enough time for that today."

"Okay by me," Kim said. "I hear the guy wears hair plugs anyway."

The girls dissolved in laughter. I whirled around and lobbed a piece of shortbread at Lindsey.

On a little Jane Austen overload, we opted for a more contemporary English film instead—*Notting Hill*. Then, in a dreamy, happily-ever-after mood after watching Hugh Grant and Julia Roberts finally get together, we clicked off the set and cleaned up.

Once everyone left, I started surfing the Net for a job, figuring my degree and experience at the *Star* would easily translate into a reporting slot at the *Plain Dealer* or one of the weeklies in town, which in turn would give me the experience I needed to eventually earn a place at the *New York Times*.

No such luck.

Over the next few days I continued to surf the Net. I also made appointments and sent out résumés and played the networking phone game with some of my pals in the biz. But newspaper after newspaper, even the alternative weeklies, turned me away, citing hiring freezes or the downturn in the economy.

Finally, on Thursday, with every journalistic fiber of my being screaming in noble protest, I tried the local PR and advertising route. After all, a girl's gotta live. But it seemed that there were no writing jobs to be had in the entire city. I was considering making a sign that said, *"Will work for food. Will work even harder for chocolate,"* when I ran across an ad I hadn't seen before. It was perfect: *Publishing position in fast-paced office for energetic self-starter.*

This energetic self-starter e-mailed her résumé and within minutes was scheduled for a job interview the next morning.

Note to self: Practice flexibility. Maybe I'm not supposed to work in newspapers right now, but instead should take a detour into the publishing world. Perhaps I'll discover fabulous manuscript at bottom of slush pile written by unknown author toiling away in obscurity. Said book will take the publishing world by storm and become a national best seller. I'll be feted and cheered and grateful author will, insist upon working with only me as his editor. Appreciative author will, of course, be single and attractive—in bookish sort of way—and fall madly in love with me. We'll marry and live together blissfully in our Manhattan loft, writing best sellers side by side while our golden retriever, Falstaff, lies at our feet. After a few years of newlywed bliss, we'll move to Connecticut, where I'll have beautiful baby (babies?) and become beatific earth mother, using only cotton diapers and making homemade baby food like Diane Keaton in Baby Boom . . .

The ringing phone brought me back to reality.

"Hello?"

"I don't believe it. You're alive."

Uh-oh. In excitement over fantastic new publishing job, forgot to screen phone calls.

"Hi, Mom."

"Honey, I think you need to get a new answering machine, because the one you have is broken. I've left a million messages since last week, but you never got them."

"Didn't Jordy give you my e-mail?"

My mother, who'd lived in the same small town her whole life, refused to join the twenty-first century and learn to use a computer. So I e-mailed her care of my happily married brother, who lived just down the street with his wife, four kids, two dogs, three cats, one goat, assorted reptiles and amphibians, and an aquarium filled with real goldfish. My good and faithful brother then delivered the e-mail to Mom.

"Yes," she was saying, "but that's not the same as talking. What's wrong with plain old-fashioned talking?"

"I've been meaning to call, but I was out of town. Didn't you get my postcard?"

"Yes, daughter. I received your postcard of the Statue of Liberty," she said. "Very nice. Thank you. Although if you were going on vacation, I'd have thought you might come home to visit your family, whom you haven't seen for the past three Christmases."

"It wasn't a vacation, Mom. I had a job interview." No need to tell her the interview was an unequivocal bust. Or that I was no longer employed at all.

But apparently she knew. Jordy must have opened his big-brother mouth.

"Why don't you move back home, honey?"

"Say what?"

"Move back home where you belong. You can have your old room. And Gordon could use a little help at the newspaper now that Esther's getting on in years."

"I'm not moving back home, Mom. I'm thirty-one years old, and I've made a wonderful life for myself here in Cleveland."

"But you don't have a job. Or even a boyfriend. How can you have a wonderful life when you're unemployed and unattached?"

"Actually, I'm about to start a new career in publishing."

Sorry, God, for that little white one. But my mother made me do it. She drives me crazy. You know how mothers can be . . .

"In fact, Mom, I really need to go now so I can get to bed and be well-rested for my first day tomorrow. I'll talk to you soon. Love you. Bye." I hung up quickly before my one white lie could morph into a legion of others in a rainbow of colors.

Famished, I opened the fridge: limp celery, ancient Chinese take-out with green growing things that definitely weren't broccoli, and a lonely shriveled apple. I checked the cupboards: half a box of pasta, a few wheat crackers, and some Nestle's Quik. Too hungry to wait for the pasta to boil, I wolfed down the crackers, which long ago had lost their snappy crunch. And with no milk in the apartment, I dumped some Quik into a mug, dribbled some hot water on top, and stirred it together to make a wet chocolate paste, which I lapped from the spoon while standing over the sink. Needing a little fiber, I dipped a stalk of celery into the chocolate mix.

Can you say "major comedown from the Plaza"?

Not to worry, I reassured myself. *This is just temporary.*

I had no idea just how temporary.

The next day I got the publishing job. Except it wasn't book publishing. And there was no writing involved. But it paid weekly, and my rent was overdue. So I became the newest data entry clerk in the office of one of those free real-estate-listing "magazines" you can pick up at the front of every grocery store. My job—along with nineteen other drones in a cavernous warehouse—was to transform each realtor's hand-scrawled listings into perky, concise ads (no more than forty words long) to be listed under each house picture in the magazine.

And this is going to land you a job at the Times?

Ignoring my depressing inner voice, I focused on the job at hand. Our instructions were to input the ads exactly as written. The only thing we were allowed to do differently was to abbreviate some of the longer words into real-estate shorthand to fit the tight space constraints. For instance, kitchen became *kit.* Beautiful was *beaut* and hardwood *hdwd.*

No problem. The problem came when I corrected the spelling errors in the realtors' copy.

Suzanne, my on-a-power-trip supervisor with electric-blue eye shadow and high hair stuck in the eighties, proofed every entry and returned the pages I'd submitted. "Just type them exactly as the client has written it out."

"But the client can't spell."

"So? That's not our job. Our job is to take what the realtor gives us and input it into the computer, making sure it fits into the required word count," she recited.

"Understood. But naturally, we'll correct any misspelled words in the copy before it goes to print."

Suzanne chomped her Trident. "No. The realtor's job is to write up the ad the way he wants it to read, and our job is to type it up just as it appears."

"But misspelled copy gives a bad impression."

"We're paying you to type, not spell."

And clearly they're not paying you *to think* . . . A variant of the Scarecrow's mournful refrain popped into my head: *"If you only had a brain . . ."*

At Lone Rangers that weekend, Phil, Jake, and Scott, along with every other guy in the group—save Christopher—were still hovering over the new girl. Lindsey and I skipped out early after doing our obligatory hostess-with-the-mostest duties and set out to buy a wedding gift for two Lone Rangers who planned to terminate their single status next weekend. Afterward, shopping bags in hand, we caught a chick flick, munching on popcorn and talking about the fickleness of men as the end credits rolled.

The next day, after church, my best friend and I headed to our favorite sushi bar for a light lunch of California rolls, marinated bean sprouts, and iced tea—courtesy of my two-for-one coupon. But Lindsey kept pushing her bean sprouts around in a circle.

"Okay, Lins. What's up?"

"Nothing. What do you mean?"

"Whenever something's bothering you or you're nervous, you play with your food."

She stopped in midswirl, speared a bean sprout, and shoved it in her mouth. "I do not."

"Yes you do. There's this whole pushing-your-food-around-your-plate-in-circles ritual you do when you're worried about something. So c'mon. What gives? Is it your family?" A terrible thought struck. "Is someone sick?"

"Oh no. Nothing like that. Don't worry."

"Well then, tell me. It can't be *that* bad."

"Promise you'll still say that after I tell you?"

"Why?" I looked at her in suspicion. "Lindsey, what did you do?"

She gulped a large swallow of tea. "It wasn't just me. It was Phil too."

"What?"

"We placed an ad in the personals for you."

"You did *what*?"

"We took out a personal ad on the Internet for you right before you got laid off."

"Lindsey, I can't believe you did that!"

She sighed. "Pheebs, there's no one at Lone Rangers you're interested in, and you haven't met anyone at work or the gym, so we thought this would be a great idea. More and more professionals—doctors, lawyers, architects—are taking out ads. There's even this elite matchmaking serv-ice for Fortune 500 types."

"And we know I certainly qualify for that."

"No. But you do qualify for an ad on Eternally Yoked. You can get e-mail responses and regular mail as well. I signed you up for both. I took out a post-office box under the name of P. Cary. Get it? Cary, as in Grant?" Lins smiled, proud of how far she'd come in her old movie-star knowledge under my tutelage. She waved a thick stack of envelopes beneath my nose. "Look how many responses you've gotten already."

Despite myself, I was curious. "So what did the ad say?"

She shoved a piece of paper across the table.

MUST LOVE MOVIES AND GOD. SWF, attractive, profes-sional, fun-loving, churchgoing woman, just over 30, seeks like-minded SM 25-45 for coffee, conversation, and movies. Must be willing to share popcorn. Only serious replies.

"Just over thirty? Well that'll make 'em come crawling out of the wood-work—emphasis on crawling. They'll think I'm some bun-wearing babe with support hose and sensible shoes."

"Shut up and start reading." Lindsey separated the stack and handed me half.

A magazine picture of Mel Gibson with his face painted blue in *Braveheart* fluttered out of the first envelope.

Dear Ms. Movie Lover:

Since you're such a movie fan, you'll love the fact that I look a lot like Mel Gibson. All the ladies tell me so. I'm a real *Mad Max, Lethal Weapon* kinda guy and would love to get together with you soon for some popcorn in a dark movie theater . . .

"Too scary." I started a reject pile with the wannabe Mel-man.

Lindsey nodded. "Too arrogant."

On top of Mel-man, I added two letters from prison inmates. Then came,

Dear Miss Must Love Movies and God:

I go to the church of I'm OK, We're All OK, and am a slightly over forty-five professional motivational speaker. I liked the energy I got from your ad and would love to get together soon over some green tea to see if our spirits are on the same harmonic convergence. Or, if you'd prefer to meet at a movie, I'll bring the soy nuts.

"Bet this one's sixty if he's a day, has a long gray ponytail, and wears hemp socks with his Birkenstocks," I said.

After the seventh reject, I looked up at Lindsey. "I'm really havin' some fun now."

"Be patient. We're not even halfway through the stack. We're bound to get a few losers."

"A few? That's being generous, don't you think?"

"You spoke too soon. Listen to this one, Pheebs:

Hi—

I've never responded to a personal ad before, but yours caught my eye with its unique headline. I too love the movies. And God. But what kind of movies are we talking about here? That's too sweeping a statement. For all I know, you could be an ardent fan of horror films or, worse yet, junior-high bathroom-humor comedies. If so, then here's where we must part company. But if you wouldn't be caught dead at either, I'd be happy to share my popcorn with you. Who knows? Maybe this could be the beginning of a beautiful friendship. . .

"He's a *Casablanca* fan!" I squealed.

"I just had one of those installed in my dining room."

"Be serious, Lins. You know *Casablanca* is my favorite movie of all time."

"I know. You made me watch it with you twice. But I still don't get it. Why Ingrid Bergman went off with that other guy when she was really in love with Humphrey Bogart . . ."

"Because it was the right thing to do," I said. "That's why it's a classic." I read the letter again. "A man who quotes from *Casablanca*? Now I'd go with him in a New York minute. He's not one of the usual suspects."

I wrote to the *Casablanca* guy—his name was Steve—at P.O. Box 24601 and pointed out that our local art-house theater, the Grand, just happened to be screening my favorite film the very next week, as part of their classic film series. We agreed to meet at the theater for the movie, followed by dessert and coffee and, perhaps, the beginning of a beautiful friendship.

chapter six

The day of the big date, I was a wreck. My teeth were screaming in torment.

I'd bought one of those over-the-counter whitening bleaches the night before and applied it to my top and bottom teeth as instructed—well, almost as instructed. The directions had said to leave on for thirty to forty-five minutes. But wanting to dazzle my date with the whitest smile possible, I'd decided to keep it on overnight instead and let it do its magic while I slept.

Big mistake.

I went to brush my teeth the next morning and thought I would die when the cold water hit them. Hoping to soothe my oversensitized incisors with a little warmth, I took a grateful gulp of my morning coffee. Now my teeth were on fire. They rebelled at anything that touched them—hot, cold, or in-between. Which ruled out eating and drinking for the day.

As if that wasn't bad enough, I also had a great big, angry zit smack in the center of my nose. It wasn't quite ready for its coming-out party, so I dabbed on a little concealer to keep it under wraps.

But now I was facing the Herculean conundrum that plagued all single women everywhere: what to wear?

Since it was just a movie and dessert, I didn't want to go too dressy, but I also didn't want to be too casual either. Jeans and a blazer? *No. Don't want to reenact infamous sweating scene.* Khakis with a light sweater? *Uh-uh. Khakis make hips look too big.* Shoes? *Hmmm, heels always make me look thinner, but I don't want to tower over him like an imposing giantess in case he's a Tom Cruise type. Ix-nay on the eels-hay.*

At the last minute, in homage to the film—"The Germans wore gray. You wore blue."—I settled on a sapphire sundress that swirled away from my hips and thighs. I added a white blouse in case the theater was chilly, slipped on flat sandals along with my favorite silver toe ring, and set off to meet my potential moviegoing soul mate.

Arriving at the theater a few minutes early, I headed to the restroom to check my makeup and to settle the monarchs in my stomach. I returned to the lobby, where a tall George Clooney look-alike wearing jeans and a button-down Oxford shirt smiled, nodded, and headed my way.

Thank you, God. I gave the George-man my most welcoming smile. "Steve?"

He sent me a puzzled glance and kept on walking.

"Hi, honey, ready to go in?" A raven-haired beauty passed me from behind and linked arms with George. I turned and watched them glide into the darkened theater.

"Hey *Feebee.*"

Looking around to see where the annoying nasal whine was coming from, I spotted a skinny little guy with helmet hair, leather armbands studded with spikes, and a long-sleeved shirt of tattoos.

Ohmygoodness, it's Harvey the ferret's younger brother. But I wonder where Steve . . . no . . . this can't be . . .

Tattoo-ferret-man shot me a snaggletoothed smile, shook his box of popcorn, and held up a package of Red Vines. Our signal.

Note to self: Look beyond superficial, external appearance. Remember, this is a creative, interesting guy who loves God and shares your taste in movies. Focus on the inward, not the outward. The inward, not the outward.

I held out my hand and gave him a friendly smile. "Steve?"

"You got it, babe." He winked, handed me the Red Vines, and slung his arm across my shoulders, wafting waves of cheap cologne.

"Um, we'd better go inside." I slid out from under his arm. "The movie's about to start. We don't want to miss any of it."

"Whatever you say, babe."

The inward, not the outward. The inward, not the outward.

But as Humphrey Bogart and Claude Rains walked off into the fog after that immortal friendship line, Steve—who'd been restless throughout the entire film—snorted. "Lame!"

"What?"

"That dude should have gone off with the chick. She was really hot for him."

"Excuse me?"

Steve took a last swig of his soda, then belched. "Like I said, babe, if it were me, I wouldn't have wound up in the desert with some dude, I'd be with the hot chick."

"Please don't call me *babe* again."

"Whatever."

"Listen, I'm a little confused. You quoted from *Casablanca* in your response to my ad. I thought it was one of your favorite movies."

"Nah, never saw it before tonight." He winked. "And I gotta tell ya, ba—uh, Feeb-girl, don't wanna ever see it again. Boring as all get-out. Not much action—and no color! Me, I like a little more blood and guts in my movies, but I know you chicks don't, so I figured, what the hey, first date and all, we'll do what you want. I try to do that with all my online dates, on account of I'm a gentleman, ya know."

"Er, do you have many online dates?"

He grinned, revealing long, yellow teeth. "You got it. I'm signed up with several services—that way you get a bigger field to choose from. Know what I mean? Anyway, this one's for you, but the next time, *I* get to pick."

Inwardly I cringed and tried to understand. "But if you're not a *Casablanca* fan, why did you say, 'This could be the beginning of a beautiful friendship'?"

He sniggered. "I'd never say anything as lame as that."

"Aren't you Box 24601?"

"Nope. 24610."

Huge sigh of relief.

"Phoebe?"

At the sound of the familiar voice, I turned around to see my former date Colin, of the hair plugs and the live-in mother, standing in the aisle with my friend Samantha. Both of them looked quizzically at me and the ferret-man beside me.

My life as I know it is over. I'll have to resign from Lone Rangers and never leave my apartment again. Oh well, at least I've got lots of movies, plus Lins can bring me food rations . . .

I squirmed in my seat and turned slightly to try and block the couple's view of my date. "Uh, hi, Colin. Samantha. What a surprise to see you. Did you enjoy the movie?"

"Oh yes," Colin said, beaming at Sam. "It's one of my all-time favorites."

Next to me, Steve snorted again.

Colin peered behind me in the dimness. "Phoebe, aren't you going to introduce us?"

"Oh. Sure," I mumbled, standing up. "Uh, Colin, Samantha, this is Steve."

My tattooed date stayed sprawled in his seat, chomping on a Red Vine and shooting an appraising look at Samantha before winking his approval at Colin. "Dude."

Sam flushed and cast me a sympathetic glance, then linked her arm through her date's. "Colin, it's getting late. We'd better be going."

"Yes. I've still got that long drive back to Toledo. Steve, nice to meet you. Take care, Phoebe."

I murmured my good-byes, then picked up my purse. Finally my horror-flick date stood up. "So, Feebee, ready for a little dessert now?" he leered.

"Actually, I'm afraid I must have eaten too much popcorn; I'm not feeling too well. I think I'd better just go home and get to bed."

Steve inclined toward me, his convenience-store cologne overpowering. "Bet I can make you feel better."

I gagged, and he pulled back in dismay. "Okay. Maybe next time then. See ya," and he and his tattoos streaked to the exit.

Saved by the gag. Thanks, Lord.

The next day, as the prewedding strains of Pachelbel's Canon filled the church air, I leaned over to Lindsey and whispered, "So, how many weddings does that make this summer?"

"Five."

"And of those five, how many of the brides were under thirty?"

"Four. No, wait—five. I almost forgot Brooke. She was nineteen."

"And how old are we?"

"Older than dirt."

"At least this time we're not bridesmaids."

"Amen to that, sister."

One of the hazards of being part of a church singles group was that people kept getting married off. Everyone except me and Lindsey, that is. And one of the hazards in being in singles leadership was that you got invited to every wedding.

Note to self after purchasing fifth wedding gift in three months: Remember to buy stock in George Foreman grills.

I took a detour down the whine path. "If I have to go in on one more filmy lingerie set for a blushing twenty-four-year-old, I'm going to spit lace," I murmured out of the side of my smiling mouth. "I've been waiting longer than they have."

"Shush." Lins hissed. "Check out Scotty. Doesn't he look adorable in his tux?"

"Sure does. He's quite the cute boy. If he were just a few years older."

The organist struck up the oh-so-familiar chords of "Here Comes the Bride," and we shut up and stood with the rest of the congregation. Near the end of the vows, Lindsey sighed, "When I get married, I want Pastor John to do the ceremony."

"Me too. Wouldn't have anyone else."

Do you, Phoebe—kind, spiritual, funny Phoebe of the exciting career and fabulous friends, who's quite content in her singleness and happy without a man in her life—take thee Adam, Bill, Charles, Alex—no, not Alex!—of the soaring intellect, sensitive nature, great sense of humor, and wonderful job, beloved by dogs and children, to be your . . .

My best friend poked me in the side. "It's time for the kiss."

And what a kiss it was.

Every unmarried woman in the church breathed a collective sigh of weak-kneed rapture as the young groom enveloped his bride's waiting lips with his own in a deep, soulful meeting of the mouths.

Kissless for a few years now, I felt my head involuntarily tilting up and yearning toward the puckered embrace. "Look how he cupped her face in his hands, Lins. So gentle. So romantic. I want my husband to do that when I get married."

"Put it in the prenup."

"Right."

The prenup was a variation on the well-known legal document that Lindsey and I had cooked up for our intendeds. But unlike the typical celebrity arrangement, ours had nothing to do with money. So far, our prenup requirement included:

1. Throughout our wedded-bliss lifetimes, husband will only have eyes for us, no matter how many firm young *Baywatch* bodies parade into view.

2. Same husband will surrender remote after four hours of weekend sports to adoring wife without being asked and snuggle in with her to watch *Masterpiece Theater*.

3. Hubby will also smile and say "Yes dear" when presented with honey-do list. ☺

And the biggie:

4. Beloved must never *ever* say yes when asked, "Does this make me look fat?"

Now we needed to add another item to the list:

5. Must cup our faces adoringly between their hands when kissing us at the altar.

The blissful, brand-new marrieds left the church, and Lindsey and I headed to the ladies' room to patch up our tear-stained makeup.

"Ugh. This zit is the size of Alaska," I said, looking in the mirror. "No wonder I'm not married." Pulling out my concealer, I went to work.

Lins lined her lips in raspberry. "That didn't stop the guy in *My Big Fat Greek Wedding.*"

"I'm not Greek," I said, powdering the offending blemish. "Norwegian girls don't have that same hot-blooded allure. I think it's all those fjords and pickled herring." Tugging on my skirt, which was doing the static-cling tango with my hips, I followed Lins to the reception in a nearby hall bedecked with white pearlescent balloons, potted blue hydrangeas, and confetti-topped tables. There, she and I sat with a group of Lone Rangers noshing on stuffed mushrooms, seafood-filled puff pastry, and cold cuts, and sloshing it all down with virgin strawberry punch. The women chatted about the bridesmaids' dresses, the flowers, and the decorations while the guys, who were playing soccer with their Jordan almonds, agreed it would be much easier to elope.

"Score!" Scott said after shooting a Pepto-Bismol pink almond through his brother's goalpost-cupped hands.

Phil shrugged and bit into the goal-winning nut.

"Hey, that was my last one!"

I pushed my heart-shaped paper cup of almonds across the table. "Here you go, Scotty, you can have mine."

"Thanks, Pheebs. Oh, that's right; you're not big on nuts, are you?"

Phil winked and popped another almond into his mouth. "That's why she's not interested in you, little brother."

Ignoring Phil, I turned my attention to Scott. "Nope, I'm more of a chocolate mints girl."

"*I* like nuts," piped up Kim's son, Teddy.

"You do, buddy?" Scott leaned down to the four-year-old's eye level. "Hey, wanna play a little table soccer with us?"

"Sure!"

Teddy flicked the next almond right between Phil's goalpost hands.

"Score!" Scott high-fived his young friend. "Hey, we make a great team, buddy."

"Yeah," Teddy said. "We're a great team. Hey Mom, we won! We won!"

"You sure did, Teddy Bear. Good job, my little man." She too high-fived her happy son and mouthed "thank you" to Scott.

Noticing the wistful gaze Kim cast her son and Scott while they were otherwise engaged, I kicked Lins under the table. We exchanged knowing smiles, which Kim saw.

"Oh look," she said, redirecting our attention. "Isn't that Samantha dancing with some older guy?"

Susan and Lindsey craned to look, but I didn't need to.

"That's Colin!" Lindsey said.

"Colin?" Susan and Kim said in confused unison.

"My boss's insurance guy and Phoebe's ex-blind date."

Kim's mouth dropped open. "You mean hair-plug guy? I thought he was fifty-something!"

"Fifty-one." I drained my punch. "And it looks like he's finally found his twenty-six-year-old."

Lindsey shook her head. "Not quite. Sam turned twenty-seven a few months ago."

"Why do guys always go for sweet young things?" forty-two-year-old Susan demanded.

Scotty shot a flirtatious smile my way. "Not always."

"Shhh, everyone," Kim said. "Here they come."

God, if I promise to be good and go on a short-term mission trip to a third-world country—without whining about the heat and bugs—can You please help them keep quiet about my wretched blind date with tattoo-ferret man?

Twinkletoes Colin whirled Samantha across the dance floor, ending with a graceful flourish in front of our table.

"Hey, Sam," Phil teased. "I didn't know you were such a good dancer."

Samantha smiled sweetly at Phil. "It helps to have someone who knows how to lead."

"She gotcha there, bro." Scotty laughed. "So, Sam, introduce us to your date."

"Um, everyone, this is Colin Ramsey. Colin, these are my friends: Susan, Kim and her son, Teddy, the brothers Phil and Scott, and, uh, you already know Lindsey and Phoebe."

Colin shook hands and exchanged pleasantries with everyone, seemingly unfazed by the memory of our blind-date debacle and my recent appearance with tattoo-ferret man. "Hi, Phoebe. Hi, Lindsey. Nice to see you both again."

Phil adopted his paternal air. "So, Colin, how'd you meet our Sam?"

"Uh, we . . ." Samantha tried to forestall her date's reply, but Colin, oblivious, beamed happily across at Sam and blurted, "Through an online dating service."

Scotty raised an eyebrow. *"Really?"*

At that moment, Lindsey jumped up. "Oh, this is one of my favorite songs. Sam, would you mind loaning me Colin for one dance?"

Samantha thanked her with her eyes. "No problem, Lindsey. Have a good time, you two. He's a great dancer." She smiled her okay at Colin, who returned it with a warm grin of his own, then whisked Lindsey away to the beat of ABBA's "Dancing Queen."

"Okay, Sam. Now, dish." Kim and Susan demanded.

Phil and Scott leaned in while Teddy busied himself with a coloring book. "Yeah, we want to know everything," Phil said. "We need to make sure he's good enough for you."

"He is," Samantha said. "He's kind, considerate, a perfect gentleman, and a Presbyterian. Plus, he has a good, steady job and isn't afraid of commitment."

The divorced Kim cut straight to the chase. "Has he ever been married before?"

Sam blushed. "No. He said he's been waiting for the right woman."

"Guess it's been a long wait," Phil said under his breath.

Scott, the diplomat of the two brothers, took a more tactful approach. "Far be it from me to rain on your dating parade, Sam," he asked gently, "but isn't he a little old for you?"

"You're the one who always says age doesn't matter," she replied, casting a sharp look in my direction. "Colin's active and in better shape than a lot of guys I know. Besides, James Garner's character in *Murphy's Romance* was almost thirty years older than Sally Field—right, Pheebs?"

"Yes, but please don't put this on me," I said. "Just because I showed you that movie in my living room, I don't want it on my head if things go south with this relationship."

"They won't," Sam said, continuing her Colin laundry list. "He's sweet, compassionate, treats me better than any guy I've ever dated— and he can dance. Besides, no guys my age are ready to settle down and start a family."

Susan's jaw dropped. "Are you already talking kids? How long have you been dating?"

"A couple of weeks. But we've seen each other every night," she said. "Besides, I learned about his longing for a family from his ad. He was straightforward and up front. Said he was tired of the dating scene and was hoping to meet the woman God had chosen for him—a woman who wanted to be a wife and mother and create a loving home. The very same things *I* want."

"But . . ." I took my bad blind-dating life in my hands and plunged in. "Did Colin mention *his* mother? And that he still lives with her?"

Samantha jutted out her chin. "Yes, he did. But that's only until he gets married. Once he has a wife, Tilly's planning to move into a seniors condo a few miles away."

"Tilly?"

"His mother. She's a darling. Fun and lively and really sharp. She always beats me at Scrabble."

Kim glanced at Susan and me, concern evident in her expression. "Sounds like things are really moving along fast."

"It may seem that way, but actually the pace is just right for us," Sam said. "We both know what we want." Her defensive posture softened, and she got a faraway look in her eyes. "Remember the pickle man in *Crossing Delancey*?"

The guys groaned. "Oh no. Not another chick-flick conversation." Scott stood, scooped up Teddy, and perched him on his shoulders. "Hey, whaddya say we leave the womenfolk to their girl talk and go score some wedding cake, huh, buddy?"

"Yeah," Teddy said, beaming down at Scott's upturned face. "Let's get some cake!"

"Coming, Phil?" Scott said over his shoulder.

"Right behind ya."

Once the men left, the discretion gloves came off.

"I think Colin might be my 'pickle man,'" Sam shyly confided to her girls-only audience.

Hair-plug and eye-lift Colin? Is she kidding?

I was the one who'd introduced my girlfriends to the movie *Crossing Delancey*, an eighties parable for single women everywhere. Amy Irving plays an uptown New Yorker with humble roots and a crush on a pretentious author. "Bubbe," her old-world grandma, who lives on the less sophisticated side of town, tries to match her couldn't-wait-to leave-the-neighborhood granddaughter with a nice, sweet local guy who owns a pickle stand. But Amy's character thinks that the pickle man is beneath her, that they inhabit completely different worlds. Almost too late, she comes to realize that her grandmother's choice is the genuine article—

kind, intelligent, funny, real, and sincerely interested in *her*, unlike the shallow, superficial author who loves only himself.

"Phoebe," Samantha was saying, "I know you had a lousy blind date with Colin. Works for me, or I'd have never met him. I know that all you see is his age, his mother, the hair plugs, and what seems to be a boring insurance job. But he's one of the most caring men I've ever met. Do you know why he became an insurance salesman?" She answered her own question. "Because when his father died, they didn't have insurance and his mother was left with nothing. Colin doesn't want that to happen to other women, especially those with a family to raise. He wants to make sure they're taken care of."

"So that's why he's lived with his mother all these years," I said, that pesky realization dawning again.

"Exactly."

I help up my hands in surrender. "What can I say? I'm a shallow woman skimming through life like a water bug. Serves me right if God leaves me single forever."

Just then, Lindsey and Colin returned. She thanked him for the dance, and he murmured a polite response, but only had eyes for Sam, whom he waltzed away to "Smoke Gets in Your Eyes."

"I have a feeling we'll be attending another wedding before too long," Susan said.

"I'd take bets on it," Kim added.

Lindsey scooted her chair over to mine. "Pheebs, guess what?" she whispered. "Colin's given up polyester. That was Ralph Lauren he was wearing!"

Thankfully, the guys chose that moment to return, bearing big slices of wedding cake.

"Yum. It's carrot cake." I grabbed the largest piece and took a big bite of sugary comfort, reveling in the thick and gooey cream-cheese frosting. Amazing how something sweet helps dispel envious thoughts. *Hmmm. I should bring that up at Bible Study.* It was a concept I'd never heard taught before. Maybe I could even start up my own study: Women of Sweetness. After polishing off the last delicious morsel, I leaned over toward Susan and Lindsey to confirm our single-girlfriends-over-thirty strategy. "Okay, the minute they start clearing the floor for the bouquet throw, we're heading to the ladies' room. Right?"

"Right."

"And we're not leaving 'til we know for sure that the floral coast is clear. Right?"

"Yep. We got your back, girl."

Our trio beat a fast track to the women's lounge, grabbing another plate of cake to share. On the way we noticed commitment-phobe Jake at a corner table, making his move on the Heather Locklear look-alike.

"Wondered where he was," muttered Lindsey, rolling her eyes.

"They probably deserve each other." I patted her shoulder loyally while eyeing Heather's sleek, orange column dress. "Anyone who can wear that color ought to be shot, anyway. Let's go."

Once ensconced on comfortable sofas in the lounge for the flower-throwing duration, we realized we'd forgotten forks for our piece of cake. I ducked back out to retrieve some, but as I bent over to grab three from the buffet table, something whizzed past my head.

Startled, I looked up just in time to see Kim catch the bouquet.

"Does that mean we get a new daddy now?" little Teddy asked his mother.

Kim blushed and buried her face into the flowers, inhaling their fragrance and thereby missing the reflective look Scotty cast her. But I didn't.

Another one bites the dust . . .

After the reception, a little depressed by all the happily-ever-after cheer, Lindsey, Susan, and I trooped over to my apartment to watch *My Best Friend's Wedding.*

No, we're not masochists. But when even Julia Roberts doesn't get the guy, we know we're in good company. Besides, that film has one of our all-time favorite funny scenes. We each grabbed a microphone—wooden spoon for Susan, plastic spatula for Lins, and ice cream scoop for me—and lustily joined in the restaurant sing-along of "I Say a Little Prayer."

The film ended with the gorgeous Julia's love unrequited forever now that her best friend was married to another woman. Sniffling over the bittersweet ending, we reminded each other, as Julia's boss reminded her, that there might not be love, marriage, or sex in our futures—perish the thought—but that there would "always be dancing."

Then we took turns waltzing each other around the room before exchanging a goofy good-friends good-night.

*a*fter locking the door behind my gal pals, I powered up my laptop and logged on to the Internet, while at the same time shedding my static-clung wedding clothes and tight shoes in favor of a favorite nightshirt and slippers.

"Ah, much better," I sighed to Gabby, my fake goldfish. "Freedom!"

I started scrolling through my messages, deleting thirteen forwards from my sister-in-law, who liked to pass on every joke and chain letter going round the Internet. Disappointed that I had nothing but junk mail, I almost deleted a message with the subject line, "Searching for lost movie lover," but stopped just in time.

The address read Filmguy791. Although I didn't recognize it, I was intrigued enough to chance opening it. *Please Lord, don't let this be a virus.*

Hi, Movielovr,

Remember me? I responded to your ad. I'm the *Casablanca* fan. You wrote back to my P.O. Box—24601—and sent me a note with your e-mail address. First chance I've had to write. Sorry. Still want to communicate? Hoping I wasn't misinformed. Would like to get to know another movie buff who's also a Christian. That's hard to find.

Here's lookin' at you—or hoping to eventually,

Filmguy791

What? I had sent my response to the wrong box and gotten tattoo-ferret man and an embarrassing evening for my pains. *So how did this guy get my address?* Maybe he was a stalker preying on lonely single women who take out personal ads.

I told Lindsey this was a bad idea . . .

Then the paranoia fog lifted.

Lindsey.

Who else besides my best friend knew every disastrous detail of my case of mistaken identity blind date, including my dyslexic transposing of the post-office box numbers? And who was the one who'd started this whole thing—including setting up my P.O. box?

I punched in Lins's home phone on my cell so I could keep Filmguy's e-mail on the screen.

"'Lo," she said sleepily.

"I can't believe you're sleeping the carefree sleep of the innocent after what you did!"

"Pheebs?" Lindsey was fully awake now. "What's wrong?"

"What's wrong is that I just got an e-mail from the *real* Box 24601!"

"Finally. So what's wrong with that? He's the one guy you wanted to meet."

"But I tried that, and it was a train wreck."

"No, you didn't. You had a lousy evening because it was the wrong guy," she said. "All I did was correct your numerically challenged mistake by sending a brief note to the right P.O. box. Now you can finally get together with the *Casablanca* fan."

"I don't think so," I said. "No more blind dates for this girl. I've learned my lesson."

Lindsey sighed. "All right, Pheebs. But at least write him back. Who knows? If nothing else, you might make a platonic pen pal who gets all your old-movie stuff that the rest of us never do. 'Kay, I'm going back to sleep now. Talk to you tomorrow." And she hung up.

Vacillating note to self: Should I or shouldn't I? If I respond right away, will he think I'm desperate? Maybe I needed to play it cool and wait a few days. But if I played it too cool, some other rabid film buff might have snapped him up before I even have a chance. *God, what do You think I should do? Can You give me a little clue here, please?*

My instant messenger popped up on the screen.

> Filmguy791: Hi. Hope you don't mind, but saw you online & wanted to say hello.
>
> Movielovr: Hi.

What else should I say that's polite, yet casual? Should I ask him what he's doing up so late, or do I really want to know?

> Filmguy791: Just back from a business trip—unwound with Casablanca. "Of all the gin joints in all the towns in all the world, she walks into mine . . ."

Ah. Safe, familiar territory.

> Movielovr: "Play it, Sam. Play 'As Time Goes By.'"
>
> Filmguy791: "I was misinformed." Speaking of info, tell me about yourself.

Danger, Will Robinson! Danger! Proceed with caution.

> Movielovr: Not quite ready for that. How 'bout you?
>
> Filmguy791: Smart girl. Safe. Never know—I could be an ax murderer. ☺ Nothing so dramatic, tho. Just a businessman doing the corporate dance.

> Movielovr: So if you dance, take it you're not Baptist?
>
> Filmguy791: Nope. But have attended Baptist churches & Episcopal, Pentecostal. Presbyterian, depend. on geography. Am nondenominational at heart. U?

Movielovr: Presbyterian now, grew up Lutheran. How long have u been a Christian?

Filmguy791: Since my teens. U?

Movielovr: Since grade school. So, what's yr fave movie? With a handle like Filmguy—are you into film noir? Not sure it's my thing. ☺

Filmguy791: Me either. Like some noir, love all kinds of movies—can't choose 1 fave.

Movielovr: OK. If you're stranded on a desert island, name top 5 you'd want.

Filmguy791: Assume desert island has electricity, TV, and video/DVD player?

Movielovr: Comes with all amenities. Except phones, pagers, e-mail, or any way of communicating with the outside world.

Filmguy791: Need 6. Here goes, in no order: Casablanca, The African Queen, Star Wars, To Kill a Mockingbird, Singin' in the Rain, & Airplane.

Movielovr: *Airplane*?! Surely that's not in your top 5! I mean 6.

Filmguy791: Yep. And don't call me Shirley.

Movielovr: Why do guys like silly movies?

Filmguy791: It's our job. ☺ Your turn.

Movielovr: Also in no order My 6: Casablanca, Gone with the Wind, Little Women (w/ K. Hepburn), Chariots of Fire, Sound of Music, *and* The Parent Trap.

Filmguy791: The Parent Trap? Why, and which version?

Movielovr: Hayley Mills, natch. Because it's sweet, funny, &
              incredibly romantic.
Filmguy791:   Romantic?

Movielovr: Uh-huh. Check it out when the mom and dad
              finally get back 2gether.
Filmguy791:   Bet it can't beat Princess Bride. Now that's
              a romantic movie—not to mention hilarious.
              "Mawwiage is what bwings us togever
              today."

Movielovr: "Have fun stormin' the castle!" Love it—but
              can't fit into my top 6.
Filmguy791:   Forgot Chariots of Fire. Might have to bump
              something. Not sure what.

Movielovr: Airplane?
Filmguy791:   Never.

Movielovr: Love that line in that great Scottish accent,
              "God made me for a purpose, Jenny, but he also
              made me fast. And when I run, I feel his
              pleasure."
Filmguy791:   I hear ya. And I can do a passable Scots burr.

Shades of Sean Connery. Hold me back.

Movielovr: Glad u like musicals. Singin' in the Rain's great.
Filmguy791:   Best musical ever.
Movielovr: No way. What about Sound of Music?
Filmguy791:   Too sappy. And no Gene Kelly. His dancing in the
              rain number is classic.

Movielovr: Agree. But the love story w/ Maria & the Captain
              is much more romantic.
Filmguy791:   Talkin' best musical, not best romance.

Movielovr: West Side Story?
Filmguy791:   Still no Gene Kelly. And too much ballet twirling
              for me.

Movielovr: Typical guy.
Filmguy791:   It's a testosterone thing. And while we're on the
              subject . . .

Of testosterone? Knew he was too good to be true . . .

Filmguy791:   . . . My testosterone, as well as the rest of me, is
              beat. Must get to sleep. Can we pick up l8r?
              Maybe in person?
Movielovr: "Don't let's ask for the moon, Jerry. We've got
              the stars."

Filmguy791:   Take it that's a no, Ms. Bette Davis?

Whoa. This guy knows his old movies. Not many men have even heard of
Now, Voyager.

Movielovr: Um, not quite at person-to-person stage yet.
Filmguy791:   "Frankly, my dear, I . . . understand." But let's
              share cyberpopcorn next.

Movielovr: Kettle corn count?
Filmguy791:   Oh yeah.

Movielovr: Deal. OK. Bye. Talk soon.
Filmguy791:   Sweet dreams. And remember, we'll always have
               e-mail.

The next morning I woke up on cloud ninety-one, recalling last night's fun cyberspace banter and eager to tell Lindsey about it. But I was running late, so I decided to call her on my lunch hour—actually a half-hour, punched out dutifully on the time clock—instead. Grabbing a quick cup of coffee, I headed for the shower, where I tried a couple of Gene Kelly moves of my own.

Note to self: Do not attempt dancing feats in small wet spaces.

Driving to work, I relived every comma and comment from my online conversation with Filmguy, humming the scores from the different musicals we'd reviewed. *Wonder if he looks more like Gordon MacRae or Christopher Plummer?* I was one happy cybercamper. Even the spelling-impaired, big-haired Suzanne couldn't get to me today.

Or so I thought.

Midmorning, I was typing away and automatically correcting—what can I say? I couldn't help myself—the realtor's misspelling of "Corian" (scrawled "Koryon") countertops, when Suzanne tapped me on the shoulder and asked me to come to her "office"—a nearby cubicle.

"How does she *know* when I'm fixing the mistakes?" I whispered to my new work pal Yolanda at the computer station next to me. "Is she Supergirl with laser vision, or does she just have my keyboard rigged so that when I ignore her typing rules, it flashes on her screen?"

Yolanda chuckled as she continued to input her ad. "Don't know 'bout that, girlfriend, but don't you pay her no mind. She's just jealous 'cause you got yourself a college degree and used to write for the *Star*. That girl never even got herself no high-school diploma."

I winked and flashed a conspiratorial smile at my comrade in monotony as I made my way to my supervisor's troll-topped desk. (The woman collected troll dolls of every shape and size and with every hair color imaginable—lime green, magenta, even screaming yellow. With effort, I refrained from mental comparisons between the trolls and their big-haired mistress.)

"Yes, Suzanne?" I asked, sitting across from my supervisor as her favorite turquoise-haired troll glared balefully at me from atop her monitor.

"Phoebe," she said, chomping her ever-present Trident as she stroked the orange hair of Carrot Top, her smallest troll, "the company is going through a difficult financial time right now and has to make some cutbacks. I've been instructed to handle the layoffs in this department. And since you have the least seniority, I'm afraid I have to give you your walking papers."

She tried hard to look appropriately professional and sympathetic. But the triumphant glint in her eye gave her away.

I wouldn't give her the satisfaction of seeing my dismay at losing a second job in such a short period. I gave her a beatific smile as she handed me my termination papers along with my final paycheck and told me I qualified for unemployment.

"No problem, Suze." *See, I've been checking into freelancing and just found an editing job where they're desperate for someone who can both write and spell. Seems more and more people these days are graduating without knowing those simple basics. So thanks for freeing me up to explore this opportunity. Oh, and unemployment is spelled m-e-n-t, not m-e-a-n-t.*

She looked bemused by my nonchalance as I held my silent smile, signed the papers, and snapped off a farewell salute.

Heading back to my work station, I picked up my purse and lunch bag, gave Yolanda a hug good-bye, and waved to my other salt-mine coworkers as I sailed out of the Dickensian warehouse, head held high.

Once I got into my car and drove away, however, that same head drooped considerably.

Lord, what is going on *here? Why can't I keep a job? Is this Your subtle way of telling me to lose those extra fifteen pounds? Or is it something else? I don't get it. What have I done wrong? And how am I supposed to keep tithing and sending money to Christopher's missionary friends in Africa who are doing Your work if I'm out of work? God, what is it You want me to do?*

Entering my lonely apartment, I vented to Gabby. "You know, these are the times it would really be nice to be married. Could sure use a nice, broad shoulder to cry on here. Or someone to just hug me and say, 'There, there, everything's going to be all right.'"

Gabby stared up at me in plastic incomprehension.

Okay, Pheebs, get a grip. This is not the end of the world, my internal cheerleader rah-rahed. *You should look at this as a blessing. You know how much you hated that job. It's not like you were using any of your gifts or talents, right? Now think: What would Scarlett do in this situation?*

That was a question I'd asked myself often, ever since I read *Gone with the Wind* as a preteen. I'd been impressed with Scarlett O'Hara's moxie and strength. She didn't wilt and tremble when tough times came; she used her wits, her wiles—even a pair of curtains—to make it through difficult situations and achieve her goals. The movie, with the beautiful Vivien Leigh as Scarlett and dashing Clark Gable as Rhett, was also one of my favorites. So it felt natural to ask myself, "Hmmm. Just what would Scarlett do?"

She'd think about that tomorrow, my procrastinating self reminded me. *After all, tomorrow is another day.*

With that important question answered, I popped in the DVD to enjoy some Scarlett time. But about halfway through the movie, I ejected it. Scarlett wasn't working her old magic today. In the past, I'd always appreciated her high-spirited gumption and tenacity, but this time was different. Instead of strength and independence, I now saw her selfishness and cruelty to others who got in the way of her plans and ambitions. She even stole her sister's well-off beau to save her beloved Tara.

I made a new note to self: *Try to be more kind and self-sacrificing, like steel-magnolia Melanie, rather than petty and self-absorbed like Scarlett . . . so as not to wind up alone with just plantation and proclivity to procrastinate.*

Though I had to admit, I really wouldn't mind that plantation . . .

Time to job surf again. I checked out some journalism and writing sites. Still nada—unless I wanted to move to Alaska or Montana. Not exactly New York.

Discouraged, I checked my e-mail. Zip—except for three for-wards from my sister-in-law. Thinking back to last night's IMs with Filmguy and the instant connection we'd shared, I decided to drop him a note.

> Hi. Enjoyed our chat last night. Watched one of my top 6 today
> (*Gone with the Wind*) but should have gone with *Chariots of
> Fire*. Needed an inspirational pick-me-up. Oh well. Next time.
> L8r . . .

Signing off, I picked up my Bible, seeking comfort and peace—which the Psalms provided as always—but also direction. These Proverbs offered the latter. "The laborer's appetite works for him; his hunger drives him on" (16:26) and "The sluggard's craving will be the death of him, because his hands refuse to work" (21:25).

With this clear biblical injunction to put my hands to good, hon-est work rather than whine, I looked at the clock and decided I had just enough time to hit one of the temp agencies before they closed for the day. I dug through my closet for my best interview suit and drove down-town. Unfortunately, the only position available was as an "associate" with Happy Holly Housecleaners. It took me just a minute or two to understand that "associate" meant "maid."

Way to put that college degree to work, Pheebs—cleaning houses. Oh well. At least I learned from the master: my mom.

Growing up, even though we lived in a rural area with cows, chick-ens, one goat, and lots of country dust, my meticulous mother always insisted on a spanking clean house with everything in its place: towels folded into thirds and neatly stacked in the linen closet by size and color (unsightly tags to the rear so they couldn't be seen), canned goods and jars of homemade preserves arranged in fruit and vegetable groupings in the kitchen cupboards (labels always facing forward so we could find what we needed at a glance), and books shelved alphabetically by title, no matter what the subject (so that when I went in search of *Gone with the Wind*, it would be wedged between *Goats and Their Dietary Needs* and *Gospel Songs Elvis Loved.*)

With that squeaky-clean background, I knew a little dusting and vacuuming would be a Cinderella cinch. I signed on the dotted line to become a Happy Holly associate.

the next morning I reported to the housecleaning headquarters in jeans, as instructed, and was handed a pale-pink polo shirt with the words *Happy Holly* stitched on the breast pocket beneath a smiley face. I'd considered calling Lindsey the night before to tell her of my job change, but wanted to see how things shook out first on the house-cleaning front. Besides, I was embarrassed.

I was apprenticed to the fifty-something Alma, the company's number-one cleaner, who'd been with the company since Holly started it fifteen years ago. By virtue of her rank, Alma got to drive one of the two pink Holly Housecleaning vans to her assignments.

"Gee, it's like Mary Kay and her pink convertibles," I joked, trying to make conversation with my new coworker as we clambered into the van.

"Except her makeup reps don't have to stick their hands down toilets."

All righty then. Now I know what I'll be doing on our first house call.

Sure enough, Alma sent me into the bathroom as soon as we arrived. "Use the squeegee on the glass shower doors, making sure not to leave streaks. Use a pumice stone in the commode to remove stubborn stains—but only after you've used Lysol and a toilet brush first. Make sure all the chrome fixtures are gleaming, and be sure to empty the litter box."

After I finished both baths, she continued her instructions, keeping one eye on *The Young and the Restless* the whole time. "Use this special cleaner on the hardwood floors, wipe down all the baseboards, and make sure you vacuum outward to the corners from the center—like the petals of a daisy—always remembering to step backward out of the room, vacuuming over your footprints. Once you've finished, try not to go back in the room and leave your foot indentations on the freshly vacuumed carpet. If you must, walk along the edge, rather than the middle."

What if I trip and fall? Talk about a big indentation. Would that be grounds for firing?

Alma stopped waxing the kitchen floor to swig from her water bottle. "Oh, and when you polish the furniture, make sure you carefully remove all the knickknacky stuff, remembering exactly where everything was so you can put it back in the same spot once you've finished."

By noon we'd finished with the first house and after a quick pass through the McDonald's drive-through for Quarter-Pounders and fries, were off to the second. Except this one wasn't a house, but an apartment—a guy's apartment by the looks of things as we walked through the front door. Empty and not quite empty pizza cartons and cans of soda littered the coffee table. Dirty socks and shorts dotted the floor. The whole place smelled like something had taken up residence under the couch.

Shaking her head in disgust at the sinkful of dirty dishes, sticky countertops, and all-around mess, Alma volunteered to tackle the living room and kitchen while I hit the bedroom and bath. "Remember, this is only a two-hour job, so we have to work fast. Although how we're supposed to get this pigsty cleaned up in just two hours is beyond me," she muttered under her breath. "Some mothers sure didn't raise their children right."

I headed down the hall to the bathroom, grabbing a gallon of bleach and pulling on industrial strength rubber gloves as I went.

It was worse than I feared. Apparently the apartment tenant—who was most definitely a guy—had never heard of cleanser. As I scrubbed the grungy porcelain bowl, my mind drifted. *My life is in the toilet. What am I doing here? For this I went to college? I seem to be regressing rather than progressing . . . God, are You trying to tell me something?*

Next, I moved to the bedroom, stepping over piles of dirty clothes to reach the dust-covered dresser. A familiar, albeit younger face smiled out at me from a college graduation picture.

You've got to be kidding me. Jake's apartment? I glanced down at the piles of dirty underwear I'd just stepped over. Ew!

When my first day's shift ended with a grudging "You done good," from Alma, I clocked out and headed home. Arriving at my apartment, hot, sticky and definitely needing a shower, I found a late-rent notice from the building manager taped to my front door. *Desperate note to self: Run away and join the circus.* I let myself in, then sagged against the wall and slid down to the floor where I had a good cry.

A few minutes later, the ringing doorbell made me jump.

What now? Mr. Allen come to evict me? Heaving myself up and wiping my eyes on my pink sleeve, I peered through the peephole.

Lindsey.

"C'mon, lazy girl," she said loudly. "We're supposed to be at the gym. I know you're there. I saw your car, so don't try and fake me out with that old pretending-you're-not-home bit."

Sighing, I opened the door.

"Hey, what's with the shirt?"

I closed the door behind her, not wanting all my neighbors to know. "Yours truly is now the newest member of the Happy Holly Housecleaning team."

"Since when?"

"Since I got laid off from my stimulating publishing job yesterday."

"Oh no."

"Yep. You're looking at a two-time flop. I'm going for a record. I figure if I work really hard and try my best, maybe I can get dumped from a third job in less than a month *and* get evicted from my apartment at the same time."

"What?"

I handed her my overdue notice.

"Oh, Pheebs, I'm so sorry. Why didn't you tell me things were this bad?"

"A little thing called pride."

"There's no place for pride between best friends." She pulled her checkbook from her gym bag. "How much do you need?"

"No way, Lins, I can't take money from you. You've already done way too much."

She ignored me and began writing. "That's what friends are for, Pheebs. Sisters in Christ, too. Remember, this too shall pass. It's just a season." Her face brightened. "Hey, I have a great idea! Why don't you move in with me? I have that empty extra bedroom, you know."

"No way, Lins. I wouldn't want to wreck our friendship."

"How would living together wreck our friendship?"

"You said it right there. *Living together.* The surest way to ruin a great friendship is to live together. Or travel together."

"We traveled to New York and did fine."

"Yeah, but that was only for a few days."

"C'mon, it'll be fun. We can stay up late, paint each other's toe-nails, and dish about guys."

"Guys." I blinked. "That reminds me! The one bright light in my disaster called a life is that I had a great IM conversation with my lost *Casablanca* fan Sunday night."

"You did? Tell all!" Lindsey said, leaning forward, then quickly pulling back. "But first, uh, why don't you go change? Love ya, but you're a . . . bit aromatic."

"Let me jump in the shower." I headed down the hall. "I'll be out in five."

"Okay, but hurry. I'm dying to know all the details. Like what's his name? Where does he live? What does he do for a living? And does he have a brother?"

We decided to eighty-six the gym. In my current dismal state, the last thing I wanted to face was perky, tight-bodied Melissa and her thong. Instead, we took the only sensible course of action: We ordered a pizza.

While we waited for the delivery, I gave Lins the 411 about Filmguy—she couldn't believe I hadn't gotten his vital statistics. Then, while we ate, we hashed over my awful day and my possible romantic prospects.

Lindsey had just bitten into the last slice of the combo pizza—tonight was not the time to skimp on carbs—when the thought struck her. She almost choked. "Hey Pheebs, do you think maybe *Alex Spencer* could be Filmguy? Remember, he's a movie buff too."

I snorted. "A little too much *You've Got Mail*, don't you think? Besides, someone with his money and connections doesn't need to play in the personals." I extended my claws. "Unless, of course, the women he meets are all put off by his height. Or lack thereof."

"Meow," Lindsey said, setting down the last piece of chewed-on crust and reaching for her napkin.

Having more or less demolished the pizza, we continued to chew the cheese for awhile. We prayed about the possibility of living together, and finally, a little after eleven, Lindsey left, after pressing the rent check into my hands. I reluctantly accepted it—but only as a loan.

Physically and emotionally spent, I began to get ready for bed. Needing a little pick-me-up first, though, I decided to check my e-mail on the off chance that Filmguy might have written.

He had. He had! And just a couple of hours earlier.

Hi. How r u? You sounded a little down. Everything ok? If u need a cybershoulder to cry on, feel free. Meanwhile, got yr kettle corn close by? Am munching some now as I prepare to watch *Parent Trap*. Thought I'd check out yr romantic sensibilities, altho I've never been a big Hayley Mills fan. Too skinny. Maureen O'Hara is another story. She even looks great in b&w. Remember her in *Miracle on 34th Street*? My fave Xmas movie (neck-in-neck with Ralphie and the Red Ryder BB gun, tho.) How 'bout you? Just top 3 this time ☺ Here's mine:

1. Tie between *Miracle on 34th Street* and *A Christmas Story* (Did u know parts of the latter were filmed in Cleveland? At Higbee's?)

2. *How the Grinch Stole Christmas*

3. *It's a Wonderful Life*

Hope we'll get to share some kettle corn in person sooner rather than later. Let me know.

God bless, Filmguy

My exhaustion vanished—and I hadn't even had a jolt of coffee. I shot off a quick reply:

Hi. Thx for the cybershoulder offer—may take u up on that sometime. Had a lousy day, but don't want 2 go there now. So, wasn't I right about *The Parent Trap*?

Speaking of movies, here's my top 3 Christmas flix:

1. Tie between *White Christmas* & *A Christmas Story*

2. *Miracle on 34th Street*

3. *It's a Wonderful Life*

Yes, I recognize Higbee's every time I watch "You'll shoot your eye out, you'll shoot your eye out!" Ralphie. As for kettle corn, how'd u like to meet at the Grand Friday at 7? They're showing 1 of your top 6—*The African Queen*. Just leave the leeches at home! ☺ I'll be dressed in white in homage to K. Hepburn's spinster missionary.

Signing off, I closed my laptop and headed to the bathroom. While brushing my teeth, I heard the phone ring. "What'd you forget this time, Lins?" I mumbled around a mouthful of toothpaste.

"Pheebert?"

"Jordy! Jus' a sec."

No one but my brother called me that. He'd assigned me the nickname when I was three and in love with Bert and Ernie on *Sesame Street*.

Setting the receiver down, I rinsed and spit, then returned. "Sorry, big brother. Hey, nice to hear your friendly California voice. What's up? Wait—let me guess. Karen's having twins?"

In their first three years of marriage, Jordy's wife gave birth to two daughters. Then she waited five years to have a son, followed two years later by another daughter. Now, three-and-a-half years later, Karen was expecting their latest and greatest, making me an aunt to the fifth power. Sixth, if she had twins.

"Nope. Actually, I'm calling from the hospital . . . Mom's broken both her arms."

"What? Is she okay?"

"Other than the double casts? She's fine."

"What in the world happened?"

"She slipped on a cow pie."

My brother cleared his throat while I was still digesting this astonishing bit of information. "Um, Phoebe, I have a huge favor to ask . . ."

chapter nine

When my plane lifted off on Friday, I settled in for the five-hour flight—which my mom had eagerly paid for—and tried to psych myself up for a hometown reunion with the woman who'd brought me into the world but had never wanted me to see more than her little corner of it.

This was the big favor my brother had asked of me. After easing my concerns over Mom's injuries, he said she'd be out of commission for at least six weeks. Also, she needed someone to help care for her. He'd invited her to stay with them, but she had refused, not wanting "to be a bother" or to leave her own home. They'd suggested hiring a nurse, but Mom didn't like the idea of a stranger in her house.

At that point, I saw the writing on the mother-ship wall. Now, just a few days later, I was on my way back to the little town where I was born. Barley, California.

Clever way of beaming me back home, Mom. You've tried everything else. No, I'm not suggesting you deliberately slipped on that cow pie . . .

Although I wondered. Mom had been around cows and their calling cards all her life. During our growing-up years, with cows in the field behind our house, she'd always teased Jordy and me, "Make sure you watch where you're stepping or you might wind up with a cow pie for dessert."

Our mother was a homespun cross between Ma Ingalls and Aunt Bee, with a dash of neatnik Monica from *Friends*. But my dream mom was Clair Huxtable of *The Cosby Show,* a cool, with-it woman who maintained a high-powered career and parented five kids at the same time, all while exchanging witty banter with Bill Cosby. My mom was no Clair Huxtable.

I knew I wasn't Mom's ideal daughter, either. For one thing, I lived too far away, a definite drawback to my homebody mother. For another, I was a huge disappointment in the domestic arena. I couldn't sew a straight stitch to save my life, the only things I could cook were grilled-cheese sandwiches and French toast. And as for that neat thing of hers, there was no way. Oh, I knew *how* to clean, as my recent (brief) stint with Happy Holly indicated. But if there was a four-letter word that applied to my housekeeping habits, it certainly wasn't *neat*. (Can you say "slob"?)

I was much more my dad's daughter. In fact, the two things that had made my hometown at all tolerable for me had been Dad and the old Bijou movie theater where I'd spent as many happy hours as I could, losing myself in the romance of the silver screen. After Dad died, I couldn't wait to leave and see the world he'd longed to see and never had a chance to. That's why, to my homegrown mother's dismay and my friends' amazement, I'd enlisted in the air force the day after I turned eighteen. Less than a week later, I'd found myself winging my way to San Antonio, Texas, and six weeks of basic training.

Now, winging my way back to California, I scribbled off grateful notes to Lins and Phil, thanking them for helping me pack and store all my stuff. (I'd decided to bite the bullet and give notice on my no-longer-affordable apartment.)

Then, all of a sudden, I remembered my date with Filmguy. Tonight.

Oh no! In all the craziness of getting ready to leave for an extended time—scrambling for affordable tickets, quitting my choice new job, and moving my belongings to Lindsey's spare room—I'd completely forgotten our *African Queen* rendezvous.

I grabbed my laptop from beneath the seat in front of me and powered it up. All I got was a blank silver screen. I hit escape a couple of times and Ctrl-Alt-Del, but still nothing. Then I shut it down and tried again.

Up popped the same blank screen.

At that moment the steward came on the air with the announce-ment to stow all electronic devices as we began our descent into Sacramento. The minute we landed and got the okay to use cell phones again, I punched in Lindsey's number, glancing at my watch as I did so. Six-fifty Cleveland time—only ten minutes before I was supposed to meet Filmguy. "C'mon Lins, pick up. Pick up."

She didn't answer, so I left a frantic voice mail asking her to please run to the theater to catch my movie-loving blind date if she received my message within the next fifteen minutes. After I punched send, how-ever, I realized the futility of it all.

I didn't have a clue what he looked like. In my starry-eyed excite-ment, I'd neglected to find out what he'd be wearing or holding in his hand—no Red Vines this time—for identification.

No, I had to go and be Miss Mysterious. And now he was going to think I'd pulled a Deborah Kerr on him, like in *An Affair to Remember.* She'd stood up Cary Grant too, although she had a very good reason. *Just hope he doesn't think I was hit by a car. Although that would almost be better . . .*

As everyone around me shoved their way into the aisle to deplane, I replaced my cell and grabbed my two carry-ons.

Minutes later, my sister-in-law, Karen, was enveloping me in a large, pregnant hug.

Three-year-old Lexie, who was just a baby the last time I saw her, looked me up and down as her mom released me. "Do you have a baby in your tummy like my mommy?"

Scooping my darling niece up into my arms, I planted a big kiss on her cheek and sucked in my stomach. "Nope. I just need to work out more."

Karen and I caught up as we made our way to the luggage carousel, with little Lexie holding tight to her mother's hand. Her big brown eyes darted everywhere, fascinated by all the people and activity, before finally coming back to rest on me. "Gamma Glory fell down and broked her arms," she announced.

"Yes, I know, sweetie." I squatted down to her eye level. "That's why I've come ho—um, back to help take care of her."

"'S'about time!"

"Lexie!" Karen reprimanded her daughter.

"Thas what Gamma said."

Karen shot me an apologetic glance. "Mom's on heavy medication right now, so she's not her usual self."

"Sounds pretty usual to me. But, hey, maybe if I'm lucky, this better living through chemistry will make her forget her 'it's time you settled down and got married' refrain."

We began the hour-and-a-half drive to Barley in my sister-in-law's SUV. I glanced across the seat at her ever-expanding belly. "So, what's it going to be this time, Karen? Boy or girl?"

Lexie interrupted before she could answer. "Wanna baby bruvver. Gots enough sisters."

Karen smiled in the rearview mirror at her daughter. "Your daddy and Jacob feel the same way, honey. That way they won't be so outnumbered." She grinned and flicked her eyes over at me. "With as many kids as we have now, we decided we'd just let God surprise us with our next one. As long as he or she is healthy, that's all that matters."

"Nuh-uh," Lexie protested from the backseat. "Wanna bruvver."

Leaning over the backseat, I patted my pouting niece's knee. "I hear ya, sweetheart. Brothers are the best. Your dad's always been a great brother."

Lexie's lip quivered and she began to cry. "He's not a bruvver. He's Daddy!"

I glanced helplessly across at Karen, who rode to the rescue. "Uh-oh. Somebody's tired," she said under her breath. Then she smiled in the rearview at her now-wailing daughter. "Lexie, honey, you know how Jacob's your big brother?"

"Yes-s," she hiccupped between sobs.

"Well, Daddy's Aunt Phoebe's big brother, and when they were little, they played together just like you and Jacob do."

Lexie sniffled and lifted her teary eyes to meet her mother's. "Dey did?"

Karen pinched my leg.

"We sure did, Lexie. And you know what your daddy used to do?"

Wide-eyed, she shook her head from side to side.

"He'd put on a red cape and pretend he was Superman, fighting the bad guys and rescuing me from them—I was always Lois Lane."

Eyes shining with pride now rather than tears: "And my daddy wescood you?"

"Yes he did. Although once or twice I had to be Supergirl and rescue your daddy, 'cause girls can rescue boys too, you know."

"Uh-huh, I know. Mommy tol' me. My Barbie wescoos Ken a lot." Bored with the I-am-woman-hear-me-roar lesson, Lexie looked at my manicured left hand resting on the back of the seat. "Look. I gots polish too," she said, thrusting her chubby little fingers toward me from her car seat.

"I see that. What a pretty pink. Did you do that all by yourself?"

She started to nod yes, then admitted, "Mommy helpded."

"I really like that color. Do you think you could help me polish mine that same pink too?"

"'Kay." My niece nodded, her eyelids beginning to droop. Seconds later she was fast asleep.

"Sorry about that," Karen said, "This is usually her nap time, and she can get pretty cranky when she's tired, but she insisted on coming to the airport to meet you."

"Not a problem. I feel the same way when I don't get my nap. So fill me in on Mom. How's she doing, really? She's not in a lot of pain, is she? What exactly did the doctor say?"

My sister-in-law fumbled in her purse for an Altoid and offered me one as she merged onto the freeway. "Other than her frustration at not being able to cook and clean and roll around on the floor with the kids like she usually does, Mom's doing just fine—not to worry. The doctor said both arms were clean breaks and will heal nicely, and she should be able to get her casts removed in another five to six weeks."

Karen switched on the cruise control, then glanced over at me. "All right, Phoebe, now spill. I can never get the full story from Jordy—you know how sketchy men are with details, especially relationship ones. Anyone special back in Cleveland?"

"Not really. As you know, I'm the queen of the bad blind date. I've really had some doozies lately. Although there's this one guy who definitely has potential . . ."

"Really? What's his name? What's he like?

"Well, uh, we haven't actually met in person yet . . ."

I filled my sister-in-law in on mystery date Filmguy and our fun movie connection, which I'd been hoping to explore in person tonight. When I mentioned we both liked musicals, Karen, who'd taught drama before she started popping out babies left and right, interrupted.

"That reminds me, the Players are just beginning rehearsals for *Oklahoma*. We've got this wonderful high-school senior, Steve Patterson, who makes a great Curly, and a terrific Laurey too, although our Ado Annie needs a little work . . ."

As Karen talked about people I didn't know, I listened with one ear while we drove by Lodi—yes, of "stuck in Lodi" fame. Moments later, we passed the green sign for Barley, seventeen miles off the main highway.

Ah, home sweet one-cow country home. Correction, one-thousand-cow home. The only thing Barley and its outlying farms had in abundance was cows—dairy cows. Everything else numbered in the single digits—one beauty shop, one barber, three gas stations (one with auto body shop, one grocery store plus a minimart attached to one of the gas stations, one feed store, one VFW hall, one newspaper with two full-time employees, one high school, and one movie theater, the Barley Bijou, a majestic place left over from the days when the railroad went through town and generations of young people hadn't left to find jobs. A handful of restaurants managed to stay in business, including Lou's Diner and Steakhouse, a Mexican dive called Tia Rosa's, and Tiny's Café downtown, which existed primarily to serve awful coffee to senior citizens at the crack of dawn. And of course there were churches—St. Mary's Catholic, several varieties of Baptist, First (and only) Methodist, Barley Presbyterian . . . and Holy Communion.

Growing up, I attended Holy Communion Lutheran Church, which my mom's family—immigrants from the Lutheran Midwest—had helped to found. It was where the women were renowned for bringing the best—and most—food to all the town potlucks and bake sales. Dad sang in the choir and often did the tenor solos while the rest of us beamed with pride.

I was in the choir, too—the tiny children's choir one of the church ladies put together. But they never asked me to sing a solo. I was always relegated to the back row.

I did, however, get to play Mary in the Christmas pageant when I was eight. Mary didn't sing or speak; she just had to smile serenely at the Baby Jesus—which was actually my Heather Serene Cabbage Patch doll—in the manger. All went well until Tommy Clark, who played one of the three wise men, cut off all the hair of my beloved Heather so she'd look more like a boy.

My traumatic youthful reverie was cut short. "Hey, what's that?"

Karen followed my gaze to a vibrant red and gold sign hanging outside the long-vacant hardware store at the town's entrance. "Peking Dragon, our new Chinese restaurant. They have great mu shu pork, and the kids love their sizzling shrimp. We'll have to take you there one night."

"Gee. Barley's really moving up in the world—what with *four* restaurants now."

"Five, actually. There's also the Barley Twist, which opened just a couple of months ago to cater to all the transplanted Bay-Area types who moved here when their real-estate prices started skyrocketing. It's mainly vegetarian, but they also serve chicken and seafood. Their lobster bisque is to die for, and Jordy loves their grilled red snapper."

"What about Mom?"

The corners of my sister-in-law's mouth turned up. She shot me a knowing grin. "You know Mom. If there's no red meat, it's not a real restaurant. That woman really loves her steak. Lou's prime rib is still her favorite. Besides, remember, this is—"

"Cow country, after all," I said in unison with Karen, repeating one of Mom's favorite sayings. Without missing a beat, we segued into another of her cooking bromides. "You need some good, hearty red meat several times a week. Especially women—we're prone to low iron."

We continued to drive through town. In addition to the two new restaurants, I noticed that Barley now boasted a craft and gift boutique, two antique stores, and, wonder of wonders, a combination bookstore and coffee bar.

In amazement, I took it all in. "Things certainly have changed in the last few years." *Maybe my six-week exile to cow town won't be so bad after all.*

At the end of Main Street, Karen turned right and drove past several blocks of houses that slowly thinned out before road became a dusty country lane that dead-ended at the white-framed, green-shuttered home of my childhood. As she pulled into the driveway, the back door swung open, and a passel of kids swarmed out. They surrounded the van, shouting, "Aunt Phoebe, Aunt Phoebe!" And, "Mom, guess what happened at school today?"

Instantly enveloped in a tangle of hugs and kisses, I looked over the heads of the affectionate mob and smiled a warm greeting at Jordy, who stood holding the screen door open with his foot.

"Hi, there, big brother. Where's Mom?"

"I'm right here," she said, making her way past Jordy. "Just a little slow with these dad-blamed casts is all."

Once disentangled from the kids, I raced over to give both my

Mom and Jordy a hug, although since she couldn't very well put her arms around me, our embrace was a little stiff.

My mother, whose now-gray hair was still in the familiar, long, old-fashioned braid I remembered from childhood, peered over her bifocals at me. "My goodness, Phoebe Lynn. You cut all your hair off."

chapter ten

We sat down for a delicious fatted-calf dinner—my mother's famous tender pot roast, potatoes, carrots, and homemade gravy (all of which, I later learned, Karen had put in the Crockpot under Mom's watchful eye), followed by her prize-winning cherry cobbler and vanilla ice cream. After which Karen, Jordy, and their brood hung around for another hour catching up.

I was just telling Jordy the sad saga of my fried laptop when little Lexie sidled up to her grandma and in a loud stage whisper announced, "An Beebee has a boyfriend."

An eager matrimonial glint shone in my mother's eye as she zeroed in on me. "Is this true, daughter? Is it serious? What's his name? How old is he? What does he do?"

I shot a bewildered gaze at Karen. "Mother, I do *not* have a boyfriend. Trust me on this."

Lexie folded her cute dimpled arms in front of her and jutted out her tiny chin. "Do so, An Beebee! You're not 'posed to lie. Else you have to go to time out."

Karen stepped in. "Alexandra Nicole, what have I told you about making up stories? I think maybe someone else needs a time out."

My niece's face crumbled, but she stubbornly stood her ground. "I not making up stories. Heard An Beebee tell you 'bout man named Poe Tentshul who likes movies jus' like her."

Jordy smothered a laugh with a cough and Karen's mouth twitched while my face flamed red under my mother's probing look. But my sister-in-law wasn't finished correcting her daughter. "Lexie, you misunderstood, sweetheart. That's why it's not polite to listen in on other people's conversations."

"But, Mommy, I couldn't help it. You woked me up when I was sleeping."

My brother tried to save the day. "Hey pumpkin, what say we have a little more of Grandma's yummy cobbler, okay? Mom, your cherry-cobbler recipe is the best around—even if we did have to thaw it out for you."

But Jordy's complimentary tactics and feeble joke were not going to deter my marriage-minded mother from her mission. "So, Phoebe, are you going to tell me about this movie-loving man with potential or not?"

Well, you see, it's like this, mother of mine. Mr. Potential is probably gone with the wind by now since I stood him up on our first date tonight in my haste to rush back home to cow-town. "Mom, there's nothing to tell. He's just someone I've been writing to online. We haven't even met in person yet."

"You haven't even met him? So how do you know he's not in prison—or an ax murderer or some kind of sex fiend or something? I saw a report on *20/20* that warned about the dangers of Internet relationships. Whatever happened to meeting a nice man at church?"

I thought I finally did, Mom, but there was that little problem of his costing me my job . . . "I know plenty of nice guys from my church, but we're just friends. Nothing romantic."

"Who says friends can't turn into something more? You never know how the good Lord's going to work," she said. "Whatever happened to that nice friend of yours named Phil?"

"Mom, Phil's like a brother to me. It'd be like dating Jordy!"

My brother licked ice cream from his upper lip. "And what's so bad about that?"

"Eew. Can you say 'icky'?"

"I don't seem to recall your protesting when I took you to your sophomore prom."

"Then you're losing your memory, brother dear—must be your advanced years taking their toll; they say the mind is the first thing to go. I'll have you know I fought long and hard against going to prom with my *brother*. Talk about looking like a loser."

"Nobody forced you to go with me, Pheebert."

"Right." I snorted. "Nobody but Mom, Dragon-Lady Dieffenbrock, and Hubert the Horrible."

I thought back to that infamous night that went down in sophomore history. Every member of the student council was required to make an appearance at prom—including *moi* as sophomore class secretary. Since nobody had asked me, I planned on going solo, and Dad supported me in my declaration of independence. But Mom wouldn't hear of it. Neither would Mrs. Dieffenbrock, our dragon of a music teacher, nor Mr. Hubert, the math teacher who served as class adviser. Apparently a girl going alone to the prom was an unthinkable scandal, so my brother got drafted as my pity date. That the same thing had happened to Judy Garland and Lucille Bremer in *Meet Me in St. Louis* was only a small consolation.

After all these years, the mortification of that moment—not only arriving at prom with my brother, but wearing my mom's twenty-year-old, out-of-style Miss Udderly Delicious Dairy pageant gown because I'd scorched my own dress with an iron minutes before we had to leave—still made me shudder in embarrassment. But that embarrassment soon gave way as I remembered what happened next. It was what turned the worst evening of my life into one of the best.

"That was the night that Dad sang to me," I whispered.

My English-teacher dad, who was one of the dance chaperones, had left home early, before I was dressed. But he caught sight of me from his place at the punch bowl next to Dragon Lady Dieffenbrock. Dad whispered something in his music colleague's ear. Dieffenbrock nodded and headed over to the band, slipping in and replacing the keyboardist. Then, with shining eyes only for me, my father approached as the music swelled into a completely different tune. He drew me into his arms and serenaded me with a show-stopping rendition of "Some Enchanted Evening" as he whirled me around the floor.

It was just like the movies.

Everyone stopped dancing and stepped back to make way for us. It was just me, my dad, and the music. Nothing else mattered. Afterward, the room erupted into applause. Through the din, my father whispered into my ear, "My little girl has turned into a beautiful young woman, just like her mother." Then, as the rock band started back in, one of my brother's senior classmates tapped Dad on the shoulder and said, "Excuse me, Mr. Grant, but may I cut in?"

"That was the night your daddy realized his little girl was growing up," Mom said, her eyes glistening as she exchanged a poignant smile with me.

"Yeah, that was also the night my buddies realized it too, and I had to start keeping 'em all in line," Jordy recalled.

I fluttered my eyelashes at my big brother. "My hero."

"Hey, hero man, I hate to be the one to break up this walk down memory lane," Karen said, looking at her watch, "but I'm afraid it's time for us to start packing up. The kids still have homework to do, and it's past Lexie's and Jacob's bedtime."

"Aw, Mom, do we have to go so early?" protested ten-year-old Elizabeth, who'd been stealing covetous looks at my double-pierced ears and *Gone with the Wind* purse all evening.

My sister-in-law stood up and began collecting empty dessert bowls. "Yes, we do, young lady. It's nearly eight-thirty, and I know someone who still has some math problems to finish tonight. Now, go ahead and pick up all the toys and put them back in Grandma's toy box, please." Next, she directed her attention to her eldest, who'd had her nose in a book most of the evening. "Ashley, can you find Lexie's other shoe and put it on her for me? And honey," she said over her shoulder to my brother as she headed to the kitchen, "can you wash

Jacob's hands and face before he gets ice cream all over your mom's furniture?"

"Sure thing, sweetie." Jordy scooped up his sticky son and headed toward the bathroom. "C'mon, buddy, let's have some male bonding time, okay?"

"Yeah," a sleepy Jacob mumbled.

Mom struggled to get up and help clear the dishes with her cast-encumbered hands, but I was too fast for her. "No, Mother, you just sit back and relax. That's why *I'm* here, remember?"

A drowsy Lexie slid over on the sofa next to Mom and, laying her head in her lap, said, "I belax wiv you, Gamma."

Entering the kitchen, I handed Karen the rest of the dessert dishes. "Hey Kar, sure you don't want to leave one of your sweet daughters here tonight?" I pleaded. "We could have a slumber party. And I'd be happy to help Elizabeth with her homework and make sure she gets up in time for school."

Then I lobbed a guilt grenade my sister-in-law's way. "Besides, you know how much Mom loves having her grandkids around."

Karen passed me some bowls to load into the dishwasher. "I also know how much she loves her only daughter and how happy she is to have you home at last. Besides," she said, "you're lousy at math. Sorry. This one you have to handle on your own. Don't worry. It won't be that bad."

"That's what they said to Tom Selleck in *Quigley Down Under* before he had to eat those big old nasty Australian slugs." I groaned. "Were you not there when she gave me the third degree about my Internet 'romance'? The minute you guys leave, you know she's going to hit me with it. She won't be able to stop herself."

Karen rinsed the last bowl, handed it to me, and dried her hands on a dish towel. "So steer the conversation in another direction. You're a reporter. You know how to ask questions. Put that journalism degree to use and simply think of your mom as someone you're interviewing for a story."

Just then, fourteen-year-old Ashley, who reminded me of an adolescent Julia Roberts—all legs, coltish awkwardness, and tumbling long hair—came in to tell her mom she'd found Lexie's shoe and they were ready to go. She cast a shy look at me through her incredibly long lashes (without benefit of mascara, thank you very much) and said, "Good night, Aunt Phoebe. It's really nice to see you again."

I hugged my bookworm niece and kissed her on top of her Julia mane. "Good night, sweetie. It's great to see you again too—you've grown so much I hardly recognized you! You've become quite the beautiful young lady, in fact. We'll have to make sure to have some fun girl time while I'm here, okay?"

Ashley nodded as a rosy flush warmed her cheeks.

After all the familial hugs, kisses, and good-nights were dispensed for the evening—a time-consuming process when four affectionate children are involved—my mother and I were alone at last.

"Mom, would you like a cup of tea or something—do you still like chamomile?" I bustled around, plumping pillows and straightening up. "Or since it's fall, would you prefer cinnamon?"

"Sit down and relax, daughter. Now that everyone's gone, you and I can finally talk woman to woman." Her motherly romantic radar began to blip. "Now, Phoebe, tell me all about this online relationsh—"

"So, Mom, uh, how 'bout them Niners, huh?"

She gave me a strange look. "Niners?"

"Yeah. You know—that football team you really like. Are they having a good season?"

"Phoebe, I like *basketball*, not football. The Sacramento Kings are my team."

"Oh. Right. So, how are those Kings doing? Do you have a favorite player?"

Mom knitted her brows. "Phoebe, you *hate* sports, always have. Where'd this sudden interest come from?" Then her face cleared. "Oh, I see. Does your Internet man like sports?"

"Um, not sure." I tried a new conversational tack. "Hey Mom, what's with all these changes in Barley? I hardly recognized the place as we drove through! Two new restaurants and a bookstore too. Wow. Tell me, Karen says they have a coffee bar in the bookstore as well. Is it any good?"

Knowing my coffee addiction and hoping it might be strong enough to lure me back to Barley permanently, she immediately took the bait. "Oh yes, honey, it's very good. You know me; I just like a plain old cup of coffee, but they have all that fancy stuff you like too—cappuccino, mocha, and . . . la-tea?"

"Latte?"

"That's it."

"My, my. Barley's certainly moving up in the world." I smiled and put on my interviewer hat. "What do you suppose accounts for all these changes?"

That was all she needed.

Grateful to have escaped the Filmguy inquisition, I listened, at least for a while, as my rural-minded Mom rattled on and on for the rest of the evening about the commuters from Sacramento and the Bay Area who'd begun encroaching on the area, although she had nothing against progress, mind you, just not at the expense of the open farmland, blah, blah, blah. I made sure to emit the occasional "Really?" "Mmm-hmm," and "You don't say?" as my mind drifted back to my friends, Filmguy, and the life I was already missing in Cleveland.

Tomorrow, the Lone Rangers are having the scavenger hunt that Lindsey and I organized. And Sunday they're going to the ballet. I was really looking forward to seeing Romeo and Juliet. *Oh well, it's not like I don't know how it ends. Hmmm, wonder if Filmguy would go to the ballet? Probably not, since he didn't like it in* West Side Story—*and since, for all he knows, I'm a total jerk. Sure hope I can get through to him on e-mail soon and explain about standing him up. Should've gotten a phone number or something . . .*

My head began to droop, and Mom stopped talking at once. "My goodness, what's the matter with me—running on and on like that when you're probably exhausted from that long trip. I must admit I'm a little tired myself too, so how 'bout if we call it a night dear?"

"Works for me." I yawned. "I *am* pretty bushed, and still need to unpack."

Together we walked down the hall to her bedroom, where I helped her change into her pj's—now sleeveless, for ease in slipping over casts—wash her face, and brush her teeth. I propped extra pillows beneath each arm so the heaviness of the casts wouldn't weigh her down. Then I bent down and kissed her cheek. "Good night, Mom."

She returned my kiss. "Good night, sweet dumpling. Sleep well, 'cause tomorrow after breakfast we need to go into town and do some grocery shopping—my cupboards are nearly bare."

Nodding, I counted inwardly to ten. I wasn't overly fond of being called "daughter"—it's not like we were Amish or anything—but I *really* hated it when she called me "dumpling." *Why don't you just call me fat, mother, and get it over with?*

I crossed the hall to my old room, still with all its adolescent movie posters intact: *Pretty in Pink*—when I was thirteen, I longed for nothing more than to have red hair like Molly Ringwald—*Top Gun* and *Raiders of the Lost Ark.* Tom Cruise and Harrison Ford, yum. And the two films that had a lasting spiritual impact on me, *Chariots of Fire* and *The Sound of Music.*

Humming "Climb Ev'ry Mountain" to myself as I unpacked, I recalled what Julie Andrews said to Christopher Plummer when they finally admit their love to one another: "When the Lord closes a door, somewhere He opens a window."

Lord, what window are You opening for me here? And as dumpling girl, will my thighs be able to fit through it?

I wandered over to the small pine table that had served as my desk and where my old turntable and tape player still sat next to a stack of albums—some standards by Sinatra, Tony Bennett, and Rosemary Clooney mixed in with a few pop favorites—U2, Amy Grant, and Billy Joel. But most were soundtracks from the movies and Broadway. I almost wore out "Corner of the Sky" from *Pippin* as I listened to it over and over again, wondering if I'd ever feel like I fit in anywhere I went.

Stashing my suitcases in the closet, I noticed the bulletin board on the back of the door filled with favorite quotes I'd tacked up during high school: "The future belongs to those who believe in the beauty of their dreams."—Eleanor Roosevelt. "We have a God who delights in impossibilities."—Andrew Murray. And my favorite scripture, Jeremiah 29:11: "'For I know the plans I have for you,' declares the Lord, 'plans to prosper you and not to harm you, plans to give you hope and a future.'"

I'm glad You *know the plans You have for me, Lord, 'cause I'm pretty clueless. Do I start sending my résumé to other New York papers? Or do I wait for Filmguy to come riding up in his white Beamer and whisk me off to movieland? Or perhaps I should just pray that during the night Mom metamorphoses into Carol Brady—with a better hairstyle—before we kill each other?*

Turning down my patchwork quilt—sewn by my domestic goddess mother, naturally—I slipped beneath its cozy warmth. Before going to sleep, though, I fiddled with my laptop again, hoping against hope that the intervening hours had somehow magically restored it.

No such luck.

Since it was too late Cleveland time to call Lindsey, I left her a cell text message instead. "Hey grl, wassup? Plz tel me u got 2 meet Flmgy! My lptp's fried ☹ Say hi 2 Phil. More l8r. P."

Flipping my phone shut, I heard a rustling across the room and glanced up to see a large calico cat standing in the doorway looking up at me.

"Well, hi there, kitty. You must be the latest member of Mom's feline family. What's your name? Here, kitty, kitty."

The cat refused to budge, just stood there staring at me. Finally I got out of bed to see what it wanted. As I drew nearer, I noticed a small dark spot on the carpet at its feet. I bent down to get a closer look, and the dark spot moved.

I screamed and slammed my door shut.

"Phoebe! What's wrong? Are you all right?" Mom yelled from her room.

"Your cat dropped a live mouse outside my door!"

She laughed. "Oh, is that what all the ruckus is about? It's probably just a field mouse. You should feel honored. That means Ginger knows you're family—she was bringing you a welcome-home gift."

"Thanks all the same, but I'd much rather have chocolate," I muttered. Trembling, I grabbed a shoe and jumped back up on the bed, pulling all the coverings up after me so the scary critter wouldn't be able to crawl up them. Then I raised my voice again. "You know how I hate any kind of rodent, Mom! Can't you tell her to take it away, please?"

More rustling outside my door.

"Mom, what's she doing? Is she eating it? Gross!"

"No, she's probably just batting it with her paw. Cats always do that. C'mon, Ginger, that's a good girl," I heard Mom coo to Killer Kitty. "Take the mouse back outside now. Phoebe didn't mean to scare you. No, she didn't. You're Mommy's good little mouser, aren't you? Yes. That's it. Good girl. Okay, Phoebe, you can relax. Ginger's taken the mouse out the kitty door."

"Are you sure?" I lowered the shoe a fraction. "What if she comes back with more?"

"She won't, honey. Goodness, you scared her half to death."

"*I* scared *her*?!"

"Get some sleep now, dear. Night-night."

"G'night."

Our Father, who art in heaven, please deliver me from mice in the night and a mother who drives me crazy. And Lord, please get me to New York soon!

a loud crash the next morning sent me flying in my pink pig slippers and Betty Boop nightshirt out to the kitchen, where I discovered my frustrated mother staring down at a black cast-iron skillet at her feet.

"Mother, what in the world are you doing?"

"I wanted to make you breakfast your first morning home."

"Thanks, but you know you shouldn't be picking up anything heavy." I sighed, then steered her over to one of her oak dinette chairs and poured her a cup of coffee. "It's a wonder you didn't smash your toes. Then you'd be the four-casted woman."

I retrieved the skillet, set it in the sink, and squirted in some dish soap, opening the fridge with my other hand to grab the milk. "I'll make breakfast. Do you have cereal?"

"Some Cap'n Crunch and Lucky Charms for the kids."

"A little too sweet for me first thing in the morning." Rooting around in the fridge for anything remotely healthy, I finally found half a cantaloupe and some grapes. "Do you have any granola or yogurt we could mix up with this fruit?"

"No, honey. I was planning to make us some bacon, eggs, and toast."

Knowing my carnivorous mom had to have her meat, I compromised. "What about a couple of slices of French toast, bacon, and some of this nice fresh fruit instead?"

"Sounds wonderful. Thank you, dear."

Quartering the cantaloupe, I placed the sections into two of my Mom's Blue Willow soup bowls, arranging the red grapes artistically on top of the melon. Then I set them on the table and encouraged her to dig in while I cooked the rest of our meal.

"Why this looks too pretty to eat! My goodness, daughter, you've become quite the gourmet since you've been gone."

The bacon started to sizzle, and I began beating the eggs for our French toast. "Not really, Mom. I still can't cook, but I've at least learned how to make food—even store-bought—look good, compliments of the Food Network."

"The Food Network?"

"It's this great station on cable that shows all these different chefs at work. Although I never have time to watch the cooking part—I usually just catch a few minutes at the end when they do presentation."

I started to dunk the bread in the egg mixture, but she stayed my hand with a question. "Honey, did you put in the cinnamon?"

"Cinnamon?"

"A dash of nutmeg too. But just a dash. That's what gives French toast its extra flavor."

And to think that all these years I've been making it, I haven't been adding that little dash—it's a wonder my friends could even bear to eat my French toast, flavorless as it was. Note to self: Remember to beg friends' forgiveness for obvious culinary faux pas.

After we finished our flavorful breakfast—complete with requisite spices—I asked Mom if she wanted a shower, but she declined, saying Karen had helped her yesterday and had washed and braided her hair, so she could wait until tomorrow before needing another one. I helped her into a loose, button-up shirt and denim skirt, then settled her in her chair to watch everyone "come on down!" on *The Price Is Right* while I got ready.

I grabbed a quick shower, spiked and tousled my hair with gel, did the makeup thing, and pulled on my Gap jeans and favorite black and red sweater, then stepped into my red knock-off Prada boots and joined Mom in the living room.

She quirked her eyebrows at me. "My, aren't we all gussied up for just a trip into town. Or do you have other plans for today that I don't know about?"

Yes, I'm planning to run away with the circus. "This is the way I always dress. All set?"

"Two more minutes. They're about to do the final showcase, and I want to see who wins."

While Mom stared transfixed at Bob Barker, I poured a cup of coffee into an oversized mug to take with me and blew on it before taking a sip. Ugh. Definitely not my customary double-shot mocha.

Note to self: First stop after Karen and Jordy's: the new bookstore/coffee bar for some real *coffee.*

"Okay. I'm ready, Phoebe. Can you turn off the TV for me, please? I just knew the guy was going to win the speedboat and the trip to Italy. That young girl clearly didn't know her living-room furniture sets."

"Obviously not a woman worth her domestic salt." Whistling the sisterhood anthem, "We Are Family," under my breath, I grabbed my laptop and we headed out the door.

My mother looked askance at the machine under my arm. "Why are you bringing that along? You're not planning to work at Karen and Jordy's, are you?"

"No, Mom. I don't *have* any work right now. And even if I did, I sure couldn't do it on this. It's broken. But Jordy said he had a couple of computer whizzes in his class and if I dropped it off, he would take it in to them after lunch today and see if they could fix it."

A few minutes later, as we pulled into my grandparents' old farm— now home to my brother, his wife, and their brood—Lexie and Jacob came bounding out the door to greet us. "Hi, Gamma. Hi, An Beebee. Gamma, gamma, wanna see the ladybugs we catched?"

And the three nature lovers were off.

My sister-in-law smiled at me from the doorway. "So, how'd it go last night? Did you get the third degree?"

"Nope. Took your advice and changed the conversational direction. Worked like a charm. But we did have an unexpected nighttime visitor that I'm sure Mom's dying to tell you all about. If you don't mind, though, before she comes back, Jordy said I could use your computer. Mine's broken, and I wanted to try and send Filmguy a quick e-mail to apologize for standing him up."

"Sure, Phoebe. No problem. It's in our bedroom. Only thing is, we have limited access out here, so sometimes it takes a long time to connect, plus we have difficulty getting onto other servers. If you have any problems, let me know."

I was unable to access my server as Karen had predicted, but she signed onto their e-mail for me, then left me in privacy while I dashed off a quick note to Lindsey and one to buddy Phil, then began composing my apology to Filmguy.

Except . . . wait—what's his exact address? Filmguy719? 1971? Or just two numbers? 71? This is why I have a mental block for anything math-related—it involves numbers. Why couldn't he keep it simple like I did with Movielovr and just be Filmguy? *Men! So complicated.*

Just then I heard the back door slam, and Mom's voice wafted in from the direction of the kitchen. "Phoebe? Where are you? We've got to get a move on if we're going to get all our shopping done."

Out of time and not wanting to face another inquiry on my Internet relationship, I decided to take my chances and send the apology to all three numerical variations on Filmguy. Then I popped into Jordy and Karen's master bath, flushed the commode, and ran some water into the sink before rejoining my relatives. "Here I am, Mom. I was just using the bathroom. Ready to go? Karen, please tell Jordy thanks again for taking in my laptop to his students."

"No problem, Phoebe. Some of those kids are technological geniuses. If it can be saved, they're the ones who can do it. Have a good day. We'll see you both later."

We said our good-byes to Karen and the kids, then headed into town. "Hey, Mom, mind if we stop by the bookstore first? I'm dying for a latte or a double mocha."

"Of course. I wanted to look at some of their gardening books anyway."

Once inside Books 'n' Brew, I settled Mom in with a couple of gardening books, then made a beeline for the coffee bar at the back. In the display case under the counter, I noticed a couple of scrumptious blueberry muffins, scones, and a lone piece of shortbread calling my name.

"Hi there. May I help you?"

Raising my eyes, I met the chestnut brown ones of an attractive—in that laid-back, hippie kind of way—thirty-something guy with long blond hair pulled back into a ponytail. He sported a small silver hoop in one ear and a gorgeous old cross around his neck—not the trendy kind everyone wears these days as a fashion accessory, but a worn silver cross with a Celtic knot.

"Hi." I flashed him a pleading smile. "I'd give my firstborn child for some *real* coffee—a tall, nonfat double mocha. Or if you don't have that, then a cappuccino instead?"

Silver Earring smiled back in caffeinated empathy. "Not a problem." He busied himself behind the counter and moments later handed me a tall, frothy mocha.

I took a grateful gulp. "Thanks. I needed that."

"Couldn't tell."

Hmmm. Funny and cute. Maybe my sentence to the sticks won't be too bad after all . . .

"Any chance that yummy-looking shortbread is homemade?"

"All our baked goods are homemade," he replied. "My wife's a fabulous cook."

Big-time crash and burn. *Note to self: Do not forget first rule of flirting. Always look for wedding ring.*

Married Silver Earring handed me the last piece of shortbread baked by his fabulous-cook wife. His silver Celtic-knot wedding band gleamed in the light, reminding me again of his cross.

Attempting to save face, as well as shift into more neutral ground, I complimented his jewelry choice. "Gorgeous cross. Very unusual."

"Thanks. I got it nearly twenty years ago at this ancient church in Edinburgh. It was my graduation present to myself for making it through seminary."

"Seminary?" I took another sip of mocha. "Don't tell me, let me guess—you're a coffee-bar pastor?"

He grinned. "Actually, I'm the associate pastor at Barley Presbyterian. However, in a small congregation, there's not enough to pay a second pastor's salary, so my wife and I run this bookstore and coffee shop during the week. On Sundays I put on my pastoral hat and teach the singles Sunday-school class."

There you go again. Don't you ever get tired of the taste of shoe leather—even when it's kicky wannabe Prada? "So, do I have egg all over my face?"

"No, just foam." He laughed. "Tell you what, coffee's on the house. And we provide it at Sunday school too. Why don't you bring that first-born child you were so willing to part with and come visit our church this Sunday? Unless you're just passing through?"

"No firstborn child yet, although I might be able to borrow a niece if kids are a requirement. I attend a Presbyterian church in Cleveland, so I would like to—"

Mom cut me off at the denominational pass. "Hello, Jeffrey. I see you've met my daughter, Phoebe. So nice of you to invite her to your church group, but she'll be attending Holy Communion with the rest of her family. Well, we must be going. Please say hi to Amy for me."

And she hustled me out of the bookstore.

I'd never seen an injured woman move quite so fast. "Mom, you know I go to a Presbyterian church now and—"

A large, red-headed bulldozer in a polyester muumuu enveloped me in a crushing hug on the sidewalk. "Phoebe? My goodness, how sleek and sophisticated you've gotten."

Sleek? Not something I usually hear. But I guess it's all relative in Barley. I struggled to breathe, balance my mocha, and reply to my mom's church lady crony. It was a bit difficult, squashed up as I was against her ample bosom. "Hello, Louise. How have you been?"

She released me and patted her lacquered hair. "Fat and sassy as always, honey, but then, that's how my husband likes me." Louise turned her attention to Mom. "Now, Gloria, the Meals to Those in-Need Committee has a schedule all worked out for the next few weeks. Tonight I'm bringing you two my Tuna Surprise. Tomorrow, Sharon Lee's going to bring her Tater-Tot casserole. And Monday, Linda Ray's going to—"

"Thank you so much for your kindness, Louise, dear." Mom smiled at her well-meaning, bulldozing friend. "But now that my daughter's home, I won't be needing any meals from the church. Besides, we already have dinner planned for tonight."

"We do?" I asked.

"Why yes, dear: meat loaf, mashed potatoes, green beans, cheese rolls, and homemade Dutch apple pie. Speaking of which, we'd better get a move on if we're going to get that pie made in time," she said, steering me with her casts toward the car. "Please excuse us, Louise. See you at church on Sunday."

"'Bye, Louise," I called over my shoulder to Mom's open-mouthed pal.

Once inside the car I whirled on my mother. "What in the world was that all about?"

She sniffed. "That Louise couldn't cook her way out of a Tupperware container. Tuna Surprise, indeed—the surprise is how many different kinds of store-bought canned food she can throw into a Pyrex dish.

Last month when she delivered a casserole, poor Lester Sims was up-chucking all night. The last thing I need right now is botulism."

I sighed. "Okay, fine. But why don't we just get some frozen dinners instead? They make some really good ones these days. Besides, I don't know how to make meat loaf."

Mom slid a triumphant smile my way. "That's okay, dear. I do. I'll walk you through it every step of the way."

After the market came the butcher shop, then the feed store (goat chow for Elizabeth's 4-H project), then the post office, with Mom show-ing me off to everyone we met: "Look, my daughter's come home."

Worn out from all the small talk, smiling, and glad-handing, I was more than ready to beat a retreat to Mom's. Then we ran into Gordon Green, my old boss from the Barley *Bulletin*, as I finished loading the groceries into the back of the car.

His face lit up. "Phoebe Grant! Aren't you a sight for sore eyes?"

"Gordon, I've missed you." I hugged him tight, relishing the familiar smell of cigars and English Leather cologne.

"Sure, sure. I know. That's what all my former employees who've made it to the big-time dailies say," he teased.

"Actually, the paper was recently bought out and they had to lay several of us off, so I'm unemployed at the moment."

Gordon cast me a sympathetic look. "I'm sure sorry to hear that, Phoebe." Then his eyes brightened. "But their loss is my gain. If you're looking for assignments, I could sure use you at the paper these days. It would be a big help to me to have your bright young mind and fast fingers around the place again." He and Mom both looked hopeful.

"That's very sweet of you, but I'm afraid I'm only staying a few weeks—just 'til Mom's casts come off. Then I'm planning to look for a new job in New York or Chicago or someplace like that."

He patted my hand. "I understand. Big city kind of gets in your blood, doesn't it? Well, whenever you get the urge to do a little writ-ing, I can always use the help."

When we got home, Mom took a nap and I put away the groceries—including a store-bought apple pie. On that I'd put my foot down. I'd make her the homemade meat loaf she was hankering for, but I certainly wasn't about to slave all afternoon rolling out crust and cutting up apples.

Not today.

I wasn't in the mood.

At six o'clock, I was just pulling the meat loaf out of the oven when a mind-numbing cacophony assaulted my eardrums. I glanced out the kitchen window and saw a Jurassic-sized black truck with tires taller than I am roar up the driveway. A cranked-up country-western tune shredded the once-peaceful air.

Setting the meat loaf down on the counter, I called into the dining room, "Mom, looks like you have a visitor."

The doorbell rang.

"Can you please get that for me, dear?"

Fanning my hot face and flapping my sticky blouse, I opened the door.

There, standing on the front porch and spitting a stream of chewing tobacco over the railing, was a modern-day Jethro from *The Beverly Hillbillies.*

a n awkward hour and a half later, when the door finally clicked shut behind Jethro—whose real name was Hank, "thirty-two years old, moved here from Lodi a few years ago, works at the gas station on the edge of town, and a nice boy, even if he is a Methodist"— I turned to the woman who'd given me life and nothing but matchmaking grief since I was old enough to say "I do."

"Mom, you've been watching *Hope Floats* again, haven't you? I know Barley's a small town, but this Hank guy is not Harry Connick, Jr. And I'm certainly no Sandra Bullock."

"Before you went and cut off all your beautiful hair, you kind of resembled her," she protested. "Besides, look how happily that movie ended, with her getting together with that handsome Harry. He reminds me a bit of your dad, you know. Sings like him too."

"Yes, I know, but Hank isn't a bit like Daddy *or* Harry Connick." I sighed but held my single-girl ground. "Mom, you've got to promise me you won't invite any more 'eligible' men over to dinner while I'm in town, okay? I'm *not* interested."

Wa-a-a-y not interested. Nice try, Mother, but there's no way you'll get me to settle down in Barley with some guy—especially not a tobacco-chewing, monster-truck hillbilly. Even if he does look a little like a tall Tom Cruise . . .

She promised as we settled in for the evening with our microwave popcorn and Cary Grant and Deborah Kerr in *An Affair to Remember.*

Later, before I went to sleep—after flossing and moisturizing, of course—I prayed for strength and fortitude to follow through with my Sunday-morning plans.

Lord, please help me to stick to my guns with Mom and please help her not to have a cow when I do. I know You want us to honor our father and mother, but I also know You don't want parents to exasperate their children. And Mom sure knows how to punch all my exasperation buttons at once.

The next morning we joined Karen and Jordy for Holy Communion Lutheran's nine o'clock service, which hadn't changed a bit in twenty years. *Same hard pews, same ancient, droning hymns, same spray of white plastic gladioli at the altar, same old Mr. Soames snoring in the back pew, and same Mom poking me in the ribs to stay awake . . .*

We filed out after service, and I gave Mom a quick peck on the cheek. "Okay, see you in a little while. You're riding back with Karen and Jordy. I'll join you all for lunch later."

She looked bewildered. "What? Where are you going?"

"Um . . ."

Karen tried to provide a distraction by saying, "The kids should be getting out of Sunday school any second. Let's—"

But my mother was not to be deterred. "Where are you going, daughter?"

"Um, I—I have a . . . date." I looked at my watch. "Whoops, and if I don't leave now, I'm going to be late. Don't want to keep him waiting, you know. Bye, Mom. Bye, Jordy." I nodded at my sister-in-law, who responded with a smile of encouragement. "See you soon." With a brief wave I scooted off, leaving an open-mouthed mother in my wake, just as the kids thronged out of the side door.

Whew. That was close. Thanks, God, for that Sunday-school reprieve.

Driving to the other end of town, I parked in front of a red-brick building and scurried inside a side door. Nervous and out of breath, I instantly realized I was in the wrong room—bursting as it was with mostly pregnant young couples.

I smoothed down my slimming, chocolate-brown suede skirt and sucked in my slight pooch as a ready-to-pop twenty-something mom-to-be waddled over wearing a pup tent dotted with black-and-white cows. "Can I help you?"

"Uh, I'm looking for the adult singles class?"

She glanced down at my now-flat stomach, then over at my naked left hand. "This is young marrieds. The over-thirties meet in the room across the way—where they keep the choir robes," she said, pointing to a small door across the courtyard of Barley Presbyterian.

This time when I stepped through the door I was greeted with open arms.

"Phoebe! Heard you were back in town. Welcome to the Church of the Fruitful Womb."

Recognizing the hearty horsewoman voice, I squinted past the choir robes to a woman who was making her way to me from a small group clustered around the coffeepot. "Mary Jo?"

"The one and only."

Although Mary Jo Roper and I had attended high school together, we'd never really hung out or talked much, other than to ask questions about homework assignments or to roll our eyes in mutual accord over the inane jokes and lame attempts of some of our teachers—especially Hubert the Horrible—to be hip. Mary Jo and I had very different interests. She was an outdoorsy, natural type; I was an indoorsy reading and movie-watching girl. While I was writing stories for the school paper, she was winning blue ribbons in all the 4-H contests. And while I was out shopping in Sacramento or San Francisco, she was out riding or cleaning out stables, always wearing her Walkman for the latter and listening to her beloved Beatles.

Always a big-boned, sturdy girl, Mary Jo had bulked up a bit over the years, and she apparently still didn't care a whit about clothes, clad as she was in a shapeless corduroy jumper, flannel shirt, and scuffed boots. But at least she didn't have cows grazing across her belly, and it was nice to see a friendly face.

We hugged. "Long time," I said. "Good to see you. So what are you up to these days? Still riding?"

Mary Jo tucked her stick-straight, muddy-colored hair behind her ear. "Yep. Only now I teach riding too out at the old Jackson Ranch. Bought the place when it came up for auction. You should come out," she said with a wink. "Maybe we'll finally get you on a horse."

I shuddered in all my carefully nurtured city-girl wussness. "No thanks. The only kind of transportation I like has wheels under it."

"That can be arranged. I still have an old set of training wheels from my nephew's bike that we could hitch up to ol' Pluto the Wonder Horse . . ."

Just then a middle-aged Barney Fife type with a bad comb-over barged over. He looked a little familiar, but I couldn't quite place him.

"Why, Phoebe Grant, as I live and breathe!"

Oh no. I remembered that nasal voice. It was Hubert the Horrible, the only teacher who ever gave me a D in my academic life—with an unsettling grin and a not-to-be-found-in-nature dye job. *Is this a sign that you want me to stay at Holy Communion, Lord?*

He leaned forward, but I cut him off in midhug with an outstretched hand and a forced smile. "Mr. Hubert. Nice to see you again."

He engulfed my proffered hand between his two sweaty palms and shook his head at me as a conspiratorial grin split his face. "Now, now, you're not my student anymore, Phoebe. No more of this Mister stuff. Name's Bruce." He winked and puffed out his chest. "Like Springsteen."

Behind him, Mary Jo rolled her eyes, and I stifled a girl-bonding giggle. "Okay, Mr. Hubert. I mean, B-Bruce. It's going to take a while to get used to that."

He beamed at me while still holding on to my hand and checking out my statistics. "No hurry. My, you've certainly grown into a lovely woman, Phoebe . . ."

"Hey, Bruce, I think class is about to start. We'd better sit down now." Mary Jo disentangled me from the H-man's moist grasp and steered me toward a chair several seats away.

"Okay." He snapped off a farewell salute, apparently in honor of my military service. "Nice to have you home again, Phoebe." Then he rejoined a fifty-something blonde in a too-tight polyester print dress whose hair looked like one of Dolly Parton's wigs. She glared at me and scooted her chair closer to his while at the same time picking off an imaginary piece of lint from his shoulder in that age-old gesture of female possession.

Mary Jo leaned over and whispered. "Better watch out for Sylvia Ann; she might think you're trying to jump her claim."

I snorted. "No worries on that score."

Our girl talk was cut short as Jeff, the coffee-shop pastor, entered. A petite redhead followed him, carrying a guitar. Mary Jo confirmed that she was Amy, the shortbread-baking wife.

"Good morning everyone," Jeff said as Amy tuned her guitar. "Shall we begin our praise and worship time?"

I closed my eyes and let the music take me away.

Now, this is more like it. Real. Lively. Rockin'. My kind of place.

Jeff taught a short lesson after worship, then divided us into two groups to discuss the story of the woman at the well. Afterward, Jeff introduced me to Amy, who invited me over to dinner the following week.

Mary Jo and I walked out together. "So, Phoebe, we should try and catch a movie while you're here so you can pay your last respects to the Bijou."

I stopped short. "Last respects?"

"Yeah. Haven't you heard? Word on the street is the theater's going to be torn down and replaced with a fast-food hamburger joint."

"What?! Drive-through cholesterol instead of my beloved Bijou? That's where I first saw Scarlett turn a pair of velvet drapes into a stylish outfit, Julie Andrews make the captain's seven children play clothes out of curtains, and Bambi's mother cry, 'To the thicket, Bambi. To the thicket!'"

"You saw those movies there? But you weren't even born when—"

"That is strictly beside the point," I told her haughtily. "They *showed* them there. And over my dead body are they going to tear down that theater!"

I raced over to Jordy and Karen's and hurried inside, ignoring the tummy-teasing scents of Sunday fried chicken, mashed potatoes and gravy, green-bean casserole, and buttermilk biscuits. "Hey! How come none of you told me the Bijou's being torn down?"

Karen looked up from the stove, where she was stirring the gravy under Mom's watchful eye. "I thought I mentioned it on our ride in from the airport, Phoebe."

"I don't think so. I'd have remembered."

My sister-in-law frowned. "But I'm sure I did. I told you all about our putting on *Oklahoma* as the last great hurrah before the doors close for good."

That's what you get for tuning out. "That does sound a bit familiar now, Karen," I admitted. "Sorry. Guess I was so surprised by all the changes downtown that I wasn't listening closely. Do you mind filling me in again? Why do they want to close down the Bijou?"

Jordy sneaked a biscuit behind Karen's back and wolfed it down. "Well, business has been bad for a while," he said. "With all the multiplexes in Elk Grove, Lodi, and Sacramento, there's no way our little theater can compete. George Henderson hasn't really made a profit in years and years."

"But it's a landmark—a historic building," I said. "That's where we saw *Star Wars* and *Chariots of Fire* and—"

Mom interrupted. "Why do you care? It's not like you live here or have a stake in it."

Can you say "awkward silence"?

Jordy jumped in to try a little damage control. "So, how was Barley Pres, Pheebert?"

Thanks, brother dear. I've always preferred the fire to the frying pan.

Karen and I both gave him dismayed looks as Mom took off on a new now-look-what-my-unacceptable-daughter-has-done tangent. "Barley Presbyterian Church? I thought you said you had a date."

"I did. With, um . . ."

Go ahead, might as well get it over with now. You can't lie, you know . . .

Taking a deep breath, I plunged in. ". . . God."

Mom's braid twitched furiously as she swung around to face me. "Are you saying God's not at Holy Communion?"

I squirmed. "Noooo . . . It's just that . . . well, personally I can relate to him better in a more modern, informal setting."

Karen tried to placate her. "Phoebe's not abandoning the family church, Mom. She'll still attend services with us every week—she just needs something different, more contemporary, too. It's more a style thing than anything else."

"It's always a style thing with my daughter," Mom said. "Style's not as important as substance."

"Barley Pres is quite substantial, thank you very much," I said. "In fact—"

My cell rang, cutting me off. "Hello. Lins? Finally! Hang on a minute." I turned the phone away from my ear to address my family. "Sorry, everyone. I really need to take this call. Lindsey and I have been playing phone and e-mail tag since I got here. I'll be back in a few. You guys go ahead and start lunch without me."

Escaping to Jordy and Karen's room, I closed the door behind me and expelled a huge sigh of relief. "You really got my back that time. Thanks."

"Why? What's up?"

"Just the same old disappointing my mom scenario. But I don't want to get into that now," I said, kicking off my shoes and settling in for a long, comfy chat. "How *are* you, best friend? I miss you! So good to hear your voice. Hey, how's my sofa doing?"

"We're both great," Lins said. "And the sofa looks fab in the apartment—albeit a little lonely. Just like me. We're both in a hurry for you to come back. Exactly when *are* you coming home?"

I sighed. "Not sure yet. Looks like it'll be several more weeks. But Lins, I'm dyin' here—tell me, were you able to make the Filmguy connection?"

"Sorry. No could do. Got there too late—the lobby was empty and the movie had already started."

"Oh well. *C'est la vie.* Guess it just wasn't meant to be."

"But guess who we *did* see there?"

"We?"

Lindsey's words came tumbling out in a rush. "Oh, Phil tagged along, and since we were already there we decided we might as well stay for the movie." She repeated her question. "So guess who we ran into in the lobby afterward?"

"Tattoo-ferret man?"

"No-o." She paused for effect. "Alex Spencer."

"You're kidding!"

"Nope. And let me tell you, I really gave him a piece of my mind too."

I smiled across the miles at my friend's loyalty. "Thanks, Lins. I'm glad you put that jerk in his place."

She hesitated. "He's really not a jerk, Pheebs. In fact, he's very nice. He's been going out with Sarah—the Heather Locklear clone, who's really nice too, by the way. And he felt really bad about your being laid off and seemed quite concerned about you."

"How do you know that?"

More hesitation. "Um, he invited us out to coffee after the movie. He and Phil really hit it off."

My pal Phil getting friendly with the enemy? How quickly things changed. What next? Were they going to become roommates?

Note to self: Kill Phil.

I changed the subject. "So how's everyone else? Susan? Scotty?"

"Actually . . ." Lindsey switched over to her ready-to-dish, tell-all voice. "You won't believe this, but Scotty's been spending a lot of time with Kim and her son. He really fell for the little munchkin at the wedding, and I think that maybe he's starting to fall for mom too."

Out of sight, out of mind, I guess. Down, twinge of jealousy, down. You didn't want Scotty 'cause he was too young for you, so you should be happy that he's found someone else—someone sweet who's closer to his age.

I am, my inner brat pouted. *But it sure was nice having someone with a crush on me.*

I forced myself to sound enthusiastic. "That's great. They'd make a really good pair."

But my best friend knew me too well. "All right Pheebs, call off the pity party. You know all you had to do was crook your little finger and Scotty would have come running. But you chose not to crook, so snap out of it." Then she softened her tone and switched over to supportive, encouraging mode. "Why don't you try again with Filmguy?"

Wallowing in my single-girl-wanting-a-guy-but-never-gonna-meet-him misery I wailed. "Can't. My laptop's on the fritz, and I can't remember the exact numbers in his e-mail." A hopeful thought struck. "Can *you?*"

Her regret resounded over the miles. "Sorry. Numbers aren't my strong suit either, remember? But hey, he's not the only guy in the world. How's the talent out there in Barley?"

I snorted. "Abysmal. Nonexistent. They either drive giant trucks or are older than dirt. I've only met one with any potential, but of course he's married."

"Hey, almost forgot! Speaking of marriage . . . guess who's planning to tie the knot?"

"Who?"

Another pause. "Colin and Samantha."

"My blind-date, polyester-wearing hair-plug Colin? You've gotta be kidding. How long have they been dating? Five minutes?"

"More like ten. And he's only wearing natural fibers these days. Samantha's really updated his wardrobe. See, Pheebs," Lindsey teased, "if you'd hung in there, you probably could have gotten rid of those little polyesters too."

"Yeah, but not the hair plugs or the mother." Removing the focus from shallow, superficial me, I added, "Gosh, they sure moved fast."

"The wedding's even faster—two weeks from now. Can you believe it?"

Dazed, I shook my head. For once I was glad to be stuck in Barley. Then I remembered Lins couldn't see my response, so injected an audible reply as well. "Wow. So is it going to be a big splashy affair?"

"No, they wanted something small and simple, so they're getting married at church and will have a brief reception afterward before jetting off to the Caribbean."

"The Caribbean?"

"Yep. They're going to St. Thomas for the honeymoon."

Great. Just great. Now they get my sandy white beach and turquoise water, too.

"Just think, Pheebs," she teased again, "it could have been you."

"Yeah, but I thought three was a crowd and didn't want to have to fight his mother for territorial rights. His mom's going with them on the honeymoon, right?"

"No. In fact, she doesn't even live with Colin anymore. The minute they got engaged she bought a condo. They're helping her move in this weekend."

All right, all right, so I was a little hasty about the mom thing too. Note to self: Remember on next date to not be so quick to judge and to take the time to go a little deeper.

We chatted a few more minutes as Lins brought me up-to-date on Christopher (away on another short-term mission) and Susan (leading a new women's Bible study) before I told her I had to get back to my family.

Flipping my phone shut, I didn't move straightaway.

Lord, how come everyone else gets a happily-ever-after except me? Am I ever going to meet the right guy? Or am I going to keep throwing away viable Mr. Rights 'cause I'm too picky? What am I supposed to learn from all this—besides the fact that I'm a superficial, self-absorbed, never-satisfied brat?

I looked around my brother and sister-in-law's room at all the happy, smiling-faced pictures of them with their children. My biological speedometer zoomed from zero to sixty in nothing flat.

What's up with that, *Lord? I've never had kid urges before. Are You trying to tell me something here? Do You know something I don't? Okay, stupid question. Of course You do. You know* everything, *while I pretty much don't know zip. Especially as far as my future's concerned . . . But God, could these feelings possibly mean that I'm soon going to meet my Mr. Wonderful, who will sweep me off my feet and give me two-point-five kids* and the golden retriever, *all while I'm working at my exciting, stimulating writing job in the City?*

I looked at the pictures of Ashley, Elizabeth, Jacob, and Lexie again—the nieces and nephew I barely knew. *Or is it just that You want me to be a better auntie?*

Note to self: Resist jealousy over coupling up Cleveland friends, stop fantasizing about phantom Mr. Right, and do more of that whole bloom-where-you're-planted thing, beginning with spending time with brother's sweet children.

With this new resolve firmly in place, I went to rejoin my family.

Karen looked up from the dining room table. "Everything okay, Pheebs?"

"Just fine," I said, ruffling my nephew's hair and winking at Lexie as I sat down between Ashley and Elizabeth. "Hey, girls, how 'bout after lunch we raid your closet and I give you some of those fashion tips I've been promising you?"

My nieces looked up at me like I was all that and nodded yes.

That night I went to sleep with visions of happy children, the Bijou, and all the childhood movies I'd seen there dancing through my head.

after a strained breakfast at the old homestead the next morning, I dropped Mom off at Karen's and went into town to learn what I could about the Bijou's closure. First stop: Books 'n' Brew for my daily mocha, a brief shoot-the-breeze with Jeff and Amy, and a couple of scones to go. Next stop: the Barley *Bulletin*.

The newspaper door jangled shut behind me. "Okay, Gordon, what's the Bijou scoop?"

My former boss peered up from his old Underwood—his up-to-the-minute computer glowing on the other side of the desk. "Good morning to you too, Phoebe."

"Morning." I handed him a blueberry scone and sat down at my old desk, sipping my mocha. "All righty then, I've brought you sustenance. Now, c'mon. What gives?"

Gordon laid down his ever-present cigar—which by California law he couldn't light inside anymore, but he still liked to chew on—and bit into his scone. Then he basically repeated what Jordy had already told me the night before about business being bad at the theater. But he filled in a few blanks my brother hadn't known—like the fact that old George Henderson, the Bijou's longtime owner, didn't particularly care one way or another if a burger joint went in or the Bijou stayed in place. He simply wanted to sell the place that had become a financial albatross around his neck and move to Montana to be near his grandkids. He leaned back in his chair and replaced the cigar in his mouth. "Can't say I blame him, actually."

The news about the Bijou left me hopeful. "So it's not a done deal yet?"

"Nope. They've just been discussing the possibility. The developer's made an offer, but George is hoping to get a little better price, so he hasn't accepted it yet. Developer figures no one else is interested in that small piece of land, so he's in no hurry to raise the price. They're in kind of a standoff right now."

Lightbulb. "Gordon, why don't *you* buy the Bijou?"

He snorted and let loose one of his frequent mild profanities. "It's all I can do to keep the *Bulletin* above water, much less invest in another money-losing business."

"Okay, then, let's look at this from a different angle . . ." I chewed my pen. "I know! The building's really old; maybe it's a historic land-mark, so they *can't* tear it down!" I moved over to his computer. "Mind if I Google that?"

"Watch your language, young lady."

"Um, Gordon . . . that's a search engine on the Internet. "

He gave me a dry look. "Really? Didn't know that, seein's how I'm stuck out here in the sticks with only papyrus and a quill pen to put out the weekly newspaper."

I stuck out my tongue at him, then began surfing the Net, where I soon discovered, much to my dismay, that the Bijou wasn't old enough or architecturally noteworthy enough to qualify as a historic landmark.

Hmmm. "Hey, Gordon, wonder if we could antique the Bijou up a bit by battering the wooden floors with some heavy chains or some-thing like they do on those home improvement shows? Or maybe—"

The bell above the door jangled again, and I looked up to see Esther Blodgett, Gordon's lone full-time reporter, entering. She'd worked for the newspaper as long as I could remember.

"Mornin', Gordon. Sorry I'm late. It's getting harder and harder to get these ol' bones up and movin' in the morning," the seventy-something Esther said, adjusting her trifocals. She plunked some smudged pages on Gordon's desk. "Here's my restaurant feature." Then she noticed me for the first time. "Oh, pardon me. I didn't see you sit-tin' there." She held out her hand. "I'm Esther."

I stood up with a smile for my old coworker. "Hi, Esther. It's me, Phoebe."

She looked at me uncomprehendingly, then bristled. "I paid the PG&E bill!"

I shot a helpless look at Gordon, who strode to my rescue. "No, Esther," he raised his voice, enunciating each word. "It's *Phoebe Grant*, come home. Remember when she worked here in high school?"

The older woman's face filled with relief, and she enveloped me in a tight embrace. "Phoebe! How great to see you. Have you come back to take my place so's I can finally retire?"

"*No* one can take your place," I said, returning her hug. "I'm just here visiting for a while and helping out my mom."

"Isn't that the darndest thing, your mama slippin' on that cow pie and bustin' both her arms? You'd think she was some city slicker 'stead of a Barley girl born and bred."

"Don't I know it?" I said under my breath.

"But never you mind," Esther continued. "She'll be right as rain soon enough. And maybe before then, Gordon here can talk you into stayin' on at the paper. I'm more than ready to relax and put my feet up and take it easy in my old age." She fumbled around the desk for a notebook. "Well, gotta go. Got me an interview with Stan down at the Rotary Club about the new scholarship they're givin' to the Miss Udderly Delicious Dairy Pageant winner this year."

Gordon sighed and moved closer so she could hear him. "Esther, Stan's not the Rotary president anymore. It's Lou Jenkins now."

"See what I mean, Phoebe?" she chuckled. "This ol' girl's mem'ry just ain't what it used to be. You'd do Gordon and me both a favor if you stayed on." And with a wave, she was off.

"Truer words were never spoken," murmured Gordon as he looked down at Esther's copy. "Doggone it, she's got the restaurant owners' names wrong again, and her dates are off too, which means some of her other facts are messed up as well. I'm going to have to go on down to the Barley Twist myself and straighten this out."

"The new vegetarian restaurant?"

"Mostly vegetarian. They serve a wonderful roast chicken and some great—"

"Grilled red snapper," I finished for him with a smile. "I've also heard the lobster bisque is out of this world."

He looked at his watch. "Well, could you go for an early lunch—the *Bulletin's* treat—say in about half an hour or so?"

Thirty-five minutes later, my old boss was introducing me to Steve and Sydney, the transplanted Bay Area husband and wife who owned the restaurant. I ordered a cup of the bisque and a small salad of baby greens with raspberry vinaigrette, while Gordon settled on a grilled chicken sandwich. As we waited for our lunch to arrive, he apologized to the couple for having to ask some of Esther's questions again.

Steve winked at his wife, then smiled at Gordon. "That's okay. We appreciate the follow-up. Last time Esther did a piece, we had some customers come in looking for steak-and-kidney pie rather than *Sydney's* cakes and pies." He skimmed the article. "Speaking of dessert, did she happen to mention that we've added crème brûlée to the menu?"

"Crème brûlée in Barley?" I took a sip of my iced tea. "Will wonders never cease? I'll have to save room for that. Oh, and Gordon, when you rewrite the article, make sure you mention this great mango tea. It's delicious."

After a cosmopolitan lunch that made me feel I was back in my old life again, I quizzed the couple on how they were adjusting to Barley.

"Oh, we love it here," Sydney assured me. "It's a much slower pace than San Francisco. Plus, with all the open space, we think it will be a wonderful place to raise kids."

"Don't you ever get bored?"

"No time to," Steve said. "There's just the two of us running the restaurant—which means we do all the shopping, cooking, baking, serving. And we're open six days a week, so it keeps us hopping."

"But don't you miss all the culture and nightlife of San Francisco?"

"Now and then," Sydney admitted for both of them. "But when we want a little culture, we just drive into Sacramento on our day off. Or catch something at the Bijou."

Here was the opening I'd been waiting for. "Speaking of that, have you heard the Bijou might be torn down?"

Sydney exchanged a disappointed glance with her husband. "We had, but we were hoping that was only a rumor. We love that old theater. Great art deco ambience, especially those gorgeous plush velvet seats—"

Steve interrupted his wife. "Although the lobby could do with some freshening up and definitely some better snack choices than dusty Raisinettes and Good & Plenty."

"Careful, there," Gordon said. "I'm a Good & Plenty man from way back." He smiled and explained to the culture-loving couple that I wanted to figure out a way to keep the Bijou open.

"Way to go, Phoebe. We'll help in any way we can," Sydney said. "Won't we, Steve?"

"Absolutely. Just let us know what you need—food, drinks, a place to meet to brainstorm, whatever."

Gordon returned to work, and I hit some of the businesses in town and did an informal survey on how the owners felt about the potential loss of my—um, *their* theater.

Jeff and Amy over at Books 'n' Brew said they loved going to the Bijou for date nights; Sylvia Ann at the Bobby Pin—whose hair was styled like Anna Nicole Smith's today—took great pains to tell me that she and Hubert-the-H went there every other Friday. The owners of the new Peking Dragon, Mr. and Mrs. Fong, said they were faithful attendees. In fact, almost everyone agreed that they hated to see the Bijou close—except for Lou over at the Steakhouse, who didn't mind one way or the other 'cause he didn't ever go to the movies.

I appealed to his wallet. "Aren't you worried about a new burger place in town taking away some of your business?"

"Honey, the day one of them places with pressed meat and plastic tomatoes and rude kids at the counter takes away any of *my* customers, that's the day it's time for me to pack it in," Lou said around the toothpick in his mouth.

After canvassing one side of Main Street, I stopped by the Bijou, where the cast and crew of *Oklahoma* were deep in the midst of rehearsal. Weary from all my research and schmoozing, I sank into a seat near the back.

Karen's right. The boy playing Curly has a great voice. So does the high-school Laurey. But I've seen better Ado Annies. Oh well. What do you expect from cow town?

Enveloped in the cushy but creaky seat, where I'd spent so many idyllic, popcorn-filled afternoons as a child, all at once it hit me. I remembered how the Grand in Cleveland had fallen on tough times and held a fundraiser by selling off theater seats. As I recalled, it was a huge success. The regulars loved the opportunity to keep their art house theater open, but they also loved seeing their names etched on discreet brass tags on *their* seats.

We could do that here! A lot of people in town would cough up the dough in a heartbeat. People in other towns too, even Lodi. And for those who don't care—like Lou—we can appeal to their commercial side. "It's great advertising for your business. Plus, think of the prestige of having your company name on a seat in this beautiful, historic theater . . ."

Then my practical side, which usually remains submerged, popped up its periscope.

Face it, Pheebs. All the fancy plaques in the world aren't going to keep the Bijou running. To do that, you have to fill the theater on a regular basis. And compete against the big multiplexes down the road. Just how are you going to do that?

My pie-in-the-sky self answered back: *We could have a film festival of old movies.*

Practical side played devil's advocate. *Yeah, and how exactly is that going to attract the millennium generation, who think black-and-white films are primeval? Not everyone shares your love of old movies.*

Then we also include modern classics like Grease, Airplane (*shudder*), *and* Young Frankenstein (*I'll get 'em to watch a black-and-white film yet!*), my visionary self argued. *We could also open it once a month to concerts from local bands and artists. We upgrade the food and drinks: throw in some cappuccino from Books 'n' Brew, toss in a few of Amy's homemade cookies and muffins, and add in Steve and Sydney's killer mango tea. That's it. That's the ticket!*

Brimming with ideas, I jumped up and sprinted for the exit.

First, I needed to do a little more research.

Then I'd ask Gordon if I could write an editorial for the paper about the Bijou.

And after that, we could really get down to work.

Over the next several days, I developed a pattern. In the mornings I'd help dress and feed Mom, then drop her at Jordy and Karen's for a few hours while I did more research and lobbying for the Bijou. Following that, I'd go over and play with the kids for a while, touch base with Karen, then take my mother home, where I'd cook down-home dinners under her eager tutelage: beef stew and biscuits, chili and cornbread, roast beef and mashed potatoes.

I longed for my favorite sushi bar.

Knew Mom would get me one day for breaking my Easy-Bake Oven. I'm turning into a regular Suzy Homemaker here. If Lins could only see me now.

I really enjoyed my theater research, though. I learned that Esther and some of her girlfriends were in the Bijou crying over *A Tree Grows in Brooklyn* when World War II ended—they interrupted the movie with the news. And that Gordon gave his first kiss at age fifteen to Betty Lu Humphries while watching Tony and Maria sing "One Hand, One

Heart" in *West Side Story*. *And* that Karen told Jordy she was pregnant with Ashley as they were leaving Disney's *Beauty and the Beast*. (That explained the Belle and Beast waltzing figurine I'd noticed on their nightstand.)

While listening to everyone reminisce about favorite times at the Bijou, I thought back to mine, most of which revolved around my dad. One Saturday a month, beginning with *The Rescuers* when I was five, he'd take me on a date to a matinee. Dad and I had both watched enraptured as E.T. flew Elliot and his friends through the sky on their bicycles, then wept when the creature with the glowing heart light said, "I'll be right . . . here." We'd enjoyed the adventurous escapades of the whip-cracking, snake-fearing Indiana Jones in *Raiders of the Lost Ark* and sung along with Fievel and his *American Tail* mouse friends on their journey to America.

The more I thought about those happy childhood days, the more I realized that old theater was part of my history—part of my life. And I wasn't going to let it go without a fight.

Finally, by Friday morning, I was ready to write my editorial for Sunday's paper. My fingers flew over the keyboard down at the newspaper office as I poured out my heart over what the loss of the theater would mean to the community. The Bijou was the spirit and soul of the town, I wrote. Just how much soul did a fast-food place have? I considered including my theater-seat auction idea, which I'd mentioned to Gordon, but since it hadn't quite gotten past the visionary stage yet, I decided I'd better not.

I hadn't realized how much I'd missed writing until I typed my last period.

Lord, please help a New York editor somehow to read this piece or to discover my sparkling résumé online soon and offer me a dream journalism job there.

I turned in my piece to Gordon with regret, my fingers itching to pound out a movie review or three, but needing to return to home-front duty.

Mom and I had spaghetti that night over at Karen and Jordy's, where we got into a Monopoly marathon with the older kids after the younger ones had gone to bed. Elizabeth moved Mom's Scotty dog token for her while Jordy and I renewed our fierce childhood competition.

My brother puffed out his financial wizard's chest. "I can get more properties than you and fill them *all* with hotels."

"Wanna bet?"

"You don't want to go down that road, Pheebert. Face it, high finance is not your thing. Have you forgotten how I always beat you growing up?"

"That was then. This is now. I'm all grown up now." I gave my brother a sweet smile. "Prepare to lose."

But Jordy quickly bought another railroad and added a couple of hotels to three of his properties. "What'd I tell you, little sister? You didn't know you were dealing with a bona fide real estate mogul here." He leaned back in his chair, a self-satisfied smile tugging at his lips. "Soon, I'll be raking in the money on rent."

"From your lips to God's ear," Karen murmured, her brow furrowing.

I glanced from her to my brother. "Why do I get the feeling we're not just talking Monopoly here?"

Jordy preened. "Actually, I'm in the process of turning Gramps' old storage area above the barn into an apartment we can rent out."

"Rent? In this town?" I hooted. "With all those Bay Area types swarming in and property so cheap these days, why would anyone rent when they can buy, Mr. Real Estate Mogul?"

Karen flushed and gave her belly a nervous rub, Mom shot me a warning look, and Jordy just looked crestfallen.

Open mouth, insert large thoughtless foot, Pheebs.

"I'm sorry, Jord, Karen. Never mind me. I have absolutely no idea what I'm talking about." I shrugged my shoulders and shot them an apologetic grin. "What I don't know about finance and real estate would fill a book. So tell me, what are you doing exactly?"

Jordy leaned forward. "Well, with the new baby coming I knew we'd need a little extra cash flow, so I'm—"

But Ashley interrupted: "Dad's doing a Ty Pennington and making this really cool apartment with a kitchen and everything over the garage," she said, brimming with excitement, "and maybe in a couple years it will be *mine*."

"Maybe," her mother reminded her. "It all depends on how things are going at that time and whether we even have a renter or not." Her brow furrowed again.

Jordy gave his wife a gentle look. "Babe, remember how we prayed about this? Not to worry. God will provide."

Mom cleared her throat. "Okay, can we get back to the game now?"

We did. Jordy and I resumed our cutthroat childhood competition. But while we were taunting each other with entrepreneurial glee, Ashley quietly picked up Boardwalk and Park Place and kicked our respective Monopoly butts.

Karen high-fived her shy daughter. "Way to go, Ash!"

Mom beamed at her eldest grandchild. "Your dad and your aunt could take a lesson from you, dear."

Who'd have thought? This is almost as much fun as game night at Lone Rangers. Except for the dearth of single, available men—not that I ever managed to find one.

I followed Karen to the kitchen for ice cream. Grabbing the cartons from the freezer, my attention was caught by a piece of orange construction paper on the freezer door beneath a SpongeBob SquarePants magnet.

I set down the ice cream and scanned the *Oklahoma* flier. "Hey Kar, is this all the publicity you guys are doing for the show?"

She scooped up some Rocky Road. "Oh no. We're taking out an ad in the *Bulletin*. Plus, there's a huge poster up at school, and Sylvia has another big one in the front window of the Bobby Pin." Karen chuckled and shook her head. "With Bruce Hubert playing Ado Annie's father, Sylvia was dead set on getting the role of Aunt Eller so she could share stage time with him. But that woman can't sing a lick. Dance, either. And Aunt Eller's got that big number with Will . . ."

"You're going to need more advertising than that," I said, returning the flier to the fridge.

"We can't afford more, Phoebe."

"Actually, you can," I said, donning my PR hat. "Newspaper advertising's expensive, so the best thing is to get a reporter to do a story instead. It's great free publicity. You need to grab their attention, though. We should really play up the Bijou closing angle more. Let's see . . ." I ticked off newspapers on my fingers. "We can send out press releases to the *News-Sentinel* over at Lodi, the *Stockton Record* and the *Sacramento Bee*. The papers down in Manteca and Modesto, maybe even a couple of the Bay-Area papers. I should find out if Steve and Sydney have any connections at the *Chronicle* . . .

"Can you do all that?" my sister-in-law wondered. "I wouldn't know where to start."

"Hey, don't worry," I said, suddenly a little giddy, "We'll do fine by Oklahoma." Then I couldn't resist breaking into song: "Oklahoma, O-K-L-A-H-O-M-A—Okla-*ho*-ma!"

Jordy popped his head into the kitchen. "What's that awful noise? Sounds like a cat in heat or something."

I threw a damp dish towel at him.

He ducked. "Nice try, Pheebert. But you still throw like a girl."

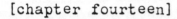

t he Midway scents of peanuts, cotton candy, and corn dogs at the Barley Fall Fair took me back to my childhood: Jordy and I ramming into one another on the bumper cars, Dad and I at the top of the ancient Ferris wheel—with my scared-of-heights mom below biting her lip—and the four of us all getting dizzy together on the Tilt-a-Whirl.

"Hey, Mom," I joked now, guiding her over the uneven ground as we passed by the familiar whirling contraption, "wanna go for a spin?"

She shot me a sly grin. "Only if you go with me to the embroidery and needlework booth."

My sewing-impaired self recoiled in horror. "Pass."

Whoa. Was that my mother being funny? Or have aliens taken over her body? Note to self: Keep close eye on Mom-unit to see if she exhibits other signs of behavior not in keeping with usual self.

We arrived at the 4-H pens, where Elizabeth was showing her pet billy goat, Justin Timberlake, and scooted in next to the rest of the family.

"I gonna get a goat when I big like Lizbeth," announced Lexie, as she watched her older sister put the animal through its paces for the judges. "Did you have a goat when you were little, An Beebee?"

"No, sweetie, I don't do so well with four-footed animals," I said. "I have a hard enough time with the two-footed ones. But your daddy had a goat. Her name was Billie Jean. And she sure didn't like me. Every time I got near, she tried to kick me. I think she was jealous and wanted your daddy all to herself."

Karen gave her husband a secret smile. "I know the feeling."

Elizabeth and Justin Timberlake took the blue ribbon, and we celebrated the win with to-die-for gourmet caramel apples dipped in rich, dark fudge and studded with chocolate chips.

"What an amazing flavor sensation," I said as I bit into my epicurean delight. "Barley used to have just plain old caramel apples—not this wonderful, palate-pleasing combo of textures and tastes." I took another delicious bite. "Mmmm, love that luscious, decadent fudge and gooey caramel, combined with the fresh, juicy sweetness of a Granny Smith . . ."

Jordy snorted, intruding upon my foodie reverie. "Hey Pheebert, forget being a movie reviewer. You should be a food critic instead."

"What time is it?" Mom asked for the seventh time that day.

"It's four-thirty. Don't worry," I reassured my casted, watchless mother, "We still have plenty of time to get to the pie and preserves judging."

She fidgeted in her seat. "Well, I just don't want to be late."

I licked my fingers, savoring the last fleck of fudge and lingering drop of juice. "Okay. So why don't we head over there now then?"

It was agreed that my brother would take the kids to see Mary Jo put her horses through their hoops while Mom, Karen, and I made our way to the food judging area. When we arrived at the tent entrance, who should we meet but tobacco-chewing hillbilly man.

Who, indeed?

"Oh, hello, Hank," Mom said, affecting surprise. "How nice to run into you. You remember Phoebe—and of course you know Karen, Jordy's wife?"

He took off a baseball cap emblazoned with a Pennzoil label across the front. "Pleasure, ladies." Then he zeroed in on me with a Tom Cruise smile that surprised me with its dazzling whiteness. "Phoebe, I was hopin' you might accompany me to the racetrack for the truck rally that's about to start."

"Truck rally? Is that like a pep rally? What do we do, cheer for the most athletic truck?"

Hank threw his good-looking head back and laughed.

I put a sock in my sarcasm as I checked this good ol' boy out. Hmmm. Not too shabby today in his pressed jeans and black button-down shirt. No telltale lump in the jaw either. *A truck rally has to be more diverting than the domestic arts drudgery awaiting me inside—especially after the home ec immersion course I've had this week. And he* does *have a killer smile . . .*

But I knew my responsibilities. "Sorry, Hank, but it's almost time for the pie judging, and I need to get Mom inside for that."

"Now never you mind that, daughter," Mom said, salivating over Mr. Eligible. "Karen's with me—I'll be fine. You two just go have some fun."

"How will you get home?"

"Karen and Jordy can drive me. Now you just go on and scoot now."

Mother, could you be *more obvious?*

My inner voices began to remonstrate. *Don't forget your recent resolution to dig deeper. There could be hidden layers to this guy like there was with Colin—who's about to marry one of your girlfriends, remember—which you overlooked in your surface rush.*

Okay, point taken. Guess he is *kinda cute. Tall. Good teeth, which is pretty amazing considering the tobacco. Nice and polite. And if I went with him I could skip the domestic goddess food-tent rituals . . .*

But I still hesitated. "You sure, Mom?"

She almost strong-armed me with her casts. "Yes. Now, you two go off and have fun."

"Yeah, Phoebe," Karen echoed. "You guys have a good time."

Great. Now my whole family's in the matchmaking business.

"Ready to go?" Hank asked.

As he led me to the racetrack, my truck rally escort said, "You couldn't have picked a better day than this to go to the fair. This here's Mud Bog Day."

"Excuse me? Mud what?"

"Bog." He looked at me, incredulous. "Haven't you ever seen a mud bog before?"

Not intentionally. Although there was that one time in basic training . . .

"I don't think so." I smiled at him. "There won't be any ROUSes, will there?"

He gave me a blank stare. "Huh?"

"Rodents of Unusual Size. Haven't you seen *The Princess Bride*?"

Hank scratched his head. "Nope. Don't go too much for chick movies and fairy tales with princesses and all that girl stuff."

Strike one.

My placating inner voice spoke up. *Aw, c'mon, give him a chance. Just 'cause he doesn't like chick flicks—that's what you have girlfriends for.*

True. But Princess Bride *isn't a chick flick,* my stubborn self argued. *I know plenty of guys who like it—actually love it.* I thought wistfully of my lost Filmguy.

So? Maybe you can introduce him to it the same way he's introducing you to this new experience. Be open to possibilities, urged my Dr. Phil conscience.

Oh, all right already.

At the racetrack, we were greeted by a raucous country song blaring from the loudspeakers. I wasn't sure I caught all the words. "Is that guy really saying, 'Don't tell Mama I'm a guitar picker—she thinks I'm just in jail'?"

"Yep," he beamed. "That's one of my favorite Jim Stafford songs."

He saw my puzzled look and explained, "You know, the guy that sang 'Spiders and Snakes'?" All I could do was shrug. He flashed his Tom Cruise teeth. "Guess you're not much of a music lover."

The song was soon overpowered, however, by a thunderous roar that drowned out everything else.

Hank urged me forward, his excitement palpable. "We have to hurry, or we'll miss the beginning," he said, ushering me past the rows of bleachers to some empty metal chairs down in front, right next to the track.

As I sat down, I smiled a greeting to the older man on my right, who returned the smile to reveal tobacco-stained teeth—my date's disgusting dental future?—and a distended jaw.

Ew!

Hank leaned over and shouted to make himself heard over the racket. "My buddy's drivin' today, so we can get up really close," he said with pride. Then he turned away, pulled a flat can the size of a hockey puck out of his back pocket, grabbed a discreet pinch of Copenhagen, and packed it into his mouth.

Double ew! Could you be any more revolting? Strike two—plus, a bonus strike.

Trying not to visibly shudder and making an effort to overlook his bad habit—after all, I'm addicted to chocolate—I focused instead on the scene before me, feigning an interest I didn't feel. "What's with the pile of wrecked cars on the other side of the track?"

My country-fried date turned his head to the side to spit into a paper cup before answering. "That's what the trucks have to drive over."

"Why?"

He cupped his hand to his ear, thinking he'd misunderstood. "What?"

"No. *Why?*" I yelled.

Are we gonna play the who's-on-first game next?

Hank dropped his hand, shooting me a look of disbelief. "Because . . . that's what they *do.*"

Noticing my blank expression, he attempted to explain the intricacies of the sport. "It's kind of like an obstacle course," he shouted above the din. "They fill up the track with muddy water and mounds of mud—mud bogs—then grind through all the mud and over piles of wrecked cars."

"Again—*why?*"

"Be-because it's fun!" he said, wiping at the corner of his mouth.

"Ah."

At that moment, two megatrucks appeared on the other side of the track, revving their engines at a deafening decibel. The shiny black one had painted orange flames racing across the front and sides; the bright yellow one sported Old Glory and a bald eagle. Sponsors' names covered the cabs and sides of both vehicles. I spotted Lou's Steakhouse advertised in metallic red letters on the yellow truck.

My date got a dreamy, far-off look in his eyes. "Someday, I'm going to have my own monster truck."

"What do you call the one you have right now?"

He guffawed and slapped his thigh. "That little bitty thing? That don't even have no hydraulics on it. A real racin' one, ya need a step ladder just t' get on up into it."

Of course you do. After all, Jack needed a big ol' beanstalk to climb up to his—well, his monster.

Hank was starting to realize just how ignorant I was about the things he held dear. So he proceeded to regale me with an educational litany of what constituted a good monster truck: engines with huge headers and massive exhaust pipes, yellow shocks, over twelve hundred fifty in horsepower, blah, blah, blah . . .

I nodded, feigning interest, but tuned out to focus on one of *my* favorite sports instead. *I wish I'd put those cute Kate Spade ankle-straps I'd seen in Cleveland on plastic. I know they were screamingly expensive, but they would have looked so great with my little black dress. Or my new black skirt. Even last year's pants. Maybe I can have Lindsey go and . . .*

Too late I realized that my mother's matchmaking pick had stopped talking. I tried to cover, searching my mechanically challenged brain for any semireasonable question to ask about the subject at hand. "Um, so what happens if they crash into each other?"

Bingo.

Hank puffed up in good-ol'-boy-helpin'-the-little-lady pride. "Crashing into another truck is an automatic disqualification," he told me. And he was off again, explaining in excruciating detail all the rally rules so near and dear to his heart.

Strike two and three-quarters. But I was saved from further enlightenment by the official start of the mud-bogging games.

The gargantuan black truck revved forward at an ear-splitting pitch, lunging ahead in a deafening roar as the crowd surged to its feet in a thunderous mass of shouts and stomps. I'd never heard such an awful agony of noise, except perhaps during the early rounds of auditions for *American Idol.*

At least there we broke for commercials. Here, there was no escaping the horror.

I clapped my hands over my ears in self-defense. No good. No matter how hard I pressed my hands against my head, compressing my gray matter into a teeny, tiny mass of imbecility, I could still hear the grinding, crunching, crashing, and overall screeching of metal as the massive machine pulverized the pile of wrecked cars in its blaring path.

"Isn't this cool?" Hank yelled across to me, eyes shining.

My reply was lost in the din—which was just as well.

At that point a guy selling refreshments walked by. "Hey, ya want something cold to drink? A beer, maybe?" Hank shouted, reaching for his wallet.

"No, thanks. I'll just take some water." I turned to the vendor. "Do you have any Evian?"

Apparently not.

I settled for a Sprite, inhaling its fizzy fragrance in a futile attempt to block out the surrounding stale aromas of spilled beer, cigarettes, diesel fuel, and exhaust fumes. Once again, to no avail.

Really having some fun now. Tattoo-ferret man's starting to look attractive. At least on that bad blind date we were in a clean, quiet movie theater. This outdoor fun business is really overrated.

And far too noisy.

I shifted in my uncomfortable seat. *Time to go to my happy place . . .*

In the cathedral hush, row after row of gleaming shoes greeted me: mules, slides, slingbacks, stilettos, strappy sandals, boots, basic black pumps. Okay, I admit it—I inhaled.

Ah, there's nothing like the smell of leather in the morning . . .

My excited date punctured my shoe-in-the-sky fantasy and brought me back down to the nightmare that was my reality. "Look!" He pointed to the far end of the track. "Here comes the other guy."

Peering into the distance to watch the patriotic big-wheeler begin its earsplitting ascent over the wreckage, I didn't pay much attention to the approach of the bad black monster truck—until it was too late.

Now I know how it felt to meet Shamu the killer whale up close and personal.

I'd been so intent on tuning out my mind-numbing surroundings that I'd failed to notice the large mound of mud just off to the side and front of where we were sitting. But the metal Creature from the Black Lagoon certainly noticed it. And plunged right through the mess.

Everything shifted into slow motion then as an arc of mud moved toward me like a tidal wave, splashing my best Guess jeans and T-shirt and leaving me covered in gross, goopy gunk from head to suede-shod toe.

Dripping with disgusting goo, I turned in horror to Hank.

My oblivious date had no drips, just a few mud flecks here and there. "Whoa! Was that cool or what?" He stared straight ahead with the glassy-eyed gaze of an addict. A true believer.

Strike ten. I am so outta here!

Squish-squishing my way from the arena, I wiped at my face and tried to remove the biggest chunks of mud from my hair, searching in vain for a nearby restroom where I could clean up before all of Barley saw me in this state. No luck—just a row of blue, mirrorless porta-potties.

I skulked to the parking lot, ignoring the stares and occasional cheer mixed in with a whistle or two. I found a little box of garbage bags in the backseat—my Mom liked to be both clean and prepared—and spread them to protect the seats. And as I drove home, steering with one hand and wringing the worst of the sludge from my sticky clothes with the other, God and I had words.

Lord, I tried to look beyond the surface, to dig deeper, but instead of gold, all I got was a pile of mud. I know You say You cause all things to work together for good, but what possible good can come out of this disgusting mess?

A putrid brown glob fell off my elbow and landed on the car seat just beyond my garbage-bag shield. I rolled down the windows in an effort to get rid of the stench, then started shivering as the cool air hit my clammy skin and wet clothes.

At least I'm in Mom's old Ford instead of my nice, shiny Bug. And speaking of Mom, Lord . . . I've tried to honor my mother, but this time she's gone too far. If it hadn't been for her relentless, insistent matchmaking, this would never have happened.

I pulled into the driveway, spinning gravel. Slamming the car door, I stalked toward the house, squishing in my soaked suede boots all the way. The kitchen door banged behind me. "Mother!" I yelled, beginning to peel off the mess that was once my clothes.

"Yes, daughter?" her voice floated from down the hall. "Did you have a good time?" Appearing in the kitchen doorway, she gasped. "Oh my, what happened, honey?" She advanced toward me, concerned. "Are you all right?"

"No, I'm *not* all right. I'm covered in icky, smelly mud!" I attempted to maintain a level tone of voice, but knew I was fast approaching the point of no return. "And your tobacco-chewing, Godzilla-truck-loving friend Hank is what happened."

Seeing the confusion in her eyes, I dialed the anger down a notch. "I thought I told you, Mom—no more setups."

"No, little dumpling," she corrected me. "You told me not to invite any single men over to dinner."

The camel's back snapped.

"It's not going to work, Mom! You can't keep me here like you did Dad, no matter how hard you try. I have bigger plans for my life than Barley. So stop trying to fix me up, quit pushing me to get married, and let me lead my own life! I'm not you—I never will be. And I'm not your little dumpling either!" I said, stomping down the hall to the shower.

"In your anger do not sin."

Too late, God. Already sinning. Might as well go for broke.

"And another thing," I said, turning back to face her before entering the bathroom, "my friends like my French toast just the way it is!"

I felt a stab of guilt when I saw the hurt on Mom's face but blocked it out as I stood under the steaming water and let my angry tears swirl down the drain with the mud. I shampooed—*three* times to get every trace of mud out of my hair, thank you very much—ranting and raving all the while.

I can't wait *to get out of this hick town! This would never happen in New York. No county fairgrounds. No tobacco-chewing rednecks. No monolithic trucks that are so ridiculously tall a woman could walk right beneath them without even bending. Although why she'd want to get that close is beyond me. If I never see one of those mutant machines again, it will be too soon.*

After blow-drying my hair, I tried to call Lins, needing to hear a friendly voice, but got her voice mail instead. "Hey Lins, it's me. You gotta break me outta here before I do some serious damage—although it may already be too late for that. You'll never believe what happened!" I gave her voicemail the *Reader's Digest* version of my terrible, awful, horrible day. I called Phil too and left more or less the same message.

Next, I called Karen and Mary Jo.

Trembling, I surveyed my wardrobe and got dressed to kill. After finishing my face, I was at last composed enough to leave my room.

When I came out, Mom was sitting in the living room with Karen and Jordy—whom I'd asked to come over—waiting for me.

"Phoebe, I'd like to talk to you."

I know you would, Mom, but I can't handle a lecture right now. I'm simply not up to it.

The doorbell rang. "That'll be Mary Jo. Mom. I'm sorry. I really have to go. We're having a girls' night out—something I really need. We'll talk later, okay? Thanks, Karen, Jordy. Gotta go."

I escaped, shaking.

I'm a terrible, awful daughter—unloading on my mother like that and then leaving. The woman's in casts, for goodness' sake! But Lord, I just can't handle any more confrontation tonight. I need a break. I promise I'll apologize later . . .

It was only once I was outside that I remembered Mary Jo drove a truck too. "At least yours has normal-sized wheels," I grumbled as I clambered in. "So, where we going?"

Mary Jo gunned the motor. "To church."

"I don't know that I'm in the best mood for church right now."

She grinned. "You will be."

When we walked into our Sunday-school classroom, I was stunned to see a half-dozen or so of my high-school classmates.

"I thought you needed a little reunion, Pheebs," Mary Jo said, "so I called some of the old gang."

Wow. I haven't seen most of these people since graduation. "Hmmm. I see a little gravity and hair loss has come into play," I whispered to Mary Jo.

Then Travis, my old high-school boyfriend, caught my eye and headed my way with a smile.

It was turning into a real red-letter day, romance-wise. *I so don't need this tonight. Lord. Please don't tell me he's still carrying a torch after all this time. I thought those particular flames had been extinguished long ago . . .*

Although Travis was cute and sweet, we'd never had too much in common, what with his abiding interest in basketball, cars, and Barley, and mine in books, movies, and big cities. Our relationship had only lasted a few months.

I steeled myself to let him down easy. Then I realized someone else was tagging behind Travis. Someone tiny with long, dark hair.

"Jenny? Jenny Flynn? I can't believe it!" I jumped up and embraced my former best friend from the tenth grade. "How are you? It's been way too long! What have you been up to?"

Jenny favored me with a cautious smile. "Getting engaged."

I squealed. "Cool! How exciting! Who's the lucky guy?"

"I am, Phoebe," Travis said, pulling Jenny close and smiling down at her.

It's an epidemic. All my rejects are hooking up with someone else.

"I'm so happy for you both," I said, catching up and making small talk for a few minutes before they walked off hand in hand.

Okay, I know I didn't want Travis, Lord, but did You have to rub it in that he's got someone too? The whole world's paired off. Even the animals in the ark had someone to walk up the plank with. It'd sure be nice to have someone's hand to hold, arms to snuggle in, lips to kiss . . .

Down, passion-girl! my G-rated single self slapped me back to reality. Then memories of my mother's hurt face intruded.

You're not the only one who's not a couple.

Sensing my discouragement, the cavalry showed up. "Hey you guys, this party's a little dead," said Mary Jo. "What say we liven it up a little?"

Fifteen minutes later found a bunch of us in a crowded karaoke place in Lodi, where who should we run into but Sylvia Ann—whose hair was down tonight and feathered à la Farrah Fawcett in the seventies—and Hubert, I mean Bruce. Bruce doing a pitiful Springsteen impression singing "Born in the USA." Then he passed the mike to his love-struck girlfriend, who sang a painful but vigorous rendition of "I Will Always Love You."

"She's sure no Dolly," Mary Jo whispered.

"Whitney, either," I whispered back.

Things improved some when Travis serenaded Jenny with his sweet interpretation of "Endless Love," but when he segued into the gooey "Three Times a Lady," it was more than Mary Jo could take.

Afraid he'd run through the entire Lionel Richie repertoire, she took the stage—and the mike—the instant that Travis finished. And no sweet, sappy love song for my country friend. She surprised me and everyone else in the room by channeling Aretha and asking for a little R-E-S-P-E-C-T.

I looked at Mary Jo with new respect when she rejoined our table. "Wow! Didn't know you had that in you."

She lifted her plastered hair off her neck, fanned herself, and then drained the rest of her Coke. "You ain't seen nothin' yet." Returning to the stage she burst into the Beatles' "All You Need Is Love" then segued into a Motown medley, ending with an "Ain't No Mountain High Enough" that Diana Ross herself would be proud of.

"Mary Jo, you need to audition for one of those TV talent shows," Jenny said when she returned.

I nodded agreement. "Who'd have guessed the next Celine Dion was hiding beneath those bib overalls and flannel shirts?"

Mary Jo glanced down at her ample hips. "I'm no Celine. Besides, I'd have a hard time climbing out of one of those celebrity sports cars."

I sighed. "That's why they have limos, my dear."

She brushed off our praise. "Besides, when I got rich and famous and went to Hollywood, who'd take care of my horses?"

"Your ranch manager," I said, "or a cute stable boy."

Mary Jo changed the subject. "All right Pheebs, it's your turn."

"To go to Hollywood? Okay. Throw me in that briar patch."

"No. To sing. Go on now—get up there."

Jenny and Travis chimed in. "Yeah, Phoebe, go on."

I shook my head. "I am *not* a singer."

"So? That hasn't stopped anyone else," Jenny said, glancing across the room at Sylvia Ann, who was hanging on H-man's every word.

I took a sip of bottled water. "My point exactly."

But my former classmates began chanting, "Phoebe, Phoebe, Phoebe," as I slunk lower in my chair.

Mary Jo stood up.

Whew. Mary Jo's going back onstage.

She was. But not alone.

My Celine-voiced friend leaned down and whispered, "C'mon, Pheebs. We'll do it together."

I had no choice. "Okay," I said, "but it's on your eardrums." Then, going for broke, I joined in the fun and warbled "The Lion Sleeps Tonight" with Mary Jo and Jenny helping me out on the *a-weema-weh, a-weema-weh*s.

We laughed ourselves silly and weema-wehed all the way home.

"It's sure nice having girlfriends for backup." *Thanks, God.*

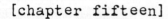

t he house was quiet when I let myself in the kitchen door at one-thirty in the morning. *Returning to the scene of my crime.* My stomach turned over as I remembered how I'd raged at my mother earlier.

She'd left the stove-hood light on for me. It illuminated a scrawled, nearly illegible note on the counter. "P—I'm sorry. Please forgive me. We need to talk. I love you, Mom."

Ni-i-ce, Phoebe. Making your broken-armed mom have to write. You should be the one doing the writing. And the groveling.

The talk had to wait a bit longer. I overslept the next morning and missed services at Holy Communion. By the time I got up, Mom had already left. I nearly missed the singles class at Barley Pres as well. When I finally walked in ten minutes late and tried to slip in the back, the room erupted in applause.

Oh no. Don't tell me everybody found out about the monster mud debacle. That's the problem with living in a small town—everybody knows everything. How embarrassing . . .

"Way to go, Phoebe!"

"Great editorial."

"Pheebs, you rock!" Mary Jo said. "And you say you have no talent."

What with everything else going on, I'd forgotten all about the theater editorial.

Gee. Doesn't take much to impress small-town folks. Wonder if Mom's read it. She didn't say anything, but of course I wasn't awake for her to say anything to. Besides, I'm sure there's lots of other things she wants to say to me.

The message in class that day came from James: "Everyone should be quick to listen, slow to speak and slow to become angry, for man's anger does not bring about the righteous life that God desires."

I slunk in my seat and tried to hide behind my NIV.

"Not a word," I said to Mary Jo as we walked to the parking lot.

"What? I wasn't saying anything."

"Your nothing spoke volumes."

As we made our way to our cars, an old family friend also stopped to compliment me on the editorial. *If you knew what a rotten daughter I was, you wouldn't be so quick to pat me on the back.*

"You know, I appreciate the praise," I said to Mary Jo, "but truth is, at this point I'd rather have money. I *so* need a job. And soon." I kicked the gravel. "I can't keep living off my Mom, and I can't keep living *with* her either. I really lost it last night, Mary Jo. That's not normal for me."

Mary Jo frowned. "Can't you do some freelance writing? Something on the Internet maybe?"

"I've tried, but nothing's come up. Well, Gordon said I could do some stories for him at the *Bulletin,* but that's definitely not what I'm looking for, and it wouldn't pay enough to live. I've posted my résumé on several journalism search engines, but so far I've gotten zip. *Nada.* Say a little job prayer for me, would you?"

"You got it," she said. "I'll also be praying for your talk with your Mom today."

Gee. Thanks for reminding me, pal. But I'll take all the prayers I can get.

Nervous, I drove home, unsure what kind of reception to expect. I pulled in the driveway and was relieved to see Karen and Jordy's car.

Whew. Saved by the brother and sister-in-law. Thanks, God. Then my neurotic self came screaming forward. *Unless this is an inquisition instead—or maybe an intervention—and they're all waiting inside to give me what for. Go on, bad girl, time to face the music.*

I stepped inside, where the music blasted me off my feet. Kool and the Gang welcomed me with "Celebration" from Jordy's CD player while everyone, even Mom, blew horns and noisemakers, Jacob and Lexie threw confetti, and my whole family chorused, "Congratulations!"

What? Did I win the lottery or something? Oh no, that's right. You have to play *the lottery in order to win it. So what's the deal? This isn't about the editorial again, is it? What gives with these people?*

Amidst the mostly feminine bedlam, a little boy raised his hand to get noticed.

I squatted down to my little nephew's eye level. "Yes, Jacob?"

"Aunt Phoebe, are you famous?"

I hugged him. "No, honey. Infamous would be more like it." Over his head, I searched for Mom. When I caught her eye, I mouthed the words, *I'm sorry.*

She nodded and mouthed back *Me too.* Then she flashed me that we'll-clear-the-air-later smile.

Mom blinked. "Who's ready for roast chicken? Karen and I tried that low-fat recipe you like, Phoebe, with wild rice and those Portybello mushrooms instead of my fried potatoes."

Whoa. What was that about an old dog and new tricks? We were just finishing our delicious, healthy dinner and starting an even more delicious, not quite so healthy dessert when a knock sounded at the door. Jordy got up, wiping his mouth, and opened the door to Gordon.

Noticing us all at the table, he backpedaled. "I'm sorry. Didn't mean to interrupt your Sunday dinner. I can come back later."

"Come on in, Gordon, and have some dessert," Mom said.

He fumbled with the top button on his ratty old cardigan. "You sure? I don't want to intrude."

"No intrusion at all." Jordy ushered him inside. I got up to get another chair.

Mom smiled at him. "Your timing's perfect. We were just getting ready to cut Phoebe's cake."

He looked stricken. "It's not your birthday, is it, Phoebe?"

"Not for another nine months or so."

Karen brought in the chocolate Sara Lee cake Mom had insisted on picking up this morning on their way home from church. Ashley had just finished writing "Congratulations!" on it in pink frosting.

"Sorry it's store-bought," she said. "If it weren't for these annoying casts, I'd have baked Phoebe's favorite from scratch. But never mind. We're celebrating my daughter's wonderful editorial in your paper this morning."

"Actually, that's why I'm here," Gordon said, sitting down. He accepted a piece of cake from Karen. "My phone's been ringing off the hook with people calling to talk to Phoebe *and* to ask where they can buy theater seats and how much they cost."

"What?" I paused, fork in midair. "Theater seats? What are you talking about?"

Everyone turned and stared at me.

Then Karen's face cleared. "Phoebe, have you not read today's *Bulletin*?"

I squirmed. *Sure, go ahead and ask me in front of the editor and publisher. Way to make me look indifferent and ungrateful.* "Um, not yet. I, uh, overslept and didn't have time before church. Then when I got home, you all surprised me and I haven't had a chance to . . ."

Jordy jumped up, grabbed a copy from a tall stack on the kitchen counter, and plopped it in front of me. "Here. Read!"

I did—with everyone's eyes, including the publisher's, on me. There, on the front page *above the fold* was my editorial in big, bold print under the dramatic headline, "Save the Bijou!"

No wonder everyone was congratulating me. Front page, no less.

"But editorials usually go on Page Two." I looked up at Gordon in surprise.

He took a bite of cake. "Not when they're about something important that affects the whole town. That's called news."

"Keep reading, Phoebe," Mom said.

I did. And what I read surprised me even more. Gordon had

followed my editorial with his own commentary: "It took a local girl who's been gone several years to make me appreciate what we have right here 'in our own front yard'—to quote Judy Garland from *Meet Me in St. Louis.* So let's pick up the gauntlet that Phoebe Grant has so ably thrown down and save the Bijou with our very own fund-raising drive. Watch for upcoming stories to learn how you can buy your own theater seat and help keep the Bijou alive for your children, your children's children, and future generations."

Can you say "speechless"?

"Wow," I stammered. "Th-thank you, Gordon." Then, curious: "So, how are you planning to run the fundraising drive? How much are you going to charge per seat?"

He fumbled with his cardigan button again. "Uh, er, I don't know exactly. I thought you would handle all that, um, in addition to your other duties."

"Other duties?"

Gordon ran a hand through his thinning gray hair. "I'm doing this all wrong. Phoebe, I'm officially offering you a job at the *Bulletin.* Temporary if you like, but full-time. With benefits. I was also, er, hoping you could spearhead the theater fund-raising campaign, since I don't have the first clue how to go about an operation like that."

Talk about fast answer to prayer. Although this wasn't quite what I had in mind, Lord. The Bulletin's *not exactly the* New York Times . . .

And you're not exactly Times *material yet,* my humbler self reminded me. *You gotta pay your dues, remember? This could help you get there, though.*

"What about Esther?"

"Esther quit," Gordon said.

We all screeched out a collective "What?"

He waved off our concern. "She's been wanting to for a long time. And this morning, after reading your piece, she said it was just what the

Bulletin needed—fresh blood. So now she doesn't feel bad about leaving. Said her blood—and the rest of her—is tired and wants to just relax and have some fun. So she booked a Caribbean cruise and leaves Tuesday for a seven-day tour with a couple of her old college girlfriends."

"Go, Esther!" Karen said.

I was pleased for her too, but then I remembered. "Thanks for the offer, Gordon, but I'm afraid I'm going to have to say no. The reason I came home in the first place was to help Mom while she's out of commission. And that's what I'm going to do."

"Nonsense," Mom said. "Don't you worry about me. Gordon needs you more. So does the *Bulletin.* You can't turn your back on them in their hour of need." Her voice softened. "You're a wonderful writer, dumpli—er, sweetheart. I never realized just how wonderful. You have a special gift, and you need to be exercising that gift the Lord has given you."

Don't start blubbering in front of everyone now. Hold it together, Pheebs.

"But I wouldn't know where to begin either. I've never set up a fund-raising campaign before."

"I have, for the school," Karen said. "I'll help."

"Me too," Mom chimed in.

Think of it as a way to start building up your portfolio. And earn some much-needed cash at the same time. Besides, my ambitious self urged, *this whole save-the-little-guy theater stuff plays really well in city arts communities.*

I looked around at my eager family and expectant publisher. And sighed. "Well, Gordon. I guess you've got a new reporter. For now at least."

A broad grin split my new boss's craggy face.

"So, what's my first assignment?"

He pulled a scrap of paper full of scribbled names out of his sweater pocket and handed it to me. "I need a behind-the-scenes look at the Miss Udderly Delicious and the local girls vying for the pageant crown. Their hopes and dreams, why they entered the competition, what led them to this point, yada, yada. A big feature piece."

My face fell. *C'mon. Anything but the bimbo beauty pageant.*

Mom knew what I was thinking. I'd never been exactly quiet on the subject. Jordy knew it too.

"Lower your feminist hackles, little sister," he said. "Didn't you see *Miss Congeniality*? Beauty pageants have come a long way, baby." He peered at me over his glasses. "Three of the contestants are in my advanced calculus class. And if memory serves, *you* barely made it through basic algebra."

I turned my nose up. "True, Mr. Left-Brain Numbers Jockey. But that's because we creative, free-spirited right-brain types are not shackled by the tedious chains of math and logic."

"Which is also why you're not shackled by a 401(k) or a balanced checkbook," my brother said under his breath.

Gordon stilled our sibling squabbling with a clearing of his throat. "Phoebe, I thought you could cover the pageant from a contemporary single woman's point of view. Bring in all the old saws about it being sexist, demeaning, and outdated. Then write what's true now. Make sure you interview both the girls and the judges."

"Uh, well, okay. I mean, you're the boss, right?"

"That's my girl."

He thanked Mom, then took his leave. Karen, Jordy and the kids followed soon thereafter. Leaving me alone at last with my mother.

The moment of truth.

"Mom, I'm really sorry for exploding at you last night," I began.

"I had Karen put the kettle on, dear. Why don't we talk over a nice cup of tea?"

I opened the pantry door and went straight to the alphabetized tea section. "Do you want chamomile, Darjeeling, Earl Grey, English breakfast, or vanilla-nut decaf?"

She glanced at the Blue Willow clock on the wall. "It's almost three. I think I'd better take the vanilla-nut."

Not me. I'm going for full-strength and then some. I grabbed both an Earl Grey and a Darjeeling tea bag and busied myself with mugs and sugar.

Behind me, Mom said, "Phoebe . . ."

I steeled myself for what was coming.

But she took me by surprise. "In high school, do you know what I dreamed of becoming?"

Um, yeah. Easy final Jeopardy! *question—I'll bet it all.* I picked up the whistling kettle and poured boiling water over the tea bags. "A homemaker."

"Nope. An airline stewardess."

I nearly dropped the kettle. Setting it down carefully, I turned to face my mother. "Excuse me, but *what?*" I placed the steaming mugs on the table and sat down, all amazed ears.

Mom blew on her tea, then took a delicate sip. She was getting a lot better with those casts. "When I was in high school, *Coffee, Tea, or Me?* came out. I loved that book about stewardesses—I guess they call them flight attendants now. It made me realize that's what *I* wanted to do—fly all over the world." She smiled at the memory. "Becoming a 'stew' was all I could think of. I went to the library, checked out every book, watched every movie with stewardesses in it. There was one with Pamela Tiffin—I think it was called *Come Fly with Me*— that I especially liked . . ."

At this point, my head was helicoptering all over the place. This was *not* the mother I'd known all my life.

She continued. "I learned the requirements and cost of the program. Then I began saving my money. Got a job as a secretary after I graduated and put away everything I could. I even applied to stewardess training school and was accepted."

I shook my head, still trying to wrap my brain around the image of my mother in full makeup and a perky uniform—and leaving Barley to do it.

I had to know: "So, what happened?"

"I sent in the down payment but was still short a large portion of the tuition fee. That's why I entered the Miss Udderly pageant. The winnings would take care of the rest."

The pageant? But that's when . . .

"Then I met your dad."

"Are you trying to say Dad stopped you from going away?" This was really hard to grasp. I'd grown up positive that she was the one who stopped him.

"No, dear," Mom said, looking down at her casts. "Your dad never knew."

"Wh-what?"

"I didn't tell him. At least not until after we were married."

"Why not?"

"Because I fell in love with him," she said softly.

Seeing my confused look, she explained. "It was a different world back then, daughter. To be a stewardess, you had to be single. Married women were not allowed. So I had to make a choice."

She looked me straight in the eye, unblinking. "I chose your dad. And I've never once regretted it."

"But didn't you resent him for holding you back? For ruining your dream?"

"Oh sweetheart, your daddy didn't ruin my dream. He just gave me a much better one. That's why I've never mentioned this before. I didn't want you to ever even think that. Besides," she continued, "your father had plans to move to L.A. or New York to teach and do some acting after a one-year stint here in Barley. I figured that if I married him, I'd still get my traveling in."

"What happened? Why didn't you?"

But I knew.

She smiled. "I got pregnant with Jordy during that first year of marriage." She cast me a tender look. "And three years later, you came."

"So we were the ones who held you and Daddy back," I said in a small voice.

"No!" Mom was emphatic. "Not in the least. You simply changed our focus. Just as I chose your dad over becoming a stewardess, he chose his family over full-time theater. He never regretted it, either. In fact, he told me right after you were born that you and Jordy were his greatest production."

She bit her lip and considered. "Jordy said I should be completely honest with you . . . Phoebe, your dad was the most wonderful man I've ever known—kind, gentle, smart, talented, and larger than life." Her eyes misted. "I loved him like I've never loved anyone, and he felt the same about me. I still miss him. Every day."

Tears leaked down my cheeks.

She gave me a gentle smile. "He was crazy about you kids. Absolutely adored you. Especially you, his little girl. You're so much like him, honey. He too was more 'right brained'—although we didn't have that term then." She hesitated. "What I mean is—I'm afraid your dad wasn't very good with numbers either. His teacher's salary wasn't much, so we were always having to pinch pennies. That's why I learned to cook from scratch and sewed most of your clothes— although that became a true pleasure for me."

Not for me. I hated those homemade clothes. The minute I was old enough, I'd found a part-time job so I could go to Sacramento with my girlfriends and shop.

Mom continued. "That's also why we never traveled. Couldn't afford to."

My tea had gotten cold. "But why didn't you ever tell me any of this before?"

"Wasn't any reason to. I'm only doing it now because Jordy and I had a long talk after you left last night, and he thought it might help us understand one another a little better."

Remembering my outburst, I was ashamed all over again. "Mom, I'm so sorry for losing it last night and yelling at you like I did. I said some hateful things, and I apologize. Can you forgive me?"

"Of course," she said. "If you'll forgive me for my matchmaking."

Mom shifted in her chair to get more comfortable. "All I've ever wanted is for you to be happy, Phoebe. And since the greatest happiness I've known came from being married to your dad, I've simply wanted the same thing for you—a good, kind man who will love and adore you."

"I want that too. But I have to tell you, Mom, it's not Trucker Hank. That's not gonna happen."

Her eyes twinkled. "I knew you didn't have a whole lot in common, but he *is* a nice Christian boy. Cute, too, don't you think?"

"True. But I stopped making mud pies in the second grade."

We looked at each other and burst out laughing.

The next morning, after settling Mom in at Karen's and grabbing a notebook and my daily mocha from Books 'n' Brew, I drove out to Barley High to interview the pageant contestants.

It was a pleasant surprise to discover that all the girls weren't skinny-minnies. Sure, of the twelve competing for the crown and the two-thousand dollar Rotary Club scholarship, there were a couple of Ally McBeal types with long legs, microscopic waists, and no hips. But most of the girls were just regular, normal, everyday girls with regular, normal, everyday bodies. There was even one who might be considered plump.

The other surprise was that these girls were smart. Way smart. Two had already been accepted to Stanford, one was planning to be a vet, and another showed me her portfolio of the Web sites she'd designed.

What? A computer nerd at the Miss Udderly Delicious? Way to get rid of lots of my preconceived notions at once, Lord.

After I finished interviewing the girls, my next assignment was to do a story on Christy Sharp Armstrong. I deciphered Gordon's scrawl: "Christy *Sharp*? Barley's 1988 homecoming queen?"

"The one and only."

When I was a freshman, Christy Sharp was a senior and the most popular girl in high school. She'd been head cheerleader, homecoming queen, the lead in the senior class play, featured soloist in the choir, and a semifinalist in the national Pillsbury Bake-Off competition. Oh yeah, she also won Miss Udderly Delicious that year.

"So what'd Christy do now?" I asked Gordon. "Win *Survivor,* the Antarctic version?"

"Nope. She has the largest salt and pepper shaker collection in the county, maybe even the state," Gordon said. "She's trying to make the *Guinness Book of World Records.*"

"I'm sorry?"

The phone rang and he waved me off. "Make sure you take the camera and get some good shots."

Gordon wasn't kidding.

Christy Sharp—homecoming queen, big girl on campus, repeatedly voted most likely to succeed—had now laid proud claim to the dubious honor of owning more than a thousand salt and pepper shakers. They ranged from plastic to fine porcelain and came in a variety of shapes, sizes, and colors.

Guess she really likes a little spice in her life.

Christy's husband, Bob, had taken their spare bedroom and turned it into a shrine for her obsession—uh, hobby.

"This is my showplace," she said proudly as we entered the room. "Bob built the shelves for my favorites."

There were hundreds of shakers on each wall of floor-to-ceiling oak shelves.

"We converted the library's old card catalogues to house the others," Christy said, pointing out cabinets that filled the closet. She twirled and did her Vanna point back toward the walls. "Each wall is a category, and each shelf has its own theme."

There must have been fifteen narrow shelves on each wall, each crowded with shakers. I pulled out the camera and took some photos as she explained. *No one would believe it otherwise.*

"This wall is for animals. This one for minerals. That wall is for vegetables, of course. And this one," she said, turning around, "is my miscellaneous shelf. I have a little card under most sets with the information about where and when I got them. Where would you like to start?"

I blinked. "Uh, 'animals,' I think."

There was a shelf just for dogs, another for fish, and one filled with frogs. The jungle creatures were separated from the forest creatures, and the farm animals had their own shelf.

We moved on to the "mineral" wall, which housed her collection of glass, porcelain, and crystal sets—I recognized a few of the china patterns—plus those made from a variety of metals.

"This is interesting," I said, snapping a photo of the frying pan and skillet shakers.

"My 'around-the-home' shelf."

I understood the washing machine and the pot-bellied stove, but the green-and-yellow tractors seemed out of place. "And those?"

"The John Deere? A gift from my father-in-law in . . ." she lifted the shakers and peeked at the card. "In 1998."

I turned next to the "vegetable" shelf, which boasted a variety of salt-and-pepper produce. "Where did you find all these?"

"Oh, all over the place! I started collecting when I was in junior high. Whenever I'm on a trip, I look for something new. And of course, there's eBay. Why, just this morning, when I was online, there were over nine thousand sets up for bid. So it's very easy to find something I don't already have." She winked. "If you play your cards right, you can get some great bargains."

"I'll be sure to keep that in mind."

"I have shakers from all over the world," Christy continued, moving to the "miscellaneous" wall. "Irish castles, the Leaning Tower of Pisa, a pyramid and a sphinx, and coconuts from Tahiti."

On the next shelf, she pointed out shakers from a little closer to home. The Golden Gate Bridge. Washington apples. Stetsons from Texas. Mount Rushmore. Red lobsters from Maine.

"I'm trying to collect shakers from all fifty states," Christy said. "But this set has rules. They have to be purchased within the actual state by me or someone I know. No mail order or Web shopping. So far, I have thirty-nine." Her breathing quickened and her eyes took on a feverish gleam. "Next spring for our vacation, though, we're taking a road trip in the Winnebago. I figure we can pick up at least eight more states then."

Growing ever more claustrophobic among the crowded walls of shakers, I quickly scanned the rest of the displayed collection. "I see you have TV shows, cartoon characters, and even a theme park shelf—Disneyland, SeaWorld, Coney Island." Then I noticed something unusual. "But what are those?"

"Well," she whispered, as she edged closer to me. "That set is not exactly from a theme park. They're unlicensed. I found them in a gift shop down the street from Dollywood."

Definitely not a photo op.

Okay, reporter girl, my now-hyperventilating self urged, *wrap this up and get outta here.*

I started to leave, then noticed the bottom shelf—full of shakers representing sports teams and equipment. "Are those hockey pucks?" I asked, bending down to get a better look.

"You betcha. Bob's a diehard hockey fan."

Diane Sawyer's got nothing on me. This hard-hitting piece is going to rock the world.

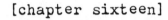

i don't want anyone messing with my feet," Mom said. "Seems the height of self-indulgence to me."

"It's good to indulge ourselves every now and then. Fun, too," I said. "Now just relax and enjoy the experience."

We were at the Bobby Pin, where I'd taken my mother kicking and screaming for a girl-bonding beauty day. It was now pedicure time, but she was digging in her dry, cracked heels. "You agreed," I reminded her. "I let you teach *me* how to cook."

She raised freshly plucked eyebrows.

"Well, after a fashion. Now you're going to let me teach you how to pamper yourself."

"But I feel funny focusing on myse—"

I played the Oprah card. "Mom, if Oprah can get Coretta Scott King to agree to a makeover, you can do the same for me, your only daughter."

That did the trick. Mom loved Oprah.

"Here," I said, selecting some polish. "I think this color would look really pretty on you."

She looked askance at the bottle I was brandishing. "Berrylicious? That's a little too bold for me, daughter. I'd rather just have clear polish. Or maybe a soft, pale pink."

"It's fall, Mom. We should go with more autumn colors. What about this taupe?"

"Is that what they call it? Reminds me of your dirty baby diapers. No thank you."

Face it, girl, your mom's never going to be one of those beige country-club ladies.

"How about this pretty bronze instead?"

She examined the color with a critical eye. "That's nice. Not too bright. Do you think it's a little too dark, though?"

"Not at all." I led her over to Sylvia Ann's just-installed pedicure throne. "It's perfect." I guided her up the two rubber-coated steps, settled her in the swivel chair, removed her loafers, and rolled up her pants legs. "Okay, swing your legs over this way and put them in the water."

She looked down at the churning water. "Why, it's like a little hot tub."

"Sure is," said Sylvia Ann, who was sporting a Marilyn Monroe hairstyle today. "Simmering spa for your tootsies." She gathered her supplies while Mom's tootsies soaked and I skimmed the latest *Entertainment Weekly*.

I lost myself in the celebrity gossip, movies, and behind-the-scenes goings-on. The faint sounds of clipping and buffing next to me barely penetrated my silver-screen reverie.

"Hey, wait a minute! What are you doing?"

Looking up from my magazine, I saw Sylvia rubbing oil on my red-faced mother's legs. "Mom, that's part of the pedicure."

"I thought I was only getting my toes polished."

"Nope. A proper pedicure includes the works: soaking, scrubbing, buffing, mas—"

She let out a little squeak.

"Massaging. Doesn't that feel good?" I asked as Sylvia began kneading her calves.

My mother's face was now stop-sign scarlet. "Um . . . er . . . nobody but your daddy's ever rubbed my legs before," she stammered.

"Well then, today's a day of firsts, Mom. Relish it."

When her newly bronze toes were mostly dry, I pulled out some sparkly black flip-flops for her to don as we made our way to the final stop on her day of beauty.

"Okay," Sylvia said, with an eager gleam in her makeover eye. "And now, for the *pièce de résistance . . .* the hair. Honey, that braid has got to go." She started to remove the bottom rubber band from the long, gray plait, but Mom swung her hair out of the way of the stylist's itching fingers.

"I've had this braid for more than thirty years," she said.

"Then you're long overdue for a change, honey."

"Well, maybe . . ." She worried the braid awkwardly beneath her fingers. "I *have* thought that it might be better to go with a shorter style. Easier too." Her uncertain eyes met mine in the mirror. "But a woman's crowning glory is her hair. And your dad liked my hair long."

I bent down and put my arm around my mother's shoulders, meeting her nervous face with a reassuring glance. "Dad's not here anymore, Mom," I said gently, fingering the thick, familiar braid. "I think the time has come."

She gulped and nodded. "OK."

Sylvia pulled a black plastic smock over Mom's front, being careful with her casts, and snapped it in place at the back of her neck. "Honey, you've got a gorgeous head of hair. Why, plenty of women your age would kill to have hair that thick. But it's way too heavy to be hanging all the way down your back. We need to lighten your load some." She picked up the scissors to make the first snip, and Mom squeezed her eyes shut.

I couldn't watch either, so I hid behind my magazine . . . until Sylvia's off-key, karaoke-club singing blasted me out of my chair. "I'm gonna wash that gray right outta your hair, I'm gonna wash that gray right outta your hair . . ."

And I thought there was no culture in Barley.

Sylvia bent over a drawer in search of a comb, and Mom caught my peeking-over-the-magazine eyes in the mirror and rolled hers. Stifling a snicker, I retreated to the safety of the latest fall movies.

An hour later, Sylvia clicked off the blow-dryer. "Okay. All done. You can look now."

The salon was silent except for the collective sound of three jaws dropping.

"Wow!"

"Gorgeous."

"Is that me?"

"Mom, you look like Cher in *Moonstruck* . . . the night she went to *La Bohème* with Nicolas Cage."

She snorted. "I'm nowhere near as skinny as Cher." She turned her head to check out her profile, a pleased smile tugging at her mouth. "Although I think I just lost five pounds with this new haircut."

Sylvia Ann spoke up. "I think you look more like Elizabeth Taylor in those White Diamonds perfume ads. The early ones."

My mother's newly mascaraed eyes glinted with tears.

"What is it, Mom? What's wrong?"

"Your daddy told me the night we met—I was thirty pounds lighter then—that I looked like a younger Elizabeth Taylor, without as much makeup."

Next stop: the Barley Twist, where I treated Mom to lunch. We each had cups of the lobster bisque and Caesar salads—plain for me, chicken for her.

"Do you want any dessert, Mom?"

"What I really want is a nice juicy steak," she muttered. "I'm still hungry."

"They've got lots of dessert choices, but I recommend the crème brûlée."

"Crim brulay?"

"Jell-O can never be crème brûlée . . ." I flashed on the scene between Julia Roberts and Cameron Diaz in *My Best Friend's Wedding.* "Custard, Mom."

She settled on a thick slice of dense chocolate cake drizzled with raspberry sauce. I stuck to my crème brûlée but took a bite of her luscious cake.

"Yum. Who needs men when there's chocolate?"

She agreed.

Just then, over her shoulder, I noticed Gordon enter the restaurant. He caught my eye and hurried over. "Phoebe, I'm glad I found you. I need to talk to you about . . ." Gordon stopped in midsentence, all of a sudden noticing my stunning lunch companion. He flushed to the roots of his thinning hair. "Oh, I beg your pardon. Please excuse me for barging in."

"That's okay, Gordon," Mom said. "Phoebe and I were just having dessert. Why don't you join us?"

"Gloria?" He did a double take. "I didn't recognize you!"

Now it was her turn to blush. She looked down and fiddled with her fork.

Mouth open, my boss continued to stare. At my *mother*.

"Gordon?" I prompted. "You needed to talk to me about something?"

Flustered, he tore his popping-out eyes away from Mom's loveliness and cleared his throat. "Uh, yes. We need to discuss the uh . . . um . . ."

At that moment, Sydney came over with our bill. Gordon used the diversion to make his escape. "Oh, look at the time. I really need to get back to the office. Phoebe, we'll talk later. Gloria." He gave Mom a brief nod and scurried out, his cardigan flapping in his bewitched wake.

I gave this femme fatale who was my mother an admiring glance. "My, my. You reduced that man to a puddle of melted Jell-O. Amazing what a mere haircut can do."

"Don't be silly, daughter. Gordon and I have known each other forever," she said, reddening again. "You're imagining things. Now let's focus on this fundraiser."

We spent the next half hour discussing the details of the buy-a-theater–seat campaign, going over the notes my sister-in-law had written up. Karen recommended that, considering the size of the town and most people's pocketbooks, we charge no more than a hundred dollars a seat. With the theater capacity of 340 seats, the maximum we could raise would be thirty-four thousand bucks. How-ever, the Bijou also had two sets of box seats on each side, with six seats in each box, for a total of twenty-four additional seats. Karen suggested that since these were premium seats, we should auction them off for five hundred dollars apiece. If all those sold, we would raise an additional twelve thousand.

I sighed. I may not be good with math, but even I knew we would need at least three times that combined amount to save the Bijou. Discouraged, I pushed my unfinished dessert away. "I wish there was something else we could do to raise more money."

"Trust God," Mom said. "He'll provide. *If* He wants the Bijou to stay."

"I know . . ." I said with a sigh.

My mother looked thoughtful. "You know, there *is* another fund-raiser we could consider that might bring in a few more dollars."

I pounced on the possibility. "What?"

"We could do what those English women did in that movie *Calendar Girls*," she said, the corners of her lips turning up. "It's based on a true story of some women in a small English village. They've raised millions as a result of their calendar."

"Mom!"

"What?" She tossed her Liz Taylor tresses and grinned. "Now that I have my new hairstyle, massaged legs, and pretty toes, I'm a brand-new woman. Maybe I should go all out."

"Uh, I don't think Barley's quite ready for that."

Although the posing aspect did give me another idea . . .

We pulled up to my brother and sister-in-law's ten minutes later, taking care to turn off the engine and simply coast into the driveway. I looked at my watch. "Three-fifteen. Okay, that means everyone's home except Jordy. You all set, Mom?"

She tittered. "I think so. Do you really think this will work, dear?"

"Like a charm."

We crept along the side of the house until we reached the front porch. "Let me make sure the coast is clear," I whispered.

I peeked in the front picture window and, not seeing anyone in the living room, motioned Mom over. She took up her position in front of the door, and I adjusted the voluminous black cape she'd borrowed from Sylvia Ann to hide her casts.

Then I nodded at her, rang the doorbell, and flattened myself against the front porch.

We heard footsteps approaching. As they drew near, Mom disguised her voice and sang out, "Avon calling."

Karen opened the door, drying her hands on a towel. She gave the black-caped woman a pleasant smile and said politely, "I'm sorry, but I already have an Avon representative."

Mom couldn't maintain the fiction. She snorted.

Karen's eyes bugged out. "Mom?"

"Who's at the door?" Elizabeth's voice floated from the kitchen.

"Shhh," Mom whispered to Karen.

From inside the house I could hear Lexie and Jacob squeal when they spotted Mom's car out the window. "Gamma's here!" They ran to the door but stopped short at the sight of the dark-haired stranger in the flowing black wrap. "Where's my Gamma?" Lexie asked.

Mom's face split into a wide smile. "I'm right here, Lexie."

Lexie's eyes grew wide as she recognized the voice, but not the face. Then she began to wail.

Uh-oh. Joke's over. I stepped into view and removed the cape concealing Mom's casts. "Look Lexie. See. It's Grandma."

She sniffled. "Gamma?"

"Yes, sweetie. It's me. I'm sorry. I didn't mean to scare you."

After Lexie calmed down and realized this strange woman was in fact her "Gamma," she kept touching her hair in wonder. "Your hair's a different color."

Mom leaned over and whispered. "So are my toes. Want to see?"

Everyone oohed and aahed over Mom's makeover. "Wow, Grandma, you look like a movie star," Elizabeth said.

"Yeah. Like Catherine Zeta-Jones—only with shorter hair," Ashley said.

Jacob chimed in. "You smell really good too."

As everyone gathered around Mother, sweet Ashley sidled up next to me. "Guess what, Aunt Phoebe? Our class is going to help you raise money for the theater too."

"They are? That's great. How?"

She glowed with excitement. "With a fashion show! We're gonna model dresses from the Miss Udderly pageants from the past fifty years." She lowered her voice and flicked her eyes at Mom to make sure she wasn't paying attention. "I'm wearing Grandma's dress, although Mom says it'll need to be taken in a little."

"A little is right, you tiny thing. When I wore it to my sophomore formal, Mom had to let it out a little to fit me."

"Aunt Phoebe . . ." my niece hesitated.

"Yes, sweetie?"

Her words came out all in a rush. "Since you know so much about fashion and everything, do you think you could teach me how to walk and stuff and wear clothes the right way? I've never been on stage before, and it's kind of scary."

Is this a precious child or what? She hasn't a clue how absolutely drop-dead gorgeous she is. "I'd be honored, sweetie. Although my stage experience is pretty limited too. But I've watched plenty of fashion shows on cable, and Lins and I even went to a couple in Cleveland. So I can definitely give you tips. In fact, why don't we start right now?"

Ashley gulped. "Now?"

"No time like the present. Let's go up to your bedroom."

I cleared a space on her bed, popped in a little Beyoncé and sat down cross-legged. "Okay, Ash. Show me what you've got."

My shy niece took a few tentative steps, then stopped. "I feel silly."

"*You* feel silly? Honey, you don't know from silly." I leaped up and struck a pose, sucking in my cheeks, flinging my hair back—which was more than difficult since I had such a short cut—and throwing haughty "I'm a gorgeous supermodel and I'm better than you" looks over my shoulder. If my thighs hadn't started whispering to each other as I strutted around the room, I coulda been a contender.

Ashley began to giggle. So did I. And so did someone outside the bedroom door.

I flung the bedroom door wide, and Lexie and Elizabeth tumbled into the room. "Wanna play too," Lexie said.

"Okay, sweetie, you'll get your chance in a little while, but right now we're going to watch your big sister. Let's let her show us how it's done, okay?" I cranked up the music. "All right. Once more with feeling."

Ashley grinned. This time nothing stopped my beautiful niece. She relaxed and pretended she was walking down a catwalk, tossing her hair and swinging a jacket over her shoulder. The only thing missing was the sullen model look. Which was a good thing.

We applauded. "That's it, Ash," I said. "You're a natural. Work it, girl, work it! Own it. Yeah. Show me some attitude. Uh-huh. That's it. You're the star, babe. It's all about you."

Then I gave my niece two pieces of advice: "Don't let them drown you in makeup, honey. You're only fourteen and you don't need it—would that I could say the same. And don't exchange that beautiful smile for the standard-issue model frown. I've never understood why all these models look so mad all the time. Although I'm guessing it's not anger, but hunger. I'd probably look that way too if all I ate all day was a stalk of celery and a little pile of bean sprouts."

"My turn, my turn, An Beebee," Lexie said. "Wanna look pretty like Gamma and Ashley."

I grabbed my cosmetics from my purse and went to work. A pat of powder here, a trace of lipstick there, and some pretty beads around her neck. When I was finished, Lexie looked in the mirror and clapped her hands. Then she wrapped her chubby little arms around my neck and planted a big, wet kiss on my cheek. "I wuv you, An Beebee."

Major kidling surge. *Now I know how Kate Hudson felt in* Raising Helen. *Except there's no good-looking John Corbett as Pastor Dan the school principal to fall for.* C'est la vie.

As soon as I left Jordy's, I text-messaged an SOS to Lins: "Help, I'm gettng hrmonl. Nd choclte, Chinese, or shppng fix quik."

She text-messaged right back: "Choclte on way! How r u? Miss u L Guess wht? Alex not dating H.L. hottie now. Someone new, Phil says. Frm work maybe?"

That night Mary Jo and I had Chinese takeout at the home of Pastor Jeff and his wife, Amy.

Passing the little white carton of sweet-and-sour pork, I asked Amy, "So, what kind of movies do you like?"

"Careful," Mary Jo warned, "this is a test."

"A test?" Redheaded Amy looked at me with confusion.

"Pay no attention to that woman behind the curtain," I said.

Jeff snapped his fingers. "Hey, that's from *The Wizard of Oz!*"

"Well you passed with flying colors," Mary Jo said. "Verdict's still out on you, though, Amy."

"Don't be silly, Mary Jo," I said.

"What?" she asked, feigning innocence. "Go ahead, Amy. Answer Phoebe's movie question. What kind of movies?"

Amy's head swiveled back and forth between us, red curls bouncing. "Well, Jeff and I have spent a lot of time in Britain," she said, "so I'm partial to English films, especially the ones based on literature—like

Persuasion or *Sense and Sensibility*. But in general I guess I like the classics. You know—old movies."

"Ding, ding, ding!" Mary Jo said. "Congratulations! You've won the grand prize—Phoebe's friendship."

I shot Mary Jo a dirty look, but she just smiled at me.

"I almost didn't make it into the inner sanctum because I don't watch movies too often," Mary Jo said. "It was pretty touch and go for a minute there, but then John Wayne and the cavalry rode up and saved the day. Whew," she said, wiping the pretend sweat from her brow, "good thing I like Westerns."

Jeff laughed. Amy giggled. And I pretended to glower.

Mary Jo winked at me. "'Course I like any movie with horses in it. TV shows too. *Mister Ed* was my favorite."

I threw back my head and laughed.

"Hey Pheebs," Mary Jo said, changing gears. "Tell us about your army days."

"Air force. Big difference."

"Sure is," Jeff said. "I'm an air-force brat—my dad was a pilot—and I know you don't dare confuse the branches of service. They've got that whole rivalry thing going on."

We smiled in mutual understanding.

"Army, air force—whatever," Mary Jo said. "So was boot camp really like in *An Officer and a Gentleman*? I loved that movie when I was a teenager."

"It's called basic training in the air force," I sniffed. "That movie was about the navy. And they were going through pilot *officer* training. I was a lowly enlisted type."

"Did you have to go through one of those awful obstacle courses?" Amy asked, crunching on an egg roll.

"Yep. Except there was no Richard Gere urging me to climb the wall. We had to do it on our own. *And* swing across this muddy pond on a rope. *And* run three miles. But that was just one day out of the whole six weeks. No big deal. It was the day-in and day-out stuff that was tough."

Mary Jo took a bite of her shrimp lo mein. "Like what?"

"Like getting up at five every single day—'It is now oh-five-hundred hours. All airmen will be up. All airmen will be awake.' Like folding our underwear into equal thirds, polishing our ugly shoes with a cut-up pair of nylons, and sleeping in a room with thirty-nine other women—no music, no TV, no contact with the opposite sex. And doing stupid things just to show that we could follow orders—like the time we had to march an errant dust bunny down to the latrine and give it a proper military send-off."

Amy nearly choked on her egg roll. "You've got to be kidding!"

"Nope. Although, come to think of it, that was kind of fun. So was the marching." I smiled at the memory. "The assistant training instructor always did one of those call-and-response cadences as she marched us to the chow hall, like this." I began marching around the room and singsonging both parts, motioning to my companions to join in:

> I got a guy in San Antone.
> *I got a guy in San Antone.*
>
> We swap kisses by telephone.
> *We swap kisses by telephone.*
>
> Am I right or wrong?
> *You're right!*
>
> Correct me if I'm wrong.
> *You're right!*
>
> Am I right, or am I wrong, or am I right or wrong?
> *You're right!*
>
> Sound off.
> *One, two.*
>
> Sound off.
> *Three, four.*

Sound off.

One, two, three, four. One-two-oo, three-four!"

By this time Jeff, Amy, and Mary Jo were laughing and signaling "enough," so I sat down, grinning.

"I can't believe it," said Mary Jo. "This from a woman who had to be coaxed and dragged up to the karaoke stage."

"Well, nobody cared what we sounded like, as long as it was loud," I said. "And like I told you, it was sort of fun."

"Sounds like a barrel of laughs to me," said Amy, shaking her head and laughing.

"What wasn't fun," I added, "was when I had to scrub every inch of the barracks latrine—with a toothbrush. I knew just how Richard felt, although I doubt he had to scrub as much as I did. His toothbrush stunt man probably took over for him."

"Well, I gotta give you your props," Mary Jo said. "When you joined the military after high school, I was pretty surprised—we all were. I mean, you'd always been such a girly-girl. We never thought you'd make it through boot camp—uh, basic training."

"You'd be surprised what you can do when you have to."

"Yeah, but that's just my point. You didn't have to. You volunteered. You *wanted* to do it."

"What I wanted was to get out of town and see the world." I gave her a mock-haughty glare. "I had my dreams, you know."

I didn't add that I'd spent most of my glamorous military career typing forms in Dayton, Ohio.

Mary Jo broke open her fortune cookie. "The thing that *does* surprise me is that after all that order and discipline, you're not more organized."

"It surprised my mom too. It's called 'I don't *have* to anymore, and you can't make me.'"

Jeff slid a smile at his wife, then raised his eyebrows at me.

"Hmmm," he murmured. "Rebellious much?"

Wednesday afternoon found me sitting in on an emergency meeting of the Board of Directors of the Barley Cemetery District. The board was voting whether or not to allow a statue of Norm Anderson's beloved pet pig, Anastasia, in the town cemetery.

"I don't see what the problem is," Norm bellowed. "Mildred Kramer put up that monument to her stupid little poodle that used to nip at everyone and do his business in everybody's front yard. My Anastasia never hurt no one, and she respected other people's space." He hitched up his below-the-belly jeans. "Besides, when I was stationed in England, I visited an old village church out in the countryside—must've been three hundred years old. When I was walkin' through the court-yard, I saw this cute li'l statue. It was Tiddles, the church cat—they'd buried him on the grounds."

"Cats are a different story," said Betty Dixon, whom everyone knew had at least three cats of her own. Probably more like six or seven, but because of the local ordinances, she just couldn't own up to the exact number.

Norm got real quiet. "Why's that?"

She flushed. "Well, because a cat's a pet, as are dogs—more like members of the family. And a pig—well, a pig's a dirty barnyard animal."

"My Anastasia never spent one night in no barn," Norm said. "She had her own special bed inside by the fireplace. Besides, I heard that actor George Clooney has a pot-bellied pig, and his relationship with that pig's lasted longer than any of his girlfriends . . ."

That would be because he's another commitment-phobic guy—albeit a gorgeous one. I think he's holding out for me . . .

"I just don't want our cemetery to be a laughingstock," Betty said, "with some big ol' stupid pig statue."

In the end, however, a four-to-three vote determined that Norm could erect a statue to Anastasia, "Just as long as it is small and taste-ful, and near the back of the cemetery."

After the meeting, several people came up to me to say hello.

"Welcome home, Phoebe. Nice to have you back! Bet your mama's real happy to have you home at last."

"Phoebe, good to see you. Tell your mother I hope she's well enough in time to bring one of her delicious pumpkin pies to the church har-vest festival."

"Nice how you've settled right back in—with a job and everything. Why, it's like you've never been gone!"

Only for thirteen years.

As I typed up my notes from the board meeting, I considered how to best attract more customers to the theater *and* write some reviews that I could collect for my New York portfolio.

"Hey Gordon, what do you think of the idea of having a classics night at the Bijou once a week to introduce a whole new generation to some oldies? I could draw attention to it by writing a preview of the movie in the paper."

"I get it." He smiled and spoke in a high, adolescent voice. "'I've got a barn, let's put on a show!'"

"Why, Andy Hardy," I replied with my best Judy Garland impres-sion, clapping my hands in delight. "What a wonderful idea. Wonderful!"

"Any thoughts on where to start?"

"How about *It Happened One Night?* It swept the 1934 Oscars—best picture, director, actor, and actress."

"Yeah." Gordon snapped his suspenders. "The only film to do so until *One Flew over the Cuckoo's Nest* in the seventies."

Oh, he thinks he knows his movie trivia, huh?

"Yes, but did you know how *It Happened One Night* changed the fashion industry?"

He shook his head.

I set the scene. "Clark Gable is getting ready for bed. He takes off his shirt to put on his pj's and he's *not* wearing an undershirt. And that was that. T-shirt sales plummeted."

Gordon scratched his head. "I didn't know that."

"Yep. And Tinseltown's been telling us how to dress ever since."

"Sounds like a great idea, Phoebe. If George Henderson's willing to run a classic at his theater once a week, I'll put your previews in the paper."

That was a big relief after all the small-town, country stuff I'd been reporting. *Look out New York, here I come!*

But Gordon was saying, "Hey Phoebe, I need you to go out to Herbert Ritter's farm and do a feature on his prize emus."

"Emus?"

"Yep. They're kind of like ostriches."

"I know what an emu is." *Just wish I was one so I could bury my head in the sand and get out of this assignment.*

It wouldn't have been so bad, however, if one of the emus hadn't decided to take a love bite out of my neck.

Most male affection I've gotten in years.

chapter seventeen

Pheebs, you have to!" my desperate sister-in-law pleaded.

I stood my ground. "No way. I'm not a singer, remember?"

"You don't have to be a singer—and besides, there's no one else who can do it," Karen begged. "Tell her, Jordy."

"Aw, c'mon, Pheebert," my brother coaxed. "Why don't you help Karen out? What are you afraid of? You know you can do it—no big deal."

I snorted. "Right. Then why don't *you* do it?"

My brother grinned. "'Cause I don't look so good in a skirt."

"There's got to be someone else . . ." I said. Just then I had an inspiration flash. "What about you, Karen? You know it backward and forward. Why don't *you* step in instead?"

My sister-in-law looked down at her eight-months-pregnant stomach and smiled, "That would give a whole new meaning to the lyric, 'I'm Just a Girl Who Cain't Say No.'"

Jordy laughed and hugged his wife. "Sure glad you didn't say no, honey."

Karen blushed. "None of that now. We're in a crisis situation here. The show opens tonight, and our Ado Annie is stuck in a hospital in Lodi with a broken leg. We have to find a replacement and you're the only natural choice, Pheebs. You've been to nearly every rehearsal since you got here and you know the show inside out."

"But—"

Mom interrupted. "That's right, daughter. Besides, I know you remember the words—you sang them for me and your daddy at your tenth birthday party."

"That was over twenty years ago, Mom."

"Maybe," she continued, undeterred, "but once you memorize something, you never forget it, 'specially when it comes to songs. You're just like your daddy that way."

Jordy grinned. "Mom's right. Besides, remember what Dad always said?"

We smiled together in fond remembrance and chorused, "The curtain must rise."

"Don't worry, Phoebe," Karen said. "Ado Annie doesn't need to have a great voice. She's the comic relief. Just play it for laughs and you'll be fine."

"Easy for you to say, Madame Director. You're not the one who's going to be onstage making a fool of herself." I sighed. "Oh well, I guess if I can sing at Carnegie Hall, I can sing at the Bijou."

Remember, this is small-town Barley. None of your Cleveland friends will ever see the show. No potential dates either, since everyone in town's already married, spoken for, or involved with monster-truck rallies. So no worries there. Plus, you only have a few more weeks left of your sentence to the sticks—and this familial favor should keep you in good standing for quite a while.

I kept reminding myself of all this as Mom and her church friend Louise, whom she'd pressed into last-minute service, conferred about the costume I needed to wear in a few short hours. I'd pulled the calico-print dress over my head, and although the full skirt slid down effortlessly, the waist was another story.

I felt like the little brother Randy in *A Christmas Story,* whose mom had stuffed him into a snug snowsuit. "I can't put my arms down!" he wailed.

Neither could I. I couldn't even get my arms into the sleeves.

"Knew I shouldn't have eaten all those nachos," I said as I tried to wiggle up into the tight bodice. "That skinny kid they made the dress for probably never lets gooey cheese, chips, and sour cream even pass her lips." *Note to self: Never eat fats or carbohydrates again—unless they're chocolate-covered.*

"That girl's *too* skinny, daughter. She looks almost anorexic. You've got curves—the way the good Lord intended women to be."

"Couldn't agree with you more, Gloria," said the self-proclaimed fat and sassy Louise. "Unfortunately, the good Lord didn't make this costume." She considered for a moment. "We can let the seams out some. That should help."

Mom circled me. "Yes-s, but I'm not sure it will be enough."

"Hel-looow," I said in my best Billy Crystal, *City Slickers* voice, muffled as it was through yards of calico. "I'm dyin' here!"

"Oh, sorry dear," Louise said, pulling the claustrophobic garment back up over my head. Then she grabbed Mom's seam ripper and went to work.

I snorted. "Good luck with that, Louise. You'll have to be a miracle worker to make up the difference."

Mom, who must have been thinking the same thing, suddenly snapped her fingers. (Yes, even with casts—although the plaster did muffle the sound a bit.) "I've got it!" she said. "Follow me, daughter." And she headed down the hall to her bedroom.

Five minutes later I was lying on my back on Mom's bed, sucking in everything I had—including my breath—as I struggled to pull the ancient girdle up over my hips.

Mom tried to help, but this time her casts got in the way.

"We need reinforcements," she declared, raising her voice. "Louise, can you come in here, please?"

"Oh my," Louise said upon entering the room. "I haven't seen one of those in years."

"Me either," I muttered, remembering back to when we were kids and Jordy and I had used a discarded one of Mom's as a gigantic slingshot.

Louise lent a hand and began tugging as well, but to no avail. "Boy, I'd forgotten how heavy-duty these things are!"

"I got it for the Miss Udderly pageant," Mom explained. "They were starting to go out of style, but I'd put on a few pounds and I—"

Just then a knock sounded at the back door. "Come in," my mother yelled, unwilling to leave her girdle-guiding position.

"Mom! You don't know who it is! It could be anyone—including the UPS man."

"Oh no," she reassured me, "he only comes at Christmas."

Karen's voice filtered down the hall. "Where *is* everybody?"

"In my room, dear. Come on down. We could use your help."

My sister-in-law appeared in the doorway with Ashley and Elizabeth. At the strange sight that greeted them, ten-year-old Elizabeth said, "What are they doing to Aunt Phoebe?"

Through her guffaws, Karen explained.

I glared at her. "You'd better quit laughing and get on over here and help, or this girl will find it very easy to say no."

She snickered and tried to rearrange her features into a solicitous expression. Failing that, she turned her face so all I saw was her profile as she instructed her daughters in the all but forgotten art of girdle application. "Okay, girls, you go on one side of the bed and grab hold of the right leg while Louise and I take the left, then we'll all pull together. Got it? Okay . . . one, two, three, *go*!"

The four females grunted and tugged in tandem while Mom murmured words of encouragement—"Heave ho! Heave ho!"—and I helped by sucking everything in, lifting my backside off the bed, and yanking on the waistband.

Success at last.

"Now I know how Scarlett felt after Mammy finished cinching her into a corset," I said. "Although even with this, I'm a far cry from her seventeen-inch waist."

That night as I stood backstage shaking in my calico costume waiting for my cue to go on, I had to admit that Mom was right—the oversized piece of Lycra around my middle definitely did hold everything in place. And then some.

How did women breathe in these things, much less move? Oh, that's right—they didn't. They just sat on the porch surrounded by beaus, sipping lemonade, and saying "Oh, fiddle-de-dee!" But never mind that. You've got more important things to worry about, girl. Like your lines. Especially the one you keep flubbing. Focus, Phoebe, focus. Whoops. There's my cue!

I strode onstage with pterodactyls doing claw-to-claw combat in my stomach. It was no stretch to affect the wide-eyed, disingenuous Ado Annie persona—my eyes were already bugging out from the combined strain of the iron corset and performance anxiety. But after my first few off-key notes, as the sound of snickers and chuckles and then full-on belly laughs reached my ears, I began to relax. Encouraged, I hammed it up for the audience even more, playing my second-banana role to the hilt and only stumbling over a few of my lines until it came time for the one I always messed up—and flubbed it yet again. Mortified, I tried to compensate by belting out my song with more off-key gusto.

When the curtain finally fell, it was all I could do not to stampede to the nearest exit. But the teenaged boy playing my fiancé, Will, wasn't having any of that. "Not so fast, Miss Ado Annie. We've still got our curtain call."

When it was my turn to take a bow, the crowd whistled and stamped its feet.

Whoa, so that's what the roar of the crowd and the smell of the greasepaint's all about. Hmmm, maybe it's time for this girl to change careers. Just call me Meryl . . .

Flush from my triumph, I attempted a dramatic theatrical bow, only to discover I should have gone for a girlish curtsey instead. Still encased in Lycra, I learned that returning to an upright position again was a bit of a challenge. Thankfully the curtain came down at that point, and the cast, led by my director sister-in-law, rushed over to help me unbend. Then they all gave me exultant high-fives.

Mom, Jordy and the kids were the first ones backstage to congratulate me. "Your dad would have been proud," my mother said with tear-filled eyes.

"An Beebee, how come your face is all red?" asked Lexie.

I smiled at my young niece past the lump in my throat. "'Cause Grandma's old girdle is cutting off all my circulation. Boy, I can't wait to get out of this thing."

"Um . . . hold that thought." My boss's voice cut through the crowd behind me. "Congratulations, star reporter. I always said you had talent."

"Gordon!" I whirled around to give him a hug.

And came face-to-face with my Cleveland nemesis, Alex Spencer.

Short, gorgeous, intelligent, snake-in-the-grass Alex Spencer.

Stunned speechless, all I could do was stare. *Of all the theaters, in all the towns, in all the world, he walks into mine.*

And then the corporate raider who'd destroyed my career dreams had the nerve to smile.

"Phoebe, nice to see you again." He moved toward me, and I backed away as fast as my girdle-encased body would allow, but not fast enough to stop him from giving me the mother of all bear hugs. "That's from Lindsey," he said. "She misses you and sends her love. Phil, too."

I refrained from slapping him silly—a little too romance-novelish for me, especially with the crowd of curious friends and family looking on. But giving him the stiff-backed, deep-freeze treatment was no trouble at all. The girdle helped.

"Phoebe, I'd like to speak to you," he said when he'd released me. Glancing around at the group of onlookers, he added. "Alone if I could."

Catching a hopeful glance between Mom and Gordon, I went into my polite but dismissive, not-in-this-lifetime-buddy mode. "Sorry. That won't be possible. I need to change and get to my brother's for the cast party. Karen, Ashley, you coming?"

Karen looked torn. "Um, Pheebs I need to get home and . . ."

"Not to worry," said Mary Jo, who'd just arrived and caught the end of the conversation. "Ashley and I will help Phoebe and join you in a few minutes."

Grateful, I said my good-byes. Then I turned and made as dignified an exit as I could with my Lycra-clad thighs swish-swishing against each other in chummy hip-hop harmony.

Ashley and Mary Jo followed me offstage and my 4-H friend whispered, "Who's the hunka burnin' love?"

I sniffed. "Just the jerk who cost me my job back in Cleveland. Although I can't imagine what he's doing here." A terrible thought struck. "Unless it's to take over the *Bulletin.* I wouldn't put that past him."

But my current state of imprisonment cut off my speculation at the waist. "But never mind about that now." I segued into Scarlett mode. "If I don't get out of this thing right now, I declare I'm going to swoon."

After Mary Jo helped divest me of the snug calico dress, I lay down on the dressing room couch, once again sucking everything in as she and Ashley each took a leg and tugged at Mom's sixties-era instrument of torture while I pushed down from the waist. Try as we would, however, it simply wouldn't budge.

Grunting from the exertion, I said, "This is my punishment for being a bad daughter—stuck forever in my mother's underwear. Guess I should have used baby powder."

Ashley rummaged around the dressing table. "There's some here, Aunt Phoebe. Why don't we try it now?"

"Great idea!" Mary Jo helped me struggle to a sitting position, then I peeled back the foundation garment waistband with one hand while sprinkling in powder with the other. But the recalcitrant restraint wouldn't cooperate. The rubber corset snapped back into place, sending a cloud of powder in the air, which set us all to sneezing and coughing.

As the powder settled, my niece looked at me thoughtfully. "You know at the fair when they have those greased pigs? Well, those pigs get real slippery, Aunt Phoebe. Maybe we could figure out a way to make you more slippery so the girdle would come off."

"What—I'm a pig now?"

Ashley looked horrified. "Oh no, Aunt Phoebe. That's not what I meant at all! I was—"

I winked. "Just giving you a hard time, sweetie. Sorry to be giving you *both* such a hard time with this ridiculous underwear."

"Guess there's only one thing left to do," my horsy high-school classmate said. "Be right back." Moments later she returned. "Time to bring out the heavy hardware," Mary Jo said, advancing toward me and brandishing a gleaming instrument of torture. "These were out in my truck. Remember the Girl Scout motto: 'Be prepared.'"

"Uh, I think that was the Boy Scouts," my niece said.

"Whatever." Mary Jo continued advancing toward me.

"Do you have a license to operate those things?"

"Don't be such a wuss, Phoebe. These garden shears will cut through anything. Why, I even used them in an emergency to cut the umbilical cord on one of my foals."

"Not that same pair, I hope."

"Yep, this same pair. Don't worry, I cleaned and sterilized them afterward. Man, you're such a priss. Don't know how you've lasted this long."

"It's called living in the city."

"Not to worry, Pheebs. If these babies can cut through an umbilical cord and a privet hedge, I'm sure they can slice their way through a l'il ol' ancient girdle."

All the same, I squeezed my eyes shut tight as she started cutting.

Mary Jo snipped the last inch of industrial-strength fabric loose and my thighs sighed in relief. At the same time, without warning, the Latex missile shot across the couch and ricocheted off the nearby wall. Thwap. On its return, one of the garters snapped me in the forehead before coming to rest in rubberized peace on the floor. Ashley and Mary Jo wound up there too, weak with laughter and clutching their sides. Rubbing my tender head, I slid off the couch in helpless abandonment and joined them in the laughing pile.

We were still giggling fifteen minutes later when we finally waltzed in to Karen and Jordy's for the cast party.

"Get this woman some chocolate," Mary Jo ordered. "She deserves it."

A hand proffered a plate bearing a slice of my mom's rich double-fudge cake with buttercream frosting. "Will this do?"

I stopped in midreach. *Is there no escaping this creep?*

"Nice outfit," said Alex Spencer, glancing at my black, straight-leg pants and red silk shirt. "Suits you better than calico."

Pulling myself up to my full height—in heels, a good couple inches taller than Tom Thumb the publisher man—I started to refuse his cake offer, but Mom chose that moment to appear at my elbow, Elizabeth close on her heels bearing a tray of desserts. "Mr. Spencer, would you care for some of my pumpkin pie?"

His eyes raked the tray with a lean and hungry look. "I've already had a piece of this delicious chocolate cake," he indicated the plate in his hand I had yet to accept. "But pumpkin pie *is* my favorite," he said, casting a longing glance at a large slice laden with whipped cream.

"We've got plenty for everyone," Mom said. "You go on now and take that one."

There was no way around it. I *had* to relieve him of the piece of cake so his hands would be free for the pie he was drooling over—although we nearly had a chocolate disaster when he fumbled the plate in the exchange.

Clumsy much?

He reddened. "Thank you so much, Mrs. Grant."

"Please. Call me Gloria. Everyone does."

He took a bite, shutting his eyes in appreciation and winding up with whipped cream on the side of his mouth. "Gloria, this is about the best pumpkin pie I've ever tasted."

Mom flushed with pride. "Thank you, Mr. Spencer. My recipe took first place at our local fair."

Elizabeth piped up. "You've got whipped cream on your face."

He flushed again and wiped his mouth with a napkin. "Thanks."

"You're welcome," my niece said. "Bet you didn't know my Grandma's pumpkin pie has won the blue ribbon the past seven years in a row."

He smiled at Elizabeth. "I'm not surprised. It's delicious." Then he addressed Mom again. "Gloria? Turnabout is fair play. Please call me Alex."

"All right," she said, succumbing. "Alex."

Needing to escape this mutual love-fest before I tossed my cookies *and* my cake, I started to move away, but my mother body-blocked me. "You know, Alex, I'm teaching Phoebe how to make all my family recipes. She's becoming quite the cook," she said, beaming at me. "In fact, she was the one who actually put together the pie—seeing as how I'm temporarily out of commission."

As she held up her now beat-up casts to demonstrate, I telegraphed an SOS to Jordy behind her back. In seconds, my brother was at my side. "Hey Mom, Karen needs your help—something about how to slice a pumpkin roll?"

She excused herself as Jordy and Alex sized each other up.

"So, you're the guy who cost my little sister her job, huh?"

Great. Let's just go from cramming my domestic virtues résumé down his throat to asking him to step aside. What's with the 'shall we take this outside, Pilgrim' protective-brother mode? For that matter, what about me? Am I the incredible invisible woman or something? Hel-looow. Still in the room here, guys.

Thankfully, the sound of someone's fork tapping on a glass of cider brought relief. "Hey, everyone, can I have your attention for a moment, please?" said Gordon, who had climbed on the fireplace hearth to be seen and heard over the rumble of the crowd.

"Will you excuse me, please?" Alex said, turning to join my boss.

I got a sick feeling not only in the pit of my stomach, as every dime store novel says, but throughout every cell in my entire body. Grabbing Alex's arm, I yanked him out of my brother's earshot. "What *is* it with you?" I hissed. "Don't you have anything better to do than to follow me around the country and pull the newsprint out from under me?"

He quirked an eyebrow at me. "It's not all about you."

You're right. It's not. I have options. But whatever is poor Gordon going to do? All he knows is this paper! He can't do anything else, and he's too old to start something new . . .

I started to voice my thoughts aloud, but poor Gordon smiled and cleared his throat, quieting the room. "Some of you have already met my guest tonight, but for those of you who haven't, I'd like to introduce him to you."

"That's my cue," Alex said. "We'll have to continue this later."

Gordon beamed at the younger man who was about to relieve him of his livelihood. "Alex Spencer here is part of the Spencer publishing dynasty, and he has a special announcement he'd like to make."

"I wonder how he sleeps at night," I muttered to Jordy, "the money-grubbing sleazebag."

"Shhh."

Power-hungry newspaper stealer took the floor. "Thanks, Gordon, and good evening, everyone. First, let me say how much I appreciate your warm welcome and hospitality. I've had quite an enjoyable night watching the funniest production of *Oklahoma* I've ever seen."

A round of clapping and a few scattered cheers from cast members greeted his remarks.

"He should start a new career as a politician," I mumbled to my brother.

Jordy elbowed me.

When the applause died down, Alex said, "An added bonus has been Gloria Grant's prizewinning pumpkin pie . . ."

Mom flushed as Gordon glowed at her and everyone applauded again.

Not wanting to be elbowed again, I kept my thoughts to myself this time. *Way to work the crowd, bucko. Give the simple folk a few warm fuzzies before you stab one of their own in the back, you corporate-raiding, pie-eating, Trivial Pursuit–playing Judas.*

He sent a Cheshire cat grin my direction as he waited for the applause to end. *How dare you find this funny, you arrogant suit! How can Phil be friends with you? I'm* so *going to let him and everyone else know what a lying, manipulative marauder you are.*

Alex continued. "This week, a new friend of mine who knows I'm in the newspaper business showed me an article a friend of his had written," he said. "His friend was your own Phoebe Grant, and the article was her recent *Bulletin* editorial about the Bijou—"

"Go, Aunt Phoebe!" Ashley interrupted.

Alex smiled at my eldest niece. "I was so taken by the impassioned plea to save your theater that I had to come see this historic building up close and personal."

Gordon beckoned me forward. I went like a lamb to the slaughter.

The phony, trying-to-make-nice media magnate reached into his pocket. "Gordon, Phoebe, as a movie lover myself, I wanted to present you with a check for five thousand dollars to help save this beautiful theater."

Esther snapped a photo of Alex handing us the check. The room erupted in applause, and several people pulled out their checkbooks and started swarming Gordon.

During the hubbub, Alex pulled me aside. "Ah, alone at last," he said, with a grin. "You were saying?"

I glared at him and cast a pointed look at his hand on my arm.

He dropped his hand. "Sorry. Look, Phoebe, here's the deal. Making a donation to the Bijou fund-raising drive wasn't the only reason I came to town."

I knew it! "Go on. I'm waiting for the other shoe to drop."

"Actually, *you're* the main reason I'm here," he said. "I'd like to offer you a job."

I gaped at him.

"Careful," he said, with a wink. "You might catch flies that way."

My mouth snapped shut.

"No, really," he said. "After Phil showed me your editorial, I was really impressed with your writing—so impressed that I went through some back copies of the *Star* and checked out your movie reviews. You're good. Very good. You should be playing with the big guys. That's why I want to offer you a position at our Boston paper. They've got an opening for an arts-and-entertainment reporter, and there's room in the job for movie reviews . . ."

He lowered his voice and looked straight at me. "This David and Goliath, tugging at the heartstrings bit can only take you so far, Phoebe," he said. "Phil says you want to write for the *Times.* And to do that, you'll need clips from another major metropolitan daily. So what do you say?"

For a minute I just stared at him. I couldn't believe I'd been offered the stepping-stone job I wanted so desperately—and by the same corporate know-it-all with the little-man complex who'd ruined my life before.

I'll admit it. I was tempted. But then I came to my senses.

"There's no way I'd ever work for you." Then I turned on my heel and left.

chapter eighteen

So, have you heard from the media mogul since he left town?" Mary Jo asked as she mucked out her stables.

I backed away from my 4-H pal as a heady whiff of manure assaulted my city-girl nostrils. "Not since I turned him down flat on his job offer. If my writing's good enough for him to offer me a job on a big daily, then it's good enough for other major metropolitan markets too. Say, New York."

Mary Jo ceased her mucking for a moment to push her hair behind her ears. "You did thank him for the donation, didn't you?"

I'd been eating thick-crust humble pie for the past few days among my family and friends ever since I'd been proven wrong about Alex Spencer and his motives for visiting Barley. "Of course. What do you think—I was raised in a barn or something?" Too late, I realized what I'd said and clapped my hand over my mouth, contrite.

She didn't take offense. Instead, she cast a wry glance at my stiletto boots as she continued raking hay. "If you were raised in a barn, you'd know better than to wear high heels in one. Have you forgotten everything you learned about living in the country?"

I picked my way daintily around my stable-mucking friend—backing up against a nearby stall in an effort to put as much distance between my precious red Anne Kleins and her pile of serious horse droppings mixed with hay. "No, but I'm trying to."

At that instant my cell rang, setting off a chain of events that remain fuzzy to this day. Startled, the horse behind me bucked in surprise, then surprised *me* by nudging me none too gently with his nose, so that I pitched forward into the pile of raked hay and unmentionables.

"Ew! Gross!" Good thing I'd instinctively thrust out my hands to protect myself. It could have been my face that landed in the stinky, smelly mess.

Lord, this would never happen in New York. Please, You gotta get me outta here. Soon!

All of a sudden, above the sound of my still-ringing cell, which seemed to have fallen out of my purse in the melee, I heard a snorting noise behind me. I glared at my four-footed attacker as I tried to extricate myself from the mess of manure and straw. "Mister Ed," I told him sternly, "if I were you, I wouldn't be making a sound right now."

But it wasn't the horse making noises. It was Mary Jo, doubled over and gasping for breath.

"Sorry, Phoebe," she said, wiping the tears from her eyes. "It's just that you looked like something from *America's Funniest Home Videos.* Where's my camera when I need it?"

"I'll camera you," I said, holding my nose with one hand and clutching my dirty cell with the other. "I don't know how you can work around all this smelly, disgusting stuff."

"You get used to it. I don't even notice the smell anymore," she said, extending her hand to help me up, while at the same time stifling another snort of laughter. "Sorry, Pheebs. I know this isn't what you bargained for when you came out to visit today. C'mon—you can take a shower up at the house. I can lend you some clean clothes."

Half an hour later, I was sitting in Mary Jo's country kitchen drinking a cup of coffee and swimming in a pair of jeans and a sweatshirt that listed ten reasons a woman's best friend is her horse.

"This is false advertising, you know." I sniffed. "I can think of ten reasons why a horse is not *this* woman's best friend."

She grinned and set a half-eaten package of Oreos on the table, then grabbed a gallon of 1% milk from the fridge and poured herself a glass. "Sorry, Pheebs, all my other shirts are in the dirty clothes." Mary Jo dunked an Oreo in her milk. "So what's going on between you and the very hot Alex Spencer anyway?"

"Nothing. Absolutely nothing. Less than nothing, in fact."

She bit into the soggy half of her cookie before it could fall into her milk, raising her eyebrows at me in the process.

"Seriously." I decided it was time to give her the short version. "I met him about a month or so ago in Cleveland, when he showed up at our singles group one night. And sure, I was attracted to him before I knew any better. Thought he was pretty good-looking—except for the height thing. I've always preferred my men on the taller side."

Mary Jo nodded, her mouth full.

"Plus he goes to church, knows a bit more about movies than the average guy, *and* plays a mean game of Trivial Pursuit."

Her eyebrows rose higher.

"But . . ." I licked the middle of an Oreo. " . . . that creep is responsible for my losing my job, my apartment, *and* my life as I knew it. If not for him, I wouldn't be stuck back here in Barley again."

"Is that such a bad thing?"

"Not if you're a horse or a cow. And only if you want a life beyond mud, manure, and motherhood." I sighed. "No offense, Mary Jo, but I'm just not a small-town girl. If you had any doubts, look at what happened here today and out at the fairgrounds last week. I simply don't fit in here."

I don't want *to fit in here.*

"Right. So that's why you've got a whole town behind your drive to save the Bijou," Mary Jo said. "Look, I'm not saying this is gospel, but could it be at all possible that Alex Spencer is just the vehicle God's using to make some changes in your life? Did you ever think that maybe God allowed all this to happen because He wanted you here for some reason?" She took a gulp of her milk. "So maybe Alex is all part of His big cosmic plan?"

I snorted. Then thought about it.

Could that be, Lord? Is *Alex Spencer a vehicle?*

Yep, my cynical self replied. *A Hummer that crushes everything in its path.*

"I wonder . . ." I said aloud. "Did God really bring that man into my life to set off that negative chain of events that had me wind up back here? It does seem a little coincidental that there were *no* writing jobs to be had in the entire city of Cleveland. And I come to Barley and get one of the only writing jobs in town." I gave serious consideration to all the cosmic-plan possibilities.

"Then again, maybe not." Mary Jo dunked another Oreo. "Maybe he's just a rich, good-looking, sparks-flying jerk."

I sprayed a mouthful of coffee down the horsey T-shirt. "Sorry. Don't hold back now, Mary Jo. Tell me what you really think." I sighed again. "I've been asking God for months what He wants, *where* He wants me, what He wants me to do, but He hasn't exactly given me any neon signs or thunderbolts. Plus, I really don't see how Alex Spencer can be part of God's plan for me. He's a rich high muckety-muck. And I— I'm simply covered in muck."

This time it was Mary Jo's turn to spray.

"Ha! Gotcha."

My friend mopped her shirt and gave me a gentle rebuke. "God doesn't usually speak to me in thunderbolts, either, you know. It's more that still, small voice thing."

I wasn't in the mood for a Sunday-school lesson. Changing the subject, I asked, "So, anyone you've got your eye on? I know it's sort of slim pickin's for male company around here—although there's a kind of cute monster-truck guy I could introduce you to, if you don't mind tobacco juice. Do you ever meet any nice traveling salesmen or anything?"

"Nah, not really. I haven't been on a date in so long, I've forgotten what it's like."

"I hear ya on that."

But something in the way Mary Jo said it made me realize it was different than when Lindsey and I said the very same thing. We whined and complained. For Mary Jo, it was a simple statement of fact—and not one she seemed to lose any sleep over either.

I cupped my hands around my coffee. "But don't you *want* to meet someone?"

"I used to, but things have changed over the years, Pheebs. If that's what God has for me, fine. But I kind of get the feeling He doesn't. I think I'm more like Paul."

"As in the apostle Paul, who said 'it is better to marry than to burn with passion'?"

She nodded.

"Er, not to be too personal, Mary Jo, but . . . don't you ever burn with passion?"

We looked at each other across her scarred oak kitchen table and burst out laughing. I still wanted to know, though—not that I had any personal passion issues. "Seriously. Don't you ever struggle with that?"

She drained her milk, licking up the crumbs of Oreo that had collected at the bottom. "Not that much anymore. It's just not that big a problem for me now, which is one of the reasons I think I'll probably stay single. And that's okay. I'm quite happy with my life. I have good friends, a good church family, *and* I get to do what I love for a living. How many people can say that?"

"True. But what about kids?"

"What about them? I'm with kids every day," she said. "I get to hang with them, have fun bonding over horses together, plus get my fair share of hugs and kisses. Besides, if I ever decide I want any of my own—and if that's what God has for me—there's always adoption. But so far, God hasn't given me any nudges in that direction, so I'm content to leave things as they are."

Lord, how'd she get it all together so quick? We're the same age, and I'm nowhere near the same spiritual plane. Must be that nature connection. Is this what they call horse sense?

"So . . . no white picket fence, adoring husband, two kids—one of each—and a dog?"

"Already got the fence and the dog. Husband, too," she said raising her eyes heavenward. "As for kids, dirty diapers aren't exactly one of my favorite things."

"Says the woman who shovels horse manure."

Recalling *my* recent run-in with manure and the ringing cell phone that had started the whole mess, I realized I'd better check my messages to find out who had called.

Christopher. From Cleveland. With a message I never expected. He was *getting married* before heading off to the mission fields of Africa and had called to invite me to his last-minute wedding this weekend.

Christopher, of all people—the guy who never dated. Go figure.

There was also a text message from Lindsey saying the same thing, but giving me the inside track that Chris had neglected to mention. "C's gtng mrryd! Ges who 2? Sarah, the Hethr-Lckler babe—she's a misonry 2!"

I shook my head as I flipped my phone shut. "Will wonders never cease?"

That night at dinner, I broached the subject of my return to Cleveland, thankful to have snared a cheap ticket on lastminute.com. My Visa had been getting quite a workout lately and, even though I was now employed, I was nervous about getting deeper in debt.

My mother blanched, but recovered in record time. "Well, of course, honey. The doctor says I'll get my casts off Monday, so there's really no need for you to stay any longer. I know how much you miss city life and all your friends. I've really appreciated your spending all this time with me, but I know you need to get back to your own life."

"Mom, I'm just going back for a friend's wedding, I'm not staying forev—"

What are you saying, girl? This is your ticket out of here!

You only came to help while Mom was out of commission, my city-girl self reminded me. *After next week, she'll be good as new. You've done your duty. What's to keep you in Barley anymore?*

How 'bout family? my loyal self answered. *You've gotten really close to them lately.*

We can still stay close, I reassured my family self. *I'll phone and e-mail a lot.*

What about a job? my practical self reminded me. *How about a place to live?*

I'll live with Lindsey, my stubborn I-want-my-own-way self argued. *We've always wanted to be roommates. Besides, Cleveland's much closer to New York, where I want to work.*

What about your job here? Planning to leave Gordon in the lurch? And how 'bout the Save the Bijou campaign? Your idea, remember? Are you just going to cut and run now?

Too many selves clamored for attention while Mom watched me with a hopeful expression.

"I don't know if I'll be staying or not yet," I told her. "Depends on whether I find a job. And of course I'd have to give Gordon two weeks notice . . ."

She tried to hide her disappointment. "Of course, daughter. Why, by now I'm sure there are lots of openings for someone with your talent." Now that she'd finally gotten off the matchmaking merry-go-round, Mom had become my biggest career champion.

Outside, a door slammed. Moments later my nephew-and-nieces menagerie came clattering inside. "Aunt Phoebe, guess what happened at rehearsal today?" Ashley said, unable to keep still. "Miss Thomas said I was the best model in the whole group. 'A natural'—that's what she called me."

I smiled at my sweet niece. "See. What did I tell you?"

"Want to practice some more with me?"

"Sure. But only if I get to be Tyra Banks this time."

While I was putting Ashley through her catwalk paces, Mary Jo dropped by.

"Hey Mar, you're just in time," I said. "We're doing the model runway dance. Want to join us?"

She backed out of the room in haste, her flannel shirt flapping in her wake. "Not this woman. Besides, uh, I just remembered, I need to go home and feed Pluto and Sugar."

Ashley and I dissolved in giggles on the bed.

"Mom, are you sure you'll be okay without me when you get your casts removed?" I asked a few days later on our way to the airport.

"Of course. Karen or Jordy can take me into Lodi. I'll be fine. Don't worry about it. You just go have a nice time at your friend's wedding."

Karen, who was driving, agreed. "Not to worry, Pheebs. We've got a handle on it."

"You're coming back, though, aren't you, Aunt Phoebe?" Ashley said. She had the day off school because of a teachers' meeting and had come along to see me off.

"Of course I am."

"But soon?"

"Um, I'm not sure yet."

Ashley looked crestfallen. "Aunt Phoebe, you'll be back for my show, won't you? I couldn't do it without you there."

I reassured my niece. "I'll be there. I promise—no matter what. Count on it, babe."

Tears glistened in both our eyes when I hugged Mom good-bye. She whispered in my ear, "I love you, daughter. Always have. And I've always been proud of you, even though I didn't always show it properly. Whatever happens, you know you've always got a home here."

Once in my seat, I selected the show-tunes channel and adjusted my airline headphones. *Hope corporate-raider-boy Alex Spencer won't be at the wedding. Phil said he's a Lone Rangers regular now.* Suddenly "I'm Just a Girl Who Cain't Say No" filled my ears. I grinned as I remembered my infamous one-night stint as Ado Annie and the before-and-after girdle tugathon.

Other memories from my time in Barley played in my head: the night sounds of frogs and crickets below my bedroom window. The theater fund-raising drive. Teasing—and getting teased by—my big brother again. Savoring the new relationship with my mom. Lexie's chubby little arms around my neck . . .

Stop it right now! my single, adventurous, cosmopolitan self scolded. So I pushed aside thoughts of my family and Barley and focused instead on the city life I'd left behind and sorely missed, but would soon be experiencing again. I recited the litany of missed things over and over: *Lindsey, Phil, the ballet, the art house, great bookstores, No More Lone Rangers, sushi, Thai food, my church, shopping, brunches out after church, my couch, my car, Lindsey . . .*

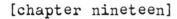

my best friend and I chick-squealed when we saw each other at the airport and flung ourselves into one another's arms. "I've missed you, girl!"

"Ditto, Pheebs. Your couch has been pining too."

Phil relieved me of my bag. "So what am I? Chopped liver?"

I hugged him and gave him an affectionate smile. "No, Phillie. You're pâté de foie gras."

"That's still liver."

"Ah, but it's the most expensive kind. And French too. Ooh la la."

My *la la* froze on my lips, however, as we exited the terminal into the brisk Cleveland air. I pulled my light jacket tighter around me. "Brrr! Guess my blood must have gotten thinner in California. I can't handle this cold weather anymore."

"Spoken like a true California girl," Phil said. "What's next? Blonde hair and tofu?"

I flashed him a sweet smile. "If you're really good, I'll whip you up some while I'm here. I've become quite the cook, you know. Except of course that my Mom would never let any red-meat imposter in her kitchen."

Phil staggered back a step and clutched his chest. "You? Cooking? Never thought I'd hear those two words together in the same sentence."

"Things change." I punched him in the arm.

"That's for sure."

My best friend linked arms with me and urged me forward. "So, Pheebs, tell us all about Barley. How're things going with your mom?

What's up with your cute nieces? Have you seen monster-truck man again? Did an emu *really* feast on your neck?"

"Lins, did you have too much coffee this morning?" I pulled back and gave her a searching look. "You're babbling like a brook on speed."

Phil laughed.

Lindsey shot him a dirty look and said, "Put a sock in it, Phil."

"Ah, that's better." *Now that's the Lins I know and love.*

As we drove to the church, Phil played chauffeur while I freshened my makeup. "Is the whole gang going to be there?"

"Most of them," Lins said, huddled next to me in the backseat so we could gab easier. "Except for Susan—she's out of town visiting relatives." She leaned over with an expectant gleam in her eye. "But another guest is going to fill her spot . . ."

I pulled out my lip liner and held it ready for a smooth stretch of road. "Okay, so who is this mystery guest you're foaming at the mouth to tell me about?"

"Samantha and Colin's *baby*," Lindsey said. "They're pregnant! Can you even believe it? They just found out."

"Of course I can. She's exactly the right age," I said. "He and his mother should be very happy." I smirked. "Must have been something in the water."

Phil snorted. "Yeah, it's called romantic tropical island, honeymoon sand and surf, and years of pent-up sexual frustration all coming together at the same time."

"Phil!" Lindsey said.

"Hmmm. Is someone a little envious?" I met his eyes in the rearview mirror. "Hey, boy, if you want the happily-ever-after and all the attendant benefits, you gotta at least start dating someone."

"Who says I'm not?"

I gaped at him, then gave my gal pal a playful punch. "Lins, you never told me Phillie was seeing someone! Who is she? What's her name? How long has this been going—"

"Phil, wasn't that our exit?" Lindsey was pointing back behind us.

He shrugged. "We can take the next one and circle around—no big deal."

"But we're cutting it a little close, don't you think?"

I looked at her curiously. This concern over being on time was definitely a newly acquired Lindsey trait. I didn't think I had been gone that long, but things just didn't feel quite the same.

Phil grinned at us in the rearview. "Maybe if certain women in the backseat would keep their mouths shut for a change, I could manage to concentrate."

We both stuck out our tongues at him, but I got the point: Don't taunt the driver while he's driving. I decided to save the delicious topic of Phil's love life for later. "Hey, Lins, where are Christopher and his bride—what's her name again?"

"Sarah."

"Right. So where are Chris and Sarah going on their honeymoon?"

Phil snorted again. So much for concentrating on his driving. "Some mud hut in the jungle. Now, that's what I call romantic. A suite at the Plaza or The Four Seasons with four-hundred count Egyptian cotton sheets, mints on the pillow, and room service is much more my style."

"I hear ya on that." I spritzed some breath spray to get rid of that stale airplane mouth. "So what's this Sarah like? I met her a couple of times, but never got to talk to her—she was always surrounded by a posse of panting men," I said, with a pointed glance at Phil in the mirror. "And didn't you tell me that Alex-the-short even got in on the action?"

Lindsey and Phil exchanged glances in the mirror and I remembered Alex and Phil were now friends. Maybe I needed to keep my big mouth shut for a change.

"Sarah is very quiet and sweet," Lindsey was saying, "and she's absolutely perfect for Christopher. She worked as a missionary at an orphanage in Romania for a couple of summers in college and couldn't care less about clothes, cars, houses, or other materialistic trappings. Unlike shallow, superficial you and me. She's not into shopping, movies, or fine dining. She'd much rather hike or go backpacking."

Phil added his two cents. "Yeah, she's nice and sweet. Drop-dead gorgeous, too, but a little too goody-goody for me. Definitely on a higher spiritual plane than the rest of us." He adjusted his silk tie. "I took her out once—to dinner at Chez Panisse—and she went on and on about how much it costs and how that much money would buy food for twenty kids in Romania and how we waste so much food in America. I mean, I know that—*everyone* knows that. That's why I sponsor that kid in Peru. But that wasn't the right time or place to spout a lecture on it. When I take a woman out to a nice restaurant, I want her to at least appreciate it."

Lindsey winked at me. "Poor Phil. The gorgeous blonde wasn't impressed with his platinum American Express."

I snapped my compact shut. "Didn't she go out with Jake too? How'd she fare with Lone Ranger's resident lady-killer?"

Lindsey hooted. "She told him he needed to stop toying with the affections of all his sisters in Christ, quit being a double-minded man, and go on a short-term missions trip overseas."

Phil caught our eyes in the rearview mirror, and we all exploded in laughter.

"Way to go, Sarah!"

We pulled up to the church moments before the wedding was to start. The three of us slipped into a back pew, with me in the middle.

As the beautiful bride walked down the aisle, I nudged Lins and whispered. "Isn't it poetic justice—God justice, actually—that Christopher, who couldn't care less about looks, gets the hottest girl in the group? And people say God doesn't have a sense of humor. I guess it's true what they say about Him bringing together unlikely—"

Just then, Phil started coughing.

"Do you need a lozenge?" I asked, fishing in my purse.

"No. Just had a catch in my throat."

The church stilled as the couple said their vows, which they had written themselves. "I wasn't looking for a wife," said my friend Christopher as he gazed deep into his bride's eyes. "I was merely following the path the Lord had laid before me. I thought it was a solitary path until one day I turned, and there was Sarah. A woman deeply in love with the Lord her God and following the same path I was—a path she too thought would be a solitary one. But God's plans were different."

I sniffled. *Are You trying to show me something here, Lord?*

He continued. "The Lord put us together, and I am blessed beyond what I could ever imagine by this great gift He has given me—this precious, beautiful woman who shares the desires of my heart. She's a gift I don't deserve, but my Father in heaven knew I needed her. Sarah, you are my heart. My love. My helpmate. I cherish you and pray I may be worthy of your love."

I sniffled again. Lindsey sniffled. And so did every other woman in the church. Even old Phil got a little misty-eyed, although he denied it later.

At the reception, I spotted Scotty and Kim on the dance floor, quite intent on each other, as were Colin and an almost-showing Samantha. I exchanged a knowing look with Phil and Lindsey. "Gee, a lot's been happening around here since I've been gone?"

"Uh, what do you mean, Pheebs?" Lins said a little testily.

I nodded toward Scotty and Kim.

"Oh yeah," Phil barked out a nervous laugh. "Those two are starting to get a bit hot and heavy."

"Don't worry on my account, Phil." I patted his arm. "Scotty was way too young for me, anyway, and I'm really happy for him. Of course, he could have waited longer than a minute to get over me. Oh well, out of sight, out of mind. Right?"

Lindsey shifted in her seat.

What was with her? Ever since the ceremony ended, she'd acted uneasy. If I didn't know better, I would think she was angry about something.

"You weren't out of our minds, Pheebs."

"Just teasing."

I looked around and saw several of the Lone Rangers, but not everyone. "So, Phil, where's your buddy Alex?"

"Out of town," he said. "I think he had some family business to attend to. Why?"

"No reason." I shrugged. "Lins just told me he comes to Lone Rangers now and that you guys were pals."

"Yep. He's a great guy," Phil said. "He said you were great in *Oklahoma* too, Pheebs—the best Ado Annie he'd ever seen. That was a surprise; I've never seen that side of you. Did anyone tape the show?"

Lord, I hope not.

Lindsey chimed in. "Yeah, Pheebs. We're all sorry we missed that. Make sure you let us know if there's going to be an encore performance."

The music started up again and Phil pushed back his chair and stood up. "Hey Pheebs, will you excuse me? I promised this dance—"

"No problem. You go on," I said. "Lins and I will stay here and catch up. We haven't had any girl time in way too long."

Phil fiddled with his collar. "Um, well . . ."

I popped a pink pillow mint, enjoying the dissolving sweetness on my tongue. "What's the matter? Tie too tight?"

"Uh, a little."

"Why don't you loosen it?" Lindsey said. "Or even take it off? This is a more casual do. Go ahead, no one will mind," she urged, then shooed him off. "Go. Dance. Have fun."

Phil left, dragging his heels.

"Okay, Lins, now that he's gone, dish!" I scooted my chair closer to my best friend. "I feel like I've really been out of the loop, what with limited e-mail, the time change, and our always missing each other. Seems like you're never home anymore."

"I know. Actually, Pheebs, there's something I want to tell—" she said, breaking off when Phil reappeared.

"Back so soon?" I looked at him in surprise. "What'd she do—turn you down?"

He yanked his chair out and started to sit. "She was otherwise occupied."

"Stay right there, big boy," I winked and stood up. "You want to dance? I'll dance with you. I love this song from *Pearl Harbor*. So-o romantic." I batted my eyes at him. "Hey Lins, hold that thought, I'll be back in a flash."

As Faith Hill sang "There You'll Be," Phil guided me around the dance floor. "Gee, Phil, I'd forgotten what a good dancer you are. Though it helps if you unclench your jaw." I looked at my friend in concern. "Hey, I'm sorry the girl of your dreams was unavailable. Want to talk about it? That's what friends are for, you know."

"Thanks," he said, "but that would be a no."

"Well, okay. Maybe later, then. But you've gotta tell me *what* is going on with Lins? Is something wrong? Is she mad at me for some reason? I feel this weird tension between us, and I don't know why."

His jaw clenched again. "Maybe you need to ask her."

"Aw c'mon, Phillie," I pleaded. "Be a pal. Can't you give me a hint? Is she upset about having to store my stuff? Are things not going well at work? Has she met someone? What's the deal?"

"Sorry, Pheebs. I'm not getting in the middle here."

"Well, okay," I said doubtfully. "But I hope it wasn't something I said. Or didn't say—was that it?" He raised an exasperated eyebrow. "Hey, I'll let you off the hook," I told him, "But I promise: before the night's out, I'll get it out of her." I did my Colonel Klink impression. "I have vays of making her talk . . ."

By the time we returned to the table, in fact, I'd pretty much figured out the problem. Why hadn't I noticed before? Lindsey had been sitting on the sidelines all night while everyone else—including her supposed best friend—danced and had a good time. Embarrassed at my cluelessness, I gave Phil a playful shove toward Lindsey. "Now, you two go and dance. Lins, you haven't danced once tonight. You've been spending all your time with me. Go ahead, cut loose! Kick up your heels before the party's over . . ."

They did. At first Phil and Lindsey were stiff and awkward with each other, but then they relaxed and moved well together. *That's what I like to see. My two good friends making nice . . .*

I sat tapping my foot to the music as I watched my friends enjoy themselves. And that was when Jake the resident flirt moved in for the kill. He gave me a welcome-back hug, then looked me up and down. "Hey, Phoebe, that country living really seems to agree with you—looks like you've lost a few pounds. Want to dance?" He slid me that lazy grin that had been known to make female hearts in three states flutter.

You're good, Jake-man. But I've scrubbed your toilet. I know who you are. I've seen where you live. And it's not pretty . . .

"Ah, Jake, you always know just what to say to a girl."

He pushed back the shock of hair that flopped endearingly down on his forehead—his trademark move—and held out his hand.

"Thanks," I said, "but I think I'll sit this one out."

He blinked, momentarily stunned that I'd resisted his irresistible charms. But only momentarily. He sonared the room, spotted a fresh prospect, made his excuses, and bolted.

"Hey, what'd you say to Jake?" a familiar voice said behind me, laughing. "I've never seen him move so fast."

I jumped up to hug Scotty, then Kim, who was holding on to his arm, uncertain. "Kim, I hope you know you've got a great guy there." I nodded my approval. "You make a good couple."

Scotty patted Kim's hand. "We think so. Hey, speaking of couples, Pheebs, what do you think of—"

Just then a breathless Lindsey appeared at his elbow with a scowling Phil trailing behind. "Hi, guys. How's it going? Hey, Scotty, that brother of yours is quite the dancer."

Scotty smiled. "You should—"

Lins cut him off and tugged at my hand. "Sorry, Scotty, I'm parched. I'm desperate for something cold. Come with me, Pheebs?"

"Sure. I'm thirsty too. Bye, Scotty. Kim, great to see you."

As Lins dragged me away, I hissed, "Okay, what was *that* all about?"

She slid her eyes to the front of the room, where the deejay had picked up the mike and the bride was moving into throwing position.

Comprehension dawned. "Ah, I'd almost forgotten. Thanks! Another minute and we'd have missed the chance for our bouquet-toss disappearing act."

We escaped inside the single girl's sanctuary, giggling as the door shut behind us, and settling onto the comfy couches for the duration.

Moments later, the door opened again, revealing Samantha. "I knew I'd find you two in here," she teased, wagging her finger at us. "How do you ever expect to get married if you don't put yourself out there for the sacred bouquet ritual?"

I sprang up to offer my felicitations. "Hey, little mama, double congrats—on your marriage and your upcoming bundle of joy. So how's married life?"

Seventeen minutes later, I was sorry I'd asked. But just when I couldn't take any more happily ever after, Lins saved the day.

"Sorry for interrupting, Sam," she said, rubbing her forehead, "but I have this killer headache. I think we're going to have to cut out of the wedding early. Do you mind, Pheebs? You must be tired after that long flight anyway."

I threw my best friend a grateful look and gave Sam a quick hug. "Works for me. Give Colin my best. Okay, Lins, let's just go say our good-byes to Christopher and his new wife."

The drive home to Lindsey's apartment was quiet. I tried to make conversation once or twice, but finally gave up. I'd just have to wait for the Tylenol to kick in.

Lins did the polite thing and invited Phil in, but he didn't want to intrude on our girl time.

Once inside, I took a flying leap and landed on my long-lost friend. "My sofa!" I said, embracing its gorgeous leather redness. Then I spotted another friend nearby. "And Gabby Goldfish. Did you guys miss me?"

A few minutes later we sat on the couch knocking back nonfat double mochas from Lindsey's new espresso machine. "Boy, have I ever missed this," I said, savoring each delicious sip.

And then: "Okay, Lins; spill. What in the world is going on with you and Phil?"

chapter twenty

Lindsey turned scarlet.

I was a little slow on the uptake, but comprehension finally dawned. "Wait a minute . . . *Is* something going on with you and Phil?"

"We've just had a few dates," Lins said, biting her lip. "Nothing serious."

"You've *just had a few dates*?!" I fell off my crimson couch. "My best friend and my best buddy? Why didn't you tell me?"

"I, um, well, we didn't know how you'd feel about it, and I wasn't comfortable telling you over the phone or on e-mail. So when we knew you were coming home, we decided to wait and tell you once you got here," she said, rushing all her words together. "But then there hasn't been a chance all day, what with having to rush to the wedding and all these people around." She shot me a worried look. "Do you mind?"

"Mind?" I yelped. "Why would I *mind* that two of my favorite people are spending time together? I think it's great!" I jumped up and embraced my best friend. "The only thing I mind is that you didn't tell me sooner," I said, sitting back down again. "In fact, come to think of it . . . you guys are made for each other. I don't know why I didn't see it before."

Because you only saw them through your friendship filter, not allowing for that male-female chemistry thing. Then another thought dawned: "Hey, I must be the matchmaker-in-absentia. I mean, the minute I leave, all these matches get made." I slid my best friend a curious look. "So what's it like—dating Phil?"

It was Lindsey's turn to smile. "You of all people should know. You guys went out for a while too."

"Yeah, but the only spark between us was when he gave my car a jump. You two have some major combustion flying around. I just mis-read it as anger."

She shot me a wry grin. "We have that, too. That boy sure knows how to push my buttons."

"Hey, I don't want to know the intimate details. Wait—what am I saying? You are walking the straight and narrow no-sex path, right?" She shot me a "well, duh" look. "Well, then, I do want to know the intimate details." I leaned forward. "When did it all begin, and how? Tell all!"

Lindsey settled deeper into the sofa beside me, tucking her feet beneath her and blowing on her coffee to cool it. "It started the night you left, when we tried to intercept Filmguy at the theater," she said. "No, wait. That's not exactly true. I guess there were little hints here and there—like the time he called when we were in New York and you were at the *Times*. He was a little flirtatious with me then, but I thought that was just Phil being Phil and didn't read anything into it. Except he'd been so sweet and gotten us that free hotel and tickets to *Phantom* and everything, and I guess I started seeing him in a different light." She sipped her mocha. "So, you're to blame."

I gave a little couch-bow. "Happy to be blamed."

"But things really kicked in when we tried to find Filmguy for you. That *Casablanca*'s a pretty romantic movie . . ."

"Haven't I always said so?"

"Yes, but I thought it was just your old movie mania speaking. Anyway, I don't know if I was hormonal that night or what, but when the movie ended I was feeling all mushy and gushy. And the look in Phil's eyes told me he was too. And then . . ."

"What? What? Don't stop there. I'm dyin' here!"

Lindsey smiled. "Then we ran into Alex in the lobby."

My best friend's romantic reverie listening screeched to a halt. "Alex? As in Spencer?"

"Yeah. Remember I told you we saw him there that night?"

"Oh, right. I forgot. So then what?"

"Nothing much. Except we all went out for coffee together, And as you know, Alex is quite the hottie, what with that whole sophisticated man-of-the-world thing, the designer suits, and those great eyes. But while we were talking, I never even noticed Alex. All I could think about was Phil and how cute he looked in his black T-shirt and jeans. How sweet and funny he was. What a good friend he'd always been. And . . . what adorable dimples he had." A devilish gleam, then. "And how much I wanted to vault over the table and grab him in a lip-lock."

"Lindsey!"

She blushed. "I didn't, of course."

"I should hope not." I gave my friend an appraising look. "So, has there been much lip-locking going on since then?"

"No. And not because we haven't wanted to. But we're really try-ing to do this whole Christian purity thing right—doing the group-date thing, attending Bible study together, staying active in Lone Rangers. You know."

"Good girl."

Lindsey took another sip of her mocha. "It sure isn't easy, though."

"I hear you on that. Not, of course, that I know up close and per-sonal—having not had a real relationship in more than *three years*. But I'm not bitter. Not at all. Not a bit jealous." I gave myself a mental shake and changed the subject. "Hey, Lins, I don't get it. Why have Phil and Alex Spencer become friends? What in the world do they have in common?"

"That's easy," she said. "God, basketball, and business. They're both doing the corporate shuffle—at different levels, of course."

"Basketball? Alex Spencer? But he's so short!"

"Not really. He's just not Ashton Kutcher."

"That's for sure."

"Anyway, Alex and Phil shoot hoops all the time. Phil says he's really good. Fast."

Fast at pulling the wool over everyone's eyes, you mean. "Whatever."

I picked up a magazine and started thumbing through it, but Lindsey wasn't finished. "Alex told us about his California trip, Pheebs. He really liked your mom—couldn't stop raving about her pumpkin pie. Liked Barley too. Listen, Pheebs, have you been lying to me all this time? Alex says it's a great little town."

"That's 'cause he didn't grow up there."

Lins gave me a speculative look. "I think Barley's been a good thing for you."

"Say what?"

"You heard me." She regarded me over the rim of her mug. "Something's different. Maybe it's because you're finally doing what you've always wanted."

"What? Living in a one-cow town?"

"No. Writing about what you love."

"Yeah, but I want to do it in New York."

"And I want to have legs up to my tonsils," she said. "Ain't gonna happen. At least you get to do something you love *and* get paid for it! Do you know how few people get to do that? I don't. Phil doesn't—"

Lindsey's hand flew to her mouth. "Oh my gosh! Phil!"

"What about him?"

"I said I'd call him after I told you about us." She looked at her watch. "It's been over an hour since he dropped us off. He's probably freaking out, thinking you're all mad and everything. I'd better call him."

"No. Wait, Lins. Let me."

She gave me a puzzled look but passed me the phone.

I punched in Phil's speed dial number and adopted my serious-with-a-touch-of-hurt tone. "Phil? It's Phoebe." (Pause.) "Could you come over here, right away please?" (Pause.) I glanced at Lindsey. "Yes, she did." (Pause.) "We'll discuss that when you get here." (Pause.) "Uh-huh. See you in a few minutes."

I hung up.

Lindsey was dying. "Pheebs, you're evil and you must be destroyed."

"It's called payback. For all the practical jokes he's played on me over the years."

She chuckled as she stood. "Well, don't get me involved. You're on your own on this one."

"Aw, c'mon Lins. Come on out and play . . ."

"No way. I'm dating the guy, remember?"

The doorbell rang.

"I'm outta here," Lins whispered, scooting down the hall to the bathroom.

I made my face solemn and opened the door. "Phil." I nodded at him to come in.

He looked around. "Um, where's Lindsey?"

"She's in the other room. I wanted to talk to you alone."

Phil coughed. "Pheebs, I—"

I cut him off at the explanation pass. "I can't believe you two! What kind of friends are you?"

He rubbed his forehead and sighed. "Phoebe, I'm sorry. We wanted to . . ."

A laugh started up from my stomach, but I turned it into a cough. I fought it so hard my eyes started to water. *Milk it, girl!* "Oh Phil." I squinted, and the tear dropped. *Hug him quick before you crack.*

He patted my back uncomfortably. "I'm sorry, Pheebs. I had no idea you'd take it so hard."

"Gotcha!" I raised my head. "You big goof. Did you think I wouldn't be happy for my two favorite people?"

He was having a hard time keeping up.

"Okay, Lins," I yelled down the hall. "It's safe to come out now."

His face cleared. My best friend rejoined us, and all was fine. Just like before.

Phil slipped his arm around Lindsey's waist and gave her an adoring gaze.

Well, maybe not just like before. Whoa. This is a little strange for me, Lord.

"Anyone hungry?" Lins was asking.

"Starving," Phil and I answered in unison.

"Pheebs, I got your favorite linguine and clams from Antonio's, some fettuccine Alfredo for me, and spaghetti Bolognese for Phil. While it's heating up, I'll make some fresh bruschetta."

"I'll help," Phil offered, following Lindsey into the kitchen.

I watched my friends as they worked together in harmony, teasing and laughing.

Well, Lord, looks like my leaving town was a good thing. Otherwise maybe Lins and Phil might never have gotten together. Guess this was all part of Your grand matchmaking plan, huh?

I'm happy for them. Really I am. But what about me? my lonely self whined. *What's my next step, Lord? Am I supposed to move back to Cleveland?* Visions of toilets clogged my head at the thought of going back to Happy Holly Housecleaning again. *Or do You want me to stay in Barley for a while for some reason, Lord? Or move to New York and hope to find work?*

"I know the plans I have for you . . . plans to prosper you and not to harm you, plans to give you hope and a future . . ."

With that thought, straight off the wall of my Barley bedroom, I looked around Lindsey's apartment. My eye landed on my beloved couch. And the phone lying next to it. And suddenly it came to me. No, not a full-blown epiphany, or thunderbolts, or anything like that. More like hearing E.T.'s gravelly voice in my head. Only instead of saying "Phone home," he was saying, "Go home."

Okay, Lord. Guess I can try this small-town life for a while. I do like my job, and saving the theater is kind of important to me. And it's been great to reconnect with my family and get to know the kids. But Lord, you know I can't keep living with my mother—we'll kill each other.

Lins set the bruschetta on the counter, and I spooned some of the fresh tomato mixture on the toasted Italian bread. *Note to self: Get the recipe.*

As I was polishing off the linguine, my cell rang. I looked at the number: Karen. "That's my sister-in-law. I'll need to take this." I excused myself. "Hi Kar. What's up?"

Ten minutes later I snapped my flip-phone shut and rejoined my friends for some spumoni. And an announcement.

"Sorry, guys, but it looks like I'm going to have to cut my visit short. My niece is making her stage debut a little earlier than planned, so I'll need to get back to Barley soon."

"How soon?" Lins asked.

I did some calculations. Or tried to. "Well, today's Saturday, and she's performing Wednesday night. And I don't think I can afford another last-minute ticket, even with a deal . . . Phil? Any idea how long it takes to drive to California from here?"

He logged on to the Internet. "Let's see . . . Cleveland to Barley, California . . . gotcha. Estimated driving time: thirty-six hours. Of course, you have to allow for gas and eating. And sleeping's always good. I'd say give yourself three full days."

I sighed. "Then I'll need to leave early, early Monday morning."

Lindsey pouted. "But Pheebs, we haven't had any time together. Surely your niece would understand."

"Actually, she does understand," I said. "They all told me not to try to come back early. But I promised Ashley, and I'm going to keep that promise. You can come out and visit me, though," I added. "Both of you. When everyone else is shoveling snow and slipping and sliding in all the Midwest slush, come on out to sunny California and I'll show you a good time."

Glancing around the apartment, I saw several of my things that my best friend was storing for me. The rest were in her extra bedroom. "Okay, Lins, here's what I think I should do. Since I don't know how long I'm going to be in Barley or even where I'm going to live—not with my mom indefinitely, that's for sure—I think it's time to simplify and get rid of some of my stuff so I can be a little more mobile."

Her jaw dropped. "You? Get rid of *stuff*?"

"Yep. We're not supposed to store up treasures on earth, right?"

Lins shook her head. "California's definitely changing you. How do you plan to do that?"

"I was thinking maybe a quickie yard sale."

"Like how quick?"

"Um . . . tomorrow after church?"

Her eyes widened, but she quickly recovered. "No problem. We are the flexible, spontaneous, seize-the-moment gal-pals after all."

"Do you mind if I have it here?"

"Of course not—as long as you don't mind that I don't have an actual yard. We'll tell the gang at Lone Rangers and spread the word."

By Sunday evening Lindsey's apartment had been stripped of all my worldly possessions. All that remained were my favorite books, clothes, videos and DVDs, Gabby the goldfish, and movie posters. Plus my shoes—lots and lots of shoes. After all, you can't expect a girl to do a total one-eighty overnight.

And of course, my beloved red couch, which Lins had done such a good job babysitting in my absence. I ran my fingers across the top of it, enjoying the feel of the cool leather. Thinking about storing up treasure—and where my heart really was.

"What size U-Haul are you going to rent, Pheebs?"

"I'm not."

Lindsey gave me a quizzical look. "But how are you going to move your couch, then?" She put her hands on her hips. "Pheebs, I know logic has never been your strong suit, but read my lips: Your couch will not fit into your Bug."

"I know. That's why I'm leaving it behind."

Her face cleared. "Oh. Okay. So you'll take it with you the next time you come. No problem. I'm happy to keep it here as long as you like."

"How about forever?" I smiled at my best friend.

"Huh?"

"Lins, I'm giving it to you."

"You are not! Pheebs, you *love* that couch!"

"Yeah, but I love you more. And this is my thanks for all you've done for me."

She protested. "I can't take your sofa. It's too expensive. I was with you when you bought it, and I know how much it costs."

"You're not taking it. I'm giving it to you. Well, sort of," I grinned. "I'll let you make the last payment."

I tilted my head. "Besides, you may have custody, but I want visitation rights."

n o way is this all going to fit, Pheebs," Phil said.

"Sure it will. We just have to move things around a little more."

"We've already done that three times."

It was late Sunday night, and Phil, Lins, and I had spent the past couple of hours cramming my car with my remaining possessions.

Unfortunately, Humphrey and Ingrid weren't being very accommodating. Try as we might, we couldn't fit my framed *Casablanca* poster into my car. Or a couple of boxes of books, either.

"Told you we should have gotten a U-Haul," practical Phil piped up.

"No time," I said. "And no trailer hitch."

I looked over my jammed-to-the-roof car and sighed.

"We can always ship it to you later," he said. "Or if you can wait a while, we can just bring it when we come out to visit—whenever that may be."

"Make it sooner, rather than later," I said. "I can't live without Bogie and Bergman for too long." I winked. "And this way you're obligated to come see me."

At six o'clock the next morning I was off, but only after much hugging and crying on both my part and Lindsey's.

I feel like Thelma without Louise—which is probably a good thing considering how they ended up. I pulled my sun visor down and popped in Willie Nelson. In general, I'm not a big country fan, but one should never leave town without "On the Road Again." I slid open the sunroof and sang along with Willie. But by the time I reached Toledo I was all Willied out.

Time for the Fine Young Cannibals and "She Drives Me Crazy."

Rocking out as I drove through the blazing fall colors of the Midwest, I thought back over the past couple days in Cleveland and how everyone seemed to be pairing up now, which was not the case when I lived there. "So since I'm leaving the land of couplehood, Lord, does this mean I'm doomed to stay single forever?"

Would that be so bad?

I thought of Mary Jo and her very full single life.

"I know the plans I have for you . . ."

Then I thought of Karen and Jordy and my adorable nieces and nephew, who I was missing like crazy.

". . . plans to prosper you and not to harm you . . ."

And Mom and our renewed relationship.

". . . to give you hope and a future . . ."

I whipped out my cell phone and placed a call to my brother. "Hey, Jordy, I think I might have a renter for you."

Fifty-something hours, two cheap motels, and nine Big Macs later, I pulled into downtown Barley. This time my return felt different. Like coming home.

Parking in back of the *Bulletin* office, I grabbed my overnight bag and my black, all-purpose, wrinkle-free slimming travel dress from the trunk—where I kept it alongside my spare tire and other emergency equipment—and hurried inside, full of delicious anticipation about surprising Ashley.

"Gordon," I sang out, "I'm ba-a-a-ck."

My midnight-oil-burning boss looked up from his desk with a bemused expression. "Phoebe?"

"I know. I know," I said as I scooted past him on my way to the loo. (*Translation: English word for* bathroom—*shorter, more fun, and more European-chic than the mundane and commonplace* restroom.) "I wasn't due back 'til this weekend, but Ashley's fashion show got moved up to tonight, and there was no way I was going to miss that." I shifted the shoulder strap on my bag. "Just got into town and don't have enough time to go home and dress, so I decided to do a quick change here. Back in a sec." I closed the door behind me.

Inside the cramped office restroom—okay, for this humdrum cubicle, *restroom* fit—I stripped, spritzed, slipped into, and freshened. After three days on the road, my makeup was screaming "Help me! Help me!" like Vincent Price in *The Fly*. I glanced at my watch: seven minutes to show time—and the theater was only seconds away.

You're good, girl. I surveyed my satisfied reflection in the dingy mirror. *Note to self: Consider becoming high-priced consultant to women on the go. Give fast-track fashion and primping seminars to busy women seeking to have it all. Charge beaucoup bucks by using natural fashion sense, then use proceeds to at long last buy a pair of Manolos—after tithing, of course.*

I gave my mirror image an approving air kiss before exiting the tiny room.

"Sorry about the employee tornado, boss," I said perching on the edge of my desk. "Just didn't want to be late. But now that Quick Dress McPhoebe has done her brilliant fashion magic, I have a few minutes to kill." I bit into a peppermint Lifesaver. "So, anything exciting happen while I was gone? Did Christy Sharp Armstrong get any new salt and pepper shakers for her collection?"

Gordon cleared his throat and shuffled some papers on his desk. "Er . . . Phoebe, I didn't expect you back for several more days."

I swung my leg. "I know, but when Karen called and told me Ashley's show had been moved up to tonight, I made fast tracks. I'm surprising her," I said.

He cleared his throat again. "I was planning to call you tomorrow."

"Why? What's up?"

Gordon gave me a hesitant smile. "Phoebe, I'm, er, retiring."

"What?!" I hopped off the desk. "When?"

"End of next month."

"But why?" I felt a cold finger of dread snake its way down my spine. "You're not sick?"

He gave me a reassuring smile. "No. Not really. Just old—too old to keep up the pace of running a newspaper. The doc says I need to slow down and take things a little easier."

"But you're going to be all right?"

"Yep. As long as I remember that I'm pushing sixty-five, not twenty-five."

I gave my journalism friend and mentor a gentle grin. "So, I take it this is your nice way of telling me the *Bulletin's* closing down and I'm out of a job."

Gee, Lord, guess I'm not staying in Barley after all. Time to dust off the ol' résumé again. Just call me Phoebe the Flexible.

"Not at all," Gordon reassured me. "Actually, the *Bulletin* will stay, and so will you—I hope. Me too, but on a limited basis. I'll still write my weekly column, but you'll take over—"

My goose bumps jumped to attention, and I no longer heard what he was saying. *Gordon's going to hand over the editorial reins of the paper to me. I'll be in charge of my very own newspaper! Note to new editor self: First thing, lose the lame joke of the week. Second, hire some bright high-school kid to write the obits from now on. Then, move the—*

I stopped short. Did I really want to run the *Bulletin*? That would mean I'd be married to this place forever. Visions of me turning into Esther—single, seventy-something, and still writing about the Miss Udderly Delicious Dairy Pageant—gave me significant pause.

"Phoebe, are you even listening?"

"Sorry. What?"

He cleared his throat again. "I'd like to ask you a favor."

Here comes the promotion offer. How should I respond? It would be pretty cool to be the editor of my own paper. But I'm not sure I'm ready to make that kind of commitment . . .

Gordon continued. "It would mean a lot to me if you'd show the new owner the ropes, give him the benefit of your expertise when I'm not around. You pretty much know how things work now."

Stop the editorial-fantasy presses. "The new owner?"

He looked at me, puzzled. "Yes. How else did you think the *Bulletin* could keep going?"

"I don't know," my impractical, illogical self replied.

"Phoebe, I'm up to my eyeballs in debt. No retirement either. By selling the paper, I'll be able to pay off my debts and still have some money to live on—even get in a little traveling." His voice took on a dreamy tone. "I've always wanted to visit our national parks— Yellowstone, Mount Rushmore, the Grand Canyon . . . I've never even seen Yosemite, and it's only three hours away . . ." He droned on about this park and that park while I reentered the job-uncertainty twilight zone.

A new owner? What kind of changes will he make? Gordon says my job is secure, but you never know . . . Maybe I misunderstood You, God, and I'm supposed to be moving on after all . . .

Then, as I pondered the scary possibilities, an even scarier suspicion dawned. I interrupted my boss's back-to-nature litany. "Gordon, who bought the paper?"

"The Spencer newspaper chain. Alex really liked the town when he came out to visit."

He was *scoping out the town before he swooped in for one of his predatory takeovers.*

"He started his career as a cub reporter on a small-town paper and wants to return to his writing roots," Gordon said. "Says his job's become more of a chore than a passion for him these days, and he misses the writing. Reminds me a little of you, in fact, Phoebe."

Not on my worst day.

"That young man and I have had some nice long talks," Gordon continued. "In fact, he was here a little while ago. You two must have just missed each other comin' and goin' . . ."

Ships in the night? No. More like the iceberg and the Titanic.

"Alex is going to pull back from his corporate role for a bit and take a sabbatical—see what it's like to run a small-town paper again."

Sure. Come out and play hometown newspaperman—slumming with the little people. And when you get bored, you can just turn the paper over to one of your corporate pencil-pushers. That way it should go under in no time.

Gordon patted my shoulder. "I know this must seem like déjà vu to you, Phoebe, but this isn't the same thing as Cleveland at all. You're not going to lose your job—I made sure of that. That was a condition of the sale, in fact, and it wasn't even a difficult one. Alex thinks you're a wonderful writer and wants you to stay on. Actually, he insisted that you do."

And what made him think I'd even consider working for him?

Just then, the clock struck eight, reminding me of why I'd raced home early. I picked up my bag and bolted for the door.

"Phoebe—"

"I'm sorry, Gordon—I have to go. I can't miss Ashley's show."

"But—"

"I'll talk to you tomorrow, okay? I really have to run now or I'll be late."

Driving down the street to the Bijou, I was tempted to keep on going and not look back.

Buck up, girl. It's not all about you. Tonight is about Ashley—her big night. Time to suck it up and be there for your niece.

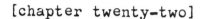

the lights had already dimmed and the music started when I slipped in a side door of the Bijou and made my careful way down to the empty seat in the front reserved for press.

As I flipped open my notebook, the first two freshman girls were already preening and prancing across the stage. I breathed a sigh of relief that I hadn't missed Ashley. But wait, where *was* Ashley? She was supposed to be in the first group. Then I saw my terrified niece—ramrod stiff and frozen near the back of the stage, her classmates hissing at her to move.

She took a few awkward steps, then stumbled and nearly fell.

My throat constricted. *Oh Ash, sweetie . . .* I fumbled in my purse in the darkness. *Where is it?* Finally, my searching fingers found what I was looking for. I grabbed my pen flashlight and clicked it on and off beneath my chin in a frantic, yet discreet, attempt to get my niece's attention. *C'mon Ash, look out here. Remember our signal.* But she was too far over to the right—she couldn't see me. *Well, it's not as if I haven't made a complete fool of myself in front of the whole town already . . .*

I slid out of my seat and, crouching down, crept my way across the floor in front of the stage, bumping into several pairs of feet in the process. "Excuse me. Pardon me. Excuse me. Sorry." Finally I was in Ashley's direct line of vision. I half stood and switched on the flashlight beneath my chin again, but this time kept it on while I sucked in my cheeks and did my Audrey Hepburn giraffe impression.

Chuckles broke out on either side of me, but it worked.

Ashley saw me, and that huge Julia grin split her face, lit up the stage, and knocked the audience dead. Then she remembered what we'd practiced and went into top model mode—minus the sullen expression—swinging her hair, scampering down the catwalk, and having the time of her life.

That's it, baby girl, I breathed. *Work it, own it—you got it!*

In the lobby afterward, several audience members grinned at me, Norm Anderson and my pals from the cemetery district board gave me a big thumbs-up, and Louise and Mom's other church lady friends from Holy Communion took turns hugging me.

Ashley flung herself at me when she emerged from backstage. "Aunt Phoebe, you made it, you made it!"

"Of course I did. Told you I'd be here, didn't I? No way was I going to miss my soon-to-be-rich-and-famous niece's first modeling gig." I held out a bouquet of yellow roses I'd snagged in Lodi. "These are for you, sweetie. You were great. Like I said, a natural."

"I was so scared at first until I saw you." She giggled. "You looked so goofy, Aunt Phoebe. It made me feel a lot better."

"Hey, that's my mission in life: one goofy aunt available for weddings, funerals, graduations, and fashion shows."

The rest of the family rushed up then, congratulating Ashley and welcoming me home. Karen hugged me and whispered in my ear, "I didn't think you'd get here in time."

"Only just," I said. "Ran into some traffic problems on the way."

Jordy placed proud hands on his eldest's shoulders. "Wasn't my daughter incredible tonight, Pheebert? Have you ever seen anything like it? She was just beautiful."

Ashley raised shining eyes to her father. "Thanks, Daddy," then turned her head into his sweater and cried softly.

My heart clenched as I remembered my own dad's pride the night of my sophomore prom. I saw Mom's tender smile and knew she was recalling the same thing.

Two of her classmates approached, and Ashley dashed away her tears. The three girls stepped aside to whisper and giggle while the rest of the family encircled me.

Mom gave me the first full-on hug she'd been able to give since I returned to Barley. "It's good to have you ho—back again, daughter. I've missed you. We all have."

I returned the hug. "Same here. But can you excuse me for a minute? Right now I need to do some quick interviews with the girls for the *Bulletin*."

Her face flickered. "You've seen Gordon?"

"Yep."

"Then you know—"

"Later, Mom." I motioned to the girls to wait up. "Right now I gotta dash. Back soon."

Ten minutes later, I'd wrapped up the interviews and returned to my waiting family.

My brother looked down at me. "Good to see you, baby sister." He lowered his voice. "Mom was worried that once you were back in your old stomping grounds that you wouldn't come home again."

"*This* is home, Jordy. For now. Cleveland isn't anymore. Things change, and I've realized that this is where I'm meant to be. For *now*," I emphasized.

Reluctant note to self: Turn in Starbucks card, cancel gym membership, and give Lins remaining season tickets to classic film series.

Jacob tugged on the bottom of his dad's coat, while Lexie grabbed at his sleeve. "Can we go home now, Daddy?" they both asked, bouncing with excitement. "Can we go home?"

"Yeah, Dad," Elizabeth and Ashley pleaded. "Can we go?"

I stared at my nieces and nephew. "Well, this is a first."

Lexie kept jumping up and down. "Wanna go home and show An Beebee the surpwise."

"Isn't it a little late?" Karen said.

"No," everyone yelled, even my mom.

"What surprise?" I said. "I thought I was the one who was surprising *you*."

Lexie chuckled and clapped her hands. "The surpwise at the

hou—" Jordy silenced his youngest by swooping her up and tickling her.

"Okay, guys, *what* is going on?"

Mom took me by the elbow and steered me outside. "If we told you, then it wouldn't be a surprise, now, would it, daughter?"

En masse, my family herded me to the parking lot, with Lexie dancing up and down with glee the entire way.

"Well isn't this the cutest thing you ever did see?" Mom said, as we arrived at my car, parked right next to Karen and Jordy's SUV. "It looks like a giant lemon cream puff." All of a sudden, Jordy blocked our path. "Okay, Pheebert, stop right there. Don't go any farther. Before you get in your car, there's something we have to do." He put on his bossy big-brother voice. "Shut your eyes."

"Shut your eyes, shut your eyes," the rest of the family chanted.

I went along with their silliness and closed my eyes. I could hear my older nieces chortling behind me. All of a sudden I felt a piece of cloth against my closed eyelids and someone tying it behind my head. "Hey! What's that?"

"Don't worry, Pheebs," Karen soothed. "It's silk."

"Only the best blindfold for my well-dressed daughter," Mom said, joining in the fun.

"Wait, don't tell me." I gave an exaggerated sigh. "I'm giving a repeat performance of Ado Annie later, so you're all taking me to try on my newest girdle, right?"

The girls giggled. "An Beebee, you're silly," Lexie said. "I's not that. It's a whole wot—"

"Shhh!"

"What? I didn't say anything about the—"

Beneath my blindfold I heard Karen distracting her youngest. "Lexie, do you want to ride with Daddy in Aunt Phoebe's pretty yellow car? Pheebs, okay with you if Jordy drives your car? You'll be riding with me."

"No problem," I answered as Jordy guided me across the parking lot. "Just don't scratch it."

"Be careful," Mom cautioned as he ducked me into the front seat of the SUV. "Watch her head now."

"Yeah, brother dear. Watch my head, or I'll be having yours."

I felt the door slam behind me and heard the rustling of assorted bodies along with several snaps, clicks, and sighs.

"Everyone got their seatbelt on?" Karen asked.

"All buckled in, and ready to roll," came Mom's voice from right behind my head.

"And we're off," my sister-in-law said.

As their mother drove and drove and drove, turning this way and that until I didn't have a clue where we were, my mother kept her grandkids occupied by leading them in choruses of "Old MacDonald." They went through every barnyard animal known to man until I thought I would scream if I heard one more *e-i-e-i-o*.

"All right. All right," Mom finally said, "One last animal." I heard whispering behind me. Then Jacob's clear voice rang out. "Old MacDonald had a farm, e-i-e-i-o. And on his farm he had a . . ." (Long, drawn-out pause.) "An *emu!*" my mother shouted. The backseat collapsed in laughter.

I rolled my eyes beneath my blindfold. "I think someone's had too much sugar," I said. "Mom, what have I told you about that too late at night? You're going to be all wound up and won't be able to sleep now."

Oh, what the heck. If you can't beat 'em, join 'em, right? Sing out, Louise! And I did. "With a neck-nip here, and a neck-nip there, here a nip, there a nip . . ."

Karen made another turn, then the SUV stopped with a lurch. Doors slammed, and everyone got out.

"We're here, we're here!" Lexie and Jacob squealed in unison.

I started to undo my blindfold.

"Not so fast," Jordy said. "Okay, everyone, go on ahead. We'll be right there."

I heard childish feet pounding up a flight of stairs, followed by slower, heavier ones. My brother carefully led me over uneven ground, then stopped. "Okay, there's a step. Careful now, lift your foot." And he guided me up a tall outdoor staircase, one creaking step at a time.

As we ascended, the wind whipped my dress, plastering it around my legs. I clutched his hand tighter. "Where *are* we?" I raised my voice. "Jordy, you better not be taking me up to the old water tower again like you did when we were little."

Above us, Mom yelped. "Jordan Richard Grant, you did *what* to your sister?"

Ah. Now, that's the mom I know and love.

"Tattletale," he muttered. "*Now* I'm going to get it. No dessert for me tonight."

We finally reached the top. I could tell we were going through a door. And somewhere in front of me I could hear my entire family tittering in anticipation. "Hurry up, Daddy," Jacob demanded.

"Yeah, c'mon, honey." Karen echoed her son's complaint. "You're taking forever."

My brother, however, could be Mr. Dramatic when the occasion called for it. He took after Dad that way. So as he began to undo my blindfold, he whispered in my ear, "Hey Pheebert, remember what Dorothy said when she missed the balloon ride to Auntie Em's and thought she'd be stuck in Oz forever?"

I nodded, clicked my aging, beautiful, but non-ruby Liz Claiborne pumps together, and repeated "There's no place like home," as my brother spun me around. Twice.

At last, he removed the blindfold with a flourish. "Voila!"

And I wasn't in Kansas anymore.

I blinked. "Wh-what is this? Where are we?"

"Your new apartment," my beaming family chorused.

"Above *our* gawage," a proud Lexie informed me.

It was as if I'd died and gone to single-girl heaven. Facing me was the most adorable studio apartment I'd ever seen: one large sunny room with French windows on either side and separated into distinct living areas—bedroom, bath, kitchenette, dining nook, and living room.

"Jordy, when I called and told you I wanted to become your tenant, I had no idea the apartment would be finished so soon. Or that it would be so gorgeous!" I looked around me in amazement. Against one wall in the living room where I remained rooted to the floor—a gleaming hardwood floor, thank you very much—stood a large, empty bookcase clamoring to be filled. Across from the bookcase, which had space for my small TV, sat a cushy, overstuffed club chair in a gorgeous black-and-white toile, with the antique cherrywood end table of Mom's I'd long coveted standing next to it.

"Oh my goodness," I breathed, sounding very like Shirley Temple in one of her early movies.

"Do you like the chair?" Mom asked. "I remembered your saying how much you like toile, but I wasn't sure about the color, so I went with black and white to go with all your old-movie stuff. If you don't like it, it can easily be changed. It's just a slipcover."

"Don't you dare change it!" I hugged my mother. "I love it. I absolutely love it. All of it!" I said, smiling at Jordy and company.

My legs finally moved, and the rest of me followed in rapt investigation. Behind the toile chair stood a wooden three-panel folding screen that separated the bedroom area from the rest of the apartment. Not just any screen either. As I drew near, I saw that it was covered from top to bottom in a quirky collage of black-and-white scenes from my favorite old movies.

I squealed. "Where did you ever *find* this treasure?"

Ashley shot me a pleased smile. "Grandma and I made it."

"You *made* it? You're kidding! It's fabulous. Wow." I traced my fingers over the panels. "I've wanted one of these dressing screens ever since

I first saw Marlene Dietrich changing behind one in *Destry Rides Again*."
I stood behind it and pretended to be a dance-hall girl from the wild
West. "Now all I need is a feather boa."

Karen slapped her palm against her forehead. "I *knew* we forgot
something." She rustled around in the bedroom closet. "One feather
boa coming right up. Ta-da!"

It's even red.

In the cute kitchenette stood the vintage red-and-chrome diner-
style table and chairs from my grandparents' house, which Mom had
always said would be mine someday. "I remember eating Cocoa-Puffs
at this table," I said.

"Hey Pheebert, over here." Jordy showed off the full bathroom he
and a buddy had managed to finish just before I got home. "I was planning to install just a shower," he said, "but Mom and Karen reminded
me how much you like your baths." He frowned. "It made the room a
little tight, though."

"It's perfect." I squeezed past him into the tiny black-and-white
bathroom with the sink, commode, and bath and shower combo. "How
much space does one person need anyway? Much more important to
have a tub. A girl needs her bath."

Miraculously, he refrained from a big-brother comment on that
one. "Okay, you need to shut your eyes again," he said.

"Oh, c'mon, Jord," I whined. "Not another blindfold."

"Nope. Just shut your eyes and trust me."

"That's asking a lot."

"I know. I know," he said. "But believe me, you won't be sorry."

Jordy led me by the hand to the area behind the screen. I heard
the opening of a door and the kids snickering nearby.

"Okay, open up."

Shirley Temple returned. "Oh my goodness!"

On either side of the small closet, Jordy had installed what looked
like an apothecary cabinet without the drawers, but which I knew in
fact to be "a shoe hive!"

I squealed and jumped into my brother's arms, wrapping my legs around him and hugging his neck. "I take back everything bad I ever said about you, Jordy. You're the best brother ever."

He winked. "Just trying to keep you organized, O messy one. We'll put the daybed and dresser from your room at Mom's here, too."

Lexie tugged at my legs, prying them loose from her dad. "An' Beebee? Come see what I did." She dragged me over to the refrigerator, where she pointed with pride at the piece of child art hanging there. "I drawed a picture of you in your new house—see? There's you at the window and underneath is me and Jacob an' 'Lizbeth an' Ashley. An' Mommy an' Daddy and Gamma. Our fam'ly."

My eyes glistened. "Oh, sweetie, thank you, Lexie, for such a wonderful present." I looked up at the rest of my "fam'ly." "I don't even know how to begin to thank you for all this. Words fail me."

"Says the writer," Karen said.

"Every woman needs a place of her own," Mom said.

I looked over at my mother in surprise. "Since when did you start reading Virginia Woolf?"

She winked at me and adopted a lofty pose. "Daughter, I have hidden depths you can't even begin to fathom."

"Oh, I heard about women needing a space of their own too," Ashley said. "On *Oprah*."

Mom laughed. "Caught me." She pointed to a large open area in the living room. "Phoebe, we kept that empty 'cause we know you have that nice red leather couch that you love so much."

Momentary twinge of regret. "Um, I *did* have a cool red Pottery Barn couch, but I gave it to Lindsey. That's okay, though. I don't really need a couch. I've got my kitchen chairs and this gorgeous toile club chair. That'll be plenty."

Mom protested. "Everyone needs a couch to stretch out on."

"It's okay. My daybed can do double duty. Or, I can always go thrift-store shopping and find a good used one."

At that, Jordy snapped his fingers. "I have just the thing."

Karen gave him a look. "No, Jordy. No way. Not that old couch you had in college."

"Why not? It's still in good condition. And really comfortable."

"And really hideous," she said. "Pheebs, you'd hate it."

I thought she was probably right. Then I took one look at Jordy's puppy-dog face.

"Maybe not," I told my sister-in-law. "My tastes are expanding. What color is it?"

"What color *isn't* it, you mean," Karen muttered.

"Brown and . . . I can't remember what else," my brother said.

"It's a stew of carrots and peas," Karen said. "A polyester one at that."

"But it's free," Jordy said.

Karen snorted. "That's 'cause no one but you would pay good money for it."

"I'll be happy to check it out," I said, wanting to avoid an argument.

Jacob let loose with a loud yawn.

Karen looked at her watch. "Whoa, it's getting late. We'd better get the kids to bed."

"Speaking of bed, Pheebs, sorry we didn't get yours over so you could sleep here tonight, but we just ran out of time," Jordy said.

"No problem," I said, looking around me in wonderment. "I'm amazed at all you did get done. Thank you so much!"

Mom yawned. "I'm a little sleepy too. You about ready to go, daughter?"

"Sure." I cast a last longing look over my shoulder at my new apartment as we left.

uess we really surprised you, huh?" Mom said as I drove us home. Correction: I drove *her* home. I had a new home now. Woo-hoo!

"With a capital *S*. I still can't believe you guys did all that."

She breathed in the fragrance of the yellow rose in my bud vase, then stole a sideways glance at me. "I had to do *something* to get you out from underfoot. I need my personal space, you know."

"Now I know aliens have taken over your mind," I hummed the theme from *The Twilight Zone*.

Mom laughed. "Okay. I know I was a long time coming to this understanding, but I'm finally realizing that the only way to keep those I love close is to let them go. 'Let Go and Let God,'" she said, parroting a plaque from her Sunday-school class. "The Lord's been trying to teach me that for a long time. I've just been a slow learner. Besides," she said with an exaggerated sigh, "you were starting to cramp my style. Since you've been home, I haven't had one date. I think the guys are afraid of getting the third degree from my daughter."

Where is my mother, and what have you done to her?

"Uh, Mom, I think your new hairstyle's going to your head. But who knows? Maybe my moving out will improve *both* our love lives." I slid her a sly glance. "I know a certain newspaper publisher who's been wanting to make some news with you for a long time."

Then I remembered my boss's recent news. I scowled and ground the gears as I downshifted. "Excuse me. I mean a soon-to-be-retired newspaper publisher. That Alex Spencer makes me so mad I could spit—pulling the *Bulletin* out from under Gordon that way." I turned the corner. "You notice he did it when I was out of town. He had to, or I'd have seen right away what he was up to and been able to warn Gordon."

Mom plucked a couple of mohair pills off her sweater. "Gordon may be getting older, dear, but he's not senile. He's perfectly capable of making a decision on his own. It's hard work to own your business. And tiring. Gordon's been struggling for years to keep that paper afloat. You see the way he dresses. Why, I don't think that man has more than one good suit to his name. And look how skinny he is. You can see his shoulder blades through his shirt. That poor man probably lives on TV dinners and takeout."

"Okay, Mom, okay. Settle down. All I'm saying is that paper is his whole life."

"It *has* been, but there's more to life than work," she said. "And Gordon has realized that. He's not a young man, you know. He's yearning to see more of this big beautiful country of ours, as he told me. This is something he *wants*, dear. Alex is doing him a favor."

"Favor, my foot. You can bet there's something in it for him. Alex Spencer eats men like Gordon for breakfast." I slammed the car door and stomped into the house. "It's not fair that he can come in here all rich and powerful and squash Gordon like a bug."

"Don't you think you're being a little dramatic, dear? Gordon wouldn't let anyone squash him," Mom said. "Tell the truth, I don't know any man who's ever gotten the best of him . . ." her voice trailed off.

I gave her a meaningful look. "Other than Dad, that is."

She blushed. "That was a long time ago, and don't change the subject. Alex Spencer's buying the *Bulletin* is *helping* Gordon. He's been working himself to death, poor man. And the doctor said he needs to slow down. If you ask me, finding a buyer for the paper is an answer to prayer."

Yeah, Alex Spencer's greedy prayer.

Seeing my mutinous expression, Mom changed the subject. "There's other news too. Theater seat sales are up to nineteen thousand dollars now. Lou Jenkins even bought two, side by side, so he could have more words on his plaque." She proceeded to bring me up-to-date on all the latest fundraiser details.

In bed that night, my last one under Mom's roof, I turned my pillow over to find the cool spot and began mentally decorating my new apartment.

I'll paint the one kitchen wall red so it will really pop. And do I want to go yellow for the rest of the walls, like in my Cleveland apartment, or bright white? Let's see, I'll hang my Casablanca *print over the bookcase and put* Wuthering Heights *over my bed. But no,* Casablanca's *still in Cleveland with Lindsey. May have to put* Gone with the Wind *over the bookcase instead.*

Wait a minute. My practical self interrupted my decorating dreams. *What about rent? You haven't even made up your mind yet if you're going to work for Spencer the Newspaper Slayer. If you don't, how are you going to pay for this great new apartment? I couldn't ask Karen and Jordy to carry me on this; they need the money.*

Had to go and bring that up, didn't you? my inner decorating diva asked. *Couldn't focus on paint and toile, could you?*

You're right, my Scarlett self agreed. *What was I thinking?* Sigh. *I won't think about that right now. I'll think about that tomorrow.*

After all, tomorrow is another day . . .

On that 'nother day, Mary Jo and I resumed our morning exercise plan. Since there was no gym nearby—and no perky, thong-clad trainers either, thank goodness—we'd settled on a two-mile walk three times a week between her house and Mom's.

It had been tough going at first to convince my country pal to join me in a regular workout program. "I get plenty of exercise working on the ranch and riding my horses," Mary Jo grumbled when I suggested it.

"Yes, but those are such solitary activities. Here you get the benefit of my girl company and scintillating conversation."

"And that's better than horses *how,* exactly?" Only when I added in the enticement of a mocha and scone from Books 'n' Brew had she finally caved.

Today though, I was too distracted to think about scones, even Amy's delicious currant ones. As we took our exercise laps, I gave Mary Jo the highlights of my Cleveland trip, and she told me the latest goings-on in her life—something about a new filly she was boarding, plus a funny story about one of her students, and we talked for a minute about my new digs.

Then we *really* got down to it.

My power-walking thighs slapped each other silly as I vented about Alex Spencer. "Can you even *believe* that guy?" I railed. "This is the second time he's come in and snapped up a struggling paper where I work." We rounded the corner to Mom's, my voice rising. "What did I ever do to him, anyway, that scum-sucking bottom feeder?"

Mary Jo cut her eyes at me.

I continued on my righteous-indignation roll. "And presenting me with that check for the Bijou in front of the whole town! Way to deflect your true intentions, Mr. Wolf in Sheep's Clothing."

Mary Jo snaked her eyes over my shoulder and blinked.

I hitched up my sagging leggings and scratched my hip. "What is *wrong* with your eyes, woman? Did you forget your contacts again?"

A familiar voice behind me said, "Morning, Mary Jo. Nice outfit, Phoebe."

Open mouth, insert cross trainer. I whirled around. "Hey! Didn't your mother ever teach you it's not polite to—"

At that moment, my mother appeared in the doorway carrying a box of my stuff. "Alex. How nice to see you. What brings you by so early?"

"I was on my morning run." He held up a basket I hadn't noticed in my whirl of wrath. "And I knew you got up with the chickens, Gloria, so thought I'd return your picnic basket while I was at it." He gave her an appreciative smile. "Gordon's right. Your lasagna's the best I've ever tasted."

Quit sucking up to my mom, you paper-stealing pirate. You may be able to fool her and everyone else in Barley, but I'm onto you. I've seen how you work, and I know where you live. Okay, maybe I don't know where you live, but I know what you're all about.

Alex looked over at me, taking in my faded, stretched-out leggings and "I Love New York" T-shirt with a grin. "So, Phoebe, will we see you down at the *Bulletin* today, or did I hear Gordon say something about a little time off?"

I shot him a withering look. "My *boss* gave me some time off. I'm not due back 'til Monday, so—"

Mom cut me off, favoring Alex with a bright smile. "We're moving Phoebe into her new apartment today," she said, shifting the unwieldy box on her hip.

Alex hurried to relieve her of her heavy load. "Here, Gloria. Let me help you with that." He frowned. "Didn't you just get your casts off? I don't think you should be lifting things . . ."

Sure. Work the concerned, chivalrous angle now. That'll score you some points with the ladies.

He glanced at the mass of boxes stacked on the porch. "Do you need some help? I don't need to be at the paper until eleven o'clock for a meeting with Gordon."

Mom shot him a grateful look and started to accept, with Mary Jo also murmuring her assent, but I cut them both off. "No thanks. We can manage on our own."

His face tightened. "All right, then. I'll leave you to it. Gloria, don't overdo. And thanks again for the great lasagna." He nodded. "Mary Jo. Phoebe." Then he jogged away down the dirt road.

"Phoebe, you were rude to Alex. Your daddy and I raised you better than that."

"Yeah, Pheebs. Cut the poor guy some slack," Mary Jo echoed. "He seems really nice."

"That's because you don't know him like I do." My face flushed at the memory of how he'd called me on my marking-time Barley motives

239

the night he'd offered me a job. "You can't trust him." I turned my attention to my mother. "I can't believe you're *feeding* him!"

"Someone has to."

"Mom, there're five restaurants in town."

She brushed a stray hair out of her face. "Restaurant food gets old really fast."

"Then he can cook for himself. He's a big boy. At least in age, if not stature."

"He's staying at a hotel in Lodi with a restaurant in the lobby, but no cooking facilities."

"Oh. Well, *now* I'm feeling sorry for him," I snorted. "The guy's rich. He can eat anywhere he wants—even fly in his own personal chef. He's just buttering you up."

"He's not that rich, daughter," Mom said. "And it's been a long time since a man buttered me up, so I'm rather enjoying it. But you and I could argue about Alex 'til the cows come home." She hoisted one of the smaller boxes marked shoes and stuck it in the trunk. "Time's a-wastin'. We'll never get you moved just standing here talking."

"Whew. That's it. The last load," I said, sinking into my new toile chair four hours later.

Mary Jo frowned. "I think I remember seeing one more box in the car."

I started to get up.

She waved me off. "Nah, don't worry. I'll go get it."

When she returned, Mom was busy lining my kitchen drawers with shelf paper and I was putting towels away in the linen closet— tags facing both in *and* out.

"Where do you want this, Pheebs?" Mary Jo asked.

Intent on my towel task, I didn't look up. "Just put it in whatever section of the apartment it's marked for."

"There's no writing on this one."

"There has to be. I marked all the boxes myself." I glanced at the unfamiliar carton. "Oh, that one's not mine. I've never seen it before. Must be yours, Mom."

She looked and shook her head. "It's not mine either. Perhaps you'd better open it, dear."

"Where're the scissors?" I asked, relieving Mary Jo of the box.

"No telling in this mess," Mom said, glancing around a room stacked with boxes and cluttered with clothes and papers.

Mary Jo reached into her pocket.

"Don't tell me you've got those big girdle-snipping shears in there." I pulled back in mock horror.

"Nope. I keep those in the truck." She pulled out a Swiss Army knife and started cutting the sides and center seam of the box. Then she helped me pull away the paper to reveal . . . a home karaoke machine. "Happy housewarming, Pheebs," she said, grinning from ear to ear. "Now you can a-weema-weh anytime you want in the privacy of your own home."

My eyes gleamed. But not Mom's. "You shouldn't have, Mary Jo," she commented. With a fake grimace, she held her hands to her ears. "Really. You shouldn't have."

"Okay, Mother dear, now you're asking for it."

Deciding it was time for a little karaoke break, I assembled the machine, started the theme from *Gilligan's Island,* and joined in with the rollicking lyrics. But when I came to the part of the song that listed the characters I stopped to impart a choice bit of TV trivia. "Hey, did you know that in some of the early shows they identified Gilligan, the Skipper, Mr. and Mrs. Howell, and Ginger, but the Professor and Mary Ann were relegated to 'and the rest'?" I jumped on my sitcom soapbox. "How'd you like to be 'the rest'? That was so not fair."

"Wouldn't bother me," Mom said. "Probably didn't bother Mary Ann, either. Now, Ginger would have been another story—accustomed as she probably was to top billing."

"Speaking of Ginger," I said. "Which one did you always want to be? Ginger or Mary Ann?"

"Mary Ann," Mom said without hesitation.

Mary Jo nodded. "Definitely Mary Ann."

"Really? I know she was cute and sweet and had that whole mom-and-apple-pie thing going," I said, "but Ginger had the best clothes. I loved all those gorgeous evening gowns she wore. Although, as a little girl, I always wondered where she got them."

"At the Neiman Marcus on the other side of the island," Mom said.

I was in the middle of unpacking some favorite childhood friends—*Little Women*, *Charlotte's Web*, *The Secret Garden*, and *The Little Princess*—when there was a knock at the door. From the other side came the sound of excited chatter.

"*There* you guys are," I said to a beaming Lexie and Jacob. "I was beginning to wonder if you were ever going to get here."

Lexie, who was clutching some wilted daisies in hands that had most likely been clean earlier that morning, turned to her mother, who was still climbing the stairs, and said, "See, Mommy. I tol' you An Beebee would miss us." She thrust the grubby flowers at me. "These are for you. I pickeded 'em myself."

I hugged my niece. "Thank you, sweetie. They'll look perfect on the kitchen table."

Just then, Karen made it to the top of the stairs and followed her youngest into the room. "I kept them away as long as I could so they wouldn't be in your way while you were moving."

"You didn't have to do that."

She grinned. "Oh yes I did, Pheebs. You don't know what it's like to have a four- and a five-year-old underfoot when you're trying to get something done." She raised the baking pan in her hands. "I made chicken enchiladas for lunch. Figured you guys might be getting hungry by now. I'll go dish it up, okay?"

"Thanks. Hey, did I ever tell you you're my favorite sister-in-law?"

"I'm your only sister-in-law," she said, heading into the kitchenette.

Close behind were Mom and a hungry Lexie, who was telling her grandma how much she liked enchiladas—"But I didn't when I was little."

I turned to my nephew, who was standing just inside the doorway, both hands behind his back. "Jacob. Come on in, buddy. Join the rest of us."

He gave me a shy smile as he crossed the threshold. "Aunt Phoebe, I have a present for you too."

"You do? What is it? I love presents!"

He puffed out his little chest. "Well, I know how scared you are of mice and stuff, an' I didn't want you to be lonely all by yourself in your new 'partment." He held out a calico kitten he'd been hiding behind his back. "This is Herman. His grandma's Ginger, Grandma's cat, but his mom lives at our house. When he grows up, he'll keep the mice away."

As long as he doesn't bring them home. "Thank you, Jacob. I couldn't have asked for a better present." I reached for Herman, but the kitten let out a loud meow and scrambled up the curtains, startling me.

Jacob patted my hand. "'S'okay, Aunt Phoebe. Don't feel bad. He's just scared of strangers. But he'll be okay."

Yes, but will I?

Below us all of a sudden came the sound of loud banging and scraping. "Hey, Pheebert," Jordy yelled up the stairs, "Make way. We're coming up."

I shot Karen a quizzical look. "Now what?"

She gave me a sick smile. "The couch."

"Ah, the infamous couch. Don't worry. It can't be all that bad."

Sure it could. And it was.

Jordy and two of his students carried in the brown *and* green *and* orange *and* gold plaid polyester monstrosity. And every fashion fiber in my being screamed in agony. *Could anything* be *more ugly?* I fingered the shiny, scratchy fabric.

"Phoebe," Mom whispered, out of Jordy's hearing. "I have some nice red chenille I think would work really well as a slipcover."

"How soon do you think you can make it?" I whispered back.

She peered appraisingly at the peas-and-carrots couch. And shook her head.

"I can have it by tonight."

[chapter twenty-four]

On Sunday morning, when we all filed into Holy Communion as a family, we got the surprise of our lives. Just inside the narthex stood my old boss in an ancient, ill-fitting suit, tugging at his too-tight collar.

"Gordon? In church?" I whispered. "Watch your heads, everyone—the ceiling might fall in."

"Shhh, Phoebe," Mom remonstrated. She welcomed her old friend with a dazzling smile. "Gordon, how nice to see you. Would you like to sit with us?"

He turned pink and nodded, then joined us. We sang the opening hymn, "A Mighty Fortress Is Our God," Mom sharing her hymnal with him. Next came "Amazing Grace."

It was pretty amazing. I'd never heard Gordon sing before. *Scripture does say make a joyful noise—and he's definitely making noise.*

Something else was going on with Gordon during that service. A couple of times I caught him stealing sideways glances at Mom when she was otherwise occupied. One time Gordon saw me looking. At him looking. He reddened and affixed his eyes on the pulpit, paying absorbed attention to the message.

After church, I wanted to stick around and find out what his intentions were, but I had to race over to Barley Pres in time to make it to Sunday school. The last thing I saw as I drove away was him escorting my mother to her car. Mom smiled and waved at me as I drove past.

I scurried into the Sunday-school room, eager to share the latest with Mary Jo. Spotting her at the coffee cart, I hurried over. "You won't believe—" My excitement nosedived when I saw who she was talking to.

"What, Pheebs?" my horsy friend said. "What's going on?"

Glad I'd worn my highest ankle-straps that day, I pulled myself up to my full height, towering over the puny publisher at her side. "Never mind. Class is about to start. I'll go grab us some seats."

"Make sure you save one for Alex," she called after me. "We'll catch up with you in a sec, as soon as we finish our coffee."

Coffee. I'd kill for some. But I wasn't about to stand around making small talk with the evil newspaper slayer, even if we were at church. I sat down and tried to focus my thoughts Godward, desperately trying to ignore the heavenly aroma emanating from the coffee corner.

Good way to practice self-control, Phoebe. Besides, you've been saying you wanted to cut back.

Mary Jo slipped in beside me and patted the seat next to her for Alex. Just then, Pastor Jeff strode into the room minus Amy, but carrying her guitar. "Good morning everyone. I'm afraid we'll have to do without our lovely worship leader this morning; she was feeling a bit under the weather today. Guess you'll just have to make do with me and the basic three chords I know." He shot a plaintive look to the class. "Unless there's someone else here who knows how to play? If so, don't be shy. Please speak up and put me out of my misery."

No one moved. But I heard a tentative Alex say under his breath, "I play a little."

"You do?" Mary Jo said. "Hey, Jeff, we got a guy right here." She urged the reluctant newcomer forward.

"Well, c'mon down, brother!" Jeff said in his best *Price Is Right* voice. He shook Alex's hand and passed him the guitar.

His hand got tangled in the shoulder strap. "Uh, why don't we pray," Alex said, taking a deep breath. "Father, as we enter into Your presence here today, help us to cast aside all the cares and difficulties of the past week and focus only on You. Open our hearts to Your leading. We lift our voices to You in praise and honor, Lord. Amen."

He strummed a few chords, then led the small class in "Open the Eyes of My Heart, Lord."

Who is this guy? It can't be the same evil newspaper publisher I know and loathe. Maybe he's schizophrenic.

Next, he segued into "Our God Is an Awesome God" while everyone joined in enthusiastically.

I've got it! It's his long-lost twin brother who was separated at birth. The good twin.

Then Alex quieted things down a bit. "I'm not sure all of you know this next one," he said, "but it's an old favorite from my younger years." He set the guitar down, closed his eyes and began to sing in a clear tenor voice "All Things Bright and Beautiful." Only one class member joined in on that one—Bruce Hubert. And oddly enough, although my old teacher's voice hadn't changed since karaoke night, something else had.

In that impromptu duet with Alex Spencer, Hubert the Horrible sounded almost like Hubert the Holy.

It was just too weird.

Okay, bad Alex twin, come out, come out, whereever you are.

I had trouble concentrating on Jeff's message that day. It had something to do with the scripture in which Paul tells us to forget what is behind us and focus on the race ahead. And I tried to listen to what he was saying about it, but my mind kept wandering. Afterward, Sylvia Ann, Bruce, and the rest of the class clustered around Alex, welcoming him and thanking him for the worship time. But all I could think of was making a quick getaway.

"Hey Pheebs, where you goin'?" Mary Jo called as I started to slip out the door. "Don't forget—barbecue out at my place in half an hour."

All eyes, including Alex's, turned to me.

"Sorry, Mary Jo. Got a family thing to go to. You all have fun, though." I gave a brief wave and shifted my eyes away from her disappointed gaze. "Talk to you later."

Stomach growling, but full of relief over avoiding more time with Jekyll-and-Hyde Alex, I sped to Mom's for our weekly family Sunday dinner.

The screen door slammed behind me. "Hi, everyone. Hope I'm not late."

No welcoming greeting returned mine. The house was strangely silent—and strangely devoid of any home-cooked aromas.

"Mom?" I sniffed my way into the kitchen.

But the only scents that met my enquiring nose were those of Pine-Sol and Mom's lemon air freshener. The stove was gleaming, but cold. As was the coffee—cold, that is, not gleaming.

"Hello? Where is everybody?" I looked around for a note. Nothing.

Concerned, I punched in my brother's cell number.

"Hello? Grantmobile here." Laughing voices and singing in the background made it difficult to hear.

"Jordy?"

"Hi, little sister. How's it goin'?"

"Where are you?"

"*On the road again . . .*" Jordy sang out in his best Willie impression to what I could hear was the loud delight of my nieces and nephew.

"To where?" I interrupted, raising my voice to be heard over the happy din.

"Old Sacramento," he said. "Gordon invited Mom out to lunch, so we thought we'd take the kids for burgers at Fanny Ann's, then maybe go to the Railroad Museum or Sutter's Fort."

"Railroad Museum!" I could hear Jacob the train connoisseur yelling in the background.

"No," Lexie argued. "Wanna go Sutter's Fort an' make candles."

Mom's having lunch with Gordon.

"What's up, Pheebert? Anything wrong? How's the barbecue?"

"Nothing's wrong. Just wanted to touch base. Hey Jord, you're breaking up. Say hi to the kids. I'll talk to you later."

My stomach growled again.

"Guess it's just you and me, kid."

Once home in my cozy new apartment, I made myself a peanut butter and banana sandwich and wolfed it down with a tall glass of milk. Then I brewed some espresso and curled up in my pretty black-and-white club chair. I tried to call Lins but got her voice mail.

Needing an old friend, I popped in *The Parent Trap*.

I sang along with the twin Hayleys on "Let's Get Together, Yeah, Yeah, Yeah" and sighed with longing as I always did when I got to the romantic part between divorced parents Brian Keith and Maureen O'Hara near the end. And for the first time in the past few busy weeks, it seemed, I found myself thinking about my Filmguy. *Wonder how he liked this movie? Never did find out.*

I sighed again, this time with regret over the loss of that potential relationship. Try as they might, Jordy's students had been unable to recover the lost information in my laptop, including my address book. They'd rebuilt my computer for me, but Filmguy and his address were gone with the wind. And though I could probably have unearthed it with some research on the work computers, so much time had gone by I was just too embarrassed to try.

Snap out of it, girl! Spilt milk. Besides, he's in Ohio, you're in California. Long-distance relationships never work. It just wasn't meant to be.

I returned my attention to the familiar, comforting movie. This time, though, when Brian kissed Maureen and held her in his arms and she said to her ex-husband, "Oh, Mitch, it's been so long. So very long," I thought of my Mom.

How many years has it been since Mom had any romance in her life? Dad's been gone almost fifteen years now, and she's been alone all that time. I thought again of how I'd misjudged my mother for so long, thinking she'd shackled my dreamer dad to small-town life and vowing that would never happen to me.

Then I thought about Gordon and Mom.

Lord, thank You for bringing Gordon to church today. Please touch him and draw him to You. And I pray for the burgeoning romance between him and Mom. Please watch over that relationship, Lord, and keep Mom's heart safe. Gordon's, too.

As I prayed, I also thought of Alex Spencer's Dr. Jekyll appearance at Sunday school today. He'd seemed so sincere—but then I'd thought he was sincere when I met him in Cleveland, too. I just couldn't bring myself to trust the man. But I was beginning to realize there might be something wrong with my attitude too.

Lord, I know You want us to love our enemies and forgive those who do us wrong. But I'm having a hard time turning the other cheek here—especially when I think he might be hurting the people I care about. Please help me to be wise as a serpent in my dealings with Alex Spencer . . .

After dinner that evening, when I was pretty sure Mom would be home from her date, I knocked on her back door bearing gifts.

"Daughter, what a nice surprise," she said, ushering me into the kitchen. "What have you got there?"

"Triple-fudge brownies with frosting and vanilla-bean ice cream. The brownies are from a mix," I said, "but I doctored them up with chocolate chips and Reese's Pieces."

Her eyes gleamed. (I come by my chocoholic tendencies honestly.) "Yum. My favorite." Then a puzzled look crossed her face. "To what do I owe this honor? It's not my birthday or anything."

I pulled two bowls down from the cupboard and started dishing up our dessert. "No special reason. Can't a girl enjoy some chocolate and just spend a little time with her Mom? We didn't get to talk at all today." I grabbed a couple of spoons from the drawer and set the now-full bowls down on the table. "So . . . how was your day?"

She laughed. "Daughter, you're about as subtle as Sylvia Ann and her hairstyles. Why don't you just come out and ask me what's on your mind?"

"Okay." I took a deep breath. "What's going on with you and Gordon, Mom? Don't get me wrong—he's a great guy and a good boss. But I don't want you to get hurt." I gave her an earnest, I'm-watching–your-biblical-back look. "Remember what Scripture says about being unequally yoked."

This time my mother snorted. Then guffawed. Long and hard.

"Phoebe," she said at last, wiping her eyes, "I'm not planning to *marry* the guy, for goodness' sakes. Can't a woman enjoy a little attention and companionship with a man without everyone trying to marry her off? Gordon's just a *friend*."

I shot her a penetrating look from beneath my arched brows. "Hmmm. I think I've heard that somewhere before."

When the full impact of my words hit her, she guffawed all over again.

I joined her. And by the time we finally returned to our brownies, they were swimming in a vanilla lake.

chapter twenty-five

h ey, Gordon, I've got that copy you wanted," I said, the bell on the newspaper office door jangling behind me the next morning. "Gordon?"

A curly brown head appeared from beneath my desk and banged into a half-open drawer. "Gordon's not here," my enemy said, rubbing his head and standing up. "He went down to the Barley Twist to grab us some lunch."

Catching my pointed look at the desk, Alex said, "I was adding some more memory to your computer. Hopefully this will speed things up for you."

I nodded a curt thanks and set my article on Gordon's desk. "Well, I'll just leave this, then."

"Don't go, Phoebe. I'm glad we're finally alone."

"I've heard that before."

"I'd really like to talk to you," he said. "I think it's about time we cleared the air, especially since we're going to be working together."

"I don't know that we *will* be working together."

"Which would be one of the things we need to discuss," he said. "Don't you agree?"

I racked my brain to think of a stinging refusal or, at the very least, a clever comeback. "I guess."

Brilliant, writer girl. You have such a way with words. No playground third-grader could have done better.

He indicated a chair. "Can we sit down, please?"

"No thanks. I'd rather stand."

Alex leaned against the desk. "Phoebe, you and I got off on the wrong foot right from the beginning." He stopped and shifted his weight. "Wait. That's not accurate. We actually *started* on the right foot when we met and played Trivial Pursuit at Lone Rangers. That was fun." He smiled at the memory. "I thought we made a pretty good team—kind of like Cary Grant and Roz Russell in *His Girl Friday.*"

Don't try and play the old movies card with me, bucko. It's not going to work.

"Anyway, I'm hoping we can do the same here at the *Bulletin,*" he said, tossing an engaging smile my way. Well, it would have been engaging if it had come from anyone other than him. And I didn't return it.

He raked his hand through his hair, wincing as he inadvertently touched the tender spot. "Sorry. I'm getting ahead of myself. Look, Phoebe, I know you're upset with me, and I understand. I realize how hard losing your job at the *Star* was for you—particularly, not getting the movie critic position."

My hands clenched.

"That night at Lone Rangers, when Lindsey mentioned you worked at the *Star*, it hit me," he said, pausing. "I put your name and the *Star* together and realized you were on the list of casualties. Obviously, I couldn't say anything—corporate confidentiality and all. The reorg wasn't public knowledge yet."

"Casualties." My hands clenched tighter. "Interesting choice of words."

"Fits, though. Don't you think?" Alex gave me a wry glance. "That's why I left in such a hurry. It put me in an awkward position. I couldn't stay, knowing what I knew." He sighed. "I'm truly sorry that you lost your job, Phoebe. And that I—my company—was the unfortunate bearer of your pink slip. It wasn't personal—just corporate downsizing."

Shades of Meg Ryan and Tom Hanks in You've Got Mail. My hands balled into fists. "Maybe it wasn't personal for you, but—"

He held up his hand. "Let me finish. Meeting you through church and then becoming friends with Phil and Lindsey has made it personal for me. I feel like I know you through them. And also, you're my sister in Christ, Phoebe." His eyes bored into mine. "I've been praying for you. Since Cleveland. Not every day, but whenever you came to mind."

I smiled reluctantly. "Not exactly what I've been doing when I thought about you."

"I'll bet," he said, shooting me a loopy grin. "Okay if we sit down now to continue this?"

I glanced out the plate glass window. Still no sign of Gordon. "I suppose."

He pulled up a chair, and I sat behind my desk. "I was pleased when I heard you got this job at the *Bulletin*. Then I read your 'Save the Bijou' piece, and I knew there was something I could do to try and make amends."

"Is that why you offered me the job in Boston?" I asked, bristling. "Because you felt sorry for me?"

"No," he said in a measured tone. "I offered you the job because you're an excellent writer and I happened to know they needed someone like you. I'm not in the habit of extending job offers out of pity. That would be bad business." He ran his hand through his hair again. "Since I—my company—was the one who delivered the bad news the last time, I wanted to be the good messenger this time." He looked up at the ceiling. "I'm glad I got to deliver the second message, Phoebe. It's how I got to meet and fall in love with—"

In spite of myself, I sucked in my breath.

"—Barley."

My breathing resumed. "Which brings us to the here and now."

"Exactly."

I leaned forward in my chair. "Why did you buy the *Bulletin*?"

Alex smiled. "Spoken like a true reporter." He glanced around the small, cluttered office, then out the front window again, a faraway look in his eyes. "I came here to breathe," he said.

"Excuse me?"

He shrugged his shoulders. "I needed to breathe," he repeated. "Your editorial about the Bijou grabbed me, Phoebe. Then I read the rest of the *Bulletin,* and I was intrigued. I wanted to see this little town with the historic movie theater for myself. So I came out to offer you a job, and yes, to check out the town at the same time—not knowing I'd get to enjoy such a delightful production of *Oklahoma* in the process," he added with a grin. Then he grew serious again. He shot me a penetrating look. "But, I did *not* come here with the intention of buying the *Bulletin.* That happened later."

"Speaking of that," I said. "I'm a bit confused. When you offered me the Boston job, you said, if I remember correctly, that I should be playing with 'the big guys.' So why do you now want me to stay at the *Bulletin?* Do you think I can't cut it on a major daily?"

"Not in the least." He gave me a searching look. "I just think you have some unfinished business here and that maybe God wants you to stay for a while."

Just then the jangling of the bell announced Gordon's return with lunch.

"Phoebe, good to see you," my soon-to-be ex-boss said, shooting a nervous look from me to Alex. "I'm sorry. I didn't know you'd be here, or I'd have gotten you something."

"That's okay. I'm not hungry," I lied as the fragrant aroma of chicken and lobster bisque wafted out of his takeout bag.

"Phoebe and I have just been talking," Alex said. "About Barley, and why I'm here."

"I'm glad," Gordon said. He reached in the bag and pulled out two Styrofoam cups with steam rising from them, followed by two hefty sandwiches. "It was a stroke of good luck that brought this guy here just when I was finally thinking it might be about time to retire." He handed Alex one of the cups of soup. "The day he came to town—no, wait, it was that night after the cast party at Jordy and Karen's—we got to talking. Alex mentioned how he liked the pace of Barley. I mentioned how the pace—running the *Bulletin,* I mean—was becoming too fast for me and that I'd like to pull back. Slow down and enjoy life a bit more. I'd been thinking there was so much I'd been missing all these years . . ." He blushed, unable to meet my eye, then hurried on. "Anyway, one thing led to another and, well, before long we'd started working on the negotiations."

Gordon unwrapped his sandwich and held up half to me. "Sure you don't want some? It's grilled chicken and avocado."

My stomach pouted when I shook my head. "So you really *want* to retire and sell the paper, Gordon? You're happy about this?"

"Very happy." He took a bite of his sandwich. "I tried to tell you that the other night, Phoebe, but I kind of made a mess of things. I'm sorry. I'm much better with words on paper than in person. And you took me by surprise when you came back early."

"Surprised me too."

Gordon sipped his soup. "I'm not completely retiring though—just semi. I'll still keep writing. But I get to get rid of all the business and management stuff I never liked anyway," he said, with a wide grin at Alex. "Yep, a stroke of luck."

More like the hand of God.

This time my stomach growled. Not a quiet, ladylike growl either. This was the queen of the hungry beasts on the prowl.

Alex pushed the untouched other half of his sandwich my way. "Eat, Phoebe. I don't want a fainting reporter on my hands." He hesitated. "At least I hope you'll still be on my hands." He flushed. "Um, the *Bulletin's* hands. Will you stay on? We really could use your help."

Gordon chimed in. "That's true, Phoebe. And don't forget the Bijou, either. The fundraising drive is in full gear, and you're the one who got folks all excited about it."

E.T.'s gravelly voice, which I'd first heard in Lindsey's apartment on my return trip to Cleveland, sounded in my head again. *"Stay home."*

Home. My darling new apartment. The kids. Jordy and Karen. Mom. "All right, I'll stay. For now."

Alex beamed. Gordon beamed. And I tore into my half sandwich, ravenous. My stomach thanked me. Over lunch, we discussed how best to transition the management of the paper as well as the new breakdown of duties.

The next day, I turned in my first assignment to my new boss. Less than an hour later, he e-mailed me his response.

> Great preview of *To Kill a Mockingbird*, Phoebe. One of my favorite movies of all time, by the way. Books, too. Hopefully the article will help introduce a whole new generation to this classic. But you might want to mention that this was Robert Duvall's movie debut as the mute Boo Radley. People who only know him from *The Godfather, Lonesome Dove,* or *The Apostle* might appreciate that bit of trivia.

My high-school French came back to me all of a sudden, and I felt a little *frisson* of excitement. *That's right, Alex really knows his movie trivia too.* Glancing up from my computer, I saw him busily typing away, his blue Oxford shirtsleeves rolled up to his elbows. And heaven help me, beginning to remember why I'd once found the man so attractive . . .

Shaking my head, I inserted a paragraph about the respected Hollywood actor—who'd also said that infamous and oft-quoted line in *Apocalypse Now,* "I love the smell of napalm in the morning"—getting his start in films by playing the gentle Boo Radley. Then I spell-checked the revised piece and resent it to my editor.

Alex pushed back his chair, stood up, and stretched. "Phoebe, I need to run down to the Bijou to check a few things out for this follow-up story. Should be back in about an hour or so. Can you hold the fort, please?"

"No problem," I said, shooting him my brisk, journalist smile with just enough of a lilt to it to help him see beyond my workplace efficiency to the fun, exciting, spiritual woman I was.

He stopped at my desk and frowned. "You okay? Did you get your coffee this morning? You've got this little twitch."

Twenty minutes later, the bell jangling at the front door made me look up. "Back so soon?"

It wasn't Alex. A slight teenage girl staggering under a huge bouquet of red roses pushed open the door with her foot. "Where can I set these?" she asked, out of breath.

Jumping up, I cleared a space on the filing cabinet next to my desk. She set down the gorgeous flowers and rushed off with a quick thanks, late for her next delivery.

"Wow. It's been ages since someone sent me flowers. And so many too. Let's see: one, two, three, four, five, six, seven . . . two dozen! Classy way to begin a working relationship, boss." I inhaled their heady fragrance, then snatched up the card from the Lodi Florist, a goofy smile on my face.

> Hey, country boy, congratulations on your latest acquisition. But aren't you supposed to go forward rather than backward? Barley?? Enjoy editing the crop reports and watch out for falling cows and their leavings. Miss you. All my love, Cordelia.

The goofy smile froze in place. "Nice, Mr. Two-Face. Go ahead and put down our town to your upscale girlfriend." I jammed the card back into its plastic holder. "Cordelia? What kind of affected name is that, anyway? Sounds like old money from Boston." I sniffed. "She probably went to Smith or Vassar and talks through her nose."

Yes, my state-college self said. *And she probably has cheekbones you could ski down, no hips at all, and thighs that have never been introduced.*

I shoved the flowers away from me and grabbed my purse. Flinging open the door, I ran smack into Gordon.

"Where are you off to in such a hurry, young lady?" he asked. "I just saw Alex over at the Bijou, and he wants to take us out to lunch. You in the mood for Chinese?"

"Sorry, Gordon. No can do. Got a couple of appointments for some stories. Must dash. Catch you later."

That night our whole family, including red meat–lover Mom, celebrated Karen's thirty-fifth birthday at The Barley Twist. Sydney showed us to our seats, and who should we see directly behind us but Alex, Gordon, and a very tanned, tropical-clad Esther having dinner together.

The trio nodded a greeting, with Gordon shooting Mom a million-dollar smile. She returned it, and I busied myself helping Lexie put her napkin in her lap so I wouldn't have to meet the eyes of the two-faced tycoon.

"You worked at the *Bulletin* for many years, Esther," I overheard Alex say. "I'd like to pick your brain about a few things."

Esther peered at him over her bifocals. "Predict if it's going to rain? I can't do that. For that you need a weather forecaster and special equipment. Although my rheumatism acting up is always a pretty good indicator . . ."

Gordon leaned forward and raised his voice. "No, Esther. He wants to *pick your brain*."

"Pick it for what?"

Yeah. For what exactly? More insights on how to trash our town to your snooty girlfriend?

"I need to go potty," Lexie announced in a loud voice.

Her mother started to get up.

"No, you stay, birthday girl," I said. "I'll take her. C'mon, Lexie." I held out my hand.

I was washing my niece's hands when the restroom door opened, admitting Esther.

"Why, Phoebe, you look downright maternal," she said. Her eyes gleamed. "Before you know it, you'll be having one of your own."

"Not anytime soon, Esther." I laughed. "I'm not even married."

She cupped her ear. "When'd you say you're gettin' married?"

"I'm *not* getting married!" I said louder into her ear.

"Well, all right. You don't have to get your knickers in a twist. I can understand your wanting to be an independent career woman. Respect it too." Esther looked in the mirror and patted her hair. "That's what I've been. But things have changed, you know. These days women can have both. And you want to be careful, so you don't wind up like me. Alone."

I sighed and patted her on the back. "Okay, Esther. See you later." Then I took my wide-eyed niece's hand, and we returned to our group.

Back at the table, Lexie let out a howl. "An Beebee's never getting mawwied. She gonna be all alone and wrinkly like my toad."

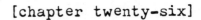

chapter twenty-six

Over the next couple days I managed to steer clear of Alex pretty well. That's the good thing about being a reporter. You can always leave the office to go do research or conduct an interview.

I made it through the rest of the week that way, and Friday night Mom and I divvied up the kids for babysitting purposes, knowing Jordy and Karen needed some romantic one-on-one time before the new baby came. She took Lexie and Jacob to her house to make chocolate-chip cookies and watch *Finding Nemo* for the trillionth time, while I invited Elizabeth and Ashley over for a slumber party.

The girls and I didn't waste any time getting into our flannel pj's and animal slippers for the night. Elizabeth's young feet sported warm and fuzzy gray kitties, Ashley wore elephants, and I'd recently traded in my worn pink pigs for some Winnie the Poohs.

We were sitting one in front of the other on the living room floor with me French-braiding Ashley's hair, Ashley doing the same for her sister, and Elizabeth holding a blissful Herman the kitten in her lap. As we munched on some microwave popcorn (light butter), Elizabeth asked me once again to tell the oft-repeated story of how her grandparents met.

"Your Grandpa came to town as a teacher fresh out of college in the late sixties," I said. "He planned to stay in Barley a year teaching English and drama, then move on to San Francisco or L.A., where he hoped to do some acting in addition to teaching . . ."

Elizabeth craned her head back to look at me. "But he didn't move, did he? 'Cause he saw Grandma on the float and fell in love with her."

"Shhh, Elizabeth," Ashley scolded. "Let Aunt Phoebe tell it. And turn around, or your braid's going to be all crooked."

I scooped up another handful of popcorn. "You're right, Elizabeth. He *didn't* move. All his plans changed the day he set eyes on Gloria Jean Johnson at the Miss Udderly Delicious Dairy Pageant."

"That's Grandma," Elizabeth interrupted again as her sister shot her a frown.

"That's right, Elizabeth," I said. "And Gloria Jean was the belle of Barley. People always said she looked like a young Elizabeth Taylor. (Grandma was skinnier back then.) So it was no surprise when she won the pageant that year."

Ashley's fingers stilled, and both girls turned around to face me, enraptured.

"When your grandpa saw this girl with the sapphire eyes, a mass of dark hair, and a tinfoil crown, riding down Main Street on the Miss Udderly Delicious cow float, he thought she was the most beautiful thing he'd ever seen. He just had to meet her. So he followed that float all the way down to the end of street. And when it stopped, he walked right up and introduced himself. 'My name is Grant. Richard Grant,' he said. 'Grant, as in Cary, so you won't forget.' Your grandma looked at him with those vivid blue eyes and said, 'I won't forget.' Later that evening, when he saw her dancing with Bud Jacobs, who'd lost an eye, an arm, and so much more in Vietnam—"

"He knew he'd found his 'Glory,'" the girls, who knew this love story by heart, said in unison.

"Yep. And six months later they were married," I said. "A year after that, your daddy was born."

Ashley sighed, "And that was how our family began. I just love that story. Soooo romantic."

"Yep." I stood up and stretched. The confectionary tale had left my taste buds primed for something sweet. "Anyone want a hot fudge sundae?"

"I do, I do," they both chorused.

We sat at my fifties diner table slurping our sundaes—no nuts—when Elizabeth piped up, "Aunt Phoebe, don't you want to get married?"

I choked. "Good thing I went the nutless route, or else I'd be asphyxiating on one right now. What makes you think I don't want to get married, Elizabeth?"

My middle niece looked across the table at me with grave eyes. "Well . . . because of what Lexie said at the restaurant. Also, you're kind of old."

"Elizabeth!" Ashley scolded her sister.

"It's true," she said. "Grandma was twenty when she married Grandpa, Mommy was nineteen when she married Daddy, and my teacher who just got married is twenty-four. Aunt Phoebe's over thirty!"

Ashley sprang to my defense before I had a chance to. "Thirty's not old. Lots of people today get married in their thirties—even forties." My once-shy older niece tossed her head. "I'm not planning to get married until I'm at least thirty either," she announced. "There's lots I want to do before I settle down—like go to Paris and London and Switzerland . . ."

I gave Ashley a warm smile, then turned to my younger niece. "Elizabeth, I *would* like to get married someday . . ." I remembered what Mary Jo had said. "*If* that's what God wants for me. Not everyone gets married, sweetie." I slurped a spoonful of hot fudge. "But if I do, I want it to be to the man God has chosen for me. When*ever* that may be—next year, ten years from now . . . Who knows? Maybe I'll be fifty."

Elizabeth looked horrified.

"Meanwhile," I shot them both an impish glance, "forget about marriage. And men. It's karaoke time." I grabbed my red feather boa, along with a pink one (for Elizabeth) and a white one (for Ashley) that I'd picked up expressly for tonight. They squealed with delight as we draped them over our respective flannel-clad shoulders and began singing, "Girls Just Wanna Have Fun."

We danced around the living room, segued into "It's in His Kiss

(The Shoop Shoop Song)" and were just beginning a new tune when a knock sounded at the door.

Expecting Mary Jo, who'd promised to drop by, I opened my front door with a flourish, thrust out my right hand, palm up, and belted out a little Supremes—or started to: "Stop in the Na—"

It wasn't Mary Jo.

"All right, already," Alex said with a huge grin on his face, "I'll stop."

chapter twenty-seven

S o then what'd you do?" Lins asked when I called her later to tell her about my flannelled karaoke embarrassment.

"Thankfully, Ashley was right behind me," I said. "She stepped right up and told Alex it was a girls' night in and he'd have to come back another time. Then she politely said goodnight and shut the door in his face. In Christian love, of course."

"Of course. Go Ashley!"

"I know. Can you believe it? My timid little niece has certainly come a long way."

Lins chuckled. "Wonder whose influence that could be, Aunt Phoebe?"

"I wonder. Hey, speaking of wondering—I've been wondering how you and a certain friend of mine are doing. How's it going with the Phil-man?"

"He drives me crazy!" Lindsey said. "He's such a guy."

"Which is a good thing."

"Except when it comes to listening." She sighed. "What is it with men and the whole communication thing?"

"You tell me."

"I hate it when I'm telling him something important, like maybe something that happened at work," Lindsey said, "and I've hardly begun talking, and his fingers are already twitching on the remote. That is so rude! You never do that. Neither do any of my other girlfriends. So why does he?"

"It's called testosterone."

Suddenly I heard a rustling behind me, and I screeched as

something cold and wet slid down my back. "Sorry, Lins, gotta go kill a couple of nieces." I hung up the phone, and Elizabeth and Ashley's excited shrieks punctured the air. "Okay, girls, prepare to die. The Phoebster takes no prisoners in the ice wars."

The next afternoon, long after the girls had left, I was reading *Little Women* for the seventeenth time when I heard what sounded like someone making their laborious way up the steps to my apartment. I hurried to the door and opened it. Halfway up the stairs stood my very pregnant sister-in-law, red-faced from the exertion and breathing hard.

"Karen, what are you doing?" I ran down the steps to her side. "You shouldn't be climbing up and down these stairs! Why didn't you just call me?"

"This kind of news you don't tell over the phone—it has to be in person. Pheebs, you'll never guess!"

I slid my arm around her thickened waist and helped her up the rest of the stairs. "You're going to have that baby right here and now on my steps?"

"No." She smiled as I led her inside and settled her onto my slip-covered couch. "Don't worry. I've still got another two weeks. And since every one of my kids has been late, it's probably more like three. Never fear. No, it's not about me, Pheebs." She twitched with excitement. "It's about the Bijou."

"What about it?"

"We did it! *You* did it, Pheebs! The Bijou's saved!"

"What?" I leaped off the couch and began jumping up and down, sending a scared Herman scuttling under the bed. Then reality intruded on my exultant display and I stopped jumping. "But how? Last I heard, we didn't even have twenty thousand dollars in seat sponsorship. Didn't we only take in a couple of thousand from *Oklahoma*?" I frowned, trying to add up the numbers. "The fashion show only brought in a few hundred, right? That leaves us with less than twenty-five thou."

Karen's eyes shone. "Right. But someone made a *huge* donation, Pheebs. I mean huge." She paused for effect. "Enough to buy the entire theater and even spruce it up a bit."

"What?! Who?"

She shook her head in wonderment. "We don't know. Some mysterious benefactor. The card included with the cashier's check simply said, 'From a movie lover.'" She snickered. "If I didn't know your financial state, Pheebs, I'd think it was you."

I sucked in my breath.

He lied. I should have known. He didn't come here to lead a quiet, simple life running a little country newspaper. No, he came here to take over the whole town. Buying up newspapers left and right around the country just isn't enough of a thrill for him anymore. He needs a bigger challenge.

"Pheebs? Are you okay?" Karen asked. "Your face is getting all red." She laughed. "You're the one who looks like she's about to go in labor."

"I'm fine," I murmured absently. "But let's get you back to the house now. I need to run into town."

"What for all of a sudden?" She put on her best teacher voice. "C'mon, now, share with the class."

"Just something I have to do. Tell you about it later."

This is just like what happened in It's a Wonderful Life *when mean old Mr. Potter tried to buy up all of Bedford Falls and turn it into Potterville,* I raged as I drove into town. *And he would have done it, too, if George Bailey hadn't stopped him. Well, I may not be Jimmy Stewart, but I can definitely bring a little Scarlett O'Hara to the table.*

By the time I arrived at the *Bulletin* office I'd worked myself up into even more of a lather. I parked my Bug right next to our publisher's—*and now theater owner's, don't forget*—shiny new Beamer. Yanking open the back door, I stormed in.

Alex looked up from his desk with a grin. "What? No red feather boa today? I'm disappointed. Not even Winnie the Pooh slippers?"

Then he took a second glance at my face. "Phoebe, what's wrong?"

"As if you didn't know!" I stomped over to him. "You come in here like Donald Trump or . . . or old Mr. Potter, thinking your money is so good and you can just buy anything you want, Mr. Rich Publishing Magnate. Well, I'll tell you something, Mr. Potter." I shook my fist at him in full "As God is my witness" Scarlett mode—not even caring that I was mixing my movies. "You can buy the paper and you can buy the Bijou, but you'll *never* own the Bailey Building and Loan!"

"The Bailey Building and Loan?" He gave me a bewildered glance. "Phoebe, what are you talking about?" He leaned closer to smell my breath. "Have you been drinking and watching old Christmas movies or something?"

"I don't drink," I said, switching to my best haughty Katharine Hepburn manner. "And you know perfectly well what I'm talking about, Mr. Ride-to-the-Rescue Millionaire. Buying up the Bijou to show everyone in town how philanthropic you are. Then playing the humble anonymous card to cover your tracks. When you and I *both* know it's just all part of your grand plan to take over the entire town."

"What?" he said, looking incredulous. "Um, I think someone forgot to take her meds today."

"Don't patronize me."

"Phoebe." I heard Gordon's voice behind me.

I held up my hand. "Not this time, Gordon. I know you two have this good ol' boy newspaper bonding thing going on, but this good ol' Barley girl is not going to stand by and watch him come in and take over our whole town . . ."

"Phoebe, Alex didn't buy the Bijou."

"Of course he did," I said. "Who else in this town has that kind of money?"

"Esther," Gordon said softly.

I wheeled around to face him. "Esther? That's impossible. She worked at the *Bulletin* her whole life and just retired. Where'd she get that kind of money?"

"She sold her land—the house and thirty acres her daddy left her," Gordon said. "Developers have been wanting to buy it for years. So Esther sold it to the developer who wanted to buy the Bijou property. Convinced him to back off the theater site and move to the other side of town. Then, with the proceeds of the land sale, she bought the Bijou from George Henderson and donated it to the community."

I sat down. Hard.

Gordon continued. "She didn't want anyone making a big fuss over her, so she asked that her gift be anonymous. Said she didn't want her right hand to know what her left hand was doing."

"But . . ." I was still trying to get my head around all this. "If Esther sold her house too, where will she live?"

Her former boss smiled. "Don't worry about that. Esther may be hard of hearing, but there's nothing wrong with that woman's mind." Gordon shook his head from side to side. "She had enough left after buying the Bijou—and then some—to get herself a nice little duplex. She's renting the other side out to one of her traveling girlfriends."

All at once I heard the back door close. I whirled around, but Alex was gone.

Way to go, impulsive, hot-headed girl. There goes your job.

Never mind your job, O selfish one. You just tried and convicted an innocent man without hearing all the evidence.

I slunk home to my cozy apartment where I spent a sleepless night pondering the error of my ways.

At Sunday school the next morning, the message was once again from the book of James: "Take ships as an example. Although they are so large and are driven by strong winds, they are steered by a very small rudder wherever the pilot wants to go. Likewise the tongue is a small part of the body, but it makes great boasts . . . With the tongue we praise our Lord and Father, and with it we curse men, who have been made in God's likeness. Out of the same mouth come praise and cursing. My brothers, this should not be."

I squirmed in my seat and stole a sideways glance at my boss—*if* he was still going to be my boss, that is, after yesterday's descent into madness—a few chairs over. But Alex was staring straight ahead, intent on the message.

You know what you have to do, girl.

I caught up with him in the parking lot just as he reached his car. "Alex."

He turned around, his face impossible to read. Especially since the sun was in my eyes. "Yes?"

"I'm sorry about my rudder."

He raised his eyebrows.

"I mean my tongue. My big mouth running away from me." I could feel the heat climbing up my face. "I have a bad habit of jumping to conclusions and speaking before I think or have all the facts. I said some awful things—thought even worse ones—" I continued in a rush, "and have been very unfair to you."

He started to speak.

I held up my hand. "No, let me finish. I need to say this. I wouldn't blame you in the least if you fired me. You have every right. I deserve it." I took a deep breath. "But I hope you won't allow my big mouth to ruin a friendship that was just beginning. Although I'd completely understand if you did. I have no right to expect anything from you after the horrible way I've behaved." I kicked a piece of gravel at my feet. "I hope, pray, that at some point you'll be able to forgive me."

Silence. Long, uncomfortable silence.

I tried. I started to walk away.

"Phoebe?"

"Yes?"

He knitted his eyebrows together. "I forgive you. I *have* to," he said with a grin, "that whole seventy-times-seven thing, you know. But only on one condition."

"Name it."

"You invite me to your mom's for one of her famous Sunday dinners."

"Done." I smiled back at him.

"And Phoebe?"

"Yes?"

"Just give me a little heads up before you start to jump off the deep end again. I want to be sure and put on my flak jacket."

That afternoon, after a mouthwatering meal of stuffed pork chops, twice-baked potatoes, steamed green beans, and sourdough biscuits, Mom asked who was ready for dessert.

Everyone groaned in protest. Except Gordon and Alex, who both started salivating. "What've you got, Gloria?"

"Homemade strawberry-rhubarb pie and warm apple crisp."

"I'd love some apple crisp," Alex said, "with a little ice cream, please?"

"I'll take some of your wonderful strawberry-rhubarb pie, Gloria," Gordon said. "Thank you."

"Not me," Karen said, patting her very pregnant stomach. "I'm watching my girlish figure."

"You and me both, Karen," I said.

Gordon sputtered. "Your figures are just fine. What is it today with all these women wanting to look like skinny young boys?" he asked. "I prefer a woman to look like a woman." He shot an appreciative glance at Mom, who blushed.

"Here, here!" Alex said, looking at me.

I changed the subject. "Who's up for a little game playing? Some Trivial Pursuit maybe—say, women against the men?"

"You're on," Jordy said.

Mom protested. "I'm terrible at this game. I never know any of the answers. I'll just watch."

"No way, Mom," I said. "It's all of us or none of us."

"Yeah, Gram, c'mon," Ashley said. "We'll help you. It'll be fun.

271

Besides," she said, sticking her tongue out at her father, "We're going to cream you guys. Women rock!"

Jordy gave his eldest a wicked smile. "Okay. Whoever loses has to do the dishes—and clean out Ginger's litter box for Grandma."

The guys got their first piece of Trivial-Pursuit pie answering a Science question, and Jacob proudly put it in the pie holder. But then they lost a Sports and Leisure question having to do with Barbie.

We women rolled the dice, and it was our turn to answer a Sports and Leisure one.

"I wish we'd gotten the Barbie question," Ashley said. It was common knowledge that the women in our family were, for the most part, sports impaired—Mom's basketball mania being the sole exception.

Jordy smirked as he pulled out a card. "Grab the dice and get ready to roll, men. This won't take long." Then he read the card to himself and paled. "This isn't a sports question," he said. "I need to pick another card."

I stilled his hand. "Not so fast. The category is Sports and *Leisure*. Ask the question, please."

He groaned and looked over at Mom. "What's the standard time for soft-boiling an egg?"

"Three minutes," she said, without blinking.

"You go, Grandma."

Next, we cleaned up on the pink wedge, which Lexie efficiently put in place. "Entertainment is my baby," I said, rolling the dice to see which color we'd get next.

"Hah! Yellow. History. Pheebs is terrible at this," my brother informed Alex. Jordy read the question. Then he groaned again. "What country's warplanes swiftly attacked twenty-five airfields in 1967?"

I gave my brother a knowing smirk but checked with my teammates first before answering. "Mom? Karen? Any idea? Ash?"

They shook their heads. "I know I *know* this," Karen said, "I just can't remember right now. Hormones."

"No problem," I said. "The answer would be Israel. Final answer."

"That's it," Karen squealed.

Jordy grumbled. "It would have to be a military question."

Alex gave him a quizzical look.

"Phoebe knows all about aircraft and warfare, thanks to being in the service."

Alex stared at me in amazement. "*You* were in the military?"

"Yep. United States Air Force," I said, snapping off a brisk salute. "Served my country with pride."

He continued to stare. "But you're such a . . ."

"A girly-girl?"

He nodded.

"Never underestimate the power of a woman," I said. "We can do anything—especially in a cute uniform."

Jordy grunted. "Okay, okay, enough with the banter. Let's get back to the battle of the sexes."

"Yeah," Ashley said. "'Cause we're going to wipe the board with you, Dad."

He winked and chucked his daughter under the chin. "Hey, show a little respect to your old man."

"C'mon guys, move it or lose it," I said. "Times a-wastin'."

Both sides kept filling up their plastic pie holders until each team was missing only one piece.

Now it was the guys' turn. They landed on pink. Entertainment.

Karen smirked and read the question. "Who played the title role in *Rebecca*?"

Alex glanced over at me and winked. "That would be no one. Rebecca is dead before the movie begins . . ."

My stomach fluttered, and I started to go down the Alex-fantasy road again, but my voice of wisdom self stopped me. *Don't go all romantic and goopy, girl. You just raked this guy over the coals yesterday, remember? Your relationship is still in that tenuous stage as you try to build a sister-in-Christ friendship with this man. Besides, he already has a girlfriend.*

I was brought back to reality by Karen and Jordy debating which way we were going to end the game—whether the guys could go to the safe center of the board and stay there, or whether they had to leave it every time they missed a question.

"If you don't give the right answer the first time, you need to go back out on the board with us," Karen said. "Surely, you can see that's the only fair way."

"Not necessarily, my sweet," Jordy said. "We've played it both ways in the past. And don't call me Shirley," he said, with a laugh.

I groaned. "What is it about guys and that movie? It's so silly. . ."

"Exactly," Alex said. "That's why we love it."

I turned to Gordon in mock desperation. "As a distinguished older man with more class than these two guys, please tell me you're not an *Airplane* fan too?" I pleaded.

He chuckled. "Sorry, Phoebe. No can do. It *is* a pretty funny movie. Silly, but funny." He paused. "Although definitely not in the same class as some of the great comedies like *Bringing up Baby* or *The Philadelphia Story*. Now, *those* are classics." He took a sip of coffee. "'Course that's because they had Cary Grant and Katharine Hepburn in them."

"I agree," Mom said. "Those two were always great together on the screen." She smiled. "Although Kate the great did a wonderful job with Humphrey Bogart in *The African Queen* too."

"I *knew* there was a reason I liked you, Gloria," Alex said, "in addition to your great cooking, that is. *The African Queen's* one of my favorites." He grinned. "Although, the last time I went to see it, I got stood up."

My head snapped up. *What did he just say?*

Jordy snorted. "*You* got stood up, man?" He chuckled. "Now I don't feel so bad about my college days. So when was this?"

"Just a couple of months ago," Alex said.

I started to hyperventilate.

It can't be.

Or can it? He was in Cleveland then. And remember he said the other day that To Kill a Mockingbird *was one of his favorites too* . . .

"Pheebs, are you okay?" Karen asked.

I nodded, a little dazed. "Uh-huh. Um, Alex, what's your favorite musical?"

He gave me a curious look. "*Singin' in the Rain.* Why?"

"Not *West Side Story*?" I asked.

"Nah, too much ballet twirling stuff for me. And no Gene Kelly."

My breathing really began to accelerate now. "So, are you a *Casablanca* fan?"

"Who isn't?" he asked. "The greatest romantic movie of all time."

I closed my eyes.

"Pheebs, you sure you're okay?" Karen asked.

"Fine." I gulped and waved off her concern. Then I looked straight at Alex. "Would you consider *The Parent Trap* with Hayley Mills and Maureen O'Hara to be a romantic movie?"

"Not especia—" His eyes widened. "Although," he said slowly, staring right back at me, "the scene near the end when Brian Keith and the gorgeous Maureen O'Hara get back together *is* pretty romantic."

Jordy looked at me, then over at Alex. "Hel-looow," he said. "Other people in the room, here. What's goin' on?"

ary Jo and I were vegging out in my apartment the next day after work, having polished off some kung pao chicken and egg rolls and dished at length about Alex and Filmguy being one and the same. When I revealed all, she chuckled and shook her head. "It could only happen to you, movie girl." Then we searched through my collection for a movie we could agree on and popped in my old video of *National Velvet*. But just as the young Elizabeth Taylor and her beloved thoroughbred won the Grand National, we were interrupted by a loud pounding at the door.

I opened the door to a white-faced Elizabeth. "Aunt Phoebe, come quick! Something's wrong with Mom."

Mary Jo and I sprinted down the stairs after my niece, quickly crossing the yard to Karen and Jordy's. Inside the kitchen, we found Karen doubled over in pain and standing in a strange puddle. Ashley hovered nearby while Lexie and Jacob stood wide-eyed in the doorway behind them.

"My water broke," Karen whispered, not wanting to alarm her children. "I need to get to the hospital."

Farm-bred Mary Jo took control. She eased Karen into a chair. "How far apart are the contractions?"

"Just a minute or so," my sister-in-law panted. "This is way too fast . . . Never like this with the other kids . . ."

While Mary Jo questioned Karen, I shepherded the kids into the living room.

Hold it together, girl. You've got to calm these children down . . .

I turned on the TV and fumbled for Lexie and Jacob's favorite

VeggieTales video. "Okay, now . . ." I gave them each a hug. "I need you guys to sit right here and watch this for a minute. And I need to call Grandma." I picked up the phone.

A pale but controlled Ashley spoke up. "I already called Grandma, Aunt Phoebe. She's on her way."

"Good girl. What about your dad?"

"I called his cell and left a message, but he's coaching a softball tournament in Stockton," she said. "Mom isn't due for two more weeks, and she's never been early with any of the rest of us, so she told Daddy to go." A tear escaped down her cheek.

Muffled moans filtered from the kitchen.

"What's wrong with Mommy?" Lexie asked. She started to cry.

I pulled her and a frightened Jacob close, reassuring Ashley and Elizabeth with my eyes. "Nothing's wrong with Mommy, sweetie. It's just time for the baby to be born, that's all, and sometimes it hurts a little bit. Maybe we should pray for your mom and the baby right now, okay?"

Just then I heard my mother's car roar up.

Thank you, Lord.

"Ash, Elizabeth, watch your brother and sister while I go talk to Grandma. In fact, tell you what," I said, squatting down to Jacob and Lexie's eye level. "Why don't you go get your shoes and socks on—'cause pretty soon we'll all be going to the hospital to meet your new sister."

I left the kids in their capable older sisters' care. "Father, be with Mom and the baby right now," I heard Ashley pray as I hurried back into the kitchen.

"Mom, thank goodness you're here! The kids . . ." I broke off as I noticed Alex Spencer standing a few feet away from my mother and Mary Jo, whose sole attention was focused on a panting Karen.

"I was at your mom's when Ashley called," he explained, "so I came along in case she needed help."

"We could use you right *now*, Alex," Mom said. "Help us get Karen into her bedroom."

"Bedroom?" I glanced from Alex to Mom. "But don't we need to get her to the hospital?"

"No time. The hospital's twenty minutes away, and this baby's coming *fast*."

Karen groaned. "Hurry. I have to push. I have to push."

"Phoebe, call 911," Mom said.

I blanched and punched in the emergency numbers. Alex picked up Karen and carried her down the hall, Mom and Mary Jo close on his heels.

After I hung up, a trying-to-be-grown-up Ashley appeared in the doorway holding her cell. "Aunt Phoebe, I can't get hold of Daddy. He usually keeps his phone on when he's coaching, but because it's the championships, he must have turned it off. He's probably only check-ing messages between innings."

I grabbed the phone from her. "Doesn't he have vibrate?"

Ashley nodded.

"Well, then, we're just going to keep hitting redial and vibrate that puppy right out of his pocket 'til he picks up."

Please, Lord, make Jordy answer the phone, whatever it takes—I don't care if You have to burn a hole in his pocket! You did the whole burning-bush thing—what's a little phone fire? Now I need to go take care of those poor scared kids. Help me think of a way to distract them . . .

"Phoebe, we need you!" Mom called. "And bring some towels."

Me? I don't know nothin' 'bout birthin' no babies. Remember, I'm the girl who can't stand the sight of blood. The girl who could never watch those films in health class. The girl they dubbed Squeamish Pheabish when I couldn't dissect that frog in biology . . .

"Phoebe, *now*!" she shouted.

I hurried down the hall, grabbing a stack of towels from the linen closet, and met Alex coming out as I went in.

He gave my arm a reassuring squeeze. "Don't worry. Those ladies know what they're doing. It'll be fine. I'll go keep the kids occupied."

I gulped and nodded my thanks. Then I entered the bedroom and saw more of my sister-in-law than I'd ever wanted to see.

Are you sure you want to do this someday, girl?

Mom and Mary Jo were crowded around Karen, stroking her hair and cheering her on. "That was a good one," Mary Jo said. "Now breathe out again."

Karen blew out short, staccato bursts of air.

Mom, holding tight onto her daughter-in-law's hand, smiled and beckoned me over. "Look, honey, Phoebe's here with towels. Think you can lift up for just a sec so we can get some under you? Don't want to mess up your pretty new sheets, you know."

Karen lifted, with Mary Jo's help, while Mom and I slid a couple of towels beneath her. Then she clenched Mom's hand in a death grip as a cry escaped. "Aaaaarrrrrgggghhhhh!"

Mom rubbed her back while Mary Jo slipped into position. "That's right, honey. Doing good. Almost there now."

Um, what can I do?

Then I remembered. In every movie I've ever seen where a woman's in childbirth, someone boils water.

Water—they'll need hot water! I can do that. How much, though? A glass? A pitcher? A bowl?

Not wanting to bother my mom, who had other things on her plate at the moment, I scurried into the kitchen to get a little of each. While I nuked a large bowlful, I overheard Alex talking to the kids in the other room.

"I never had a brother, either," he was reassuring Jacob, "but I have a sister who played as good as a boy. Her name is Cordelia."

Cordelia? His sister?

"Cordelia?" Jacob asked. "What kind of name is that?"

"It's English."

"Are *you* English?"

"Part English. And I lived in England when I was a kid."

"Do you know the queen?" Elizabeth asked.

"I've met her."

"You have?" Ashley and Elizabeth said in awe. "What about Prince William?"

When will this water ever get hot?!

"No, but I saw his younger brother Harry at a polo match once."

"You *did*?"

He's quite a natural with kids. And I never knew he lived in England . . . though I guess he has just a little trace of an accent when you think about it. I can't believe he's actually met the queen . . .

Hearing Karen cry out again, I looked up to see the microwave had already dinged and the water was boiling happily. I grabbed a couple of hot pads, raced gingerly back to the bedroom with the hot water sloshing dangerously, and arrived just in time to see my newest niece enter the world.

I swayed, then sat down hard.

She's so tiny. And beautiful. And, uh, messy. Okay, Pheebs, don't focus on the blood. Don't focus on the blood and all that other goopy stuff. Fainting would not be good. . .

I raised my eyes to see Mom, who was still holding Karen's hand, motioning me over.

Idiot—get that water over there! I hurried over with the bowl, sloshing some on the carpet and barely escaping a scalding. "What should I do with this?"

"Just set it down, honey, and come here," Mom said, patting the bed. "We don't need it." She transferred my weary sister-in-law's hand to mine and stood up. "I'm going to help Mary Jo now. You sit with Karen."

Mary Jo passed Mom's wailing new granddaughter to her. My mother held the infant close, cooing all the while, while my 4-H pal moved in with a small pair of scissors. *Not the garden shears this time, praise God. Still, Squeamish Pheabish will skip the ceremonial cutting of the umbilical cord, thank you very much. Way too much information.*

"Isn't she perfect?" Karen said, as Mom placed the blanketed baby into her mother's arms for the first time.

"Exquisite," I said. "And look at all that hair! Good thing she takes after your side of the family, Karen." I bent closer over my newest niece. "Little girl, you're going to be a real heartbreaker, I can already tell. You just stick with your Aunt Phoebe, though. I'll show you the ropes."

"Did you and Jordy finally decide on a name?" Mom asked.

Karen smiled. "Yes. After much deliberation." She shifted the baby so we could both see her sweet little face. "Gloria Phoebe, meet your grandma and your aunt."

Mom and I looked at our namesake, then at one another. Then we both burst into tears.

Moments later, the paramedics arrived and bundled mom and newborn onto a gurney. Just as they were loading Karen and little Gloria into the ambulance for the ride to the hospital, Jordy pulled up and clambered in alongside his wife and his brand-new daughter.

Needing some time alone, I headed to the bathroom. Once inside, I collapsed against the sink and wept wondering tears. *I can't believe what just happened here.*

I thought about Karen and what she'd gone through—the whole mother-giving-birth miracle of it all. And about how God, the Creator of all, so perfectly created women's bodies for such a time as this.

"You knit me together in my mother's womb . . ."

Then I thought about Mom and Mary Jo and how amazing they were. How they knew just what to do. And how we all pulled together to help Karen bring this tiny creature into the world.

Women rallying to help each other. And I was a part of it. So cool. Except the afterbirth part, that is . . .

Within the hour, all the excitement had died down. Jordy, Karen, and little Gloria Phoebe were at the hospital. Mary Jo had gone home. Mom was watching the kids, and Alex walked me back to my apartment.

Brain-dead and exhausted from all the emotions of the day, I cast about for something to say. "So, um, you have a sister named Cordelia."

"Yes, but how did—"

"Overheard you talking to the kids."

"Oh."

We walked a few more steps.

"Uh, thank you again for all your help tonight, Alex. I'm sure it was the last thing you bargained for when you stopped by Mom's."

He grinned. "That's putting it mildly. But I'm glad I was able to help."

He gave me a long, searching look. I stumbled on a stone. *Now who's the clumsy one?*

He grabbed my arm and righted me.

We arrived at my staircase, his hand still on my arm. "Well, uh, thanks again—"

But he wasn't going anywhere.

"All right, Miss Movielovr," he said gravely, "I think it's time we had a talk."

My heart fluttered just a little. We hadn't really had an opportunity to discuss what we had learned about each other the previous night. Was Alex glad or disappointed that I turned out to be Movielvr?

"I'm sorry I stood you up," I fumbled. "That was when I found out about Mom, and I just—"

He smiled across at me, and I realized how nice it was to be able to look a man straight in the eye. "You can redeem yourself, you know," he told me.

"How—"

"By joining me for the 'Save the Bijou' celebration next week. They're playing—"

"I know," I said. "*Casablanca.*"

The following Friday, I'd just gotten out of the shower and was blow-drying my hair when I thought I heard a knock on the door. I turned off the blow-dryer and glanced at the clock. Too early for Alex. "Who is it?" I yelled.

No answer.

Probably just the kids goofing around.

Finishing my hair, I began to apply my makeup. *I'd better go check just to be sure.*

Pulling on my robe, I opened the front door to find a huge package on the landing. "What in the world?" I looked around but saw no one. So I lifted up the flat, heavy box and took it inside.

I grabbed the scissors and cut open the cumbersome package, then pushed away a layer of foam peanuts to find Ingrid and Humphrey gazing into each other's eyes.

My *Casablanca* poster!

Carefully I peeled off the card attached to Humphrey's lapel and opened it to read, "Of all the newspapers, in all the towns, in all the world, I'm glad I walked into yours. Looking forward to tonight. Alex."

I melted. *How did he . . . But no time to worry about that now. He'll be here in ten minutes.*

I dressed with care for our first date: my favorite not-too-dressy, not-too-casual sleeveless black dress topped by a gorgeous red pashmina (from last year's after-Christmas sales) that showed off my shoulders. Funky silver earrings and coordinating—but not matching—bracelet.

And my lowest pair of red heels.

"Wow!" Alex said when he picked me up.

We walked shoulder to shoulder into the Bijou, and he steered me over to the new and improved snack bar, where he stocked up on Red Vines, kettle corn, *and* Junior Mints.

He winked at me. "Woman does not live by licorice alone. Neither does man. We like that salt-and-chocolate combo too."

"I think this really is the beginning of a beautiful friendship," I said as we walked into the movie.

When the lights came back on after the credits rolled. I realized with a start that something inside me was different. What was it? Something was missing, and yet its absence felt good. It felt right.

And then I realized what it was.

What was missing was that oh-so-familiar pang of sadness, of regret that the movie was over. That dull, depressed feeling signaling the end of the movie and the resumption of "real life."

This time, "The End" was just the beginning.

[phoebe's top-five (um, six) guide to (the best) old movies]

People always ask me, "So, what's your *favorite* old movie?" That's like asking a mother, "Who's your favorite child?" It's impossible to answer.

That's why I decided to share with you, my *Bulletin* readers, just a few of my favorite oldies but goodies from the world of cinema, divided by category (Romantic Comedies, Dramas, Musicals, etc.) and listed alphabetically. To keep the list manageable, I've tried to limit it to films from the thirties, forties, and fifties—with a few notable exceptions. (No way could I have left out *The Sound of Music* or *West Side Story*.)

Overall, I limited my choices to the top six in each category. On occasion, however, even that was impossible, so you'll notice that a couple of times I broke my own rules.

But you know what? That's okay. I made the rules, I can break 'em.

So here you have it: my guide to the best old movies from the thirties, forties, and fifties. I hope it gets you running out to the video store to rent some classics you may have never seen before—or better yet, to support your local movie theater when they actually show them on the silver screen.

Grab your popcorn and settle in. It's going to be a bumpy ride. (Guess who said *that*?)

classic love stories

An Affair to Remember—Cary Grant and Deborah Kerr. This five-hanky drama was the one featured in *Sleepless in Seattle* that Rita

Wilson was so wonderfully sobbing over when describing to her 'brother' Tom Hanks. A must!

Casablanca— Humphrey Bogart and Ingrid Bergman. The crème de la crème. "We'll always have Paris . . ."

Gone with the Wind—Clark Gable and Vivien Leigh. There's a reason Clark Gable was considered the King of Hollywood. And Vivien Leigh was a perfect Scarlett.

Random Harvest—Greer Garson and Ronald Colman. Oh my. Just thinking about this tearjerker makes me cry.

Wuthering Heights—Laurence Olivier and Merle Oberon. Talk about a fatal attraction.

honorable mention:

The African Queen—Katharine Hepburn and Humphrey Bogart. What a pair!

Pride and Prejudice—The delightful Greer Garson as Elizabeth Bennett and Laurence Olivier as the overly proud and disdainful Mr. Darcy, who comes around. (Colin Firth was wonderful, too, in the more recent BBC miniseries, but that's not technically a movie!)

West Side Story—Natalie Wood, Richard Beymer, Rita Moreno. (Okay, I know this is most definitely a musical—and one of the best ever—but it's also a fabulously sad love story, so I stuck it here instead.)

dramas

The Best Years of our Lives—Fredric March, Myrna Loy, Teresa Wright. Grab a whole box of tissue for this one. Can you say "poignant"?

The Bridge on the River Kwai—William Holden and Alec Guinness and that great whistling song.

Casablanca—The best movie ever. Bar none.

Citizen Kane—Orson Welles's masterpiece—and on everybody's "Best" list.

The Grapes of Wrath—A young and amazing Henry Fonda.

To Kill a Mockingbird—Gregory Peck. One of the best films and books, ever—I have it on good authority.

honorable mention:

All About Eve—Bette Davis, Anne Baxter (answer to the earlier trivia question).

Mr. Smith Goes to Washington—Jean Arthur and a stirring Jimmy Stewart fighting against political corruption. His amazing filibuster scene in Congress is the heart of the film.

Mrs. Miniver—Greer Garson, Walter Pidgeon, and Teresa Wright. (Get out the tissue, girls.)

mystery/suspense

Casablanca—Will Rick give the letters of transit to Lazlo and Ilsa? Who will stay? Who will go?

Gaslight—Ingrid Bergman and a chilling Charles Boyer. Great psychological suspense.

Laura—Gene Tierney, Dana Andrews, Clifton Webb and a gorgeous theme song.

Rear Window—Jimmy Stewart, Grace Kelly, and Raymond Burr (before *Perry Mason*). An Alfred Hitchcock classic.

Rebecca—Laurence Olivier and Joan Fontaine. Also Hitchcock—his first American feature.

Suspicion—Cary Grant and Joan Fontaine. What can I say? You can't beat Hitchcock for suspense.

honorable mention:

The Big Sleep, Key Largo, and *To Have and Have Not*—a Humphrey Bogart and Lauren Bacall triple treat.

The Maltese Falcon—Bogie again, plus Mary Astor, Claude Rains. A must-see classic.

romantic comedies

The Awful Truth—Cary Grant and Irene Dunne. A great thirties screwball comedy.

Bringing Up Baby—Cary Grant, Katharine Hepburn, and a leopard named Baby.

Casablanca—Definitely romantic. Though not traditionally thought of as a comedy, there are some pretty funny lines.

His Girl Friday—Cary Grant, Rosalind Russell, and fabulous rapid-fire dialogue.

It Happened One Night—Clark Gable, Claudette Colbert, and a slew of Oscars.

Woman of the Year—Katharine Hepburn and Spencer Tracy—an inimitable team.

honorable mention:

Roman Holiday—I couldn't leave out Audrey Hepburn's dazzling film debut, which netted her an Oscar. (Nor forget the delicious Gregory Peck. Sigh.)

musicals

Casablanca—Okay, not technically a musical. But there are several songs, including of course, the incomparable "As Time Goes By."

The King and I—Yul Brynner and Deborah Kerr. Makes me want to polka—but only with Yul. And only in that gorgeous gold ball gown.

Oklahoma—Gordon MacRae and Shirley Jones. Oh, what a beautiful show! (I also recommend the 2004 English stage show remake with Hugh Jackman—the guy can sing *and* dance!)

Seven Brides for Seven Brothers—Howard Keel and Jane Powell. Seven strapping single men dance their hearts out to win their ladies' hands. They've got mine.

Singin' in the Rain—Gene Kelly, Debbie Reynolds, and Donald O'Connor. The best. (*The Sound of Music*—see below under family—is still my favorite, but I wanted to keep my job.)

A Star Is Born—Judy Garland and James Mason. A little overwrought today, but Judy's mesmerizing performance of "The Man That Got Away" makes it all worth it.

honorable mention:
Carousel—Gordon MacRae and Shirley Jones again.

Yankee Doodle Dandy—Memorable George M. Cohan soundtrack with the great tap-dancing James Cagney playing Cohan himself.

family

Casablanca—A great movie to teach kids about the values of honor, nobility, and sacrifice.

Little Women—the Katharine Hepburn version only. No one else plays Jo as well.

Meet Me in St. Louis—Judy Garland and Margaret O'Brien. Judy never looked lovelier or sounded better than in this family classic (also a musical). Includes her wonderful "The Trolley Song" and the evergreen "Have Yourself a Merry Little Christmas."

The Parent Trap—Hayley Mills, Maureen O'Hara, and Brian Keith. Fun and *romantic*!

The Sound of Music—Julie Andrews and Christopher Plummer. Universally beloved and rightly so.

The Wizard of Oz—Judy Garland and that yellow brick road. Need I say more?

honorable mention:

Cheaper by the Dozen—Clifton Webb and Myrna Loy (*not* the recent remake).

I Remember Mama—Irene Dunne and Barbara Bel Geddes. (A must for aspiring woman writers. Especially Norwegian ones.)

National Velvet—Mickey Rooney and a young Elizabeth Taylor.

Any Shirley Temple movie—from *The Little Princess* to *Rebecca of Sunnybrook Farm*. Don't fall for the common opinion that Shirley is saccharine and simpering. The kid was *good!*

And of course, all the early Disney animated classics: *Snow White and the Seven Dwarfs, Bambi, Cinderella, Lady and the Tramp, Pinocchio, Sleeping Beauty* . . .

westerns
a.k.a. the-mostly-john wayne film festival
(with thanks to mary jo roper for her invaluable input)

Casablanca—Um, isn't Africa west of the United States?

Destry Rides Again—Jimmy Stewart and Marlene Dietrich. There's another Destry with Audie Murphy in the title role, but nobody can beat Jimmy Stewart.

High Noon—Gary Cooper and Grace Kelly. Not your standard Western hero by any means. But definitely one with more depth. And Grace Kelly's screen debut.

Stagecoach—John Wayne and Claire Trevor. Where the Duke first really made his mark.

The Searchers—John Wayne, Jeffrey Hunter, and Natalie Wood. Heartbreaking. Sad. Magnificent.

The Man Who Shot Liberty Valance—John Wayne, Jimmy Stewart, and Vera Miles. Jimmy Stewart getting the girl over John Wayne gives this a nice twist.

honorable mention:

Shane—Alan Ladd, Jean Arthur, Jack Palance. Honestly? This "classic" doesn't do much for me. I never quite understood all the fuss about it, but maybe I was just tired or having a bad day when I watched it. (I knew if I didn't include it, I'd be getting angry cards and letters from some of you saying, "What are you talkin' about? It's the greatest Western of all time!")

inspirational

A Man for All Seasons—Paul Scofield (who won an Academy Award for his brilliant performance), Orson Welles, Vanessa Redgrave.

Ben-Hur—Charlton Heston, Stephen Boyd, and that chariot race

The Bishop's Wife—Cary Grant, Loretta Young, and David Niven. Charming and touching. (Remade as *The Preacher's Wife* in 1996 with Whitney Houston and Denzel Washington. Not as charming, but Denzel is easy on the eyes and that Whitney girl can sing.)

Casablanca—Okay, maybe not in a spiritual sense, but definitely inspiring!

The Inn of the Sixth Happiness—the luminous Ingrid Bergman as a missionary in China.

Lilies of the Field—Lilia Skala and an Academy Award-winning Sidney Poitier. His joyous singing of "Amen" captivates me every time.

honorable mention:
Going My Way—Bing Crosby and Barry Fitzgerald.

NOTE: Although I said I wouldn't include anything past the seventies, I changed my mind. I had to include two of the films that had a lasting spiritual effect on me and continue to move me every time I watch them:

Brother Sun, Sister Moon—Franco Zeffirelli's wonderful story of St. Francis of Assisi. A moving scene near the end with Alec Guinness as the Pope makes me weep me every time.

Chariots of Fire—Ian Charleson and Ben Cross. Would that we were all willing to stand up for our faith so publicly, and at the expense of our personal dreams.

[acknowledgments]

Writing my first novel has been a labor of love. But I'd never have been able to do it without the following:

I owe a huge debt of gratitude to the Mount Hermon Writer's Conference and Davis Bunn's amazing fiction class. Davis, if not for you, my foray into the world of fiction might still be but a dream. Thanks also for introducing me to Ami McConnell. I owe you.

Special thanks to my writing pal and humor partner-in-crime, Dave Meurer, who upon hearing my opening lines, laughed until he cried. Further gratitude to Dave and his precious wife, Dale, who met Phoebe in her infancy and kept me going by saying, "What happens next? Write more!" Thanks, guys, for the great meals, conversation, and the "leeches" teapot. Particular thanks for the mud bog scene idea. (Although Dave, I'm not sure I want to thank you for introducing me to, "Don't Tell Mama I'm a Guitar Picker (She Thinks I'm Just in Jail.")

Thanks also to Wendy Lee Nentwig, whose passing comment about books "for single women whose lives haven't turned out the way they said they would in Sunday School," helped shape Phoebe.

Warm gratitude to Randy Ingermanson, another of my funny—and brilliant—author friends, who kindly read early chapters even though he wasn't a chick and spurred me on with his enthusiasm and adverb-killing advice.

Ditto to Anne Peterson (who is a chick) for early Phoebe feedback and support.

To Cindy Martinusen: a heartfelt thank-you for loving Phoebe and for the small-town tips. I treasure our friendship and our meeting of the writing minds—even though your mind is much deeper than mine. (Thanks for the bed, Weston—even though your shark poster scared me.) Thanks too, Cindy, for introducing me to Cathy Elliott. And Cathy, thanks for opening up your cute home during my writing getaway and for the gorgeous blue-and-white canisters.

To my brother-in-law, Jim Jameson: This clueless city girl thanks you for taking the time to vet the monster truck scene. Any errors are mine.

I owe a special debt of brainstorming thanks to Amy Bartlett, who provided a today's-single-woman's perspective and gave up several afternoons and a long weekend to read several chapters and give me crucial feedback. We'll always have Santa Cruz.

To my wonderful agent and friend, Chip Macgregor, thank you for making me cry when you said, "Congratulations, you have a new career as a novelist." I'm grateful for your continued guidance and support. Play it again, Chip.

Here's lookin' at my brilliant and enthusiastic editor-par-excellence, Ami McConnell. Thanks for falling head over heels for Phoebe and for making my lifelong writing dream come true! I've learned so much under your expert tutelage. Thank you for making my first novel experience such a joy. And to think it all began over a game of Trivial Pursuit . . .

Thank you, Allen Arnold and WestBow Press, for welcoming me with open arms. With special thanks to Amanda Corn Bostic.

Everlasting gratitude to singular sensation Anne Christian Buchanan for her amazing editorial eye for detail, logic and numbers—the latter two of which have never been my friends. Thank you for helping to make Phoebe shine so brightly. (I'm keeping the e-mail with all the girdle-research details for posterity.)

For Phoebe's fashion and coffee advice I must thank Kari Jameson, Michelle Gadwa, Ami McConnell, Michelle Skinner, Andrea Thomas, and Lana Yarbrough—with extra thanks to my niece, Kari, for all the fun, single-girl reality check stuff.

To Lana: thanks for being my Lindsey.

Particular thanks to my sweet, small-town, Southern-fried friend Annette Smith, who walked the fiction road just before me, and held my hand when I got scared. Thanks also for reading chapters and cheering me on when I was crunching on deadline.

For the authenticity of the childbirth scene, I need to thank Lori Birtwell, Clark and Lisa Crebar, and Annette Smith, since like Phoebe, I don't know nothin' 'bout birthin' no babies.

To my wonderful pastor, Clark Crebar: thank you for modeling Christ daily.

To my yada-yada California writing girlfriends Jan Coleman and Judi Braddy, thanks for all your support and for the (mostly) monthly get-togethers that help keep me sane. We're overdue. I'll put the kettle on.

Everlasting gratitude to our Monday night Acts2U group and to Janice Elsheimer's *The Creative Call* for pushing me to step out into the scary and unknown fiction waters. And to Lonnie for always being in my cheerleading corner.

Thanks also to friends and family who mostly "get" when I'm on deadline and still love me. With deepest gratitude to my mother, my sister, and my beloved husband, Michael, who have all been nagging me for years to write fiction. You believed I could do it long before I did. I love you.

And thanks, honey, for researching all those dreaded details. And for everything else. You complete me.

Everyone's favorite film geek Phoebe Grant
heads off to Merrie Old England—
and changes her dreams from *black-and-white* to
technicolor.

Look for the next Phoebe Grant novel,

Dreaming in Technicolor

available everywhere
SEPTEMBER 2005!

Discover other great novels!
Join the WestBow Press Reader's Club at
WestBowPress.com

WestBow
PRESS
A Division of Thomas Nelson Publishers
Since 1798
visit us at www.westbowpress.com